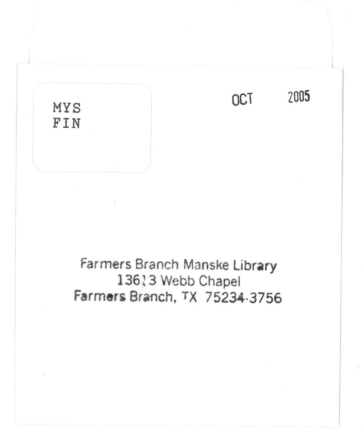

A Bitter Chill

Also by Jane Finnis
Get Out or Die

A Bitter Chill

Jane Finnis

Poisoned Pen Press

Poisoned Pen Press
6962 E. First Ave., Ste. 103
Scottsdale, AZ 85251
www.poisonedpenpress.com
info@poisonedpenpress.com

Printed in the United States of America

For Leebags, Pennyo, Philpott, and all my other good friends
from Westfield days, of whom it has often been said…
but never mind.

Part of the province of Britannia in 95 AD

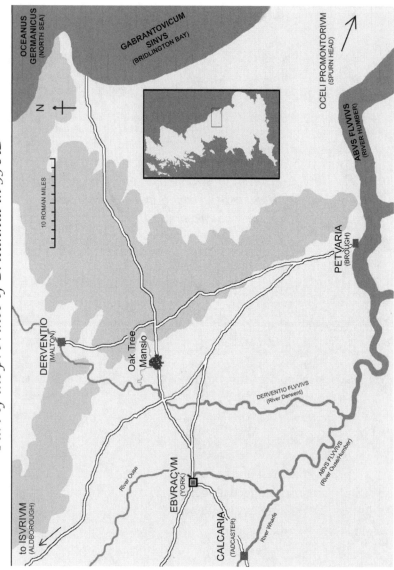

OCEANUS GERMANICVS (NORTH SEA)

GABRANTOVICUM SINVS (BRIDLINGTON BAY)

OCELI PROMONTORIVM (SPURN HEAD)

ABVS FLVVIVS (RIVER HUMBER)

N

10 ROMAN MILES

DERVENTIO (MALTON)

Oak Tree Mansio

PETVARIA (BROUGH)

DERVENTIO FLVVIVS (River Derwent)

ABVS FLVVIVS (River Ouse/Humber)

River Ouse

EBVRACVM (YORK)

CALCARIA (TADCASTER)

River Wharfe

to ISVRIVM (ALDBOROUGH)

Chapter I

It might all have been different if I hadn't burnt the mistletoe. Our troubles started on that freezing December day, and I've often wondered about it since. Did I bring down the vengeance of the old gods of Britannia, because I, a Roman, dared to destroy one of their sacred plants?

Who knows? I don't. But I'd do the same again, if I had to.

We were collecting greenery to decorate the mansio for Saturnalia. Well, I was supervising, rather than actually collecting. It's something we do every December, and as usual I'd given the slaves a half-day off to help. They were all joining in, house servants and farm hands, scouring the woods around for the best branches of holly and laurel, and the longest strands of ivy. Despite the winter cold, they were in holiday mood, skipping about and singing as they brought their trophies back to the paved forecourt where my sister Albia and I were waiting outside the bar-room door.

"It's like a forest of dancing trees!" Albia laughed as a couple of the young maids jigged along, almost hidden by laurel branches as big as themselves, while one of the horse-boys wound ivy round his head to make a comic green helmet. "And look at Taurus. He's got a whole holly-tree there."

"I told him we wanted a big tree to stand in the middle of the bar-room. He's taken me literally!" I smiled as our giant handyman strode across the forecourt holding a huge holly-bush at arm's length to avoid the prickles.

He proudly put it down in front of us. It was even taller than he was, which meant it towered half a foot over Albia and me.

"The biggest I could find, Mistress Aurelia," he declared. "Like you wanted for the bar-room. It'll look good, won't it?"

"Wonderful." It was about three times bigger than we needed, but I hadn't the heart to spoil his pleasure. "Yes, Taurus, it's a beauty. And what lovely berries!"

"All the bushes and trees have brilliant berries this year," he said. "Plenty for us, and the birds as well. Sign of a hard winter, the natives say."

"I shouldn't be surprised. It's cold enough to freeze the horns off a bronze bull." I shivered in spite of my warm bearskin cloak, and looked up at the sky, where yellow-grey clouds were being driven towards us by a sharp north wind. "We'll have snow by tonight. You've made sure we have plenty of logs close to the house?"

"Course I have. Logs for the fire and the furnace, and charcoal for the braziers. We'll be warm inside, however hard it snows."

"The first real snow of the winter." Albia pulled up the hood of her cloak. "Lovely! It makes even ordinary things look pretty. Yes, that's right, Carina," she added, as the senior barmaid brought yet another armful of green boughs. "Smaller sprigs here, larger branches over there. Pick out the very best bits for the bar-room and the dining-room, and make sure there are some good small pieces for our private rooms—mine and Relia's, and don't forget Master Lucius' bedroom. He'll be here any day now."

"Taurus," I said, "you may as well start nailing up some of the smaller bits of holly round the outside of the door and windows. Use thin nails, so as not to damage the wood...."

I caught him and Albia exchanging a smile, and stopped. He'd been nailing up decorations at the mansio every Saturnalia for sixteen years, and if he didn't know how by now, he never would.

"I'll choose the pieces for our bedrooms." I bent to pick out the choicest scarlet-studded sprigs of holly. "Ouch! I wish I'd brought some mittens. Will we have enough for the guest wing as well, Albia?"

"Oh yes. The three main bedrooms definitely, and probably the smaller rooms too." She giggled. "Not that we want the place full of overnight guests just now, so close to the holiday."

"I think we're safe enough. Nobody travels the roads of northern Britannia in December. I'm looking forward to a nice peaceful time, with no guests staying and only a few locals to serve drinks to in the daytime."

All right, I know that's not quite the proper attitude for an innkeeper, but we're only human, although our customers often seem to forget the fact. Most of the year I'm delighted to welcome guests to our mansio—soldiers, messengers, government officials, and private travellers when we can get them. They come to stay, to eat or drink, to change horses, and people say we run the best guest-house and posting-station between the River Humber and Eburacum. I say it quite regularly myself. But from mid-December to New Year, I always hope that we'll have a few days of doing nothing, or as near to nothing as we can manage.

"Can we take some berries to decorate the slave quarters, Miss Albia?" Taurus carefully secured the first sprig of holly to the door-frame.

"Of course, Taurus. Just let us choose what we need here, and then have as much as you want."

He grinned. "I like Saturnalia. The presents, and lots of good food and wine, and the games. It makes everyone equal, just for a while."

"It reminds me of when we were children," I said. Perhaps that's why it's my favourite of all the festivals, with its cheerful, anarchic celebrations, the silly jokes, the over-eating and drinking, and even the banquet where masters and mistresses wait on their slaves. And then once the shortest day of the year is past, I can tell myself that it won't be so very long until spring. A slow, late spring on this northern edge of the Empire, but when the days begin to lengthen and the first flowers appear, at least it's on its way.

Next spring would bring Albia's wedding to Candidus, and she'd be leaving home. She was counting the days, glowing with excitement every time the subject was mentioned, which was very often. I was counting days too, my pleasure tinged with foreboding. She was my housekeeper at the mansio, my indispensable right hand. Of course I wished her all the happiness in the world in her new life, but how I was going to run the Oak Tree without her, the gods alone knew. Or perhaps not even they had worked it out yet.

But I didn't want to think about it now. "This will be the best Saturnalia ever," I said, "with Lucius coming home."

"And Candidus here too," Albia added. "The whole family together." She began sorting through the largest heap of mixed greenery. "Oh look, pine branches, and even some cones! Do you think we can use these, or will they make people think of funerals?"

I walked over to join her. "Let's use them. They look good, and I always love that resiny smell." I stooped down and rummaged through the pile. "How much is there?…*Merda*, what's this doing here?" There was a large bunch of mistletoe among the other branches. I jumped back as if I'd seen a snake, then bent forward again, grabbed the foul stuff in both hands and flung it away from me as hard as I could.

I'd sooner have found a snake than those evil glossy leaves and creamy-yellow berries, the Druids' revered holy plant. And don't try telling me that Druids are outlawed in this Empire of ours. Outlawed or not, they still exist and practice their abominable ceremonies in secret. We had reason to know that, because only four years before they'd incited the native Brigantians to try to kill us. For a few heartbeats my mind went back to a moonlit woodland clearing, where white-robed priests cut mistletoe from an oak tree, as a prelude to sacrificing a boy on their altar. I pushed the memory out of my head.

"We must get rid of it," I said. "I won't have it anywhere near our good Roman celebrations. Who collected it, I wonder?

They all know how much we hate the Druids. If I catch whoever brought it in...."

"Calm down, Relia," my sister said reasonably. "It must have been one of the newer slaves, or a child. Someone who wasn't here then, and couldn't know what happened."

"I hope so, because if I find we've any Druid sympathisers among our people, they'll go straight to the next slave auction."

"I'm certain we haven't. Don't let it bother you. We'll just burn the stuff, and that'll be the end of it."

"Yes, you're right. Taurus, take the mistletoe and throw it into the furnace, please."

The big man took a pace backwards. "Me? I mean, well, are you sure?"

With any other slave, I'd have said, "Don't argue, just do it." But Taurus is almost part of the family, one of the few servants we brought with us when we came to Britannia years ago. He's not the brightest slave in the world, but he's the most completely loyal.

"I'm quite sure, yes, Taurus. You know as well as I do how the Druids hate all of us Romans. We can't have their plants in the mansio."

"But the gods the Druids worship are scary." He gazed at me unhappily. "They won't like me burning mistletoe, and maybe they'll put a curse on me. Or all of us. Like they did before."

"Nonsense!" I smiled, trying not to show my irritation. "The old gods have no power these days. Our Roman gods are much stronger. There's nothing to be afraid of."

"Aren't you afraid of them, Mistress?"

"No, of course not. Not one bit."

"Well, you're not afraid of much." Not strictly true, but I didn't see any need to correct him. "Then if you're not afraid of the Druids' gods, why do you need to burn the mistletoe, instead of just throwing it away?"

It was a fair question, and to be truthful I couldn't explain my reasons properly. I only knew for certain that the stuff had to be completely destroyed. Deep down, I was a little frightened of what the Druids stood for, having seen their power to whip up hatred and violence against us. But I wasn't going to admit that to Taurus, especially as several of the other slaves were listening to our conversation.

"I want it burnt because it reminds me of bad times. The Druids tried to have us killed, and they didn't succeed, so I'm not afraid of them or their gods. To prove it, I'll burn the stuff myself, out here where everyone can see. Fetch me a brazier and some dry wood, will you?"

As Taurus disappeared, much relieved, I realised that the whole forecourt had gone quiet. All the slaves had stopped what they were doing and were watching me warily. I noticed Albia having a quiet word with Carina, and the two of them went into the bar-room. Gods, I thought, surely neither of *them* is worried by what I'm doing? I could have done with Albia's support over this, but...well, too bad. I was going to have to manage without her support altogether before long. The prospect didn't improve my temper.

I stood there by the bar-room door, smiling and outwardly relaxed, till Taurus came back with a brazier. He added some dry sticks to it, and a good fire sprang up. I marched across to where the mistletoe lay and picked it up. Holding it high in full view, I walked back and hurled it into the flames. It made a fine blaze, the waxy berries spitting and spurting. There was a small murmur, almost a sigh, from the watching slaves, and I sensed that they shared Taurus' unease. Most were natives, born and bred in Brigantia, closer to Druid beliefs and legends than we Romans could ever be.

So I said, "Mistletoe is evil stuff, but now it's gone, and we're safe. I call on Jupiter and Juno and Diana and all the gods of Rome to protect us, and give us peace for Saturnalia."

Soon there was nothing left but a few charred twigs, and ashes vanishing in the wind. But the holiday atmosphere had vanished too, and the slaves stood about in subdued groups, saying little. It was a pity to have lost the light-hearted mood, and I was wondering how we could recover it, when Albia and

Carina appeared, carrying two large steaming jugs of hot wine and a tray of beakers.

"Now, we've got to get this finished before the snow starts," Albia called out. "A drop of wine will keep us warm. Come on, everyone, help yourselves!"

There was a cheer, and the atmosphere lightened at once. Two of the horse-boys began a mock fight using holly branches for swords, and the rest of us stood cheering them on like spectators at a gladiator show. Before long everyone went back to the decorating, happy again.

"Well done, Albia," I murmured as I sipped the spiced wine. "Thank you."

"You look as if you need it," she answered softly. "Don't pay any attention to Taurus and the others. We couldn't have those berries indoors. You were right to burn them."

"I had no choice." I still believe that. But sometimes I can't help wondering.

Before long the front of the mansio was as green as a summer bower. I smiled and joked with everyone, and almost managed to shake off the uneasy feeling those bad memories had caused. As the light faded the outdoor slaves dispersed, and Albia led the house servants inside, to begin the decorating there. I stayed on the forecourt, alone under the big oak tree that gives our mansio its name. I was so lost in my thoughts that I hardly felt the cold, or noticed when the first snowflakes fell.

Then out of the dusk appeared a slight dark figure, carrying a hunting-bow and followed by a large dog that looked more wolf than hound. My spirits lifted as I recognised Hawk, my favourite native huntsman, and the best tracker I ever saw. Also a friend, and a good one.

"Hawk, you're a welcome sight! Come in and have a drink. We've been collecting greenery, and I could do to warm up a little."

"Thank you." He gave his rare smile. "You owe me at least one large jug of beer. I've had a cold and empty afternoon trying to hunt in the woods, with all your people charging about like a herd of aurochs. They've scared away every animal and bird between here and Eburacum."

"I can well believe it," I smiled back, and we headed for the bar-room. "But everything stops for Saturnalia, you know."

"So I see." We hung up our cloaks and stood watching the girls decking the room out with the green boughs. Taurus' holly-tree had been given pride of place in the middle, and looked magnificent.

I went to the bar and collected a tray with mugs, beer, and wine. "At least we only take three days off, not like in Rome where the whole city is on holiday for seven." I led the way to my study.

"Very restrained, I'm sure. Is that due to the famous Roman self-discipline, or the even more famous Roman meanness?"

I laughed. "Probably both. You ought to know by now, we're rather good at making a virtue out of a necessity." I always enjoyed the banter I had with Hawk, and as usual, I talked to him in Latin, and he replied in British. We each speak one another's languages well, but from long habit, we each used our own. It must sound strange to other people, but it suited us.

The study was comfortably warm, thanks to a big charcoal bra-zier, but as we entered, Hawk exclaimed, "By the Three Mothers, it's too hot for me in here!" He pulled off his woollen over-tunic, and nodded his thanks as I poured his beer. "I thought you Romans were supposed to be tough. But the first little snowflake that falls, you heat your houses up like furnaces."

"It's horrible to be cold. And if we don't have to use up all our energy shivering and stopping our teeth from chattering, we'll have all the more strength to be tough when it counts." I raised my beaker. "To your good health, Hawk. And to peace and happiness for all of us this winter."

"To your good health." He took a long drink of beer. "I'm a bit less sure about the rest of your wishes. That's why I wanted a word." His expression became serious. "I think you may be in for a spot of trouble."

"As long as it doesn't come till after Saturnalia," I joked, but his piercing black eyes continued to survey me gravely.

I felt a stirring of the uneasiness I'd had earlier. "Not the Druids again? I found some mistletoe in among our green branches this afternoon. I don't know how it got there, presumably by accident, but I burnt it just to be safe. I don't want reminders of the Druids or their gods anywhere near this mansio."

"I've no quarrel with the old gods," Hawk said seriously. "I hate Druids though, as much as you do."

He had every reason, but I didn't want to dwell on the horrors of the past. I took a good swallow of wine. "Then if not the Druids, what's wrong? I hope we haven't upset one of the neighbours?" We always try to get on well with the native Brigantian farmers. "We're on good terms with all of them. Or I thought we were."

"You are, as far as I know. This is something different. I suppose you weren't out and about in the woods last night?"

"Not me. I was safe and snug in front of a log fire."

"Then you didn't hear a wolf howling?"

"No," I said, surprised. "I wouldn't expect to. There aren't any wolves left in these woods now, they've all been killed by hunters from Eburacum. That's what you're always telling me, isn't it?"

"Quite right. So when I heard a wolf-howl, clear and distinct and not far away, I went to investigate. I found it came from a two-legged wolf prowling around your farm buildings down-river, and presumably signalling to another of his kind."

"Did you see him?"

"No, only his tracks, but that was enough, because I've seen them before. There's a gang of Brigantian lads, young toughs who'd rather steal than work. They're supporting themselves by thieving and intimidating farmers, and they call themselves the Wolf-pack, of all silly names. The man signalling last night was one of them."

"The Wolf-pack? Now you mention it, I've heard of them. They caused a bit of trouble east of here in the wold country earlier this year. I remember last June the army at Eburacum sent out a couple of foot-patrols to try and catch them, but of course they hadn't a hope. They might as well have sent an elephant to chase a shoal of fish."

He nodded. "A gang like that always has the advantage over the army. They know every yard of the countryside, and every hiding-place for miles. Catching them is a job for a proper investigator like your brother. How is he, by the way?"

"He's fine. You can see for yourself in a day or two. He's coming home for the holiday."

"Excellent! Tell him I know where there's an interesting wild boar, if he fancies a spot of hunting."

"I will." Lucius would jump at the chance of going after a wild boar that an experienced huntsman described as interesting. "But go on about this gang, the Wolf-pack."

"They're moving down off the hills for the winter, which means they'll be around Oak Bridges for a while. They won't go much nearer to Eburacum, because a couple of ex-army types have joined them lately, and they won't want to risk being recognised near the fortress. I've seen their tracks. They're still using their hobnailed army boots, though I assume they're wearing Brigantian clothes otherwise."

"Ex-army? That's bad. From the Ninth Legion, I suppose."

"No. One of the auxiliary units."

"Gods, how in Hades do you know that? You'll be telling me next which unit, and who commands it."

"It's not so hard to tell auxiliaries from legionaries by their tracks. Their boots are slightly different in design, that's all. But as to the name of the commander, I didn't think to check. Perhaps I should go out and take another look?"

I laughed. "Well, I appreciate you coming to warn us. But I honestly don't think we have much to fear from that sort of band. They'll pick on easy targets, small hamlets and isolated farms, and single travellers on foot. We've got a big complex of buildings here, and plenty of men. They surely wouldn't try to steal from us?"

"They might during holiday time." He sipped his beer. "You said yourself, everything stops for Saturnalia, and they know that as well as you do. They may try to catch you napping, or at least over-indulging."

"You're saying, be on our guard. Thanks, we will."

He nodded. "You're a harder nut to crack than a family of Brigantians in a roundhouse, but that just makes you more tempting. You've got valuable horses and mules that would fetch a good price, and farm animals if they fancy a free meal or two. You can't keep all the stock in barns for the whole winter."

"No, but we can keep them well protected, and we will."

"Make sure you do, especially just now. Enjoy Saturnalia, but don't relax too much."

He went away soon after, leaving me to work out how we could keep a reasonable guard on the mansio and farm, while still letting ourselves and our household enjoy the holiday. I shared the problem with Albia, and we decided to warn the senior servants in the morning, and draw up a rota of men who would take it in turns to patrol round outside during the dark night hours.

"Oddly enough," I said, "I'm not too bothered about this. If anything, I'm relieved."

"Relieved? You mean you were expecting something worse?" She looked at me keenly. "Because of the mistletoe?"

"I don't know. But if I have annoyed the old gods, a gang of outlaws trying to disrupt a Roman festival is exactly the sort of spiteful revenge they'd throw at us, isn't it? Unpleasant, but not catastrophic."

"For Juno's sake don't put that idea into the slaves' heads! Anyhow, I still think you're taking the mistletoe too seriously."

"You're right, I'm making far too much out of a trivial incident. This Saturnalia will be wonderful, and nothing is going to spoil it."

I was never cut out for a prophetess.

Chapter II

The night brought a heavy snowfall, and my brother arrived in the middle of it.

I was dreaming about my old home in Pompeii. It was sixteen years since I'd seen the place, but in my dreams it's as real as if it still basks in the Campanian sunshine.

I was lazing on a cushioned couch in our sunny secluded roof-garden. Below me I could see the sparkling blue bay, and the town streets spread out like a coloured map under a perfect summer sky. The garden was beautiful, with tubs of flowers scenting the air, and best of all, it was *hot.* The blissful southern sun burned into my bones, and I loved it.

"Aurelia! Let me in! Aurelia! Let me in!" My peaceful solitude was broken by a man's shout, and a fist hammering like a drum. The noises didn't belong in my dream, so I ignored them. If I keep quiet, I thought, they'll go away.

"Aurelia! Let me in! Aurelia! Let me in!" The voice was familiar, and it seemed to be coming from the street door below. I should go down and see who was there, but I wanted to stay in the sun, and I knew that outside the door it would be icy cold. Reluctantly I walked to the low parapet and looked down over the roof's edge, trying to glimpse the importunate pest who was disturbing my peace. I clambered onto the wall for a better view, and then I felt myself falling…

Disappointment washed over me as I woke up and realised where I was. Not in summery Pompeii, but in my freezing December bedroom in Britannia, in the middle of a pitch-black night. I pulled the blankets over my head and shut my eyes tight, trying to return to the warmth of Campania, but the dream was gone. Pompeii was gone too, buried deep by an erupting mountain. The only way that I or anyone could ever visit it again was in dreams.

"Aurelia! Let me in! Aurelia! Let me in!"

So that at least wasn't a dream. Someone was out there, yelling and knocking and presumably freezing in the snow. Still half asleep, I wondered who in Hades it could be. We get very few travellers arriving after dark in winter. And even fewer who know where to find my bedroom window at dead of night.

I came fully awake, flung off the blankets, and reached for my heavy wool cloak and warm sheepskin shoes. Lucius! It was my brother Lucius out there. I hadn't seen him for three months, and it was typical of him to arrive at the least convenient time.

The hammering and calling were still going on. Well, if it was unpleasantly cold in here, it must be icy outside. "Hold on, Lucius!" I shouted. "I'm coming! Go round to the garden door!" There was a muffled answer, and the noise stopped. I picked up the candle I keep by my bed. It was about half burnt away, which meant there were six hours or so till dawn. I walked along the passage to the door that leads from our private wing into the garden. I put down the candle and shot the heavy bolt back. Lucius stood there, alone and covered with snow.

"Aurelia! Thank the gods!" He hurtled in, bringing a blast of cold air and snowflakes. I bolted the door again quickly, and gave him a big hug. We've always been close, because we're twins.

"What time do you call this?" I grinned at him, stepping back as I realised I was getting covered in snow from his cloak. "Do you think we're running some fancy Londinium wine-shop, with a door slave on duty all night long to let the late revellers in?"

"Terrible service at this mansio, Sis!" He laughed, his green eyes sparkling in the candle-light. "A man could freeze to death waiting for the lazy innkeeper to open up. I thought I was going to have to sleep in the stables." He began to stamp the snow off his boots.

"Serves you right for arriving when all sensible folk are tucked up in bed. But it's good to see you, Lucius. Really good. We were only saying today, it'll be an extra special holiday, having you here with us."

"I'm glad to be home, believe me. I've had a bad journey."

"You must be mad, travelling in such foul weather in the dark. Couldn't it wait till morning?"

"It's a long story. Let's go through into the kitchen where it's warm."

"Good idea. Wait though—what about your horse? Shall I wake one of the boys? Or have you seen to it?"

"I haven't got one. I walked from Eburacum."

"Now I know you're mad! But come and get warm."

He followed me along the corridor. "I didn't want anyone to know I'd come here, and it's no distance really, you can do it in four hours. It isn't snowing there, at least it wasn't when I left." He sighed. "It probably is by now. The storm started when I was about five miles from here, and I just had to push on and get through as quickly as I could. It was quite bad. I'd a job to see my hand in front of my face, let alone the road under my feet. It's a good thing I was coming home, on a road I know well."

"You've walked *five miles* in this weather?"

"Not a carriage to be had," he joked. "It's why I'm so late."

Our large kitchen never gets cold even in winter, because we keep one brazier going all night, damped down with turf, to make it easier to get hot food and drink ready in the morning. Sure enough, it was quite reasonably warm, and Lucius relaxed as he took in the familiar room, with the cooking hearths and store-cupboards, pots and pans hanging along one wall, the enormous scrubbed wooden table, and the fresh tangy scents of bunches of dried herbs hanging from the ceiling. He stripped off his travelling cloak, boots, and leggings. The thick wool tunic he was wearing underneath the cloak was damp, and he was shivering, chilled to the bone. I stirred the brazier into life, made a small fire on one of the cooking hearths, and put a bronze pan of wine on a tripod to heat.

He went to warm his hands over the brazier. "Is Albia at home? Or staying with Candidus?"

"At home, at least till after Saturnalia. Candidus will come here and have a few days with us." I unlocked the cupboard where our precious spices were kept, and found a couple of cloves, which I dropped into the wine. I added a pinch of ginger and some honey and began to stir it, and a good rich smell wafted through the room. "She'll be thrilled that you've arrived. We've both been looking forward to having you here for the holiday."

"There's something I want to tell you before she comes."

A fierce voice called out from the hall, "What in the gods' name is going on here? Oh, *Lucius!*" and Albia herself rushed in. He got another warm hug.

"I heard noises," she explained, "and I thought it must be some of the slaves messing about in here. I might have known it was our wandering boy." She looked him critically up and down. "You've gone thin. Don't they feed you properly in Londinium?"

"Not as well as you would, Albia. But I'm fine, or will be when I've managed to get warm again. And you're looking terrific. Being engaged to be married obviously agrees with you. How's Candidus?"

She began to recount their latest doings, and I kept quiet, concentrating on stirring the wine. Eventually when there was a lull, I said, "Lucius, your bedroom will be as cold as ice. I mean literally—there'll be ice on the inside of your window, like there is on mine. I'll wake one of the slaves, to put a brazier in there. We've already nailed up your Saturnalia greenery, so it'll feel like home."

"I can only stay for tonight," he said. "I shouldn't even do that, but I'll wait here till daylight, as the weather's so bad. Then I must be off again. I've got to be back in Eburacum by noon, snow or no snow. So I'll sleep in here, where it's warm already. I just need a couple of good thick blankets."

"Only tonight?" Albia asked. "But you're coming back for the holiday?"

He shook his head sadly. "No, I'm not. I've got to lie low. I'm sorry," he added, seeing our disappointed faces. "I was looking forward to it, but there's been a change of plan. This is the only chance I have to see you at all, then I'm going invisible in the Eburacum area for a while, maybe a month or two."

"Going invisible" meant he'd be on an undercover assignment. I opened my mouth to protest, but shut it again, because there was no point. We knew Lucius' secret investigations often interfered with his personal plans, but we'd wanted so much to make this Saturnalia a real family occasion.

Albia, ever practical, broke the sombre silence. "Well, at least you've time to get warm and dry. Are you hungry?"

He laughed. "Does Caesar win all the chariot-races?"

She crossed over to one of the store-cupboards. "Bread and sausage all right? And a few olives?"

"Food for the gods! And are there any of Cook's honey cakes?"

"I expect I can find some."

"Then while you're eating," I said, "you can tell us what's so important it stops you coming home for Saturnalia, but brings you into freezing cold Brigantia in a snowstorm. One of the usual reasons, I suppose—either you're in trouble, or you want something. Or perhaps both?"

He nodded. "You know me too well, Sis. I'm afraid it's trouble, and not just for me. Gods, I'm still frozen! Let me go and change into dry things, then I'll tell you."

He went off to his bedroom, where he always kept a good supply of clothes, even though he was hardly ever at home to wear them. Albia and I didn't trouble to speculate about what his news might be. Lucius had been an agent for the Governor for years, and if his work was bringing us trouble, it wouldn't be the first time. She put out a plate of food, while I lit some lamps and hung up the cloak and leggings my brother had left in a soggy heap on the floor.

Soon the three of us were sitting at the big pine table with steaming beakers of spiced wine, and Lucius was eating as if he hadn't seen food for a month. I found I was hungry too and helped myself to a few black olives, while he got through a doorstep-sized hunk of bread thickly covered with sliced sausage. Finally I said, "Come on then, what's this all about? What are you investigating in this part of the world? I thought you were permanently based down south these days. We all know you enjoy loitering about in Londinium, spending every afternoon at the baths and every evening in a tavern."

He didn't smile. "Londinium isn't a good place for me just now. Titus has sent me up here." Titus was Lucius' immediate boss on the Governor's staff. "There's been some trouble, and before I go invisible, there's something I have to tell you. I couldn't risk a letter. I haven't told anybody except Titus I'd be coming here, and if anyone asks, you haven't seen me since I was home in September." His green eyes flashed, giving him the look of a child who's about to reveal some clever piece of mischief he's just perpetrated. And suddenly it was as if we were all children again, sharing with each other the misdemeanours we could never tell the grown-ups. I found myself asking a familiar question.

"Lucius, what have you done?"

"Nothing." His answering grin was familiar too, an absurd mixture of sheepishness and defiance.

"What sort of nothing?" That was the next question in the time-honoured sequence.

"Have some more wine." He offered me the jug.

"Don't change the subject. *What have you done?*"

"Well…I've been a bit of an idiot. I had an affair with the wife of somebody rather important in Londinium, and he found out."

"Is that all?" I scoffed. "I thought that was what you young officers spent your whole lives doing. What's so different this time?"

"This time, the man I've offended chose to make an issue of it. He complained to the Governor, and as a result I've been dismissed from government service."

I couldn't believe it. "Dismissed? For something like that? Surely there's more to it?"

"No, not really. The woman's husband is an imperial freedman, one of the Emperor's hand-picked officials. He threatened to report the whole thing to Caesar if the Governor didn't get rid of me. So he's sent me back north in disgrace, with my tail between my legs."

"You're right, you have been an idiot!" I snapped.

"That's putting it kindly," Albia exclaimed. "So what happens now?"

Lucius began to laugh, and he laughed till tears filled his eyes. Albia and I sat staring at him, not knowing what to say or do. Our brother had lost his career as an investigator, the job he enjoyed and did supremely well. With it had gone his favoured position in official circles, his good name, his monthly pay—and all he could do was laugh?

Finally he spluttered into silence. "That's exactly the reaction I was hoping for." He drew a deep breath, and I thought he was going to start laughing once more, but he controlled it. "I'm sorry, but you should just see your faces! And you two know me better than anyone else in the world! Yet you believed me when I said I was in disgrace. That's excellent!"

He was serious again. "My so-called dismissal and disgrace are only temporary. They're a cover for the investigation I'm about to start on."

I felt relief mixed with annoyance at his nonsense. "You rat," I growled. Another of our childhood expressions.

"I know. I'm truly sorry, but I had to be sure my little tale of woe would work." He cut himself more sausage. "The point is, the Governor's been under pressure to dismiss me, but not because of anything I've done. So Titus invented a story that would give His Excellency a pretext for getting rid of me, and then we can use my sad fall from favour to help in an assignment here. Once I've completed that, I'll be reinstated."

I was puzzled. "The Governor's been under pressure to dismiss you? But the Governor is the chief man in this whole province. Who has the power to bring that sort of pressure on him?"

"And why would they?" Albia added.

"As to who, it's someone in the Imperial Palace in Rome, who's got the ear of Caesar and wants to persuade him that I'm involved in a conspiracy, and you two are helping me. As to why…that someone is an old enemy of ours, who's doing his best to get the whole Aurelius family branded as traitors and destroyed."

"An enemy in Rome? We don't *know* anybody in Rome," Albia objected.

"We do now. The Shadow of Death is there."

The mere mention of the name made me shiver. The Shadow of Death was the brilliant, devious rebel leader whose war-band almost destroyed us four years ago. We thought we'd seen the last of him. But now he was in Rome, at the very heart of the Empire, and he was still our enemy.

"The Shadow of Death." I could hardly bear to say the words. "Has he acquired so much influence at Caesar's court that he can really hurt us, so far away in Britannia?"

"I don't know. I hope not. But he's trying to, and that puts our Governor in a difficult position." He sighed. "Things are bad down in Londinium. I hate to think what it's like in Rome itself. Everyone's running round in circles, afraid of their own shadow. The Emperor…. Listen, I know I can speak freely with you two, but it's a luxury I don't enjoy often, and what I'm going to say has to stay within these walls."

"If you're about to tell us," I said, "that the Emperor Domitian is wrecking the government of the Empire because of his paranoia, that's hardly a state secret."

"You're right, the mere fact itself is no secret. But people outside government circles haven't any idea how serious things are. Domitian is getting more and more unstable with every month that passes."

Albia poured him more wine. "Unstable? Mad, in plain Latin?"

"Not completely mad, but certainly obsessed with the idea of treason. He sees conspirators behind every screen, killers under every couch. I don't suppose you get much palace gossip from Rome up here, so you won't have heard what happened to the last Governor, Sallustius Lucullus."

"The one that was in charge four years ago when we had all that trouble?" I reached for a honey cake. "He was recalled to Rome, and then…I suppose he got posted to another province. Or is he enjoying a well-earned retirement, living on the money he made in Britannia?"

"Neither." Lucius got up and started pacing about the room. "Caesar had him executed."

"For treason?" I began to see dimly where he was driving.

"The official explanation," Lucius smiled without any humour, "was that he allowed a new type of spear to be named after him. You may well look blank, I never heard of a Lucullan spear either. I suppose it may have existed in some outlying fort, but it was hardly the talking-point of Britannia. Anyway, the true reason was that Lucullus was one of several leading politicians whom Domitian suspected of treason."

"It sounds like a nightmare," I said. "It makes me glad we live far away from palaces and courts."

"Yes, but we're still in the Empire, so we're not far enough away to be completely safe. If someone decides to whisper in Caesar's ear that the army in northern Britannia is looking about for a new Emperor, *and* is being actively supported by a certain investigator with family connections near the Eburacum gar-rison—well, he wouldn't take much persuading."

"*He* might not," I said, "but the Governor here is a different matter. He employs you! He trusts you. Doesn't he?"

"He does, or I'd be dead already. But he's got to look after his own interests. If he did nothing at all about the rumours from Rome, and it turned out that we *were* somehow involved in a conspiracy...."

"What sort of conspiracy?"

"Oh, the usual kind. A plot to choose a new Caesar from among the generals here in Britannia, march on Rome, and assassinate Domitian."

"*Merda!* And is there a real conspiracy, or has the Shadow of Death made the whole story up?"

"That's where he's been so clever. There isn't any such plot that we know of, but there are whispers of trouble in the garrison at Eburacum, the kind of discontent that could develop into a full-blown plot, if it isn't stopped." He strode over to the hearth, picked up the pan of wine and brought it to the table, but didn't sit down. "So far it's only rumours, loose talk, and a higher than usual number of soldiers deserting from the garrison. But if the discontent gets more serious.... That's why the Governor wants me to appear to be seriously discontented too, so I can find out what's going on."

"It's just the sort of assignment you do well," Albia said. "But I still don't see why you have to go through this play-acting about being in disgrace."

"Because I come from this area, and too many people know me, including the lads at Eburacum. They know I'm on the Governor's staff, so I'm just the sort of man that conspirators would never confide in—unless I behave like a disgruntled former officer, wanting to get my own back and make some mischief."

I didn't much like the sound of that. "This is devious business, even for you, brother. You're accused of taking part in a conspiracy, so you pretend to be in disgrace and investigate it? If the Governor isn't satisfied with the outcome, you'll be in disgrace for ever. If the conspirators find out who you're really working for, you'll be dead."

Lucius grinned suddenly. "I never said it was easy. But I can do it."

I saw Albia's face twitch into a smile, and I felt myself smiling too. This whole crazy assignment was the sort of adventure

Lucius loved. He was brave, reckless, clever—and he was our brother.

"Well, since you're in this pickle, I suppose Albia and I had better help you out of it." I glanced at my sister, who nodded. "What do you want us to do?"

"Thank you." He sat down again, making a visible effort to relax. "First and most important, I want you to be certain that I'm not doing anything dishonourable or treasonable. Whatever rumours you hear about my dreadful behaviour—and I need my character blackened, if I'm going to succeed—they won't be true. I hope they won't damage you and the Oak Tree too much, but what I care about most is that you shouldn't be personally hurt by believing them."

"Where will these rumours be coming from?" Albia wanted to know.

"My former colleagues in the Governor's office, to begin with. Since I've been dismissed, they've been putting the word about that I'm no longer, as they term it, 'completely sound'. That sort of bad news spreads quickly, and once the gossips get to work, you'll hear all sorts of tales from unexpected sources."

"Right then. You said Albia and I are suspected of helping you, in other words we're potential traitors too. Will anyone try to investigate us here at the mansio?"

He nodded. "Quite likely, yes. A spy, perhaps more than one, may come snooping about, looking for anything that can be used against you. They'll discover no evidence of treason, of course, but they could try to find or fake some other reason to get you thrown out of the Oak Tree. Stealing official transport. Not paying your taxes. Upsetting important travellers. Something serious enough to make the Governor sit up and take notice. So if you have any unusual guests, you'll need to keep your wits about you, in case they're looking for ways to catch you out. Luckily you don't have many visitors in winter. By the spring I hope this will all have blown over."

"I'll drink to that," I said.

"Now, there's just one more thing you can help me with." He sipped his wine. "Something that's right up your street."

"You want a free cart-load of beer to help you get to know the conspirators?" I suggested.

He laughed. "I'll let you know! But for now, tell me what you can about morale among the military in this area. You get soldiers dropping by here all the time. Has there been more grumbling and grousing than usual lately?"

"Oh yes," I said. "It's been quite noticeable this year, especially with more and more men from the far north being moved back into our part of Brigantia. Not that I'm complaining, our bar takings have benefited from plenty of unhappy infantry drowning their sorrows."

"Good. What have they been moaning about?"

"You mean besides their food, their pay, and their centurions? Mostly the way so many troops have been withdrawn from Britannia, to fight wars in other parts of the Empire. They feel the army here is being weakened, losing too many good men."

He nodded. "Are they complaining specifically about Caesar? Or just about their commanders in general?"

"More about Caesar himself," Albia answered. "They've been telling each other how Governor Agricola was all set to conquer the whole island of Britannia twelve years ago, but then Caesar threw away the chance, and it'll never come again. Especially the older men, who served under Agricola himself."

"And you think it's more serious than usual?"

I considered it. "It's unusual for them to be blaming Caesar in person, I suppose. Domitian has always been popular with the army."

"But we're talking about bar-room grousing, not serious plotting," Albia said. "And a good measure of bragging mixed in with it. If I had a gold piece for every soldier that's told me how he was personally commended for bravery by Agricola on a battlefield, I could build myself a palace."

Lucius scratched his head and sighed. "I've some sympathy with their grumbling, you know. No, don't worry, I'm not turning into a conspirator already! But Agricola was a brilliant general, and he was here for long enough to do really good work. He could have extended the province of Britannia to cover the whole of the island, or his successor could have done it. There was only the very northernmost part left to conquer when he was recalled."

"There's nothing much up in the far north, though," I put in. "Just mountains and mists and a bunch of wild Caledonian tribesmen. I always thought it would mean a lot of hard fighting for very little gain. If the barbarians can live there, they're welcome to it."

"That seems to be what Caesar thinks too," Lucius said. "With all his other wars, he hasn't left us enough soldiers to advance further into the Caledonian lands, or even hold on to all the territory that Agricola conquered. So the frontier's being pulled back little by little, and some of the legionaries don't like it. It wouldn't be too surprising if a few hotheads think they'd prefer a Caesar who takes Britannia more seriously. Well, if they're based at Eburacum, I'll find them." He yawned suddenly. "Gods, the wine and food are making me feel tired. I may as well grab a couple of hours' sleep, I think. And thank you both." He smiled at us. "You never let me down, and I appreciate it."

"We're family," I answered, "and families stick together, no matter what."

It snowed for the rest of the night, but Lucius insisted on leaving for Eburacum as soon as there was enough light to see the road. He wouldn't take a horse or a mule, because he'd have to account for how he came by it. So he put on dry boots and a fresh cloak, and Albia packed him a bag of food and a wine-skin.

I went out as far as the main road to see him off. "Lucius, what was it you wanted to tell me that wasn't for Albia's ears?"

"Ah, yes, I almost forgot. About Candidus."

"What about him?"

"Something I overheard in Eburacum yesterday—only tavern talk, there may be nothing in it, but we can't be too careful just now. He's supposed to be mixed up in some sort of shady dealing there. Not major crime, but smuggling, evading taxes, that sort of thing. Keep an eye on him, and warn Albia if you think you should. With the family's affairs liable to be under suspicion anyway, the last thing we need is Candidus getting himself into trouble."

"I like Candidus, but he strikes me as naïve, and perhaps too soft. It wouldn't surprise me if he got himself involved in something not quite legal, but out of ignorance, not villainy."

We reached the road, and Lucius turned and looked at me seriously. "I'm sorry you two are involved in all this. Just remember—whatever you hear about me, I won't do anything to be ashamed of."

I gave him a hug. "We know that. We'll survive, don't you worry. And if you need us, you know where we are. Now off you go, and the gods go with you."

Chapter III

Back in the kitchen, Cook had just brought fresh bread from the bakehouse, and its delicious smell made me feel hungry. Cook was grumbling that someone had been "messing about in here in the night." I told him I'd felt restless and made myself a warm drink, and Albia had heard me moving around and come to investigate. He muttered darkly about people not clearing up properly, and asked why two of us had used enough crockery for three, but when I didn't respond he let it drop. He knew as well as the rest of us that some visitors were not to be gossiped about.

After breakfast I put on my warmest cloak and boots and went out to do my morning rounds. The snow and wind had finally ceased, and the sun was rising in a clear sky. There were perhaps four inches of crisp snow crunching underfoot and gleaming on the roofs of the buildings. The whole world sparkled dazzling white with a pinkish tinge, and the beauty of it all made me catch my breath.

I headed for the stable yard, where my stable master Secundus was keeping a watchful eye on the morning chores of feeding, mucking-out, grooming, and exercising. Though winter is a quiet time, if you have livestock to care for, you can never relax completely. True, there weren't many travellers' horses or mules to care for, but our own animals still had to be looked after.

Nearby I spotted Ursulus, my farm manager, setting men to work clearing the snow from the forecourt and the track. I called him and Secundus over for a quiet word. They were my senior men, the ones we'd be relying on to make sure we were well guarded against trouble. When I passed on Hawk's warning about the Wolf-pack and suggested night-time guards, they agreed readily.

"Especially during Saturnalia," Ursulus said. "Don't worry, we'll make sure everyone does a turn on guard."

"We'll take no chances," Secundus agreed. "Can't guarantee they won't moan a bit though."

I walked past the stables to the big paddock, stopping by the fence to look over our animals. The official livestock was a real mixture. Just about any size, shape and colour of beast that could be ridden or driven came our way sooner or later. Mixed in with them were some of our own black horses, my pride and joy. I'm building up a herd of good breeding stock, and last year's crop of foals had been excellent.

Two of the horse-boys were feeding them hay. They were both good lads: Castor, tall and square and brown-haired, and Secundus' son Titch—or Victor as he liked to be called now. He was a lively red-headed lad, and he'd always been known as Titch because of his small size. Now that he'd reached the age of seventeen, though he wasn't exactly of Herculean build, he wanted to lose his boyhood nickname, and I did my best to remember. But I still thought of him as Titch, and probably always would.

"Morning, boys," I called. "Everything all right?"

Titch stopped and came running over to me. "Good news, Mistress. Poppaea's had her pups, and they're all fine."

"Gods, that's a relief!" The lad's little brown bitch had spent the last few days looking as if she'd drop her litter any time, and he'd been consumed with pre-natal nerves. "How many has she got?"

"Six. Four brown like she is, and two black and white. Four dogs, two bitches. She had 'em in the night, in the tack-room. I stayed up with her. It was hard work, but we managed it."

"'We'?" I laughed. "Isn't that just like a man? It sounds to me as if it was Poppaea who did all the managing!"

He laughed too. "Aye, well, it's true, she knew what to do without me. But I wouldn't have missed it." He embarked on a blow-by-blow account, and I let him tell me all about it. He loved that little dog, and this was her first litter. "Do you think Cook'll give me some extra meat scraps to feed her? She's hungry all the time."

"I'm sure he will. Tell him I said it's all right."

"While I was up last night," he said softly, "or this morning I mean, I saw…." He hesitated, which made me look at him sharply.

"Saw what?" I thought I could guess.

"Did I dream it," he lowered his voice still more, "or did we have a visitor?"

Yes, if anyone in the household had spotted our unexpected guest, it would be this observant lad.

"You dreamt it, Titch. Nobody came here last night."

He winked to show me he'd understood. "I thought not. In my dream, it was Master Lucius."

I nodded. "By an odd coincidence, I dreamt about my brother, too."

"Is that right? Well in my dream, he didn't bring a horse with him. Did he walk through the snow?"

"He must have done, if you dreamt it that way. Have you told anyone else?"

"Only me dad. Very private things, dreams, aren't they?"

"Very. And we all know that Lucius hasn't been here since last September. He came to stay for a couple of days then, didn't he?"

"Aye, I remember."

"Good. Now, will your Poppaea let me look at her pups?"

It was a pleasant leisurely morning, with only a handful of customers in the bar, so we left Carina to take care of them. Albia and I checked our Saturnalia preparations, making sure we'd enough food and plenty of presents. Even the lowliest slave received a gift at this time of year. Then we compared notes over what we would wear at Chief Councillor Silvanius'

Saturnalia banquet, the social highlight of the holiday. We'd both had new tunics made, but we still had to choose the right shoes, brooches, and ear-rings. These were momentous decisions, because it would be a very grand affair. As Chief of the Oak Bridges Town Council, Silvanius celebrated all the Roman festivals in the most extravagant style, and expected his guests to do the same. I couldn't help smiling sometimes, when I reflected that he was born here in Britannia, yet now as a Roman citizen and public figure he took Roman traditions even more seriously than people like us, who were born and bred in Italia.

We only referred once to Lucius' visit. We were in my study out of earshot of the household, and I said, "I suppose we'd better think about what we'll do if we find ourselves with a guest who tries to spy on us. It's a nasty thought."

"Yes, it is." Albia was gazing at a large black spider that had stationed itself high up in a corner. "I must remember to tell the maids that this room needs a good clean."

"Don't you dare! When they clean in here, I can never find anything afterwards."

She giggled. "You can never find anything anyway. A spy who seriously wants to go through your papers will spend the first few days trying to understand your filing system, until he realises you haven't got one. Then he'll give up in despair and go home."

"I knew the gods had made me untidy for a good reason. Your kitchen notes and records are all so neat, they'd make any snooper jump for joy."

"Except I can't see what there is worth spying on in the kitchen, unless it's a rival mansio wanting Cook's recipe for honey cakes."

"I remember a trick Lucius told us once, for checking if someone's been searching a chest or opening a cupboard. Put a single hair across the hinges, or the place where a lid or a door opens. Anybody snooping about won't notice if they disturb something so small."

"Not a bad idea, if we get any visitors who seem too nosey. You know, Relia, last night when Lucius told us about the Shadow of Death, it all seemed very threatening. But now, in the daylight, with no spies in sight, it's hard to take it seriously, isn't it?"

Just before noon Candidus arrived. We were in the bar by then, and he burst in, gave his fiancée a huge embrace, and called out, "You must all have a drink with me. I've got the most wonderful news!"

His enthusiasm was infectious. "That's the best offer we've heard all morning," Albia said. "What shall we drink?"

"A jug of the very best, because my news deserves a proper celebration."

He's really a good fellow, I thought, as Albia fetched the wine, and he's devoted to my sister. Why do I have these reservations about him? What makes me think that under all his boyish charm he's somehow unreliable?

I pushed the thoughts aside and handed round beakers to the half-dozen or so customers, as I listened to what he was saying.

"You know that I've been looking for premises in Eburacum, for my new business. Oak Bridges is all very well, but I need a bigger town to work in. Now I've found just the place—a house by the river, with a warehouse building attached, and its own jetty. I've taken a lease on it, and I'm moving in straight away."

"That's wonderful!" Albia exclaimed. "Let's drink a toast…."

"Not so fast," I said. "Of course we will, but let's hear more details first." He'd proposed various business schemes over the past few months, and I couldn't be sure which one was his current favourite. "Now, tell us the whole thing, Candidus. This is your river trading venture, is it?"

"Yes, and I've saved the best till last. I've gone into partnership with a local river pilot, and bought a half share in his boat. He's a real old-time sailor, they all call him the Skipper, and he knows everything there is to know about the tides, and the safe channels, and the tricky shoals and sandbanks. We'll be able to carry cargo along all the rivers that you can reach from Eburacum, probably even down to the sea eventually. He'll handle the transport, I'll do the negotiating. It's perfect!"

It sounded fine, but Lucius' warning about shady dealing forced its way into my mind. "What sort of cargo?"

"To start with, building materials, which cost an arm and a leg to move by road because they're so heavy. Just think of it— limestone from the quarries at Calcaria, timber from the woods around, iron, roof-tiles—they can all be brought in by water. And I've got one or two other good ideas, but I'm keeping the details under my toga for the present. Too much competition."

"And too many inconsiderate tax collectors wanting their share?"

"Aurelia, how could you even think it?" He grinned broadly. "I have the deepest respect for tax collectors."

"And I'm the Queen of Brigantia! We're honoured to have such a virtuous citizen in our midst, aren't we, Albia?"

"Stop teasing him and let him talk. Go on, Candidus."

"The point is, Eburacum is growing like a mushroom in a muck-heap. There are new houses going up everywhere, and workshops and warehouses. The whole place looks more like a building-site than a town. And people from the surrounding area are starting to buy town houses there."

I thought this was going too far. "Really? Anyone we know?"

"Yes. Chief Councillor Silvanius has bought one for his sister Clarilla. Since she moved to Oak Bridges to keep house for him, she's been fretting about not getting to town as much as she used to."

If our esteemed Chief Councillor was buying property there, Eburacum must surely be the coming place, and Candidus' scheme had more to recommend it than some of his other ideas for turning a quick denarius. "Good. Then I wish you every success."

Albia beamed, and raised her beaker. "When we're married, I'll be able to help you with all the paperwork. Now here's a toast—to Candidus, the successful businessman."

"And Albia, his successful wife," he answered, and we all drank.

We ate a cheerful midday meal, and just as we were finishing it, a sudden wild gust of wind drove a heavy shower of hail against the mansio walls. The customers in the bar drank up and headed for home, and Candidus decided to do the same.

"I must start organising my move to Eburacum. There's so much to do! But I'll come again tomorrow, I promise."

Albia and I lazed by the fire, enjoying the luxury of a quiet afternoon, and the feeling of being snug and warm while the wind howled round outside. The hail showers came and went, and then turned into snow flurries. I roused myself to do my rounds before dark, and as I stepped outside I was surprised to hear a clatter of hooves and a rumble of wheels. I looked up towards the main road.

Three of the biggest carriages I'd ever seen were turning off the highway and heading down the track to our forecourt. They rolled in a slow, stately procession towards me, and I stood there gaping for a few heartbeats, taken completely by surprise. I don't think I could have been more astonished to see Caesar on a white elephant leading a parade of golden chariots.

They were large, elaborate closed carriages, with ornate brass on their bodywork that would have been gleaming brightly but for the thin coating of snow, and some spatters of mud that had the effrontery to cling to them. They were pulled by beautifully matched chestnut horses, and accompanied by four well-mounted bodyguards. The guards and the carriage drivers wore dark blue cloaks which exactly matched the blue of the curtains drawn across the vehicles' windows.

It was a thoroughly Roman procession, rich and powerful enough to crush anything or anyone that got in its way. I didn't need the Delphic Oracle to tell me that whoever owned it would be much the same. What in the gods' name was it doing here? My surprise turned to unease.

Albia came out to stand beside me, smiling as she looked the entourage over. "Somebody rich, Relia. In fact *very* rich. And at this time of day, they must be intending to stay, not just dropping in for a quick drink and travelling on. Good."

"Rich, certainly, but I don't know about 'good'. I was looking forward to some peace and quiet, and rich guests are normally nothing but trouble, rude, demanding, and ungrateful, whatever you try to do for them."

"I know. But they're still rich. Just concentrate on how nice it'll be when they leave again, and we collect all those big fat tips." Albia always looks on the bright side; it's one of the things everyone loves about her, even me, when I can't share her optimism.

"They probably won't stay long," I said, trying to find something positive to contribute. "It's Saturnalia in two days. They'll want to be in their own home for that, surely."

The carriages juddered to a stop in a neat line right outside the front door. They couldn't have been better positioned to be in our bar customers' way, if we'd had any customers, but that's rich people for you. The guards dismounted and stood to attention beside their horses, trying not to shiver too obviously. The leading driver got down and opened the door of his carriage, and unfolded a set of steps, placing them ready for the passengers to descend. The other vehicles remained closed up. It was like a stage ready set for someone to make a grand entrance.

An insignificant little weasel of a man teetered down the steps, glancing quickly around him. He was slightly built and sharp-faced, with a thin mouth, and touches of grey in his dark hair. Though he was neatly groomed and wore a good fur-trimmed cloak, he wasn't the owner. My guess was a secretary or clerk, though a favoured one, to travel in the leading carriage.

He looked at me like a senator who's just stepped in a dog-turd. "You there! Young lady!"

"Good afternoon." I didn't step forward. The grand personage behind the curtains might make me jump to it, but not this dogsbody.

"We want accommodation for a night or two." He came a couple of paces nearer. "My lord and lady will take your best rooms, and we'll need rooms for the rest of the party too. I'll look the place over first, of course, and have a word with your cook. I assume you have reasonable quarters for the slaves, and proper stabling."

"Certainly, it'll be a pleasure. We've plenty of rooms at this time of year." I started working out how many of them there must be: fifteen at least, maybe twenty. An unusually large group any time, and in winter, almost unheard-of. The extra trade would be welcome. Maybe Albia was right to look on the bright side.

"Well then, don't just stand there," the weasel ordered. "Fetch the innkeeper."

"I am the innkeeper. Aurelia Marcella, at your service."

"Oh." Not the most enthusiastic reaction I've ever had, but I'm used to it. I took a couple of steps forward, and even managed a smile. "Welcome to the Oak Tree Mansio. We'll be pleased to provide everything you need."

He was distinctly put out. "*You* can't be the innkeeper! Surely there must be a man in charge of an official mansio."

"My brother and I run the mansio. But he's not here at present."

"When will he be back?"

"Well," I pretended to consider it, "next month maybe, or the month after that." I enjoyed his baffled expression, and then took pity on him and explained. "My brother Lucius Aurelius and I are joint proprietors here, but he's mostly away on army service, so I and my sister run the place." I indicated Albia, but he barely gave her a glance.

"I see." He surveyed the wide forecourt with its thickening carpet of snow, and then he looked in through the open front door to the bar-room. I followed his gaze, trying to see everything afresh, as if for the first time. I thought, it all looks in good order, the walls white and clean, the room well-lighted and prettily decorated, and that big inviting fire must appeal to anyone who's spent all day on the road. So if you're thinking we've let standards slip because we haven't got a man in charge, then think again.

A gruff female voice called from inside the carriage. "Mustela! What's going on? Are you proposing to stand chattering all day?" The curtain on the side window nearest me was twitched back a little way.

Mustela? So I wasn't the only one who thought he looked like a weasel! I almost felt sorry for the poor chump, being addressed as one—almost, but not quite, because I caught a quick flash of anger in his black eyes when he heard the nickname, and saw the way he suppressed it and put on a smiling deferential mask as he turned towards the carriage. It isn't only Janus who has two faces.

"I'm sorry, my lady," the Weasel answered. "It's just that…I'm wondering if we should stay at this mansio after all. There's no landlord here, it's very unorthodox. This young person says she's the innkeeper."

"Oh, don't *fuss,* Mustela," came the voice. "The place doesn't look too bad, and anyway you know my nephew said it was the only possible one in this area. Go and see if the rooms are acceptable, and be quick about it. I'll die of cold if I have to sit out here much longer. Margarita, you'd better go with him."

"Very good, my lady," the Weasel said meekly.

A pretty young woman in a cream fur cloak trimmed with black stepped down from the carriage. She had blue eyes, and long fair hair tied back under a fur cap. She was either one of the family or a favourite slave or freedwoman. The way she didn't stand next to the Weasel told me she disliked him, so she had good taste.

"My sister Albia is my housekeeper," I said. "She'll be pleased to show you our guest wing."

"Of course." Albia smiled at them. Albia is pretty, and her smile usually gets a favourable response, especially from male guests, but not from this toe-rag. The girl Margarita smiled back though, and murmured, "Thank you."

"We've no overnight guests at present," Albia continued, "so our seven guest-rooms are at your disposal, and there'll be plenty of room for the servants in our slave quarters at the back."

"And Margarita, tell them to make sure the bath-water is hot," the disembodied voice called from the carriage. "You have got a bath-house suite here, haven't you?"

"We have. And it'll be hot, I promise." Albia gestured for the Weasel and Margarita to follow, and took them round the outside of the building to the guest wing. The mansio is built around a big courtyard, like a hollow square. The bar-room is at the front, with two wings sticking out behind it—the guest wing on the right, and our private quarters to the left. The bath-house is at the back.

The door of the second carriage opened softly, and a slim young man with beautiful dark chestnut hair jumped down. Greek, from his appearance, and extremely handsome, with the sort of fine, regular features that sculptors like to model. He gave me a courteous nod, then walked over to her ladyship's window. "How is his lordship now, my lady?" he asked, with just enough of a Greek accent to be attractive. "Shall I make up some more of his medicine?" Ah, so he was a doctor.

"He's resting, Timaeus," the gruff voice said. "Best thing for him. We'll get him into a warm bed as soon as we can. Yes, you may as well go inside and get some of his mixture ready."

The doctor turned enquiringly to me, and I beckoned one of the maids and told her to show him through to the kitchen. I could guess how Cook would react to a stranger trespassing on his territory, and hoped that "getting the mixture ready" didn't involve anything more complicated than warming up a pan. But customers have to be humoured, especially rich ones, and this customer had made up her mind to stay at least for tonight, by the sound of it. But she wasn't leaving her vehicle till her minions had gone through the motions of checking the rooms, so to get a look at her I strolled over to the carriage. I tried to peer in through the half-drawn curtain, but the interior was dark, and I saw her only as an indistinct figure wearing a red travelling cloak with a bulky fur collar and hood. As she noticed me at the window, she leaned closer, and I got an impression of a nose like a beak and sharp bird-like brown eyes. Next to her was another well-wrapped figure, his lordship presumably, lolling back against the cushions. All I could make out was a very pale face, with some wisps of grey hair showing under the edges of his hood. I caught the sound of his heavy breathing.

"May I bring you some warm wine, my lady?" I said into the semi-dark. "You and his lordship? It's chilly weather for travelling."

"That's the first sensible thing anybody's said to me since we got here. Yes, I will take a drop. And make sure it's really hot. Nothing for his lordship, though. I'm afraid he's far from well. The quicker we get him into bed, the better."

"I can speak for myself, Sempronia," came an old man's growl from the depths of the carriage. "I'll have some wine too. It will help to warm me up."

"Now, you know what Timaeus says…" his wife began, but he made a disparaging remark about the medical profession, and she subsided. I hid a smile as I went into the bar and fetched some hot spiced red wine. I handed two beakers through the carriage window, and there was a muttered exchange from within, followed by satisfied slurping noises. Soon the lady passed back the empty mugs. "That's better. What did you say your name is?"

"Aurelia Marcella. I'm the innkeeper of the Oak Tree Mansio. My brother and I…."

"Yes, yes, I got all that. I've got no memory for names these days, that's all. My secretary tends to fuss sometimes, and he's so conventional. *I've* no objection to a woman in charge of a mansio, provided she does a good job."

"Thank you."

"However, I won't stand for any nonsense from innkeepers, male or female. I hope you understand me?"

"Of course, yes."

The door of the second carriage opened again, and I saw that its driver had placed steps ready. Three people got out: a sandy-haired man of about thirty in a well-made cloak, an old grey-haired servant, and a small fair page-boy, only five or six years old. He was a striking-looking child, with fine features, huge blue eyes, and dark gold curls.

The third carriage opened too, but nobody bothered with steps. Six slaves piled out, four lads and two girls, dressed in matching blue cloaks. All the travellers stretched and shuffled, gazing round rather nervously, and pulling their cloaks tighter against the wind. Nobody said anything except the page-boy, who went to pet one of the bodyguards' horses, talking to it gently.

"Have you come far today, my lady?" I make no apology for always asking the same question, because it never fails.

"About eighteen miles, I think. Far enough, in this weather. We seem to have been travelling through this benighted back country for months! We left Londinium ten days ago, and mostly we've stayed in friends' villas along the way. We spent last night on the coast, where an acquaintance of ours has an estate—of course he wasn't there himself, and I don't blame him. They did their best, but you can't expect much in the way of civilisation this far north. I thank the gods we've got here at last."

I didn't feel like joining her in grateful prayers to the Immortals. That last sentence made it sound as if she'd be staying with us more than just the one night. Were we going to be stuck with her for the whole of the holiday? I asked, "Did I hear you say your nephew recommended you to stay here?"

"He didn't precisely recommend, he said it was in the most suitable location for the business we have in hand."

"Has he been a guest of ours?"

"Dear gods, no, he's used to better than this."

Well, naturally! But I supposed he deserved some compensations for having such a dreadful aunt. Come to that, why wasn't *she* staying with friends or family tonight, instead of at a mansio? Maybe she wasn't welcome among her nearest and dearest? "It was kind of him to think of us. Is your nephew coming to join you here?"

"No, he's far too busy. Paperwork a mile high, court cases to try, petitions to deal with—not to mention all the preparations for next year's military campaigning. He has to spend most of his time in Londinium nowadays, but mind you, he makes sure he's in touch with everything that's happening all over the province."

So he must be quite an important nephew, or maybe his fond auntie just thinks he is. "He's in Government service, then?" I asked.

"You could say that," she declared triumphantly. "His name is Metilius Nepos."

"The Governor!" Holy Diana, she was saying her nephew was the Governor of Britannia, the most powerful man in the entire province!

She gave a quiet, rasping chuckle. "Yes. I'm his father's sister, Sempronia Metilia."

"We're honoured to have you here." I actually meant it. Although she would be a colossal pain in the backside, she was genuinely as important as she made herself out to be. If we managed to keep her happy, we'd definitely be going up in the world. But, gods alive, if we didn't.... My foreboding of trouble grew. If she wasn't satisfied with every last detail of our service, she could get the Oak Tree closed down, or maybe she'd just have us thrown out and hand the mansio over to somebody else.

The weaselly slave emerged through the bar-room door, followed by Albia and the fair-haired girl. He strode round to the open carriage window and announced, "I've looked over everything, my lady. It'll do for two or three nights."

"I sincerely hope we shan't need longer," Sempronia answered.

So do I, I thought, but however long she stays, we'll keep her sweet somehow. We must. The alternative, a bad report carried back to the Governor of Britannia, didn't bear thinking about.

Chapter IV

Sempronia slowly descended from her carriage, helped by her secretary, who hovered close to her. She pushed back her hood and stood gazing around like a general assessing a battlefield. I tried to estimate her age, fifty-five at least, maybe sixty. She was thin and pale, with wrinkles and white hair, but her beady eyes missed nothing.

I noticed Margarita had gone to stand beside the sandy-haired man, and there was a fleeting look between them, a quick smile. The weaselly secretary saw it too, and his face took on an unpleasant gloating expression, then his deferential mask slid back.

Sempronia turned to me. "This is my son, Aulus Plautius Priscus." She indicated Sandy-hair, who gave a supercilious nod. I couldn't decide whether he was haughty, or simply shy. "Margarita is my maid and companion." The girl smiled at me, and I reflected that it comes to something when slaves have better manners than their owners. "You've met Diogenes—" she nodded towards the Weasel—"my confidential secretary." No smile there, and no manners either, but I already knew that. "The Lord Gnaeus Plautius, my husband, will go straight to his bed. I'm afraid he's very unwell, and will keep to his room, but our physician, Timaeus, will look after him. Oh, and the child there is Margarita's son Gaius." The page-boy stopped stroking the horse, and looked round at mention of his name. "Keep an eye on him, and let us know if he gets into mischief. I won't tolerate unruly children." She glared at the boy. "Do you hear me, Gaius? You're to behave yourself, or I'll be angry. And you know what will happen if you make me angry."

"Yes, my lady," the boy answered, lowering his eyes.

"And Horatius." Sempronia looked round. "Where's Horatius got to?"

Priscus gestured towards the second carriage. "He's sound asleep inside. I don't know how he does it. I'm freezing cold, and all my bones ache from bouncing around on the road, and *he's* been snoring away most of the journey." He banged with his fist on the carriage's side. "Horatius! Wake up, or you'll be spending the night with the horses!"

"All right, all right, I'm coming!" A large florid man of about fifty came slowly out, rubbing his eyes and yawning. "No need to shout. Have we arrived? Jupiter, it's cold! I need a drink."

"Ah, there you are at last. Horatius is my husband's cousin," Sempronia explained for my benefit. "Also our lawyer."

One look at his veined red face was enough to show how he'd contrived to sleep so soundly: with the aid of Bacchus, no doubt of it. And the wine he'd drunk hadn't improved his temper. "I don't know what I've done to offend the gods," he grumbled, "that they give me clients who insist on trundling halfway round the Empire in raging blizzards, and because the clients are also my relatives, I can't escape being dragged along with them."

"Oh do stop whining, Horatius," Sempronia exclaimed. "If I can endure it, and my poor Plautius in his state of health can endure it, then *you'll* surely manage to survive."

"I wouldn't bank on it," he growled. "This whole expedition is a complete waste of time, as I've said before, and if you ask me...."

"I am *not* asking you. I am simply requiring you to help me by doing the work I need you to do. You know why we've come here. If there were any other way to find my son, do you think I'd be trailing round this appalling countryside to look for him?"

"I expect so, yes, just to spite us all." He glowered at her. "Oh well, at least we're at journey's end now. I'm going to get a drink. I assume you're not planning on doing any work today, Sempronia?"

"Then you assume wrongly, Horatius. I shall have a hot bath, and yes, probably a little refreshment, and you can do the same if you like. After all it must be at least two hours since you had anything to drink." He opened his mouth to answer, but she waved him silent. "Then I shall start our enquiries. Be ready for a meeting in about an hour. Now that we're here, I want to make good use of the time. The quicker we start, the quicker we can finish, and get home to civilisation."

"I agree with you there, at least." Horatius headed for the bar-room, adding in a loud stage whisper, "Rush, rush, always rush! We'll all be dead before our time at this rate. Or one of us will," he added, but the last bit was a real whisper.

"Now don't stand there day-dreaming, the rest of you," Sempronia boomed. "Diogenes, get the luggage unloaded. Aulus dear, make sure the boy doesn't go wandering off. Nestor," she nodded towards her carriage driver, "make sure the animals are all properly cared for, and get the carriages cleaned up. We'll need them first thing in the morning. Hector," she indicated the leading bodyguard, "make sure the accommodation for the slaves is adequate. Margarita, you come with me, and we'll investigate the bath-house. And you, Aurelia Marcella," she rounded suddenly on me, "you'll oblige me by joining me in my room in about one hour."

Gods, what now? "Of course, if I can help."

"I need someone with local knowledge. We have business in this district, and you'll be able to give us directions, I daresay. I'll send for you when I've had my bath. Kindly be ready."

Sempronia took the largest guest-room, and adopted a smaller one adjoining it as a sitting-room. Her husband chose the next biggest, which adjoined the sitting-room on the other side. Timaeus helped him to bed, making it clear his master needed rest and quiet and no interference from strangers. Priscus, Horatius, Diogenes, and Margarita and Gaius took the other rooms. Timaeus said he would sleep on a couch in the sitting-room, so he could be near his patient. There was plenty of space in the slave block for the other servants.

But even getting the sick man settled caused a squabble. Horatius wanted that second-best room for himself, and so did Priscus. They both complained to me loudly in the corridor outside that his lordship could have managed with a smaller bedroom. I was wondering whether to fetch Sempronia to arbitrate, when we all heard the old man say, "Sempronia, tell them I'm taking this room, and there's an end of it." He didn't raise his voice, but they stopped protesting at once.

I found the handsome Timaeus in the kitchen, warming up a disgusting-smelling potion in a small brass pan. To my surprise, not to say relief, Cook was chatting to him amiably, so at least someone in this bickering bunch knew how to be diplomatic. I watched him stir the pan. He had good hands, well-shaped and with long slim fingers, and he wore an iron ring. So he was a citizen, perhaps a freedman, one of Plautius' clients. I'd taken him for a slave.

He gave me a dazzling smile. "I'm afraid we're putting you to a lot of trouble."

"Not at all. We hope you'll be comfortable here. I'm only sorry his lordship is so ill."

"It's hardly surprising. He should be at home in bed, not careering around the countryside in the cold. Anyway, you can leave it to me to care for him." His smile widened. "And of course, if any of you lovely ladies need any medical attention, you know where to find me. Now, this mixture should be hot enough, I think."

"He can give me an examination any time he likes," one of the maids commented when he'd gone.

There was general agreement from the kitchen slaves, and I thought, however troublesome most of the new guests are, the handsome doctor has only to whistle and everyone will come running. I might even come running myself.

Just before full dark I went out to the stables to make sure our lads were taking good care of the expensive transport, which they were, so I didn't linger long. The wind was bitter, and the snow was a continuous curtain now. We were in for a cold night.

But the bar-room was warm, and empty except for Albia.

"All alone?" I asked. "Have we finally got everyone happily settled?"

She nodded. "Settled, anyhow—to say 'happily' might be overdoing it. I never saw such a quarrelsome lot!"

"Nor I. It's probably a combination of the bad weather, plus having Sempronia barking at them all the time. And that little weasel Diogenes is a nasty piece of work."

"'Weasel' suits him. Sly and cunning, with sharp teeth. But Margarita seems pleasant enough. And what a gorgeous little boy!"

"That doctor's quite good-looking, isn't he?"

She giggled. "I thought you'd noticed him. Oh yes, definitely fanciable. Not that I'm interested for myself, but there's no law against looking. Well, Candidus will be here tomorrow to cheer us up. I hope it doesn't snow too much tonight. If the roads are blocked, he might not be able to come."

"Get on with you, it'll take more than a few feet of snow to keep your gallant fiancé away! What's worrying me is, if the weather turns really bad, Sempronia's party might get snowed in here, and we'll be stuck with them for days and days!"

She gave an elaborate shudder. "I'd like to know why she's dragging them all across Britannia in the dead of winter. Her husband especially. I only got a glimpse of him, but he's thin as a rail, and sort of grey and drawn-looking."

"I'll find out soon enough, I expect. She says she needs my local knowledge, so perhaps I'll tell her this whole district is suffering from a terrible infectious plague, and she'd better move on tomorrow before she catches it."

"Just say the word, and I'll get all our slaves to paint red blotches on their faces, and sneeze a lot."

In due course Diogenes came in and said, "My lady will see you now," as if I were some petitioner going to ask a favour. We walked together to the guest wing, but he didn't escort me into her ladyship's presence. He went into her bedroom, leaving me standing alone outside the sitting-room door. This turned me into an unintentional but not exactly unwilling eavesdropper. I couldn't help but hear raised voices coming from inside, so I stood quietly with my hand raised to knock, listening for all I was worth. Well, a girl can't help being curious.

"How many times must I repeat this, Horatius?" Sempronia was exclaiming. "Being here in person is the only way to convince Decimus we mean what we say. All of us—me, Gnaeus, and you."

"But if Decimus has decided to live with the girl, then he'll live with her, whether they're formally married or not, and regardless of what any of us say," Horatius retorted.

"Over my dead body," Sempronia snapped.

Timaeus came past just then, so I had to knock on the door, but I got no answer, and I whispered, "They don't seem to hear me," as if this was at least my third attempt to attract attention.

He murmured, "Go on in, I should. Her bark's worse than her bite."

"That's reassuring."

"Usually, anyway." He grinned and went off to Plautius' room, and I rapped extremely loudly on the door. This time Sempronia heard me and called, "Come in."

The visitors had lost no time in rearranging the room. The bed had been pushed into a corner, and a couple of reading-couches and several chairs and stools were arranged around the walls. There were two tables, and two bronze lamp-standards. All of this furniture had been moved in here from other guest-rooms, and so had two big braziers, which were throwing out heat like furnaces, making the whole room hotter than a bath-house caldarium.

Even so Sempronia was wrapped in a thick shawl, and had a bright wool rug across her knees. A fluffy yellow-and-white cat sat in her lap, looking bored. Horatius was there, and Priscus, and Margarita. Diogenes was sitting calmly at one of the tables. The little toe-rag had entered the room through the bedroom door, which had given the impression that I was late in answering her ladyship's summons.

"Aurelia Marcella! You've taken your time." Her look would have curdled milk, but innkeepers are tough, and I just smiled and made a silent vow to get even with Diogenes later.

"Well, now you've deigned to appear, sit down, and let's get on." She waved me towards a stool, and glanced round the room. "Are we agreed then? Horatius?"

He sighed. "I suppose so. Yes, agreed."

"Aulus, dear? You agree?"

"Yes," Priscus said. "If we must."

"Good. Because the quicker I can go back south where it's warm, the happier I shall be. What do you say, Medusa?" She paused to stroke the cat, which stared disdainfully at her, and then began washing itself. "I can't think how anyone survives in such a climate. Frost and snow and hail, and freezing winds! No wonder only natives and ne'er-do-wells live up here."

Which category does she think I fit into? I wondered. "You get used to it, my lady. I've been in Britannia sixteen years now, and it doesn't seem so bad."

"Where are you from originally?"

"From Italia. Pompeii."

Most people make sympathetic noises at this point in my life story, but all Sempronia said was, "There, Horatius, I told you she isn't a native."

"I only said she has native colouring," Horatius objected. He was sitting next to a table piled high with scrolls, but I noticed he'd made room on it for a wine jug and beaker. "Easy enough mistake to make. She's tall and fair, like all the natives. But now I look closer, her eyes are green, and the barbarians here have blue eyes. That right, m'dear?"

"That's right," I agreed, trying not to feel like a slave being auctioned and having my good and bad points discussed by potential buyers.

"And your housekeeper's not a native either, I'll bet," Horatius went on, reaching for his drink. "All those brown curls, and brown eyes. Where's she from?"

"My sister Albia? She's from Pompeii too."

"Your sister?" he said in surprise. "You don't look much alike, the two of you."

I wish I had a gold piece for every time I've heard that remark.

"We're half-sisters. We had the same father, but different mothers."

He sipped some wine. "She's a pretty little thing. Nice smile. Is she married?" Another often-repeated question.

"Not yet, but she's engaged. The wedding will be in the spring."

"Pity," he grunted.

I agreed with him.

"Now I trust I can rely on your discretion," Sempronia said. "I don't want every minute detail of our business to become common bar-room talk. So no tittle-tattling to the customers."

"Of course not. Absolute discretion."

She pushed the cat gently onto the couch beside her and held an imperious hand out to Horatius. "Pass me the letter, will you. The quickest way to give her the facts is to read it."

The lawyer picked out a slim scroll and tossed it to Diogenes, who got up and brought it to her ladyship.

Sempronia cleared her throat as she unrolled the papyrus. "This is from my elder son Decimus. Now, let me see…." She paused for a couple of heartbeats, making sure she was the focus of everyone's attention. She needn't have worried, we were all ears. Even the cat looked interested.

Decimus Plautius Curio to his dear father and mother, greetings. I have some marvellous news, which I hope will make you both happy for me. I've decided to settle here in Brigantia for good, because I've met the most wonderful girl, and have asked her to marry me. She's the kind of girl I've always wanted, beautiful, intelligent, and practical too, ready and willing to help me make a success of my new life in the north. We are both so happy, and plan to be married next year. Do say you'll come to the wedding and give us your blessing.

She gave a contemptuous snort. "My blessing, indeed! Does he seriously think I'll give my blessing to the marriage of my son to a native peasant girl?" She turned to me. "So you see the problem, don't you?"

"I see that you don't want your son making a marriage that you consider unsuitable," I said carefully.

"'Unsuitable' is putting it mildly. Decimus is well aware of his duty. He must make a marriage that will help his political career. We've already arranged a future wife for him, as he knows full well, a girl from the Fabius family. Most of the Fabii still live in Italia, and he'll join them in Rome. With their influence and money he'll get into the Senate as a matter of course, as his father did."

I wanted to say, maybe the poor boy doesn't fancy a political career, if it means leaving Britannia and having his life, and his wife, organised for him by his mother. But apart from that not being my business, everyone knows that with these rich senatorial families, the marriages are nearly always arranged by the parents, often when the prospective bride and groom are mere children. What those children might or might not want didn't count.

"Well, Aurelia Marcella," Sempronia barked, "you'll help us, I trust? You'll tell me where my son is?"

So the runaway hadn't given his dear mama his new address. I didn't blame him. "He's in this district somewhere?" I asked.

"Obviously. That's why we're staying here." She absently stroked the cat's head. "He's got a house between Eburacum and some obscure little town—Stone Bridges, is it, Horatius?"

"Oak Bridges?" I suggested. "That's our nearest town. About a mile from here."

"Yes, yes, that's right. I'm told it's a small place. Nothing there." Oak Bridges isn't a bad little town, but if you're a grand lady from Londinium, that's how the place would strike you, I suppose.

"He says he's going to start *trading!*" She almost spat the word out. "He says—where is it now? 'Eburacum is an expanding town, with a lot of new property going up. I'm sure there's a fortune to be made in trade, and I hope to move there….'" She threw down the scroll violently, making the cat twitch its ears. "I've never heard anything so ridiculous. Members of this family do not go in for *trade.*" She made it sound like the worst kind of abomination, treason, or cannibalism, or maybe both at once. "So we've come to find him and forbid this whole ludicrous enterprise, and insist that he returns home with us, and does his duty."

"That's where I come in," Horatius added. "Forbidding and insisting are always more effective when they're backed up by the majesty of the law."

Now I saw why Sempronia had brought her lawyer and her ailing husband with her. The classic way to persuade a runaway son to do his duty would be to threaten that if he didn't obey his parents, he'd be disinherited, cut out of his father's will without a copper coin.

"What I don't know," she said, "is exactly where to find Decimus. It's near here, so presumably you do. You'll give me directions to his house, if you please, and we'll go there tomorrow."

"I'm sorry. I don't know anyone called Decimus Plautius Curio."

"Don't be ridiculous! Or are you being deliberately unhelpful?"

"No, I'll help all I can. But I don't recognise the name."

"Surely you're aware what Roman settlers are buying property in these parts?"

"Many of them, yes. Especially if they're unusually successful, or if they're in trouble. But I haven't a complete list. If an ordinary young man is quietly setting up as a trader, courting a native girl, and not attracting any special attention, I may not hear of him for years."

She looked ready to explode, but said only, "That is *most* annoying. I'm extremely disappointed."

"I told you this was a fool's errand," Horatius commented.

She ignored him and continued to glare at me. "Well then, if you haven't the information yourself, you can make enquiries for us, can't you?" Her sharp eyes bored into mine. We both knew she wasn't asking a question, she was giving an order.

"Yes, I can ask around, certainly. My sister's fiancé lives a couple of miles from here, beyond Oak Bridges. He'll be likely to know about new settlers arriving between there and Eburacum. Of course it would help if you could offer a reward."

"Pay for information that leads me to him?" She sighed. "Very well. I suppose the days are gone when people will do one a service because it's their duty."

Gone and good riddance. But I just said, "I'm sure your generosity will produce results. We'll begin the search tomorrow. Albia's young man is intending to visit us then, and if he doesn't know of your son, I'll send to the Chief Town Councillor."

"You have a town council here? I'd assumed you would come under the military administration at Eburacum."

"Oak Bridges has its own council. The Chief Councillor is Silvanius Clarus, and he's a good friend of ours. I'm sure he'll be pleased to help if he can." He would, too, I was certain. As an important local magistrate with an eye to his town's future, he'd do anything at all to earn the gratitude of people related to the Governor.

"If the worst comes to the worst," Sempronia said, "I'll go out and search for him myself. We've come this far, and I can endure a few extra miles of travel, if the journey leads me to Decimus." She rolled up her son's scroll with a snap, and contemplated me sourly. "Oh well, I suppose that's the best we can do for now. Thank you. That will be all."

Chapter V

We gave them a good dinner. I'd told the maids to arrange the private dining-room so that the guests could recline on couches with their food on small tables, as they would at home. I thought it suited them better than our usual arrangement of one long table with chairs and stools round it. The big table remained in the centre of the room for carving and serving. Once our slaves brought the food in, the guests' own servants waited on them during the meal.

They had smoked oysters and cold sausage to begin with, then roast pork with sauce made of apples, and a variety of winter vegetables including some delicious white carrots. The dessert course was fruits marinated in wine, and some of our own goat's cheese. It was richer fare than we'd normally have had on a snowy winter evening, but luckily we'd just killed one of the pigs, which meant there was plenty of meat to go round, and the smoked oysters and preserved fruit were in the larder in preparation for Saturnalia.

Despite the good food, washed down with some of our best Campanian red wine, it wasn't a happy meal. The guests were no ruder than we'd come to expect, but they indulged in bouts of quarrelling, broken up by long tense silences. I was beginning to realise that Sempronia and Horatius argued almost as a habit, or a game, which neither of them took very seriously. But Horatius disliked Diogenes—and who could blame him?—and the nasty little weasel had some sort of grudge against Priscus. Whenever he addressed him his words were outwardly servile, but subtly contemptuous, like a peach laced with vinegar. Priscus ignored the barbs, either through arrogance, or because he wasn't sharp enough to realise what Diogenes was doing. Timaeus might have livened things up, but he took his meal in old Plautius' room. The sick man himself kept to his bed and ate nothing but a bowl of thin porridge. Margarita and Gaius were cheerful, the little boy full of questions and unconcerned by the preoccupations of the adults, but his childish chatter soon annoyed Sempronia and she ordered him to be quiet.

After it was all over, I went to talk to Albia and Cook in the kitchen about making sure we'd enough suitable food for the next few days. Nearly a score of extra mouths to feed at this time of year might pose a problem for some establishments, but Albia's a brilliant organiser, and Cook is inventive and resourceful. And if you're an innkeeper faced with feeding an unexpectedly large party without warning, then you're lucky if they descend on you in the few days before Saturnalia, when there's a bigger than usual store of fancy food and drink.

Albia had as usual stocked up with enough to feed a legion, and we intended to visit the Oak Bridges market in two days' time for vegetables and cheese, so our shopping list could be easily expanded. Meanwhile, I'd have a word with Hawk about bringing us extra game from the woods. Deer and hare would supplement our own animals and fowls nicely.

As we finished our discussion, Timaeus came looking for me. My pleasure at the prospect of his undivided personal attention was short-lived though. "My lord Plautius would like to see you in his room, if you can spare a little time. He apologises that it's so late, but it's taken him a while to regain his strength after the journey."

Plautius was sitting up in bed, propped on a mound of pillows, with a wool shawl around his shoulders. He was thin, and his face was lined and almost as grey as his wispy hair. Yet the impression he made wasn't of a pitiable invalid. His grey eyes were intelligent and full of life, and held mine in an intense gaze. He may be sick in body, I thought, but the mind behind those eyes is clear and formidable.

"Sit down, Aurelia Marcella. Thank you for coming so promptly." His voice was steady, but soft. I perched on a stool near his bed, and waited.

"I believe Lady Sempronia has talked to you about the purpose of our journey here?"

"Yes, my lord. She has asked me to help find your son Plautius Curio. I'm afraid I've not heard of him, but I'm going to make enquiries."

"Yes, yes, I'm sure you will do your best. And if and when you find any information about him, I want you to bring it to me first."

"First?" I was puzzled, and it must have shown in my face.

"I'm not saying you shouldn't tell Sempronia," he continued quietly. "You've undertaken to do that, and I don't want you breaking your word. What I *do* want is to be the first to know about whatever you find, before you report to anyone else. Just bring me word quietly, without troubling the rest of my household. And," he continued, not giving me time to comment, "if you should find Decimus yourself, I want you to bring him to me. I'd like the chance to talk to him alone. This is important, and I should like your promise." His bright grey eyes stared into mine, and for the second time that day, I realised I was being given an order, not a choice.

"You don't want much, do you?" The words flew out before I could stop them. Oh, me and my big mouth! Why couldn't I have just said "Yes, my lord"?

He didn't seem offended. "You consider my request difficult?"

"Well, yes. Lady Sempronia—what I mean is…."

Suddenly he laughed. "Just promise me that you'll do the best you can."

I didn't like it much, but couldn't think of any way of escape. "I promise."

"Good." He moved slightly on the pile of pillows, still watching me intently. "My wife can be very determined sometimes. It's a quality I admire in her, even though it doesn't always make for an easy life." He laughed once more, and then without warning his laughter changed to a fit of coughing, and he seemed to be having trouble breathing. He gasped several times, and put both hands to his chest. He was in pain, and I felt a sudden panic.

"What is it? Is there anything I can do?"

He pointed to a small earthenware flask and cup on the table next to his bed. "My medicine," he said between gasps. "Pour me some, will you?"

I did so, and held it to his lips, and he drank it down and waved away my offer of more. "Can't take too much. It's powerful stuff." He lay back on the pillows. He'd stopped coughing, and his breathing was easier. "Don't be alarmed. I get these bad turns now and then. My chest hurts, and I can't breathe properly. They're a nuisance, nothing more."

"Shall I fetch Timaeus?"

"There's no need. I'm over the worst. He'll be here soon anyway, to bring my sleeping-potion." He coughed again once, but was now breathing more or less normally, and my panic receded. Clearly he was more used to this than I was. He paused, and then asked, "Have you ever been in the situation of feeling yourself surrounded by enemies, and yet not being sure exactly who they are?"

The unexpectedness of this made me answer simply and straight out. "Yes, I have. It was dreadful. Having an enemy is bad enough, but having to suspect everyone around you makes it a nightmare."

He nodded. "Exactly. Now, there's just one more matter that needs to be clarified. My doctor insists I must be extremely careful about my diet. It's imperative I stick to the foods he has prescribed. Tell your kitchen staff that I do not want anyone other than Timaeus preparing my meals. Not anyone at all. I'll only eat food that Timaeus has got ready with his own hands. Please make sure that is understood."

What in Hades was going on here? It almost sounded as if he thought someone was trying to poison him.

"I'll make sure. I promise."

"Good. And my dietary requirements are the only part of this conversation that will ever be referred to outside this room."

"I understand. But…."

"Yes?"

"Please don't think me presumptuous, but my brother is an investigator for the Governor, and as I've said, I've had some experience myself of dealing with secret enemies. Is there anyone in particular who should be watched?"

A mischievous twinkle appeared in his eyes, making him look twenty years younger. "Secret enemies? Whatever brought that into your head? I'm just an old man, rambling on about nothing in particular."

"Of course. But whoever your enemies are, I'm not among them." I don't know what made me say that, but it was true. I liked the old man, though I was slightly afraid of him too, and in any battle between him and Sempronia, I knew which side I would support.

"This son of ours," he mused, more to himself than to me. "The trouble is he's not living out the dreams we've always had for him. Especially his mother. But I must confess that in a way I envy him. Well, no matter. I won't keep you any longer. Good night."

I found Timaeus waiting just outside the door. He put a finger to his lips and walked with me to the end of the corridor. I beckoned him through into the hall.

"Can your patient spare you for long enough to have a glass of wine?"

"Thanks, I'd like that."

The bar-room was empty, and we made ourselves comfortable on a bench by the fire, with beakers of spiced wine to hand.

"Gods, it's good to be away from them all for a while." He stretched his long legs to the warmth, and moved closer to me than bar-room etiquette usually dictates. But I remembered a saying of our grandmother's: a girl should never let etiquette interfere with enjoyment.

"I sympathise. Looking after an invalid must be very tiring." We were finding the healthy members of the party hard work after just one afternoon.

"Oh, he's not such a bad old boy." He hesitated, as if deciding how much of his thoughts to reveal. "It's the rest of them. They can be a little, well, argumentative."

"You're a master of understatement. Are they always like this?"

"Pretty much, though the journey has brought out the worst in them. These cold winters are enough to make anyone bad-tempered."

"I gather you haven't been in Britannia long enough to get used to the weather?"

"I've been away for five years, in Crete. That's my original home."

"Crete? Where the archers come from?"

"That's it." He laughed. "Where all the boys want to grow up to be famous bowmen. Luckily most of us grow out of it. But I still hunt with a bow when I can."

"So what made you become a doctor?"

"I'd always dreamed of being one, and when I was fourteen I heard of an old Greek physician who was looking for a lad to help him because he was going blind. I offered to be his assistant. It was a wonderful chance for me, but it meant going to Londinium, because he was moving there with his patron. I was just a boy then, and leaving my parents and my sisters was very hard. But he was a brilliant physician—he taught me a great deal. We lived in Londinium for several years, and I got to like it. That's when I first encountered the Plautius family."

I refilled his beaker. "Was Plautius a friend of your patron?"

He nodded. "Some kind of distant relation, I think. My master was sent to look after Plautius once or twice—even in those days he didn't have very good health. And after my master died, I was the one who was sent to treat Plautius."

"But then you went home to Crete?"

"I got word that Father was seriously ill, and I thought I should go back to take care of him. And it coincided with a bad time for me here…I lost my girl. She was a slave, and a rich man bought her and wanted her all to himself. Without her, Londinium wasn't the same. After Father died, I stayed in Crete for several years. But doctors are as common as cats in those parts, so I came back to Londinium last summer to find work. In September Plautius hired me as his personal doctor. By then he was really ill." He shrugged. "I had a good idea what I was getting into. Compared with an arena full of lions and tigers, they're not so terrible."

"I'd say they're evenly matched."

"Look, Aurelia," he said, moving still closer. "I feel I can trust you. I've been hoping for the chance of a quiet word."

"Well, here I am." I didn't add, "What can I do for you?" because from the look in his eye, he might have told me.

"About Lord Plautius." Oh well, I must have misread the look. "He's been a bit worried about his personal safety for a while now. I heard what he said to you, and he's said the same to me more than once."

"You obviously take good care of him. And he could have a guard at his door, if he's so concerned."

"He doesn't want that. The point is, don't take it personally. It's nothing to do with your mansio."

"Thanks, but I never thought it was. What's behind it, do you know? When I asked him, he simply dodged the question—well, you heard. Does he have a real reason to be worried?"

Timaeus smiled his dazzling smile. "If you're asking me whether anyone is trying to kill him, the answer is, I've no idea."

"It's all in his imagination?"

"I didn't say that. If you're asking me who might *like* to try and kill him, the answer is, nearly everyone in our party." His smile was gone, and his words struck a bitter chill in the room, despite the blazing logs.

"You can't seriously mean that, surely."

"I'm sorry, it was a touch over-dramatic. But he's upset several people, with his talk of altering his will."

"His will?" I decided to risk being nosey. "I did wonder why he'd brought a lawyer along. Is he thinking of disinheriting this wandering son of theirs?"

"Sempronia wants him to, and he's half persuaded. It could still go either way."

"But how would that affect anyone else? Is it because they all think it's unfair, and they're angry on the son's behalf?"

"More than that. Sempronia's trying to make him draw up a completely new will, and alter several of the terms of the old one. Plautius made his will years ago, and most of the household know what's in it by now, so she's going round telling everyone it may be changed, and threatening them with what will happen to them if they displease her. It's one of the methods she uses to get her own way." He added in a soft growl, "Someone should put an end to that evil old woman."

I agreed wholeheartedly, but I'm not quite stupid. Even a handsome and fanciable man can't talk me into making death threats to a customer. Instead I said, "She can't force Plautius to change his will, though, can she? Nobody can. When all's said and done, he's the head of the family, and he can do as he likes."

"In theory, yes. In practice, I only hope so. You must have noticed what a prize bully Sempronia is."

"But even in the short time I was with Lord Plautius, I got the impression that he's more than a match for her."

"You're a shrewd judge. I think you're right. Sometime though, when he's really unwell and in a lot of pain, he might give way to her just to get a bit of peace."

"Is his illness serious?"

He nodded. "I'm afraid it is. He can't last much longer. That's why this whole business about changing his will is more than just a philosophical debate. It's becoming urgent. It's divided the household into two camps."

"How do you mean?"

"Some of our people are scared that he'll change his will, and they might want to make sure he never does."

"The runaway son for one, presumably."

"I suppose so, though he's been away from home some time, and may not realise just how ill his father is now. I was thinking more of the Weasel. He gets his freedom under the old will, but under the new one he's bequeathed to Sempronia. She'd never release him, he's far too useful to her."

They deserve each other, I thought, but kept the observation to myself.

Timaeus poured more wine. "But there are other people who'd do better out of the new will, and they might wait until he's signed and sealed it, and then want to put him out of the way before he changed his mind yet again. Margarita's the obvious example there. She would get *her* freedom under the new will, as long as she'd agree to leave Sempronia's household. They want her out of Priscus' reach, so he'll forget about her and marry some high-class girl whose father will help him get into the Senate. Under the old will, she's bequeathed to Horatius, of all things. He's always fancied her, randy old goat." He sipped his drink. "See what I mean about two camps?"

Oh yes, I saw all right. And which camp are you in, Timaeus, I wondered?

It was as if he heard my unspoken question. "I'm not in the running for a legacy under any will, in case you're wondering."

"Our grandmother used to say, if you want a long life, don't put the doctor in your will."

He smiled. "A wise woman. Plautius said much the same to me the other day when he and Sempronia and Horatius were having one of their endless discussions about legacies. 'You may as well know you'll get no bequest from me, whether I die now or in ten years' time.'"

I stared into the fire for a while, pondering how seriously to take all this talk about wills and secret enemies. One thing I had to take seriously though. If Plautius came to harm while he was staying at the Oak Tree, it would of course be a tragedy for him, but it would be a complete disaster for us. "Look, Timaeus, I can be discreet, I think you've already decided that for yourself. If you know of a definite threat to Plautius, I wish you'd tell me about it. I've a duty to protect him, and I need to be forewarned. If anything happens to him while he's under my roof…."

"Yes, I see that, but it's difficult." He sat staring into his beaker for what seemed like an hour. I tried to be patient, listening to the crackling fire, the wind rattling the shutters, and voices drifting faintly in from the kitchen next door. But I realised he was so deep in thought, he'd forgotten I was there.

"These alterations to the will—have they been put in writing yet?" I asked, by way of reminding him of my existence.

He looked up at me, shaking his head. "It's just talk, endless arguing, and various sets of notes, but nothing formal yet. I hear most of it, because Plautius is involved, and I'm either in his room, or very near it."

The door from the kitchen opened with a bang, and Albia came through almost at a run, and slammed it behind her. "Pour me some wine, Relia, for the gods' sake, before they all drive me mad! Oh—I'm sorry, Timaeus, I didn't realise you were here."

He smiled. "They're driving me mad too. I've escaped for a little while. Here, let me pour you some."

She took it gratefully, and flopped onto the bench opposite to ours.

Timaeus turned to me. "Thank you for your company, Aurelia. I'd better be getting back to his lordship."

"Look in for a drink any time you feel like a chat."

"I will. Tomorrow, perhaps?"

"Tomorrow."

"Good night to you both."

As he left, Albia looked up from her wine. "Sorry if I've interrupted something. I needed to get away from the kitchen."

"What's up? Guests getting you down?"

"A bit. That horrible Diogenes is a real weasel."

"Timaeus, on the other hand, is rather good company."

This should have provoked some teasing, but she stared dumbly into the fire.

"Albia, what's wrong?" I went to sit next to her, and put my arm round her. "Has something upset you?"

"I'm just tired. I'll be all right." Indeed she was looking exhausted, and I thought, despite her earlier optimism, she's finding Sempronia's party hard work. But Albia's never been afraid of hard work, so there must be something more.

"What is it?" I asked. "I can probably help, but not if you don't tell me."

"It's that slimy Diogenes. He keeps coming in and out of the kitchen, saying he's under Sempronia's orders to supervise his lordship's meals, but Timaeus insists that nobody but him should touch any of the food that's going to the sick room. They've had a couple of arguments, and Timaeus has won so far. I'm delighted to see him send the Weasel off with a flea in his ear, but the atmosphere is awful. It's upsetting Cook, and you know how grumpy he gets."

"Come on, you can always manage Cook's temperaments when you have to. They're certainly not worth getting into a state over. Has something else happened? Or is it your time of the month, making you tense?"

"Don't be silly," she retorted. "Oh, sorry, I shouldn't snap at you. Take no notice, it's nothing. I'm just worn out, and disappointed because I was looking forward to a holiday. Pour me some more wine, would you? That's what I need. And tell me why Plautius wanted to see you."

I handed her the wine and told her about my meeting with the old man. "If Plautius wants me to report to him first, that must mean he's planning some course of action that he knows Sempronia won't approve of. I'm in between Scylla and Charybdis, and I don't like it one bit."

Albia nodded. "Not a comfortable position, caught between those two. Remember that old joke of our grandmother's: what's the military term for someone who stands between two armies, trying to stop them fighting?"

"A corpse," I answered.

We both stared into the fire for a space, till Albia broke the silence. "Margarita has told me a bit more about this runaway son of theirs. All he wants is to live his own life in his own way, not have to conform to what his family expects. Not much to ask, is it?"

"It doesn't work like that though, with these rich political families."

She looked at me gravely. "Relia, I realise you'd no choice but to agree that we'd help them search for their son. But...."

"But we don't need to be too energetic about it?" I smiled. "Just what I've been thinking. We'll go through the motions, ask around a bit, send out a few messages, but this isn't our quarrel, after all. If we don't find any trace of him, then Plautius and Sempronia will just have to admit defeat and go home."

"Let's hope so. The sooner they're on the road back to Londinium, the better."

"There's something to be said for not being born into a rich and powerful senatorial family, isn't there? At least we Aurelii can marry whoever we like." I picked up my mug. "Here's to freedom to choose a good husband. Here's to your marriage. It won't be long now, and then you and Candidus will live happy ever after."

To my astonishment Albia thumped her beaker down on the table and almost shouted, "Relia, how can you be so blind?"

"I'm sorry?"

"Don't you see? It's staring us in the face!" She was really shouting now. "I thought I could keep it to myself somehow, but I can't. I *can't!* Haven't you realised yet?"

"What in the gods' name are you on about?"

"Their son! When I was talking to Margarita, I suddenly understood. I've worked out who he is. We know him. Gods, it's a disaster! What are we going to do?" She burst into tears.

"We *know* him?" I stared at her, appalled. "You mean...*merda,* Albia, it can't be!"

"Yes," she answered miserably. "Their runaway son is my Candidus. *I'm* the girl they won't allow him to marry!"

Chapter VI

Have you ever been strolling on a sunny hillside and suddenly fallen down into a deep dark cave? Or wandered along by the sea and felt your feet sinking into a quicksand? Then you may have some idea of what Albia experienced that night.

It took a couple of hours and several more beakers of wine to calm her down. I realised why she'd seemed so tired and downcast, from the effort of holding her emotions firmly in check. Now she'd released them, they bolted like scared horses, and she went from anger to misery to panic and back again, as she faced the appalling fact that the man she thought she was marrying had as much chance of getting his parents' consent as a frog of becoming Caesar. Without their consent he couldn't marry her, however much he wanted to. It was a harsh law, but still law, and there was no getting round it.

"How could he lie to me like this?" she demanded over and over. "He said there'd be no serious problem about his parents agreeing to the wedding. He did tell me they wanted him to marry some rich girl down in Londinium, that was the main reason he'd run away from home. But he said that was just their snobbery, and he'd be able to persuade them that we were right for each other. Oh, how *could* he? He must have known in his heart how they'd react!"

I was sad for her misery and I shared her anger. Candidus had been at best naïve, at worst downright deceitful. But I did my best to comfort her. "He was hoping against hope, I imagine. He loves you, and he can't bear the thought that his parents won't approve. So he's convinced himself he can win them round, because he desperately wants to. Maybe he can, at that. He's a persuasive talker, isn't he?"

"Talk's not enough!" she retorted. "I doubt if he or anybody can persuade Sempronia to do something if she doesn't want to."

I couldn't disagree. "I must admit she was adamant when she was reading out his letter and telling me about the situation. I have the feeling Plautius might be more sympathetic though."

"But Candidus should have been honest with me! His parents aren't just too snobbish to have me in their family, they've actually got someone else lined up for him, some senator's daughter with powerful relatives in Italia. Margarita told me. His parents and hers have agreed everything, and they're talking about drawing up a marriage contract and ordering Candidus to marry her. Plautius has the legal right, as head of the family."

"Perhaps Candidus doesn't know things have gone that far. And anyway, Plautius may have legal right on his side, but Candidus loves you, you know he does."

"I thought I knew it."

"You do know it, Albia. He'll simply refuse to marry the other girl."

"But without his father's approval, *we* can't be married."

"You can still live together as man and wife—lots of couples do. Nobody can stop you doing that."

"Yes, I suppose so." Perhaps that's what Candidus had been planning, if they were denied a marriage ceremony to give everything the seal of legality. Or perhaps he'd decided that they could go through a full wedding, telling everyone their parents consented to the match but couldn't be present themselves. That wouldn't have made the thing legal, but after all, Brigantia is a long way from Londinium, and he wouldn't be the first man to have run away from home to marry. He'd have counted on the fact that his parents would remain at a safe distance, so the matter of their approval wouldn't be challenged.

"The important thing," I said, "is that he loves you, and you love him. You'd be prepared to live with him even without a formal marriage, wouldn't you? I know you'd be disappointed not to have a wedding ceremony, but you could still be together."

She thought about it. "I *would* be disappointed. But yes, if it's the only way, of course we can just set up house together. Oh, but then what about the children? If we aren't married, they'll be illegitimate, which means they can't be Roman citizens without a special dispensation!" She buried her head in her hands.

We kept going over and over the same facts, as if by repeating them often enough we could change them. But the longer we discussed it, the worse the situation seemed to be. If Albia was right, and she was certain she was, then she and Candidus were set on a collision course with Sempronia, like galleys racing across the water to ram one another into wreckage. However we tried to delay the hour when she discovered where her Decimus was, and the identity of his sweetheart, we couldn't prevent her finding out eventually, and the resulting explosion would rival Vesuvius erupting over Pompeii.

What would Sempronia do, besides ranting and roaring like a lioness with belly-ache? We'd joked, well half-joked, that she could get the Oak Tree shut down if we didn't give her good service. Was she vindictive enough to try to close it down because her son wanted to marry its housekeeper? If first impressions were anything to go by, she was.

And then there was the whole question of Lucius, his public disgrace, his private arrangement that the Governor would reinstate him once he'd completed his assignment. Sempronia boasted of her kinship with the Governor, but how close were they in fact? Could she persuade him to make my brother's disgrace permanent?

And I had a private worry which I couldn't share with Albia. I know my sister can be as stubborn as a pack-mule, and if she decided to share her life with Candidus whatever anybody said or did, she would stick to her decision. But I was less sure about Candidus. He'd always shown himself to be a charming young man, but I couldn't help wondering whether underneath all his educated good manners and hopeful plans for the future, he was weaker in character than Albia, and might let his parents bully him. On the other hand, he'd had the strength of mind to leave home in the first place. In any case I kept my doubts to myself. I knew I didn't want Albia to leave the mansio, and a small corner of my mind kept suggesting that I was being selfish in my reservations about her fiancé, and that nobody she chose would ever seem quite good enough.

"One thing I can do," Albia said finally. "I'll get a message to Candidus about what's happened, before he arrives tomorrow. Otherwise he'll walk straight into Sempronia and find himself in the middle of a huge row, without any warning."

"Good idea. Post a lookout a couple of hundred paces down the road from here. He can tell Candidus to approach the mansio carefully, so you've a chance to meet him before Sempronia does."

"I'll see to it first thing." She yawned suddenly. "Gods, I'm tired. Let's try and get a bit of sleep in what's left of the night, shall we?"

But I don't think either of us slept very well, and I was glad when morning brought other matters to occupy my mind. The guests woke up with the daylight, and Albia got busy organising their breakfast while I went out to do my rounds. The snow had stopped, but the sky was full of heavy cloud, so we weren't done with it yet. I strolled over to the big paddock where Titch and Castor were feeding the horses and mules. I was pleased to see little Gaius with Titch, holding out bunches of hay on his small hands. I thought the poor brat would be happier with our people than under the eye of her ladyship.

"Morning, boys," I called out. "Have you recruited a new assistant today, Titch—er—Victor?"

Titch ran over to me, and Gaius trotted after him.

"Morning, Mistress. Aye, this is the latest horse-boy. Is it all right if he helps us for a while?"

"Fine by me, as long as his mother doesn't object. Well, Gaius, do you like helping Titch do the feeding?"

The child said "Yes, thank you," and looked shyly down at his boots.

"He reckons he's in trouble, aren't you, kid?" Titch grinned down at him. "He thinks he'll be safer out here with us till her ladyship calms down."

"That sounds sensible. What's happened?"

"I let Medusa out," Gaius said, in a solemn tone that a tragic actor would have envied.

"Who's Medusa?" The name would have suited Sempronia, but anyone who dared to call her after a Gorgon wouldn't live to tell the tale.

"Yon fat yellow cat," Titch said. "Gaius wanted to show it the snow."

"She's never allowed out," the boy explained. "I thought she'd like it. But one of the dogs chased her and now she's up in the big oak tree. Lady Sempronia is *very* cross. So's Diogenes. If Medusa doesn't come down soon, my lady will make him climb up there and fetch her."

I laughed. "I've climbed that tree many times. It's not hard. But Medusa will come down when she's ready, and not before. That's what cats are like. You can't tell them what to do all the time."

"I wish I could be a cat," Gaius remarked, "even if dogs did chase me sometimes."

"The cat wasn't hurt," Titch said, "she just had to run a few yards. She's that fat, I don't suppose she does much running."

Gaius said, "Victor took me to see the puppies in the stable. They're very new. Their eyes aren't even open yet. But they've got all their paws and tails and fur and everything."

"Shhh!" Titch ruffled the boy's curly hair. "Don't go telling the Mistress we've been skiving, playing with the dogs when we should be working."

"Shall I fetch some more hay?" the child asked eagerly.

"Aye, go and see if Castor needs a hand. I've some business to discuss with Mistress Aurelia."

Gaius trotted off obediently, and I looked at Titch enquiringly.

"That Diogenes," he said quietly, "he's a rude 'un, isn't he? Can you persuade him to go for a ride on the old black stallion, then maybe he'll get chucked off and buried in a snowdrift."

"Has he been giving you trouble?"

"He was snooping around here just after daylight this mornin'."

"Was he now? Where?"

"All over—the paddocks, the orchard, and the stable yard. He went into the stables and pretended to be making a fuss of the horses there. I asked if I could help him, but he told me to push off. I didn't go far, and when he saw I was still watching him, he went back in the house."

"I don't trust him, Titch. Keep an eye on him, will you? And anyone else in their party who seems to be sneaking around where they aren't expected. Lucius—I mean in my dream the other night, I had a warning that there may be a troublemaker among the guests."

"I'd say there are several," the lad grinned. "Well, I'd best be getting back to work, or me dad'll play war." He looked across to where Gaius had started building a snowman. "You coming to help me, Gaius? Or d'you think you ought to go inside now?"

"May I stay out here?" He came over and gazed up at me with his beautiful blue eyes. "I don't want to make my lady any more angrier than she is already. She gets so cross sometimes, and then she says—she says she's going to...." He trailed off unhappily.

"Going to what?" Titch grinned. "Going to give you a good beating? Well, I've had a few of them, and they've not done me much harm."

"No. I don't want to tell." His face crumpled, and he put a fist in his mouth and looked about to cry. "It's something horrid."

Titch put a hand on the boy's shoulder. "People say things when they get angry, but they don't mean 'em afterwards. And nobody's going to do anything to you, while you're with me. You know why?"

"Why?"

"'Cos my name's Gaius too, just like yours. Gaius Varius Victor. Which makes you kind of my little brother. That means, if the mistress says it's all right, you can stay out here for a bit." He looked at me, and I nodded. "Fine. I'll see he doesn't get into any trouble. He's good with animals. And he 'minds me of my kid brother Marcus."

I nodded again. Titch rarely mentioned his younger brother who'd died of a fever aged seven, but I knew he hadn't forgotten. "Then I'm sure you'll take good care of him. But don't stay outside too long, Gaius. Your mother will be wondering what's happened to you."

Presumably Albia had posted her lookout to intercept Candidus, because if the weather was no worse than this, he would certainly ride over to see her. What would he do when he heard her news? I suspected he'd ride straight home again, which was the sensible if rather tame course to take, and would delay his discovery for a while longer. But I couldn't help hoping he would stay with my sister and face his mother's wrath. This would show how much he loved Albia, even though it would cause a very disagreeable row.

I warned Carina she might have to run the bar without Albia or me. If Candidus arrived, we'd both be too busy to pay attention to customers. Not that there would be many of those, perhaps the occasional courier, and a few natives looking in for a beer and a bite at midday. Then I reluctantly decided I couldn't think of any more excuses to put off saying good morning to our guests.

They were in the dining-room, eating bread and honey, apples preserved in ginger, raisins, and warm watered wine. Even before I opened the door, I heard raised voices. Sempronia and Horatius hadn't lost any time in resuming whatever squabble they'd been having the previous evening.

"Good morning, my lady," I said brightly. "I hope you were comfortable and slept well?"

"As well as I ever do in a strange place." She spread some honey on a piece of bread. "At least the beds were clean, and there were no fleas."

"They've probably all frozen to death in this ghastly climate," Horatius chipped in. I managed a smile, but it was an effort. Fleas indeed!

"Well, please do tell me if there's anything you need."

I turned to go, but she barked, "Wait, will you? Don't go rushing off!"

I waited while she spread more honey, took a couple of mouthfuls of bread, and had a sip of wine. Finally she deigned to transfer her attention to me.

"You said yesterday that your sister's young man intends to visit her here today?"

Here we go, I thought—I must say as little as possible, without actually lying. "That's right. Candidus, the man she's engaged to. But with the weather being so bad, we're not sure when he'll arrive."

"If he hasn't reached here by noon, I shall visit him at his house. I don't propose to waste all day doing nothing."

Gods alive, that's all we need! Horatius, predictably, objected. "Really, Sempronia, in this weather? Are you mad? Why in Hades can't you just show a little patience?"

Just as inevitably, she ignored him. "Our carriages are big enough to cope with a few flakes of snow." (There was about half a foot of the stuff outside, but I let it go.) "You and your sister can accompany me to show me the way there. She will probably want to visit her intended if he doesn't reach here, and I shall need you to come with me in any case."

"Me? Why? I mean what use can I possibly be?"

She sighed irritably. "If this young man gives us any useful information, I may be forced to travel further afield perhaps, to make more visits, and I shall need somebody who's familiar with the area." She gave another sigh. "Do you approve of your sister's choice of husband?"

"Yes, I do."

"Then you're fortunate. I only wish Decimus…ah well, never mind. If your sister's fiancé can lead me to my son, I'll be glad to show my appreciation by giving the pair of them a wedding present." She stared at me for a few heartbeats, a token pause only—we all knew I wouldn't refuse to make the journey. "Good, that's settled. Mustela, order two carriages and the guards to be ready to set off at noon. We can always change the order later if necessary. You'll come, Aulus, and you of course, Horatius. Margarita, there's not much point in you and Gaius travelling with us, you can stay here for the day, and for the gods' sake try to keep the boy out of mischief." She glanced round, challenging us to demur. None of us did.

But I decided to assert a small measure of independence. "We won't need to take up space in one of your carriages, my lady. Albia and I will be riding on horseback. We enjoy the exercise, and the horses need it."

She shrugged her bony shoulders. "As you wish. We shall only need one carriage then, Mustela."

Suddenly I thought about Silvanius Clarus, who would be sure to want to help. "May I suggest something else that might help your search?"

"Well?"

"I think I mentioned that the Chief Town Councillor of Oak Bridges is a good friend of ours. I'm sure he'll wish to pay his respects to you when he finds out you're in the district. Shall I send him a message, letting him know that you're here, and asking for his help?"

She thought about it. "I don't know. These native politicians can be a trial. I don't want to waste time being entertained, and having to be gracious to the locals."

The idea of Sempronia being gracious to anyone made me want to laugh, but instead I nodded and said, "I realise you're busy, but Clarus can provide entertainment fit for a consul. He has the best chef north of Londinium."

"Really? But he is a Brigantian native, I presume?"

"Born here, yes, but Roman educated, and prides himself on being a citizen and living a thoroughly Roman life."

"H'm. What sort of establishment does he have? Two round-houses and a herd of pigs?"

"He has a large villa just outside Oak Bridges. It was designed by a Roman architect, and it's very fine. His rooms have some of the most beautiful floor mosaics I've ever seen. He's a widower, and his sister Clarilla keeps house for him."

"Does he have any decent wine?" Horatius put in. "Or does he drink beer, like most of them?"

"He loves good wine, and prides himself on having only the best." I would say that, of course. All his wine was supplied by us.

"Very well." Sempronia actually smiled. "You may inform this Silvanius Clarus that we shall be pleased to receive him. It can't do any harm, and it might even be useful."

After the meal they dispersed, except for Priscus, who hung back, shifting awkwardly from foot to foot. His sandy hair was untidy, and he looked tired. "May I have a private word, please?"

Merda, I thought, someone didn't enjoy his night's rest. "Of course. What can I do for you?"

"Is there somewhere quiet where we can talk?"

This sounded more serious. "Yes, certainly." I led him through to my study. "We won't be disturbed here."

We both sat down, and he sat staring at the floor, as if he didn't know how to begin. I hadn't got all day to wait, so I grasped the bull by the horns.

"Is everything satisfactory, Priscus? I hope you were comfortable last night?"

"Oh, yes, thank you, quite comfortable." Another pause. "It's just—I'm not very happy about Mother's plan to go and visit your sister's fiancé."

You're not the only one, I thought. "I don't think it'll be necessary. He'll come to the mansio if he possibly can."

"May I speak in confidence?"

Holy Diana, not *another* confidential chat! But I could hardly refuse. "Yes, of course."

"If Mother decides to go in search of this young man, I'll have to go too. But I don't like to leave Margarita unprotected here. My mother's maid, you know? While I'm away trailing around the countryside, anything could happen."

"She'll be safe at the Oak Tree. Our staff wouldn't dream of laying a finger on her." Well they might dream, but they wouldn't do it, unless she encouraged them.

"Oh, no, of course not! It's Mustela—Diogenes."

"Ah. But won't he be accompanying your mother on her travels?"

"That's just it, he's told her he's not well, and asked to stay here today. He says he has a stomach complaint. I don't believe it—he seemed healthy enough at breakfast. I think he means to—to pester Margarita. She doesn't like him, but she may find it hard to stop him if I'm not there."

"Couldn't you take her along with you then?"

He shook his head. "Mother's already told her she's not wanted on the journey."

"Not wanted by your mother, no. But if *you* want her to travel with you, what's to stop her? Especially if Diogenes isn't going. You two could have a little time to yourselves." Yes, I know, I shouldn't interfere in the guests' business like that. But I felt sorry for Margarita, and there was no doubt she'd be safer with Priscus than at the mercy of the Weasel.

He looked at me in surprise. I think it was the first time he really saw me properly. "Against Mother's wishes? I mean—that is, she wouldn't be very pleased."

I mimicked the famous line in the comedy about the forty sailors. "And do you always do everything your mother tells you?"

He smiled as he recognised it, and gave me the next line in a comic falsetto: "Oh yes, sir, always, unless I don't want to."

We both laughed, and I realised I was seeing a different side to Priscus. Maybe what I'd taken for haughtiness was just shyness, and all he needed was a bit of encouragement to stand up to his dreadful mother. "You're right, of course. I can take Margarita with me. I *will* take her. Though the gods know what Mother will say."

"If you don't manage it," I put in, "I'll tell my senior barmaid to keep an eye on her, and make sure she's not on her own. She can help with the Saturnalia preparations, something like that."

"Thank you. Oh, but what about Gaius? Mother really will object if we take him as well. After all it may be better if she stays behind. You've probably noticed, my mother has no patience with small children. She likes the idea of having a page-boy, because it's the fashion, but she forgets he's—well, just a small boy."

"He can stay here on his own, if you like. One of my horse-boys has made friends with him—a good lad, he'll keep Gaius amused. And quite safe, I promise."

"Thank you. I expect you think I'm making a great deal of fuss about a couple of slaves. But I'm very fond of her. Of both of them."

"Really?" I prompted.

He smiled. "I love them, if you want the truth. And I hope that some day we can all be together as a family. But we need to be patient for now, and it's not easy."

"Couldn't you buy their freedom?"

"My parents won't hear of it. Mother says Margarita's far too useful, but the real reason is that she and Father want me to make a political marriage. And even if Margarita were free some day, I could never marry her. You know the silly laws about who senators' sons can and can't marry."

"I do, yes. But you could take her as your concubine—a wife in all but name. You'd be together then."

"It's what I dream of. Some day." He looked at me wistfully, and then got to his feet. "I'm sorry, I shouldn't be burdening you with all this."

"That's all right. You can trust me to be discreet. And you can trust me to help keep Diogenes away from Margarita, whether you're here or not."

"Thank you. And, as you say, if your sister's fiancé comes…."

"He'll come. Love's a wonderful thing, isn't it?"

"It is." The smile he gave me lighted up the whole room.

After he left, I found myself thinking over what he'd said, especially his remark about wanting to live with Margarita and Gaius "as a family". He'd given the impression that he and Margarita had been fond of one another for years. Could Gaius be his son? They didn't look much alike, but they both had blue eyes, and the child's golden hair might turn sandy as he grew older.

I shook myself out of these romantic ponderings, and remembered my conversation with Albia about being on our guard against spies. We'd even joked about it, but I didn't feel like joking now. Sempronia's party could well include the spy Lucius had warned us about. Not her ladyship or Plautius of course, but almost any of the others—perhaps Diogenes, who'd already been observed doing a little snooping. I couldn't easily protect my everyday papers and notes, not without considerable inconvenience anyway. But I could at least be warned if anyone searched them. I laid a single hair across the hinge of my small oak document chest. The hard part now would be remembering to check it from time to time.

I went to the front door to look at the weather. I was glad to see that the sun was doing its best to burn away the clouds. Candidus would surely be here soon. I stood quietly, breathing in the good air and savouring the peace and quiet which I knew would be shattered once he arrived.

I remembered I'd a job for Taurus, mending a rickety bar-stool, and I stepped out onto the forecourt, which some of the farm boys were busily clearing of snow. As I got to the workshop, I almost collided with the big man as he came hurrying out, looking worried.

"What's up, Taurus? Something wrong?"

"Mistress Aurelia, I can smell smoke."

"I expect you can." I sniffed the air. "After all, there's the bar-room fire, and the furnace. We're burning more logs than usual with all these visitors."

He shook his shaggy head. "No, not wood-smoke. More like burning grass—or hay. That's it! Saturn's balls, it's hay on fire!"

I glanced round the stable area. "It's not coming from near here. It must be in the rick-yard. One of the stacks must have caught alight. Come on!"

We set off at a run.

Chapter VII

The rick-yard, where our precious hay was stored, was nearly a
quarter of a mile from the mansio, among a cluster of old buildings. Well before we reached it we could see the smoke rising
into the still cold air. I began to be frightened. Those stacks of
hay were our main store of winter feed for the animals, and it
would be a disaster if we lost any of them.

Suddenly a voice shrieked out, "Fire! Fire!" It was a man's
voice, high and panic-stricken. We ran faster, and I put two
fingers into my mouth and whistled long and loud. My men
knew that signal, and would come to help.

Sure enough, one of the hay-stacks was well alight. The hay
itself, and its straw-thatched top, were dry as tinder, except for
the sides which had been dampened a little by the snow. Large
flames and thick smoke shot upward from the stack's base. It
wouldn't take long to burn through. Fortunately there was hardly
a breath of wind, so the fire hadn't carried to the stacks on either
side yet. But small burning bundles of hay were floating about
and scattering, so it was only a matter of time.

I was relieved to see that half-a-dozen men were already on the
scene, doing their best to douse the blaze. There was a well in the
rick-yard, and they had formed a human chain for hauling and
passing wooden buckets of water, but there weren't enough of
them. Taurus went at once to take over the heaviest task, pulling
the full buckets up from the well. His huge strength made the

job look easy. I stopped for a few heartbeats, taken aback to see that the four men and two boys who were fighting the fire were complete strangers, not our own farm hands. But there wasn't time to wonder about it now, and I joined the bucket chain, standing beside Taurus.

The native next to me looked up in surprise. "You sure you can manage?"

"Yes." We didn't waste more words. It was heavy going, but I'm strong for a woman, not one of those feeble females who become exhausted when they have to lift a comb and mirror simultaneously. Besides I was frightened, and when you're frightened the gods give you more than usual strength.

Our own farm boys started arriving, bringing pitchforks and more buckets. Some joined the bucket line, and I wasn't sorry when one of them took my place. I picked up a pitchfork and helped chase and extinguish the burning bundles of hay which continued to spew out of the stack as it collapsed in on itself. Soon we knew we had the blaze under control, but it seemed to take forever before it was completely out.

I stood still, sweating and aching and stretching my sore muscles, and looked over the devastation. That one stack was gone, nothing but a soggy charred heap on the white snow, but at least the flames hadn't spread to the rest of the hay. It was bad, but it could have been so much worse.

I called out, "Well done, everyone, and thanks for coming so quickly. Make absolutely certain there's nothing still smouldering. We don't want it starting up again once we've gone." Then I walked over to the group of natives I didn't recognise, who were standing together near the well, taking it in turns to drink from a big mug of water. Their homespun cloaks were rough but serviceable, and they had good boots. They were prosperous Brigantian peasants, and from the way they chatted quietly together, men who knew one another well.

"Thank you, boys." I spoke to them in British. "I'm in your debt. If you hadn't got here so quickly, we could have lost the whole yard. Did you see the smoke from the road?"

A stocky man with bright red hair and beard, apparently their spokesman, stepped forward. "Glad we could help, Mistress. Fire's a terrible thing on a farm."

I was still curious who they were. I shouldn't have been surprised if neighbours had come to our aid. I know all the Brigantian farmers in our area, and whatever our differences, we always help each other in an emergency. But I definitely hadn't seen these men. "I don't think we've met. I'm Aurelia Marcella, innkeeper at the Oak Tree Mansio just along the road here. If you'll come back to the bar-room with me, I can promise you as much beer as you need to get rid of the taste of smoke, and a good meal to go with it. You've certainly earned it."

Several of them looked interested, but the leader shook his head. "Thank you, but some other time. Of course I hope there won't *be* another time."

Was that a threat? I couldn't be sure. "Well, the offer's there, next time you come by. May I ask your name?"

"My name's not important. But you may have heard of my boss, he's called Otus." He turned to his band. "Let's go, lads." And without more ado, they moved off, out of the yard and across the nearest field in the direction of the road.

Otus? An unusual name. It reminded me of a Greek story about a giant who tried to storm Mount Olympus, but I didn't know any living man who used it. And there was something disturbing about the way the group had behaved.

Albia arrived just then, complete with her bag of ointments and bandages. "Is anyone hurt? No? Thank the gods for that! Who were those natives, Relia? Not very talkative, were they? And I can't remember the last time I heard a thirsty man refuse beer."

"They were the first on the scene when it started. You didn't recognise them either? I wish they'd let me give them a thank-you drink, at least."

Ursulus was prowling the yard, supervising his men as they tidied up the mess. He walked slowly all round the burnt-out area, his eyes on the ground, but having made a full circuit, he simply shrugged helplessly. "They were on the spot a bit too quick for my liking. There's no traces here, but all the same, it makes you wonder."

"You think they started the fire themselves?"

"Perhaps not on purpose, but maybe they took shelter here last night in the snow, and made a fire to keep warm, and it caught the stack."

"It's possible. They were all strangers to me." I asked our men, "Have any of you seen them before? Or heard of a man called Otus?"

As they all shook their heads, Albia gestured to a small dark man who was helping to rake the charred remains of the hay into a pile. "Otho, what are you doing here? All right, I suppose you came to help, didn't you? But you're meant to be on the road, watching out for Master Candidus. It's important that you stop him coming onto the forecourt till I've seen him."

"Sorry, Miss Albia. But I couldn't just stand by doing nothing when I heard someone calling out about a fire."

"It can't be helped. Get back there now, will you please?"

He strode off, and Albia and I began to walk briskly towards the mansio. Now the exertion was over, I was starting to feel the biting cold. "There's something not right about all this, Albia. I agree with Ursulus, those natives must have been very close by when the fire started. How did it start, anyway, in the dead of winter with everything covered in snow? Haystacks catch fire on their own in the summer, yes, but I never heard of one doing it in December. And that remark by their leader, 'I hope there won't be another time.' Some kind of threat, do you think?"

"Perhaps." She was only half listening, her mind on Candidus and the prospect of a row with Sempronia.

As we came round onto the forecourt, we heard hoof-beats on the road, and saw a rider trotting down the track towards us. He was muffled up to the eyeballs in a heavy sheepskin cloak, with a hood pulled well down to shield his face, and he and his horse had a covering of white snow. But all the same we knew him at once.

"Candidus!" Albia called out, and ran to him. "Candidus, my dearest, thank the gods!"

"Now that's what I call a welcome!" He threw back his hood, laughing as he dismounted. "Did you think I wouldn't come? It takes more than a bit of snow to keep me away from my girl!"

"You mustn't stay out here," Albia said. "Something bad's happened, and I need to talk to you before we go inside. Come round into the stable yard where we can't be seen. Quick, hurry!"

"This is all very mysterious," he smiled, but he got no further. Gaius came running out, yelling excitedly. "Master Decimus! Master Decimus!" and raced up to Candidus, who stared down at him in astonishment.

"Gaius! What a surprise!" He picked the boy up and swung him onto his shoulder. "Well, how's my little soldier?"

Gaius hugged him. "I'm so glad you've come. Everybody's been grumpy and miserable, because they didn't know where you'd gone to. Lady Sempronia will be pleased. She wants to see you. Shall I run and tell her you're here? Oh look, there's Mustela." Before any of us could stop him, he was waving to Diogenes, who'd appeared at the main door. "Diogenes, go and tell her ladyship that Master Decimus has come!"

Diogenes gave Candidus a slight bow. "Good morning, sir. I'll go and tell my lady at once." And he turned back into the bar-room.

"Oh gods," Candidus groaned. He gently put Gaius back on the ground. "How long have you been here, Gaius?"

"Since yesterday. If you've got to see my lady, I'm going back to the stables for now. I'm helping the horse-boys," he added importantly, and trotted off.

Candidus turned to Albia. "Are Mother and Father both here?"

"I'm afraid so. And a lawyer called Horatius."

"They got my letter then." He sighed. "Oh well, I didn't expect them to be overjoyed, but I never thought they'd come looking for me. I was hoping they'd calm down after a while.

Do they know yet that it's you I'm going to marry, Albia? Is that why they're here?"

"Not yet. They just arrived to stay for a night or two while Sempronia searches the district for her runaway son."

"Decimus Plautius Curio," I said. "Not a name we recognised."

"But I realised it was you," Albia put in, "and I only wish you'd told me. You could have been honest about all this, Candidus."

"I'm sorry, love. I just kept hoping and hoping that I could persuade them." He looked at her sadly.

I said, "Let's think what's best to do, but for the gods' sake let's get out of sight of the house. We'll go round to the stables. Then if you decide not to stay, Candidus...."

"Not stay? You don't think I'll turn tail and run away, and leave Albia to face my mother alone?"

"It might be a sensible move. It would give you a little time to work out what to do."

He shook his head. "I already know what to do. No, I'm not leaving. My mother—well, you've met her."

"We have."

"Then you know what she's like. If we have to face her, my girl and I will do it together." He took her hand.

I was pleased by this show of strength. "Good. Then all we have to do...."

"Decimus! Come here at once!"

Sempronia stood framed in the bar-room doorway. As we all spun round to face her, I fancied I could feel fury radiating out of her, like heat from the haystack fire I'd just faced.

Candidus muttered, "Wish me luck," and winked at us. He added in a louder voice, "Good morning, Mother. I was just on my way in to see you."

He walked swiftly forward, erect and determined, like a standard-bearer marching to death or glory. Albia fell into step beside him, her head up and her chin out.

As they approached her, Sempronia began to shout. "How dare you, Decimus, how *dare* you bring such disgrace on your family? Forcing your poor father to come traipsing halfway across the province, just because you're so inconsiderate, so stubborn!" Candidus and Albia reached the door, and all three of them went inside, so I couldn't hear any more.

I wished I could do something—anything—to stop battle being joined. But I couldn't, and I didn't have enough nerve to follow them to watch what would happen next. I felt helpless, until I remembered there was one useful thing I could do. Yes, surely it was worth trying. I hurried away to the guest wing to tell Plautius his son had arrived.

Chapter VIII

I got no reply when I knocked on the old man's door. Timaeus wasn't in evidence, in fact the whole guest wing was deserted. Presumably everyone had followed Sempronia to meet Candidus, or more likely found some vantage point from which to observe the forthcoming row.

So I knocked again. This time a grumpy voice called, "Go away and leave me alone."

"My lord Plautius, it's Aurelia Marcella. You asked me to bring you news of your son Decimus as soon as I had any. May I come in?"

"Not now, not now." The voice was muffled, as if the old man had pulled a blanket over his head. "Come back later."

"Is everything all right? Would you like me to fetch Timaeus for you?"

"No. Just clear off." That's a polite rendering of what he said. Have you noticed how swearing sounds even ruder when uttered in a patrician accent?

Anyway, his instructions were plain enough, if rather surprising. He'd made such a point of asking me to report directly to him, and now he wouldn't hear my news. It must be because he was feeling ill. I decided I would find Timaeus anyway. He'd know what to do about his patient's tantrums.

I walked out and round to the forecourt, and seeing the bar-room door still standing wide open, I went inside. A very odd scene confronted me. There was no sign of her ladyship or the young lovers, but a small crowd had collected—Priscus, Margarita, Horatius, Diogenes and several more of the visitors' party, as well as a handful of our own people. They were all staring at the door that led to the private dining-room, which was partly open, and they were completely silent, like the audience at a poetry-reading.

Sempronia and Candidus were in the dining-room, arguing violently. We could hear them clearly. As I came in, Sempronia was in the midst of a tirade, and I caught the phrases "unsuitable peasant girl", and "ruin your life". But I couldn't give her my whole attention, because I wanted to find Timaeus, and he wasn't here. I pushed my way through the listening crowd to Margarita, and whispered urgently, "Lord Plautius isn't well. Where's Timaeus?"

She nodded towards the kitchen door. "Through there. Shall I tell him?"

"No, I'll do it."

The handsome doctor was in the kitchen, sharing a joke with Cook and pounding up some grainy dark powder in a mortar. I called out, "Timaeus. Plautius is ill, I think. I went to his room but he wouldn't let me in, and said he wanted to be left alone. I thought I ought to tell you, just in case."

He put down the pestle and gave me his brilliant smile. "I'll go and check. He gets these strange moods sometimes, but I'm sure there's nothing to worry about. I'm due to take him his next dose of medicine soon anyway."

"Thank you. I'd feel happier if you made sure."

"I'll be there soon."

I slipped back into the bar-room, where they were all still silently concentrating on the unseen quarrel next door. From the angry tone of the voices coming out, it wasn't hard to picture what was happening. Mother and son were confronting one another, so intent on their argument that they had no thought of being overheard. Albia wasn't joining in, but I assumed she was there too.

"Mother, I'm not prepared to argue any more," Candidus was saying, or rather yelling. "My mind's made up. I've chosen how I want to live, and the girl I want to share my life with. I'm a free man, and I can do as I please. I don't have to take orders from you, or father, or anyone else."

"You can't marry this girl without our consent!"

"That's of no importance. We shall live together, man and wife in everything but name. We love each other, and love is enough."

"Then you will face the consequences." Sempronia's voice had dropped, as her anger turned into the quiet, deadly rage that everyone instinctively knows is more dangerous than the loudest shouting. "You will no longer be part of this family. You'll get no help or support from your father or me ever again, and you'll inherit nothing from us when we die. You choose to abandon your duty? Very well. You also lose the privileges that go with it."

"What do I care about that? I can stand on my own feet. I can make my way in the world, and nobody can tell me what to do, or what to think."

"Think?" she said, in a kind of growl. "*Think!* That's precisely what you haven't done, Decimus! You've rushed into this ridiculous decision, your new home, your impossible liaison, and you haven't given a thought to the future. So consider now, before it's too late. You've always had the support of a wealthy family. Without that support, how will you manage? What will you live on? Even a peasant girl will expect a roof over her head and clothes on her back. And how will you manage when children come? Even little bastards will expect food on the table."

"When children come, I'll treat them with more respect and kindness than you've ever shown *me!*" Candidus shouted. "I shan't threaten and bully them all the time. And will you stop referring to Albia as a peasant girl. She's no such thing. She's a free citizen, a centurion's daughter, born in Italia."

"Housekeeper at a mansio," Sempronia sneered. "*Not* the wife for my eldest son! Oh, I know she's pretty and pleasant, and I daresay she's intelligent, if you tell me so. But *your* future isn't with an innkeeper's family. You know where your duty lies, to accept the marriage your father and I have arranged for you, with Fabia Jucunda. To follow in your father's footsteps, in a public career. You'll become a senator, stand for the various political offices, perhaps even the consulship...."

"Never!" There was a crash, as if he banged his fist on the table. "I'll follow my own road in my own way. One day you'll be proud of me. Till then, you may like it or lump it, but you can't change it." The door from the dining-room flew wide open, and Candidus strode out, red-faced and literally shaking with anger. Behind him Albia followed, calm but very pale. They walked to the main door and out onto the forecourt. Nobody broke the total silence.

But I wanted to find out what the lovers intended to do, so I followed them. They walked hand in hand across the forecourt to where Candidus' horse waited patiently by the railings. There they stopped, and he took her in his arms.

I caught up with them, and said, "Albia! What's happening? I heard most of that. What will you do now?"

She disentangled herself, and I saw there were tears in her eyes. "Candidus is going away."

"Going away?" Surely he wasn't giving in to his mother now, after he'd stood up to her so bravely? "Candidus—you're not leaving Albia?"

He laughed and put his arm round her shoulders. "Of course not. But I've got to be in Eburacum for a couple of days, while I sort out my new premises."

"You won't be at the Oak Bridges house at all?" Albia asked.

"Only now and then, for flying visits. I've such a lot to get ready in Eburacum, starting the new business, furnishing the house. I want everything perfect for you."

"Our new home!" Albia was radiant with excitement now. "Won't it be wonderful?"

"A friend is helping me move my things. He's lending me an ox-cart and a couple of slaves, and two trips should do it, as long

as the snow doesn't get any worse. Then I'll come back for you."
He kissed Albia. "If Mother and Father haven't gone away, or at
least seen sense, there'll be nothing at all to stop you coming to
live with me then and there. After all, if we can't have a proper
marriage, we needn't delay setting up home together."

I didn't know whether to applaud him for his courage, or
blame him for wanting to take my sister away even sooner than
I'd anticipated, so I did neither. "There's one thing, before you
go, Candidus. I had a meeting with your father last night, and
he wants to see you, to talk to you alone. Alone—he was most
particular about that, and I get the feeling he's more sympathetic
to your situation than Lady Sempronia."

"Father!" He was scornful. "Don't you believe it. He's just a
good deal more subtle than my dear mama, that's all. She could
bully a tiger into giving up its meal, whereas he'd talk to it so
sweetly that it'd surrender a whole carcass without a growl."

"All the same, it couldn't hurt to have a quick talk with
him, could it? If we can manage it without your mother being
there?"

"Not a chance, Aurelia." He released Albia and turned to lead
his horse to the mounting-block. "Sorry, but the answer's no."

"Then have you a message for him?" I don't know why, I felt
it was important. "I promised I'd try and bring you to see him.
If that isn't possible, at least let me take him a message."

He paused by the block. "Well, yes, you can tell him this.
I'm going to live with Albia whatever he and Mother try to do,
and I'm going to set up my business in Eburacum and make my
own way and my own life there. Will you tell him that?"

"All right." I shook his hand. "Good luck, Candidus. We'll
see you in two or three days?"

"You can bet your boots on it." He hugged Albia, mounted
his horse, and rode up the track and onto the main road. We
stood and watched him out of sight.

"Come back soon, Candidus," she murmured. "Oh Relia, I
love him so much."

"I know."

"You should have heard some of the foul things his mother said. About him, and about me. She's a monster!"

"She is. But you've both stood up to her, and she must realise you won't give in. Surely she'll leave and go back home now, won't she?"

"I hope so. And meanwhile, I'll have nothing to do with her. If anyone has to supervise meals, or deal with their silly complaints, I'm afraid it'll be you. Perhaps I should go and stay with Candidus? Then I could help him move his things."

"Don't even think about it! I need you here, Albia, and Candidus wants to get everything ready for you. We'll cope, don't you worry. And talking of meals," I glanced up at the sun, "it's nearly time for their next one. How are things in the kitchen?"

"Surprisingly good. I thought we'd have no end of trouble with Cook, but he's enjoying himself, amazing everyone with the wonderful food he can conjure up at short notice for such a big party. Timaeus and Margarita have both made a point of complimenting him on the meals so far, which helps."

"Good, because if you can manage without me for half an hour, I'm going to take a bath and change. That's the trouble with fire-fighting, you end up looking as if you've been dragged through a hedge backwards."

She giggled. "That's putting it kindly. You don't exactly smell like the roses of Damascus either."

The water was deliciously hot and relaxing, and I spent longer over my bath than I need have done. I admit I was putting off my next task, which was to give Candidus' message to Plautius, and tell him in detail what was going on, though he'd probably have heard all about it already. But I didn't want him to imagine I'd forgotten my promise to bring him news as soon as I could. He'd think less of me if I didn't keep my word, and I needed as much of his good opinion as I could earn.

By the time I emerged, Sempronia's party were midway through their lunch. Good, that meant if I went to see Plautius now, there'd be less chance of interruptions. Certainly the guest wing seemed to be completely empty as I entered it.

There was no answer when I tapped at the sick-room door. I knocked a second time, and still there was silence. This was ridiculous. I must see him and give him the message. Irritated and anxious, I gave a very loud rap which rattled the door on its hinges. Nothing. I decided to go gently into the bedroom. If he's sound asleep, I thought, that's that, but if he's only dozing, he'll wake up and at least be aware of me. So I eased open the door and looked in.

Plautius was lying in his bed, covered in blood. Standing over him, holding a small bloodstained knife, was my sister.

I strode into the room. "Albia, what's going on?" I stopped, as she gestured for me to be quiet and close the bedroom door. I saw that she was shaking.

"Thank the gods it's you!" she breathed. "I've just found him like this. I don't know what to do. He's dead, and they'll think I killed him!"

"They will." It was the obvious conclusion. But surely my sister could never be a murderer? Still, I had to be certain. "Albia, I have to ask you—did you kill Plautius?"

"Of course not."

I let out a heartfelt sigh of relief. "Then let's be practical. For Jupiter's sake drop that knife. Where did you get it?"

She pointed to a sheepskin rug beside the bed. There were drops of blood on it.

"Put it back then. Is there blood on your hand?"

She dropped the knife and held out her right hand. It was clean. "The blood's dry on the knife, but it looks sticky on the blankets still."

"He was alive when I came before. That was just after Candidus arrived. I wanted to tell him, but when I knocked, he just swore at me and said go away. That was—what, two hours ago?"

"Yes, about that."

"So I thought I'd come and see him now, while the others are safely occupied in the dining-room."

"Me too! I wanted to put my side of the story, talk to him about me and Candidus. You said you thought he wasn't so set against our marriage as Sempronia."

I looked down at the bed. "Let's see what we can find out about how he died, and who killed him. Quintus always says, start with the body."

"I wish Quintus were here now."

"So do I." But simply thinking of him made me feel calmer. He was an imperial investigator who'd helped us solve murders at Oak Bridges four years ago. When he was in our part of the world, which was all too rarely, he was my lover. It must be six months since I'd seen him, and I remembered…but there wasn't time for that sort of memory. I concentrated on what he would do if he were in this room now.

"Was Plautius like this when you found him?"

"Yes, I haven't touched him or the bed. I don't know what made me pick the knife up, it was a stupid thing to do."

"I won't argue with that." I looked at the old man lying on his back, bundled in blankets which were pulled up so they covered his face. All you could see of him was the top of his grey head. The bright red stains which coloured the fawn wool of the blankets were about where his neck would be. I walked to the bed and gingerly moved the blankets down a few inches, so I could look underneath. His throat had been cut, and his neck and chest were soaked in blood. But the blankets themselves weren't torn, so whoever had killed the old man had pulled them up over the body afterwards, to hide his handiwork.

I suddenly felt sick and turned away, as the enormity of all this overwhelmed me. I've seen dead people before, including some who have died violently, and it always makes me queasy. But that was only part of it. I know this will sound callous and unfeeling, but at least half of the appalling panic I felt was because Plautius was not only dead, but was an important man, a relative of the Governor, and he was under our roof. He had even mentioned that he feared secret enemies. Could I have done more to protect him? We had secret enemies too, and this disaster could give them just the excuse they needed to destroy us. As Albia had said already, she would be seen as the most likely person to have killed him, even if she hadn't been found in his room holding the weapon that had dispatched him to the underworld.

I stared out of the window till I'd got sufficient control to be sure I wouldn't throw up all over the bed. When I could bear to look at Plautius again, I was relieved to see that Albia had pulled up the blankets, arranging them so his gruesome wound was hidden from sight, along with most of the blood. "Are you all right, Relia?"

"Just about. And you?"

"I'll survive." She shuddered, realising it wasn't the most tasteful expression to use in the circumstances. "Do you think we can find out who's done this?"

"I hope so. Because otherwise we're first in line to be suspected."

"Should we tell someone, or leave things as they are and let one of his own people find him?"

"We can't just pretend we don't know about it." Tempting as it was to walk away, or preferably run, we would risk looking even guiltier, in the eyes of someone wanting a scapegoat for this horrible crime. "No, we've got to tell them. And the sooner the better."

"Aurelia Marcella!" The voice came from behind us. We both whirled round, to see the door opening slowly, and a man standing there watching us and blocking our way of escape.

I heard someone cry out, and realised it was me. The man in the doorway was Lord Plautius.

Chapter IX

"Holy Diana protect us!" I breathed, and I heard Albia mutter a prayer to Juno. We both stood staring, unable to speak, unable to think clearly. Was this Plautius' poor wandering shade, who could not enter the underworld until it had taken vengeance on whoever had killed him? Did it think *we'd* killed him?

"Aurelia Marcella," the apparition repeated. The soft voice was calm, slightly amused even. "And this is your sister, the housekeeper. I heard people talking, and came to see who was in my room. What are you doing here?"

Neither of us ventured to answer. He sounded like a mortal man, and he seemed like one, as he began to pace towards us into the room. I tried to stand my ground, but my feet took a step backwards, beyond my control.

"What's the matter?" he asked. "You look as if you've seen a ghost."

That ordinary, casual expression was what convinced me that I hadn't seen one. I took a deep breath. "We came to look for you, Lord Plautius. And instead we found...." I gestured towards the bed. "We thought it was you. I don't understand. Who is he? What's he doing here?"

"Don't be concerned." Plautius walked calmly towards the bed. "My slave slept here last night instead of me, that's all. I used one of the other rooms. I suppose he thinks as he's in the master's bed, he's allowed to laze about all day. You can get up now, Idmon, and be quick about it."

He began to pull back the blankets, and stopped as he saw what was beneath them. He gazed down for a couple of heart-beats, then he swung round on us. "Who's done this? You have, I assume! Now I understand why you're looking at me as if I'm an apparition from a tomb. You thought I was dead! You thought you'd killed me, and have just discovered your mistake! No, you've only killed poor Idmon, one of my guards."

"*We* didn't kill him!" Now that I saw the master and servant together, I realised there was only a moderate resemblance between them. They were both thin and grey-haired, but the dead man's hair was in fact a grey wig, and his face lacked Plautius' sick-room pallor.

The old man frowned. "Then kindly explain how you come to be standing over his corpse."

I made an effort to gather my wits. "We found him like this. We thought we'd found you—as presumably whoever murdered him did." Desperation made me bold. "Last night you said some-thing about secret enemies. That's why you took the precaution of not sleeping in your own bed?"

"I had reason to be afraid, it seems."

"But not of Relia and me!" Albia exclaimed.

"No?" He said coldly, and studied us for a while. "I've felt for some time that I had an enemy, someone who wanted me dead."

"That proves it can't be us," she said. "We've known you less than a day."

"True. But my enemy is manifestly clever enough to persuade or bribe another person, or persons, to do the killing. I assume you were well paid. Not that money will help you now." He swayed a little on his feet, and I went to support him, but he waved me away.

"We didn't do this dreadful thing," I repeated, as calmly and firmly as I could.

He steadied himself against the side of the bed. "Let us go next door into the sitting-room. We can talk there. I'll get one of my people to see to poor Idmon."

He picked up a little silver hand-bell from the bedside table, and rang it loudly. Its sweet note made a disturbing contrast to the bed's gruesome inhabitant. Then, still holding the bell, he led us into the sitting-room, and we all sat down. He looked from one to the other of us with those unnervingly bright grey eyes. I gazed back at him, scared and shaken and yet impressed by his coolness. If he seriously thought we had tried to murder him, then staying calmly here in a room with us was extremely brave.

Nobody came in answer to the bell, but it would only be a matter of time before a slave showed up, or even one of the family. We hadn't long to convince the old man that we were innocent, and I decided that attack was the best form of defence. "My lord Plautius, you said just now that you heard us talking. If we'd really come to do you harm, do you think we'd have stood about at the scene of the crime, drawing attention to ourselves by talking? Do you think we'd have spoken at all? We'd have crept into your room, done what we had to do, and got out again in a dozen heartbeats."

"You thought this part of the mansio was deserted. Which it seems to be," he added irritably, and shook the bell again. "Ah, here comes someone at last!"

We heard the sound of footsteps in the corridor outside. "Guard! Here!" Plautius called out. "And where in Hades have you been?"

But it was Horatius who appeared at the door. "Oh, you're out of bed, Gnaeus. That's good." He stared round at us. Even from a distance I could smell the wine on his breath. "Why are you all looking so serious? What's wrong?"

"Go next door to my room, and see for yourself."

"Eh? Your room? Oh, all right." Horatius wasn't gone long, and when he came back his red face had gone pale. "Poor Idmon. So you were right about someone wanting to kill you." He looked at Albia and me, with a surprised expression that would have been laughable if it hadn't been followed by the question, "Did these two kill him?"

"No, we did not…" I began, but Plautius cut me short.

"Be quiet! Yes, Horatius, it looks as if they did. I found them in the room there, standing by the bed, with Idmon covered in blood, and a bloodstained knife on the floor."

"There's no blood on us though." I'd suddenly seen where our best hope lay. "Look—we haven't a spot of blood on our clothing or our hands, either of us. You two gentlemen surely both have military experience. We ourselves are from an army family. So we all know that if a person stabs someone and spills that much blood, some of it is bound to get onto him, or his clothes." I held out my hands, and Albia did the same. "See? Not a trace of blood anywhere."

Plautius surveyed each of us in turn, then looked at the lawyer. "She may have a point there, I suppose. What do you think, Horatius? And neither of them has a reason to kill me. Unless they were being paid by someone else, of course."

"Ah, but you haven't heard the latest developments! They might have a good reason, especially the housekeeper." Horatius nodded towards Albia. "Decimus has turned up, here at the mansio. He and Sempronia had the mother and father of all rows." He glanced round the room and spotted a tray with a wine-jug and half-a-dozen mugs. "I could do with a drink. Like one, Gnaeus?"

"No, thank you. Decimus is found, you say?"

I seized my chance. "Why do you think we came to see you? I promised to bring you news of him, and…."

"I told you to be quiet. Have you seen him yourself, Horatius?"

"I have, and that isn't the half of it." The lawyer chuckled and sat down with his beaker of wine. "I've also seen the woman he wants to marry." He gestured towards Albia.

"The housekeeper?"

"The very same. And now you tell me she may have tried to kill you?"

"Yes." Plautius turned on me angrily. "So you've known my son's whereabouts all along, and have been withholding the information? I thought better of you than that."

"Certainly not! It was a while before I realised that your son is someone we know. He's changed his name, he's known locally as Perennius Candidus, so when Lady Sempronia asked me yesterday to help search for him, his real name meant nothing to me."

"And *you* are the woman he wants to marry?" Plautius stared at Albia.

She sat up straight. "I am. And proud of it."

"Even in the face of his parents' strong disapproval?"

"Yes. We would rather have your consent, but we want to live together, and we will, with or without it."

"Where is Decimus now? I want to see him."

Horatius shrugged. "Where he is *now*, I don't know. He left the mansio after he and Sempronia had finished quarrelling. Or perhaps she hadn't finished, but he'd had enough."

It was my turn for Plautius' piercing stare. "You didn't bring him to see me, as I asked."

"I tried to persuade him, but I couldn't. *And* I tried to tell you what was going on, while he was still here with her ladyship. You wouldn't see me, or I suppose that was your slave. I realise now why he told me to go away, but at the time I thought you were just feeling unwell. I did tell Timaeus to come and make sure you weren't seriously ill."

"He wouldn't bother to, I imagine. He knew it was Idmon in my bed." He relaxed a little. "So Decimus and his mother had an argument. Did any of you hear what was said?"

"I did," Horatius answered eagerly, "and so did everyone for ten miles around, I expect. A real battle they had! Well, you can imagine. Sempronia going through all the reasons why Decimus shouldn't marry an innkeeper, and Decimus insisting he'll live with her anyway, with or without your consent. He plans to set up in business in Eburacum as a trader. He wouldn't give an inch, even when Sempronia told him about the will."

"He won't change," Albia put in. "Neither will I."

"Even though you'll be the cause of my son's being cast out by his family—deprived of his chance to make a political career?"

"He doesn't *want* a political career."

"And you realise that if I alter my will, he won't inherit a single copper coin when I'm no longer here?"

"I'm not marrying him for his money, and he won't give me up for it, either."

Plautius sat in thoughtful silence for a while. Then amazingly he started to laugh, his whole body shaking with merriment. "I wish I could have been there when they met. Sempronia isn't used to people saying no to her, especially in the family. And Decimus can be as stubborn as she is!"

"That's true enough," Horatius smiled. "Normally I'd put money on Sempronia getting her own way in the end. She usually does. But in this case...."

"She won't," Albia declared.

"Anyhow," the lawyer refilled his beaker, "that's why I came looking for you, to give you the latest news. I came earlier, but you were asleep, or rather Idmon was." Interesting, I thought, that Plautius hadn't even told Horatius about the change in sleeping arrangements. "So I went and had some food. Very enjoyable it was too." He gave a satisfied belch and looked at Albia with a beaming smile. "At least if Decimus does marry you, m'dear, he'll never be short of a good meal! Ah well, I suppose one shouldn't joke." He put down his mug. "So then, are you going ahead with altering your will, Gnaeus?"

"I've still not made a final decision. I want to give Decimus one last chance to change his mind." He looked at Albia. "I'll be frank with you. This is nothing personally to do with you, but we want our son to follow the political career we have planned for him, including marriage into a senatorial family. Both Sempronia and I will do our best to see that he does. I hope I make myself clear?"

"Very clear," my sister said. "But you won't succeed. I hope that is clear too."

Plautius appeared not to have heard. "First we must find out who killed Idmon, mistaking him for me. After what you've just told me, Horatius, I'm fairly certain it must have been these two women, or perhaps just the one Decimus thinks he's in love with. If she knew I was intending to alter my will, she—or they—might have decided to dispose of me before I could."

"How many more times must I tell you, we don't care about your money!" Albia almost shouted. "I love Candidus. He loves me. We two can make our own living, and we will!"

"And if they need any help," I added, "Albia has family who'll stand by her and support her, even if Candidus hasn't."

"Admirable sentiments, to be sure. But does standing by your sister include committing murder for her, or assisting her to commit it?" He turned to the lawyer. "What's your view, Horatius?"

"Oh, if you want my opinion, I don't think either of them did it." I could have hugged him, but it wouldn't have helped.

"You don't? Why not? They were almost caught in the act."

Horatius shook his head. "She's right about the blood. Whoever stabbed Idmon will be carrying some traces of it. And now it's public knowledge that you're likely to be altering your will, there are several people in the household who might want to...well...." He trailed off, but Plautius smiled.

"Put an end to me while the old will is still in force?"

Horatius nodded. "There's bound to be all sorts of gossip about whether you're making other changes too."

"Yes, you may be right." Plautius rubbed his chin thoughtfully with his thin hand. "Diogenes—Margarita—Decimus himself, of course, if he didn't ride away, but stole back to the mansio."

"But not me." Horatius chuckled. "I prefer the new arrangements we discussed, given a choice. No, this isn't a clear-cut case. However, we can't take any chances. Tell me," he faced the two of us squarely, "who's the chief magistrate in this area? You were telling Sempronia about him at breakfast."

I nodded, remembering at the same time that, in the confusion of the morning, I had forgotten to send him a message, as I'd promised Sempronia. "The Chief Councillor of Oak Bridges is Publius Silvanius Clarus."

"And will this Publius Silvanius Clarus vouch for the two of you?" Horatius asked. "Will he declare on oath that you're not murderers, and that you won't attempt to run away until we've found who killed Idmon?"

"Certainly he will. I'll send a message now, and ask him to come here, so you can talk to him yourselves."

"*I'll* send," Plautius corrected. "We need to notify someone in authority about this anyway. Killing a slave isn't a serious matter, but attempting to assassinate a senator is. And especially in an official mansio."

I tried not to show the sinking feeling his words gave me. "Silvanius will be happy to help in any way he can. His house is a little over a mile away. He can be here before dark."

"Good. And meantime, what shall we do with these two, Horatius? Lock them up somewhere?"

"I don't know about that, Gnaeus." Fortunately Horatius realised what shaky ground he would be on if he imprisoned two citizens who turned out to be innocent.

I said quickly, "Lock us up? I'll have you know we're citizens, with a brother in the Governor's service, and nobody is going to lock us up when we've done nothing wrong!"

"Besides," Albia added, with a mischievous gleam in her eye, "if you lock us up, who's going to run the mansio? Provide your meals, look after your animals, make sure your rooms and the bath-house are well heated? These things don't happen by themselves, they have to be properly supervised. By us."

That wasn't strictly true. It was our proud boast that we'd trained our staff so well that they could run the place without us. But the boast hadn't reached Horatius' ears.

"Very well then, suppose we compromise," the old man said. "You give us your word not to leave the mansio, and you also promise to stay together till this magistrate gets here."

"Of course," I said. "I promise not to run away. I've no reason to."

"I promise too," Albia agreed.

"As an extra safeguard," Plautius added, "one of our household will stay with you at all times."

I assumed my best dignified manner. "Our word should be enough."

"That depends, doesn't it," he answered, not unkindly, "on whether you're innocent or guilty. For people who have tried to murder a senator, breaking a promise would probably seem a trivial misdemeanour."

I couldn't fault the logic, so I simply said, "In our family, if we make a promise, we keep it."

"Margarita can stay with them," Horatius suggested.

"Margarita? That proves you don't believe they are guilty. If they're murderers, you'll be exposing her to some personal danger. Very well, let Margarita act as our watch-dog."

The lawyer looked thoughtful. "If they didn't kill Idmon, then whoever did is still at large. So you ought to have a guard at your door from now on, Gnaeus."

"I shall, never fear. I should have taken that precaution before. Now, Horatius, if you wouldn't mind finding Margarita, I'll draft a note to this Silvanius." He looked at me and Albia like an old tomcat playing with a couple of field-mice. "Don't think that you are no longer under suspicion. We shall be making strenuous enquiries into Idmon's death."

I said, "We've nothing to fear. They can only find us innocent." As Horatius left to fetch Margarita, I sent a silent prayer to Diana to let my brave words prove true.

Chapter X

Sometimes you feel the gods are on your side, and sometimes not, but usually it's hard to tell. I didn't know which of the Immortals sent the sudden snowstorm that arrived just as Plautius finished dictating his note for Silvanius, but I was angry to start with. I badly wanted Silvanius' friendly support, which I knew we would get if we asked for it. But how could we ask for it? No messenger was going to travel anywhere till the blizzard stopped. As it was still piling down thick and fast at dark, that meant Plautius' letter couldn't reach Oak Bridges at least till morning, but neither could any message from me. Or could it?

That's when I realised the storm might be a gift from Diana in answer to my prayer. It gave us a slim chance of making contact with Silvanius before Plautius did, and telling him what had happened. The visitors' men, being strangers, wouldn't want to travel unfamiliar snowy roads at night, but we had several lads in our household who'd be prepared to venture to Oak Bridges in the dark, if only the snow would stop falling. The problem was going to be arranging it without being seen by Margarita, who politely but quite firmly stayed with me and Albia, and made sure we kept dutifully together.

The afternoon dragged by. Sempronia and Priscus and nearly everyone else in her party, except for Plautius and Timaeus, enjoyed long leisurely baths, and then retired to the guest wing, leaving only Margarita with us. We stayed in the bar-room, chatting to the small band of customers clustered round our fire, but they went home well before dark. Then we moved to the kitchen, still with Margarita in tow, and staved off boredom by helping with the preparation of the evening meal, although Cook and the maids could perfectly well have done it without us. We were serving cold sausage with olives for starters, then geese with damson sauce, and plenty of vegetables. Honey cakes, cow's cheese, and a bowl of walnuts and hazelnuts were the dessert. I suppose the kitchen girls knew why we were all there, but they were too busy making a pet of Gaius to worry about it. They fed him such a mixture of rich titbits that I was afraid he'd be sick. But he was cheerful and well-behaved, and Margarita was good company. I was thankful that if we had to be dogged continuously by a couple of Sempronia's people, we had at least been assigned the pleasantest ones.

Not that we were left entirely to our own devices. About an hour before dinner, Diogenes came into the kitchen and addressed Albia with his habitual disdainful sneer.

"My lady wants to see you, Miss. Please come with me to her sitting-room now."

Albia put down her sewing. "Did she say what it's about, Diogenes?"

"No. But I daresay we can all guess."

"Do you want me to come with you?" I offered.

Albia shook her head. "I'll be fine. I'm sure it won't take long." She left with the Weasel through the hall door, and almost instantly, Timaeus came in from the bar-room.

"Aurelia, my lord Plautius asks if you can spare him a little time. He's in his bedroom."

"Yes, of course." We entered the guest wing only a few paces behind my sister and Diogenes. They went into her ladyship's sitting-room, while Timaeus ushered me into Plautius' room, past the looming shape of a bodyguard standing to attention in the passage.

"Ah, there you are." The old man was sitting up in his bed, wrapped in his shawl, but looking none the worse for his earlier shock. "Sit down, please."

I took a stool, and Timaeus remained standing by the door. They were taking no chances with a possible murderer.

"Lady Sempronia has told me," he said slowly, "the details of her discussion with Decimus, and how he is refusing to change his mind about your sister, or about returning with us to Londinium. I want to ask you to be honest with me. How can your sister be persuaded to withdraw from her attachment to our son?"

"She can't, my lord."

"If it's a question of money...."

"It isn't. She loves your son, and she won't give him up."

"You're certain of that?"

"Absolutely certain."

"From her point of view, marriage to Decimus would allow her to move up in the world, I suppose. I'm not trying to be offensive, just realistic. Innkeepers don't usually marry into powerful senatorial families. However, I can't approve of it. I mean it when I say that I may disown Decimus altogether. Your sister is aware that I'm considering this, but it has not deterred her. Is that because she thinks I won't go through with it?"

How many more times must I repeat this? "No. It's as I said, she loves your son, and that's enough for her. I warn you, she has a stubborn streak as wide as the Appian Way. She won't give him up."

Suddenly he rapped out sharply, "I asked you to bring Decimus to me this morning. But you said he refused?"

"I'm afraid he did, quite categorically. He sent you a message."

"Which is?"

"He said, 'You can tell him this. I'm going to live with Albia whatever he and Mother try to do, and I'm going to set up my business in Eburacum and make my own way and my own life there.'"

"Do you know whereabouts in Eburacum he plans to live?"

"No, I don't. All he's told us is that he's leaving his house near Oak Bridges and moving to new premises in the town. He didn't tell me where."

"Your sister knows, perhaps?"

"If she does, she's not saying."

"If she really doesn't know, she must be expecting my son to return here, or at least send her a message telling her where he is."

"If you say so." There was no fooling this shrewd old man.

"Don't play games," he snapped, staring at me hard. "What arrangements have they made to stay in contact?"

"I've no idea. They haven't confided in me." It was the first lie I'd told him, and only a small one at that, but it was an effort to return his stare directly. I was finding this interrogation unpleasantly scary.

"Are you prepared to help find him and bring him here to see me? I'm reluctant to go back to Londinium until I've spoken to him face-to-face. I'm sure that you and your sister between you can trace him quite quickly, if you choose."

That was the last thing we'd choose, but I could hardly be so blunt. "I don't quite see what more I can do. We don't know Eburacum at all well, it's just somewhere we visit occasionally. Looking for one newcomer who'd arrived there to make his fortune would be like hunting for a pin in a pine-wood. It'd be beyond us, I'm afraid. Couldn't you send men to Eburacum yourself to search?"

"I could, but it would take time. And money. I thought, if you were prepared to assist—but never mind. There's an easy alternative. I'll arrange to have your sister arrested for attempted murder, and kept in custody for a while. Oh yes, I'm aware she's a free citizen, but the Governor will authorise it, if it's necessary. Decimus will come back then, to see her and perhaps try to get her released. Instead of seeing her, he'll find he has to see *me.*"

And so, of course, I agreed that we would try to find Candidus and bring him to talk to his father. What else could I do? As I left his room, I reflected that every time I had a conversation with Plautius, I ended up being forced into some course of action I'd rather not undertake.

Albia was in the bar-room with Margarita. She was flushed and furious, and as I entered I heard the words "obscene old harpy," so I guessed she was speaking her mind about Lady Sempronia.

"What's up, Albia?" I settled myself down by the fire. "As if I couldn't guess. You've had a bad meeting with her ladyship?"

"She tried to buy me off! Can you believe it? She offered me money if I'd give up Candidus. That's *after* she'd tried threatening me, saying that her nephew the Governor could always find ways of dealing with 'people of your sort'. The cheek of it! I told her, 'I'm a Roman citizen, a centurion's daughter, and I'm well aware of my rights. I'm sure the Governor is too.' So then she tried bribery. She actually thought all she had to do was offer me a few gold pieces, and I'd walk away from the man I love!"

"You wouldn't be the first."

"And finally she said that she'd forbidden the marriage, and it would take place over her dead body. I tell you, Relia, it was all I could do not to say that I'll be happy to see her dead body, if it means I can marry Candidus!"

Once the guests had eaten, Albia and I took our own food— cold pork, vegetables, and a jug of Rhodian—into the bar-room, and Margarita and Gaius joined us for supper. The boy ate very little, having, as his mother said, made a piglet of himself in the kitchen. He soon fell fast asleep on the rug in front of the fire, and we chatted comfortably. Margarita was pleasant company, and the more I saw of her the more I liked her. But I urgently wanted a private talk with Albia, and I racked my brains for a ruse to get our watch-dog out of the way for a space.

Eventually she put down her knife and said, "Aurelia, Lord Plautius told me what happened to Idmon, but he warned me to be discreet about it, so I didn't say anything in front of the others. I just want you to know that *I* don't think you two tried to kill him. It's a ridiculous idea."

"Thank you, that's a relief. But I can't deny it must look suspicious, from Plautius' point of view." I helped myself to more leeks and carrots, and passed round the dish.

Margarita wiped her plate clean with a piece of bread. "Plautius has talked about secret enemies before. I'm afraid we all thought it was just a case of an old sick man with an over-active imagination. He must feel vulnerable, being so ill and away from home. Only now I wish we'd taken it more seriously."

I finished my meat and helped myself to some walnuts, cracking them in my hand the way we did as children. "The guard Idmon can't have thought there was any danger. He felt safe enough to fall sound asleep in his master's nice comfortable room."

"At least it wasn't Timaeus who was killed," she said. "Or maybe if he'd been there in Lord Plautius' place, he'd have stayed awake and caught the murderer."

"Timaeus? How do you mean?"

"This isn't the first time Plautius has put a decoy in his bed. He's done it on several nights, especially lately. The slaves take it in turns. Idmon, a couple of the other guards, and even Diogenes once, though he made an awful fuss about it. Last night Timaeus had volunteered, but because Lord Plautius felt so ill after the journey here, Idmon took over."

Albia passed round the bowl of nuts. "There's no more we can do now. Let's just relax and enjoy a bit of peace and quiet. Margarita, are you and Gaius staying over in our part of the mansio tonight, or does Plautius trust us not to make a run for it when everyone's asleep?"

She smiled. "He didn't exactly say what's to happen tonight, but I think I can risk leaving you alone over here, don't you? We're all putting you to enough trouble already, and Sempronia will expect me to sleep near her."

That's something, I thought, taking care not to look too pleased. "Whatever you think best. Is it still snowing?" I got up and opened the big main door, letting in a draught of cold air which made Gaius stir, half-awake on his rug. The storm had spent itself, and it was a still, starry night now, with a sliver of moon reflecting off the white ground. I shut the door again, and crossed the room to the fire. As I sat down, the hall door opened, and Diogenes entered. His sharp eyes focused on Margarita.

"My lady sent me to fetch you, Margarita."

Margarita sighed and got to her feet. "I'll come, if she's sent for me, though it's too early to go to bed yet. She wants me in her sitting-room, presumably?"

He smiled at her, like a crocodile surveying a trapped fisherman. "No. I'm to escort you to your room. Now."

"That's not possible," I cut in. I'd caught the fleeting look of panic in her eyes, and it made me angry. It was only too obvious what was in his mind. It was equally clear that Margarita wanted none of it.

"Margarita is sleeping over in our part of the house tonight." I looked the Weasel straight in the eye.

"Oh? That's the first I've heard of it. Is this true, Margarita?"

"Yes, it is. My lord told me to stay here till tomorrow."

"I thought everybody knew," I continued. "Those are Lord Plautius' strict instructions."

"She's supposed to be keeping watch," Albia added, "in case we decide to run away." She managed a cheery laugh. "Yes, I know it's hardly likely in this weather, but there it is, we all have to do as we're told, don't we? If you take her away now, we'll *all* be in trouble with his lordship."

He didn't miss the emphasis on "all". "Lady Sempronia will be displeased," he threatened.

I produced an unanswerable winning throw of the dice. "Perhaps we'd better check with his lordship, Margarita, in case there's been some sort of misunderstanding. We'll all have to go and see him, as we've got to stay together, so will you come with us, Diogenes?"

"No, if my lord has spoken, there's an end of it." His deferential mask, which he hadn't bothered assuming for us, was back in place for a few heartbeats, but then it slipped again, and he cast a sulky look at Margarita. "I'll see you tomorrow then."

"All right."

"You'll make sure Lady Sempronia knows that Margarita is with us tonight?" I said, in what Albia likes to call my "honey-sweet" tone. "And tomorrow morning as well, at least until Chief

Councillor Silvanius gets here. I don't know when that will be exactly. I hope he comes early, so Albia and I can get over to the Oak Bridges market in the morning. If we delay too long, all the best stuff will have gone."

"Oh, a market, eh?" Diogenes laughed softly, as if this was some private joke. "You'd better take young Gaius with you. He'll enjoy that. Won't you, my lad? A nice trip to the market tomorrow?"

To my astonishment, Gaius let out a heart-rending wail.

"You've done it now," Diogenes remarked. "Sweet dreams, Gaius!" He banged the door behind him as the boy's howls grew louder.

Margarita picked him up in her arms and sat down with him on her lap. "It's all right, love," she soothed, stroking his hair. "I'm here, and there's nothing to cry about. Hush now! He's gone, and we're safe."

"No!" he shrieked. "Not the market! I don't want to go! Please, Mamma, don't make me go!" He dissolved into loud sobbing.

"Don't cry, little one," Margarita rocked him gently back and forth. "We won't go to the market, if you don't want to."

I gazed helplessly at the pair of them, trying to work out what had frightened Gaius so. A trip to the market? For a boy of his age, that would be exciting, surely, not alarming, especially with Saturnalia almost here. Any child as attractive as this one would get more than his share of treats and presents.

When eventually she had calmed him down, she smiled at me and Albia. "Thank you. Thank you both. You've no idea what you've saved us from."

"I think we have," I smiled back at her. "That man's a pig."

"It was good of you, really kind. Usually I have to barricade my door so he can't get in."

"Can't you just tell him no and send him off with a flea in his ear?"

She shook her head. "It's not so easy. If it was just me, perhaps—but it isn't. And my lady believes any spiteful tale he tells her, of course. Well, thanks to you, we're safe for now. And if there's anything I can do in return...."

"As it happens there is." This was just the chance I'd been waiting for.

"Tell me."

"I need a quarter of an hour on my own. I give you my word I'm not running away, or planning to hurt anybody. But there's a message I have to send to a friend."

"It's time I put Gaius to bed." She got to her feet a little clumsily with the child in her arms. "Albia, is there a spare room somewhere we can use? Or we can sleep in here, whichever is least trouble. It usually takes me at least a quarter of an hour to settle him down," she added, and they went out together.

I hurried to the kitchen and sent one of the maids to find Titch. "He'll be in the tack-room playing dice with the other horse-boys, I expect. Tell him I want to see him straight away, please."

I sat down at the big table and wrote a quick note to Chief Councillor Silvanius. I used ink and papyrus, to make it look more formal and official.

> Aurelia Marcella to Silvanius Clarus, greetings.
>
> We need your help urgently, and beg you to come to us as soon as you can. Albia and I are falsely accused of murder by our guests here, Lord Plautius and Lady Sempronia Metilia. They are people of power and importance. We need someone of power and importance on our side, to convince them we are innocent. They'll listen to you, if you speak for us. Please help us.

By the time I'd sealed the note Titch was standing watching me. "Victor, I've a favour to ask you."

He looked at me in surprise. Usually I just tell the horse-boys to do things, and they do them. So he realised I wasn't giving him an order, and he could refuse if he chose. But he was always ready for adventure. I was relying on it.

"What is it?" He ran a hand through his red hair, making it even more untidy than usual. "You know I'll do owt I can."

"I need a man to take an urgent message to Councillor Silvanius' villa at Oak Bridges. Someone who'll get it there tonight and not blab about it."

He didn't hesitate. "Aye, I'll do that. The snow's stopped, and it's a grand night now. I'll go on foot, it's safer than riding when the roads are slippy."

"Good, thank you. But don't go alone. Take one of the other boys. Two's better than one on a winter night."

He nodded. "Castor will come. We'll manage fine."

"Here's the note. Make sure you give it to the Chief Councillor himself, or to his major-domo, or…."

"Or someone who knows what they're about. I will." He hesitated. "The only thing is, if I get held up waiting to deliver it, or it snows again and I don't get back here till daylight, can you make sure someone sees to Poppaea? She's that hungry, feeding all her pups. I've moved them into the old cart shed, the one nobody uses now. Me dad complained that they were in the way in the tack-room."

"Don't worry. If you're not back, I'll feed her myself, I promise. But you should get home easily, unless it snows again."

He tucked the note into his belt-pouch. "Is this to do with the feller that got stabbed?"

"You heard all about that?"

"Oh aye, the whole place is buzzing like a beehive. Their lads are saying you and Miss Albia murdered him, in mistake for their old master, cos he won't let her marry Master Candidus."

"And what are our lads saying?"

He laughed. "We all think that's daft. You and Miss Albia wouldn't murder a guest."

"Of course not."

"But if you did, you'd be too clever to get caught, wouldn't you?"

I decided it was best to assume this was meant as a compliment.

Chapter XI

As Titch was leaving by the kitchen door, I heard him talking to someone outside. He turned back into the room and said, in an over-loud voice, "Does anyone know where Mistress Aurelia is? Hold on, I'll go and see."

He shut the door and crossed the room to me, saying softly, "There's someone out there wants to see you. Big man with a black beard. Dressed like a native, but stands like a soldier. I don't know him."

"Is he alone?"

"He's alone at the door, but while we were talking, his eyes flicked sideways once, just quickly like, as if he might have a pal standing guard in the dark."

"I'll see him in my study. Probably just someone after a job, though it's an odd time to come calling. You and Castor get on your way."

The black-bearded stranger was tall and broad, and dressed in a good wool cloak, like a prosperous farmer or merchant. But I agreed with Titch that he had the bearing of a soldier, in the way he walked and stood and glanced around the room. He also had stout army boots. So he probably wasn't seeking a job, but trying to sell me something.

He greeted me politely and held out his hand. "Mistress Aurelia Marcella? I'm sorry to come disturbing you after dark, but I've a bit of business I'd like to discuss with you." He spoke good Latin, but with a slight accent. I've a good ear for accents, and this man wasn't a local Brigantian tribesman, but originated from further north.

We shook hands, and I answered in British. "Certainly. May I ask your name?"

He smiled, showing a broken front tooth. "I'm Otus."

"Otus! I'm very pleased to meet you. It was some of your boys who helped to put out our haystack fire this morning, wasn't it?"

"It was, aye."

"We were extremely grateful. You must let me get you a drink."

"Thanks, I'll take a glass of wine with you."

"Would your friend outside like a drink too?" It was an arrow in the dark, and I was pleased to see a flicker of surprise in his eyes.

"I've come on my own tonight," he answered.

"Have you? Then I ought to warn you, my horse-boy saw somebody following you."

He laughed. "Your boy can see in the dark, seemingly. All right, I did bring a man with me, but he'll do well enough outside without a drink, thank you. There have to be some advantages to being the boss."

I rang for one of the maids to bring wine, and he took a long swig and sat back in his chair.

"I hope you don't mind me asking, Otus, but am I right in guessing that you've got military connections? I'm a centurion's daughter, and I can usually spot our brave lads, even off duty."

He nodded. "Used to be a soldier, yes, but I've done my time and come out, and now I prefer a peaceful life. I run a group of contract workers, doing a bit of this and a bit of that."

And a bit of thieving and a bit of extortion? Was Otus part of the gang Hawk had warned me about? I must play this carefully. "Well, your lads were in the right place at the right time this morning. Thank you."

"I'm glad they could help. A dreadful thing, fire."

"Dreadful. And hay is even more precious than usual this year, after the bad summer. We'll only just have enough feed to see our animals through till spring. We can't afford to be losing any."

"All the farmers round here say the same," he agreed. "Hay and corn, they're scarce now, and they're going to be worth their weight in gold by April." He put down his mug. "Which is why I think we can be of service to you."

"You're a supplier of hay?" I knew that anyone with spare forage would be able to name his own price by the winter's end and then double it, and still have buyers beating a path to his barn door. Especially a man with military contacts, who had access to army stores. But in that case, why was he making his offer as early as December?

I sipped my wine and leaned forward, ready for a bit of hard bargaining. But he shook his head. "I'm not supplying it, no. You might say I'm preserving it."

"I'm sorry?"

"Me and my lads, we're offering a security service."

"Security? To stop our hay being stolen, you mean? You think things will get that bad?"

He gave his broken-toothed smile. "We run watch patrols to protect farmers from the risk of fire. You do us the occasional small favour in return, and we guarantee that your barns and stacks will be completely safe."

With a shock, I grasped what he meant. He was threatening that if we didn't do what he wanted—and who could guess what these "occasional small favours" would be—he and his men would burn down our barns and stacks. Only next time they started a blaze, they wouldn't linger to extinguish it.

I sat still, keeping my expression blank. Above all I mustn't look as scared as I suddenly felt. I took another swallow of wine and said, "It's an interesting offer, but I've got plenty of good men, and we can guard ourselves, if there's any real danger. I can't afford to be paying someone else to look after us."

"I'm not talking about money. Just a good turn sometimes. Give us a bit of help, like."

"Such as what? Free drinks for you and your men for the next hundred years, is it?"

He laughed. "Well, for instance, sometimes when we're out on patrol, me and my lads need a place to sleep at nights. Somewhere local and out of the way, like. I noticed a big old roundhouse near to your rick-yard. Doesn't seem to be used at all these days."

"No, not now. It belonged to the family who had the farm until we took it over."

"Well then, if you was to allow me and my boys to use the place sometimes, just for the odd night, we could keep a good eye on your property and make sure no harm comes to it. As you said yourself, your winter stores are important. Can't afford to lose them."

I tried to look as if I was thinking deeply, while in reality wishing I had the first clue what to do next. I'd never been faced with someone dealing in this sort of threat before. But I knew for certain I didn't want to do business with him. It was all very well for him to talk about "the occasional small favour". The favours would grow and multiply, and once I'd begun to co-operate with them, there'd be no going back. I'd have climbed onto a treadmill, with no hope of ever climbing off again.

I gazed down into my beaker, maintaining my thoughtful expression, but my mind was racing. There was something else he wasn't telling me. I'd no objection to a few local men using a building that we ourselves didn't need, and he must know that. So why hadn't he come openly and asked me about it? I'd have rented it to him for a few copper coins or the occasional deer carcass. I wished I could consult Lucius. I don't often feel the need of a man to help me, but I was well out of my depth here. My brother, as a secret investigator, must have experience of this kind of situation…. Yes, of course, how naïve I was being. *Secret* was the clue. They wanted a place to hide where no questions would be asked and no answers given to anyone who came prying.

"Well then," Otus asked, "is it a deal?"

"You left out something, I think. You'll expect our little arrangement kept completely private. You'll want to keep yourselves as secret as a wolf-pack in a den."

He nodded. "You've got it."

"Then I'm afraid I can't oblige. This is an official mansio. However much I'd like to help, it isn't a good place to keep secrets. For most of the year, it's full of people travelling on the Empire's business, soldiers, government officials, messengers, people trained to have sharp eyes. I can't guarantee that none of them will see you or your men, and if they spot you, they'll start getting curious."

"We're used to keeping out of folks' way," he said. "And I'm only talking about this winter. I'm sure we won't need to trouble you in the spring or summer. Sensible wolves," he added with a grin, "change their hunting-grounds with the seasons."

I shook my head. "Sorry, Otus. I don't think it's a good idea. Even in winter we have guests. We've got a houseful now, as it happens, some relatives of the provincial Governor's. And my own brother is coming to stay over the holiday. He's an army man, based down south, but he comes up here when he can, and he often brings friends along for a spot of hunting." Two days ago that would have been true, and it still sounded convincing.

He shrugged. "Well, don't say no straight away. Think about it. These are dangerous times, and I'd hate to see you having any trouble here."

"That's good of you. Look, I really am grateful for what your lads did today. I'll be glad to buy you all some Saturnalia refreshment." I fished in my belt-pouch and found a couple of silver pieces, which I handed to him with my warmest smile. "But it's not possible to do any more. I hope you understand."

"Oh aye. I understand all right. But if you change your mind, you can reach me care of the Wolf's Head tavern in Eburacum."

"I shan't change my mind."

His smile as I ushered him out still showed his broken tooth, but lacked any warmth at all.

Albia was alone in the bar-room, so I quickly told her about my message to Silvanius. She'd realised what I was up to, and was pleased. But when I went on to report my meeting with Otus she looked alarmed.

"It's worrying, but you did the right thing. We can't start buying protection from local gangs. And we've already decided to keep ourselves well guarded over the holiday. We'll just have to make it a regular routine for a while, till they find some other poor victim."

"Yes, it's all we can do. I'm beginning to think Taurus was right about that mistletoe. Nothing seems to be going smoothly just now, does it?" I threw another log onto the fire. "Have the other two gone to bed already?"

"Margarita's settling Gaius down. He's still a bit upset, poor little mite."

"What was all that crying about? Why did he get so upset when we mentioned the market?"

"If he misbehaves, Sempronia quite often threatens him that she'll send him to market to punish him. And Diogenes, of course, does the same when he thinks he can get away with it."

"But why is going to market a punishment?"

"Not just any old market, Relia. A slave market."

"*Merda,* no!"

"Yes. It's foul, isn't it? The poor little boy's got the constant threat hanging over him, that he'll be sold off to strangers if he displeases her ladyship. Margarita says he has nightmares about it. She probably does too."

Margarita came back into the room just then, and sat down by the fire. "He's asleep, thank the gods. He's had a busy day, and he's tired out. He'll be fine now."

"I'm sorry my chatter about the market scared him so. I'd no idea."

She shrugged, "How could you have? It's typical of Sempronia to use that sort of threat to a child. It's horrible, but from her point of view it works, because it's enough to keep him under control, and me too. She likes power, and she likes us all to know that she has it." She shivered. "And now all this business about altering his lordship's will—oh, she's having fun with *that*, making us all run round in circles and jump through hoops."

"I thought they were just changing the will to disinherit Candidus," Albia commented.

"That's the main reason, but Sempronia wants Plautius to make various other alterations at the same time. The old will is—well, old, out of date, apparently."

I remembered what Timaeus had told me about the division of opinion between those who favoured the existing will, and those who wanted a new one. "Are you affected yourself, Margarita? I mean, if they change it?"

"Yes. There's some talk of the master giving me my freedom. As things stand now, I'm bequeathed to Horatius. Gaius too, if we both behave ourselves."

She said it in such a matter-of-fact manner. Yet it struck me as a new thought, how horrible it must be for an intelligent, hard-working woman to be disposed of in a will, like a set of cooking pots or a mule.

"To Horatius?" Albia said. "But I thought Priscus...."

"Exactly. Priscus loves me, and would like me to live with him, but of course his parents want him to make a political marriage."

"And you? Do you want to live with Priscus?" Albia asked.

She answered bleakly, "It would be all the same if I didn't, wouldn't it? When you're a slave, the very last thing anyone considers is what you want." She finished her wine. "Oh, don't mind me, I'm just feeling sorry for myself. Priscus is a good man." She yawned and stretched. "It's time I was in bed. I don't want Gaius to wake in a strange room and find I'm not there." She picked up a small lamp and smiled at us. "I trust you're not planning to run away tonight?"

"Not me," I answered. "I've got to wash my hair."

"Nor me. It's too cold," Albia added.

She nodded. "Then good night, and thank you both again, with all my heart."

We lingered a while by the fire, glad of its warmth as we listened to the night wind rising outside. "I wonder where Lucius is now?" Albia mused. "I suppose he's in Eburacum, playing the part of a disgraced investigator, looking to stir up trouble."

"Do you think the spy he warned us about is someone in Sempronia's party? It seems likely, doesn't it?"

"It's Diogenes," she declared. "Slimy, sneaky little Weasel. He's a spy, I'd bet any money."

"Lucius would say he's too obvious, and a real spy would be more discreet."

"Poor Lucius! Gods, Relia, I hope he's all right, out on his own like that."

"Let's go and say a prayer for him, and then get an early night. We've another busy day tomorrow."

So we went to the household shrine and stood before the dear, familiar statues of the gods there, and I asked them to protect Lucius, and us too. Praying made us feel better, though it's hard to say why, since we couldn't know whether the Immortals had heard, let alone answered. All we did know was that the Aurelius family needed all the help it could get.

Chapter XII

I rose at the first crack of dawn, remembering my promise to Titch to look after his dogs. The air felt cold still, and the snow crunched under my boots as I walked to the stable yard. When I reached the old cart shed, I saw Titch waiting at its door, barring my way in.

"Mistress Aurelia, thank the gods! I was hoping you'd come soon."

"Good morning, Victor. Of course I've come. You didn't think I'd forget my promise, did you? But I see I could have had an extra quarter-hour in bed. You're back safe and sound."

"Aye, thanks for remembering. But I didn't mean that. The dogs are fine."

"Did you deliver my letter?"

He nodded. "We saw Councillor Silvanius hisself, and he read your letter straight away. He said to tell you he'll come and sort everything out this mornin'. And he'll make sure to put on a proper show to impress the guests."

That sounded like Silvanius, who never missed a chance to present himself as an important pillar of provincial government. "You told him a bit about the visitors, then?"

"Just a little." He lowered his voice conspiratorially. "I thought he ought to be prepared. He was real interested. And real nice, too. He gave me and Castor some wine, and offered to let us stay the night, but I wanted to get back here."

"Good, that's fine. Thank you."

"It was easy. Except now I'm not sure if I'm glad or sorry to be home."

"Why, what's happened?"

"I've found something bad. I didn't know what to do, and there wasn't any point wakening anyone up. I was hoping you'd be the first to see it."

"Thanks very much!"

He grinned. "I mean you'll know what's to be done. You always do. The others'll just flap around like a box of birds."

"Then you'd better not keep me in suspense. Tell me the worst!"

"I'll show you, better still." He turned towards the old shed. It was dilapidated and shabby, and we used it only to dump odds and ends, since we built our smart new stone carriage-house. The door was half off its hinges, and creaked as Titch pushed it open. "Sorry, this isn't very nice, Mistress."

It was gloomy inside, with only one unglazed window at the back to let in a small amount of the dawn light. The earth floor was strewn with sacks, broken tools, wheels, and old harness parts, and in the corner furthest from the door Poppaea and the puppies were ensconced in a big wooden box half-filled with hay. As I came in, the bitch sprang up and barked, her hackles rising.

"All right, girl, quiet now. She's a bit jumpy, and no wonder. There, Mistress, look." He pointed to the window.

A man was lying beneath it—a man's body, I should say, because even from a distance I could tell he was dead.

I made myself walk over and look at him. He was a well-built brown-haired man in his twenties, with a pleasant face and wide-set brown eyes staring up at the ceiling. His pale features stood out starkly against his blue tunic, and the layer of snow that had floated in through the window couldn't quite hide the blood that stained the cloth. There was a lot of blood, because he'd been stabbed in the neck, not very neatly. I assumed he'd done this himself, because his right hand lay across his chest, his fingers loosely curled round the hilt of a sword. His left was at his side, touching a folded piece of papyrus on the floor.

Gods, two dead bodies in less than twenty-four hours! I swallowed hard and managed to turn away only briefly, then I looked again more closely. "One of Sempronia's bodyguards, wasn't he?"

Titch nodded. "Aye. His name was Leander."

"Poor lad. I saw him helping groom their horses yesterday. And you found him here—when?"

"First thing, before it was even light. I came in to feed the dogs, and there he was."

"And he was dead when you found him? You're certain?"

"No doubt of it. Stone cold and stiff."

I reached down and felt his face. It was like ice. "And you haven't touched anything?"

He shook his head. "I didn't like to."

"I suppose nobody uses this place now. When did you move the pups in here?"

"Last night, just before dark. He wasn't here then, and neither was anyone else. And see, there's some snow on him. It's blown in through the window."

"Yes. So he's been lying in that spot since before it stopped snowing, which means about—what time did it stop? Somewhere round the third hour after dark?"

"I think so. It was clear and still when me and Castor went to Oak Bridges."

I gently brushed the snow from the dead slave's tunic, then gingerly tried to release the sword-hilt from his fingers, but I couldn't. The stiffness of death held him fast. Another fact that pointed to early last night as the time when he'd been killed.

I straightened up again. "I don't recognise the sword. It must belong to one of the visitors."

"Aye, it does." Titch indicated the hilt. "All their weapons have the letter P on them, for Plautius. Their lads were telling us about it, boasting that nobody could steal their gear and get away with it. But I'd say poor Leander wasn't all that used to handling one. It's not a very clean wound, is it?"

We heard footsteps outside, and then Albia's voice spoke from the doorway.

"Relia, here you are! We've been looking everywhere. Margarita was getting quite worried—I think she thought you'd run off. Gods, what's happened here?" She came into the old building and stopped short. Poppaea jumped to her feet and growled.

"Don't worry, girl." Titch went over and stroked his dog. "Saturn's balls, something's given her a real scare. I can't leave her in here if she's this upset."

Albia gazed at the dead slave. "How dreadful! Leander, isn't it—one of the bodyguards?" She came to stand beside me and examined him carefully, without touching. "He must have been here all night. And it looks as if he took his own life. Poor man!"

"Why, I wonder?" Titch said. "Just before the holiday, and all."

"What's that in the dogs' box?" I walked very gently across to their corner. Poppaea eyed me warily, and then relaxed as I began to stroke her. I reached my hand down into the hay, but she growled again and bared her teeth. "This isn't like her, Titch. Whatever happened here last night must have frightened her. Look, can you reach into this pile of hay? There's something half buried in it, something blue."

The dog made no objection as Titch plunged his hand into the hay and brought out a piece of blue woollen cloth.

"That's come from one of Sempronia's slaves," Albia said. "Their cloaks and tunics are all that colour. The edge is frayed, look, so it's been torn off somehow."

"Bitten off by Poppaea, I reckon." Titch patted the dog's head. "Leander came too close to the pups and you went for him, didn't you, girl?"

Albia took the cloth and held it rigid between her hands. "Yes, there are holes in it, and blood on it too."

"Victor! Victor! Are you there, Victor?" a shrill childish voice called from outside.

"Gods," Albia exclaimed, "it's Gaius. He mustn't see this. Make sure he stays out of here, Titch, won't you?"

The lad nodded. "I'll be glad to be out meself, now Mistress Aurelia has some company. I'm going to move the dogs out too. They'll have to go back in the main stable block."

"Victor! Where are you?" The child was closer, and Titch hurried out.

I went over again to where Leander lay, and examined his cloak. As far as I could see it was undamaged. "That's odd." I pulled the cloak back, but there were no bruises or bites on his legs or arms. "If she didn't bite this poor man, then somebody else was in here last night."

"Have you had a look at that piece of papyrus yet?" Albia asked.

"No." I reached down and picked it up. "I assume it's a note explaining why he killed himself." I unfolded the paper, which was oddly-shaped, a small uneven scrap torn from a larger sheet. It had a few Latin words scrawled on it. The letters were crudely formed but legible enough.

I'M SORRY FOR DOING SUCH A WICKED THING. PLEASE FORGIVE ME.

I handed it to Albia. "Does that give us the answer? He took his life in a fit of remorse?"

She stared at it doubtfully, pushing a loose strand of hair out of her eyes. "He doesn't name the 'wicked thing' he's done, but he doesn't need to."

"I'm not so sure. Did he mean it was wicked to try to kill Plautius, or to murder Idmon by mistake? I'd say that's two wicked things."

"Stop being pedantic. We're discussing a suicide note, not a work of literature."

"Yes, I suppose so." Suddenly a new thought struck me. "If Leander killed himself and admits trying to kill his master, then Plautius will have to accept that we're innocent. This poor man's death puts us in the clear."

"By the gods, so it does!" We turned and hugged one another, taking in the relief of knowing we were no longer under suspicion. I realise this must sound horribly unkind, but after the tensions of the last day, all I could think of was that the slave's suicide must put our innocence beyond a shadow of doubt.

I was impatient to tell Plautius, but it was too early yet to go calling on a sick man, so I snatched a hurried breakfast and then went outside to do my morning rounds. Everything was in order in the stables, and Ursulus told me he'd set some of the farm boys to carting hay from the rick-yard into the barns and store-rooms closer to the house. "Can't be too careful, with these young scamps about."

"You're right, we must be on our guard. By the way, I met the man Otus last night, the boss of the lads who helped us put the fire out. He asked me if a few of his men could sleep in that old roundhouse near the rick-yard now and then. In exchange for keeping an eye out for fire-raisers, he said."

Ursulus raised an eyebrow. "Oh aye? And what did you say to him?"

"No."

"You did right. Give people like that an inch, they'll take a mile. I'll warn my lads to keep their eyes open. I know, how about if I tell a couple of them to sleep in the old house themselves, just till we're sure the gang have moved on?"

"Good idea, Ursulus, yes. And I'll go and tell Secundus and the horse-boys."

Secundus' reaction was almost word for word the same as Ursulus'. "You did right. We can't be doing favours for people like that. I'll tell everyone to keep their eyes open."

Titch and Gaius came out of the tack-room just then. When he saw me Titch said something swiftly to the boy, and came running over to me alone.

"I've been thinking, Mistress. About that note that was lying next to Leander in the shed. What did it say? Can I see it?"

I showed it to him. He read the words aloud slowly: "'I'm sorry for doing such a wicked thing. Please forgive me.' Aye,

I thought so!" He tossed the papyrus in the air and caught it neatly. "Meant to look like a confession, as if he was doing away with hisself because he tried to kill his master."

"Meant to? You don't think that's what it is?"

"Nah." He shook his head emphatically. "Leander didn't write that note. He couldn't read nor write."

"How do you know?"

"I found out yesterday, but I didn't think anything about it till now. Several of their boys came round to the stables to play dice after dark, when it was snowing and we hadn't any work to do outside. We cleaned 'em out good and proper." He grinned. "We all got on well, and afterwards some of them stayed for a beaker of beer. Then they all went, except this Leander, and he asked me if I'd write a message for him, to go with a Saturnalia present that he'd got for one of Sempronia's maids. She can read a bit, seemingly, and he wanted to impress her. So I wrote it out nicely for him."

"You're sure he literally couldn't write at all? Maybe his writing was very bad, or he couldn't spell his words properly."

"Mebbe. But this note is spelt right."

"It is, and the writing's not much worse than mine. But I need to be sure about this, Victor. He could have got someone else to write it for him, just as he asked you to do the Saturnalia message."

"Dictate a suicide note? I don't reckon so, do you?"

"No, you're right. In fact the whole idea of Leander committing suicide seems pretty unlikely, when you stop to think about it. Nobody suspected him, they were all too busy accusing Albia and me. So if Leander really was the murderer, all he'd need to do was lie low, keep quiet, and let me and Albia take the blame. Unless he truly was overcome by guilt, of course."

"You can get overcome by guilt and not do away with yourself," Titch commented. "If he felt badly, or thought he was going to be found out, why didn't he just run away? Or steal a mule and ride away, more like."

"So then," I said slowly, "if Leander was murdered, that means the murderer is still alive. And Albia and I will be under suspicion again. Plautius will say we killed the slave, to cover up the fact that we tried to kill the master. He's bound to."

"Why then; tell him it was suicide."

His words shocked me. "Conceal a murder? I couldn't do that."

"*I* could. If I was in the mess you're in, I definitely could. Now *I* won't tell anyone, and you don't need to, neither. It'd only be for a while, after all, till you've caught the real killer. But if you go and blab to everyone that Leander was murdered, you won't be given the chance. Like you say, you and Miss Albia will be the main suspects, and they'll keep you guarded all the time, even if they don't actually lock you up."

"That's true, but still—to know about a murder, and not tell anyone?"

He nodded seriously. "Either way, the murderer is still free. If you keep quiet, you'll be free too."

I thought about it, and there was no doubt he was right. Perhaps not morally, and certainly not legally, but by all the laws of common sense, he was right. If I wanted to catch this murderer, I must keep my own counsel for a while, tell nobody, not even Albia. It wouldn't be easy, but it could be done. It *must* be done.

"Victor! Victor!" Gaius' shrill cry brought me out of my pondering. I couldn't see him, but his voice came from among the trees on the far side of the paddock. "Come and look at what Poppaea's dug up!"

"Saturn's balls," Titch said, "what now? I hope she's not found anything too disgusting."

We hurried across the paddock and found Gaius standing on the edge of the trees a couple of yards from the dog. Poppaea was under a scrubby bush, crouched down and guarding a long blue shape that lay on the ground. For a few heartbeats I thought it was another body, but as I got closer, I realised it was just a rolled-up cloak, bulky and nearly the length of a man, but with nothing inside it.

"She dug it out of the snow," Gaius shouted excitedly. "I think it must belong to one of our boys. But she won't let me go near and look."

Titch strode to the dog, which didn't make a murmur as he picked up the bundle and brought it into the open. He began to spread it out, then stopped, but not quickly enough.

"Yes, it's a cloak!" Gaius squeaked. "It's got all red and brown marks on it! Is it blood? Ooh, yes, how horrid!" He crouched down eagerly to take a closer look. "Lady Sempronia will be very cross. She hates it when we get our clothes dirty."

"Then don't you get messy yourself," Titch said, quickly rolling the cloak up again. "Leave it for now."

"But what's it doing out here under a bush?" the child persisted.

I caught Titch's eye, and he gave an almost imperceptible nod. We both knew the answer: it had been hidden by the man who killed Leander. But that wasn't for the child's ears. "I expect one of the boys cut himself while he was shaving," I suggested.

Titch, who'd only recently begun to shave, rubbed his chin and nodded. "Aye, it's very easy done. And then the poor lad knew his mistress would play war about it, so he hid the cloak out of the way." He grinned at the child. "Let's keep it a secret, shall we? Just between us three. Then he won't get into bother."

"Good idea," I agreed. "Our own special secret. All right, Gaius?"

"All right. I don't want anyone to get into trouble." Gaius smiled, then lost interest. "Shouldn't Poppaea be with her pups? They must be getting cold without her."

"She needs to get out of there sometimes, and they'll keep each other warm for a while," Titch said. "But why don't you run along and make sure they're all safe and sound? I'll be there in no time."

"Well done," I murmured, as the child trotted off happily. "And getting him to keep it a secret—a nice touch, that."

He spread out the blue cloak, and we could see that the front of it was well and truly splattered with blood. Some was brown and dry, but other patches were still sticky and reddish. Near the hem of the garment on the right side the cloth was torn and frayed, and there was another patch of reddish blood.

"Get a sack to put it in, will you," I said, "and hide it somewhere out of the way. We may need it as evidence, but whoever hid it won't be best pleased if he finds out it's come to light again."

"D'you mean he'd try and get you or me next time?"

"I mean I want to make sure there isn't any next time. Now I must go and report to Lord Plautius."

Chapter XIII

I could have entered the guest wing by its outside door, but I wasn't sure whether it would be unlocked, so I went the long way, through the bar-room and the hall. I opened the door from the hallway and was about to step through, when I saw two figures at the far end of the corridor. The light was dim, coming from a single torch on the wall, so I couldn't tell who they were, only that they wore dark clothing and were embracing. Well, good luck to them. Servants in that household deserved their fun, even if it had to be snatched in dark corners.

I began to edge back without a sound, and as I started to shut the door, a woman's voice half-whispered, "No, we mustn't. I can't...." That was all I heard before I closed it. I pushed it open again as noisily as I could, at the same time half-turning and calling over my shoulder, as if talking to someone in the hall. "All right, but you'll have to wait a bit. I'll be as quick as I can." This time when I stepped through, the only person in sight was Timaeus, standing just outside the sick-room door.

"Good morning, Aurelia. I was on my way to find you. My lord's awake, and a little better I think. I'll tell him you're here. And after you've seen him, could we have a quick word, please?" He winked. "About the kitchen arrangements?"

"If that's Aurelia Marcella, send her in," came Plautius' voice. "I may be ill, but I'm not deaf."

"Very good, my lord." Timaeus made a comic face and opened the door for me.

Plautius was propped up on a pile of pillows and was indeed looking better, with more colour in his thin cheeks. He gestured for me to sit on the stool next to his bed. "So, Aurelia Marcella, I hear that one of my slaves has confessed to attempted murder, and taken his own life. Which means you and your sister are innocent. It's proven beyond doubt."

I opened my mouth to agree with him, but no words would come out. I knew it was the wise thing to do, eminently sensible, convenient, reasonable. But when it came to the point, I couldn't brazenly sit there and lie about something so serious.

He noticed my hesitation. "Well? Have I been misinformed?"

I took a deep breath. "I'm afraid it isn't as simple as that. The fact is, if poor Leander was a murderer then I'm the Queen of Brigantia."

"You surprise me. You're admitting that you and your sister are guilty after all?"

"Of course not! I don't know who's guilty. I only know Leander isn't, any more than we are. Someone else killed him, having tried to kill you, and wrote the suicide note to cover his tracks."

"An interesting theory. Perhaps you'll explain how you arrive at it?"

I told him how Titch had found the body, and how the man must have been killed last evening before the snow stopped. I showed him the note with its brief sad message, and he examined it thoughtfully, then put it down on the small bedside table. His steady grey eyes returned to my face. His stare was unnerving, but there was no going back.

"Leander didn't write that note," I said finally. "He couldn't read or write."

"Aha!" He laughed, and clapped his hands. "And you believe if the confession was a fake, so was the suicide."

"Yes."

"Good! I knew Leander couldn't write. Most of my body-guards can, but it's not essential. It's not what I buy them for. Interesting that you should have discovered it, and been prepared to tell me. Either you're very stupid, or very wise. Because now I'm compelled to suspect you and your sister once again. Either of you could have written the note, and then killed the slave."

"If we'd written the note, why would I be standing here telling you it's a fake?"

"That's easy. You discovered when it was too late that the man couldn't write, so the easiest thing to do was point the fact out. You could still have done the killing."

"No. Leander was stabbed yesterday evening, which is proved by the snow that's fallen on top of his body. Fallen naturally, not heaped there by hand. Albia and I were closely watched by Margarita at that time, as you'd instructed. Despite," I added maliciously, "Diogenes' attempts to entice her away, which she refused."

"Who can blame her?" Plautius murmured.

"There's one more thing. It's something else which doesn't exactly help to prove me or my sister innocent, but you've a right to hear it, just the same."

I told him about the blue cloak, and he remarked thoughtfully, "I'm coming to the conclusion you're not stupid."

"That's a comfort, I suppose. Some folk would say I'm being very stupid indeed, not accepting the facts at face value."

"No, I applaud your wisdom in being honest. On the other hand this murderer, whoever he is, hasn't shown himself to be over-bright. He killed Idmon instead of me, and then he spoilt his second murder by forging a note for an illiterate slave."

"Killers don't have to be very clever to succeed," I pointed out. "They just need to be persistent, and have enough opportunities."

"So this one could try to murder me again? Another comforting thought." The old man flexed his thin shoulders and leaned back against the pillows, smiling. Whatever else he was, he was no coward. In his army days, he'd have been an officer to be reckoned with.

"Haven't you any idea at all who your enemy could be?" I asked him. "Someone who feels strongly enough to kill you, someone in your own household?"

"Quintus Antonius was right. He told me you're inclined to be nosey. He also said you're not stupid. Perhaps the two things go together."

"Quintus Antonius? You know him?"

"Yes, quite well. He's helped me out once or twice in the past. It was he who recommended that we should stay here. Don't tell Sempronia, she thinks it was her nephew's suggestion. I'd never have persuaded her to stay in a mansio if the idea hadn't come through the Governor. But *he* got the recommendation from Antonius."

"Quintus Antonius and I are old friends. And if I may advise you, my lord, I'll propose a course of action that Quintus himself would suggest."

"Which is?"

"That you publicly accept that Leander killed himself, having tried to kill you, and therefore Albia and I are no longer under suspicion."

"So the murderer will believe his deception has worked?"

"Exactly. And Albia and I will be free to go where we like and see who we like, so we can help protect you and track down the real killer. And you still want us to find your son Decimus, don't you?"

He nodded. "Your suggestion makes sense." Suddenly he smiled. "I should warn you, Sempronia sent a messenger off yesterday, carrying an urgent despatch for her nephew in Londinium."

"Gods, that's all we need!"

"Don't look so panic-stricken. I sent another message with the courier, explaining that I'm safe and well, and he is not to trouble himself about coming north in the dead of winter. But he'll take a personal interest in the outcome. So you'd better catch this killer as quickly as you can, hadn't you?"

"Yes, my lord. We will." One of my more useful skills is sounding confident even when I don't feel it.

"Meanwhile," he still sounded amused, "you want me to lie here on my bed of sickness, expecting another attempt on my life. Not exactly how I'd choose to spend Saturnalia."

"You'll be well guarded from now on. We'll see to that."

"Ah, but if I'm supposed to be satisfied that Leander was the killer, how can I justify posting guards outside my door?"

It was my turn to smile. "When we talked the other night, you said something about the way an old man rambles on about nothing in particular."

He gave his rasping chuckle. "Good! I accept your suggestion. But I shall delay making a final announcement until this Chief Councillor friend of yours arrives. I'll let it be known that he's vouched for your innocence, and I'm being guided by his opinion. That is, assuming he *does* vouch for your innocence?"

"He will." This time I didn't have to pretend to be confident. "And he's honest and honourable, a man to be trusted."

"Yes. Quintus Antonius told me that. He said the man's ambitious and pompous, but intelligent, and utterly loyal to the Empire, above everything else."

"That's a fair summing-up. He's one of the modern type of native. He believes in the Empire, and passionately wants to be part of it."

"And now we've dealt with that situation, you can tell me about your plans to find Decimus. What do you intend to do?"

"Albia and I will be going to Oak Bridges later, and we'll ask for news there. If we have time, we'll visit his house."

"Make time," he said.

"Very good. But he probably won't be there, as he's in the throes of moving all his personal effects to Eburacum."

"If the house is empty, you could search the place for information about where his new premises are located."

"No, I could *not!*" I was suddenly angry. He'd given me one too many orders. "He's a free citizen, and a friend, and I won't break the law to spy on him."

"You're probably wise. If I need a professional investigator, I can always hire one." As I left his room, I wished I'd had the effrontery to ask what else Quintus had said about me. More, I hoped, than that I'm nosey, and not stupid.

Silvanius Clarus was quite magnificent. He arrived about an hour later, riding in his most elaborately decorated carriage, which normally I considered ridiculously ornate. But today I was delighted to see it, because it was even larger than Sempronia's. With its superb horses and an escort of six mounted bodyguards, it only needed to be preceded by a company of lictors and you'd have thought it contained a consul.

Clarus himself was at his most imposing. Tall and fair, in his late forties, he was perhaps a little stouter and less athletic than he'd been as a young man, but freshly bathed and shaved and in his best toga, he looked every inch a Roman grandee. He came to me across the forecourt, with a slow dignified step, but a warm smile.

"Aurelia, my dear." He shook my hand formally. "I came as soon as I could."

"Thank you, Clarus. I really appreciate this. I need a friend— well, Albia and I both need one."

"You have one." He squeezed my hand.

I led him through to my study. When we were seated and he'd taken his first sip of wine, he leant back in his chair and smiled. "I couldn't believe my eyes, when I read your message. Such distinguished guests! I'd have paid you a visit yesterday, if I'd known, just to welcome them to Oak Bridges. To have some of the Governor's family here—it brings honour to the whole district."

"I hope so. From where I'm standing, all I can see is dishonour for the Oak Tree."

"You mustn't worry. I'm certain we can resolve this—ah— misunderstanding about the murder of their slaves. Now, as well as your message, I have received a short note this morning from Lord Plautius himself. He explains briefly that you and Albia are suspected of trying to kill him, but that he is uncertain whether you are guilty. Please tell me as much as you can, so that I shall know how best to reassure him."

I gave him the details of both murders. "I think they realise now that we're innocent, but your word as a senior magistrate will convince them."

"Leave it with me. Is there anything else I should know?"

"I'm afraid there is." I told him about the discovery that their runaway son was Albia's fiancé, and about how much they disapproved. He listened attentively and made sympathetic noises. Just as I finished, there was a knock at the door, and a voice I recognised called out, "Mistress Aurelia?"

"That's Sempronia's secretary," I whispered. "An arrogant little swine. Keep him in his place." I said aloud, "Come in, Diogenes."

The Weasel, impeccably groomed and smiling deferentially, came in and halted before Silvanius. "Do I have the honour of addressing Chief Councillor Silvanius Clarus?"

"Yes indeed. And you are?"

"I am Diogenes, confidential secretary to Lady Sempronia Metilia. My lady will see you now, if you please."

Silvanius stiffened and looked down his long nose. "I'll be honoured to meet Lady Sempronia. Please tell her I'll attend on her directly, when I've finished my business here. Aurelia will show me the way."

"But...." We both saw the brief glint of anger in his eyes, but he couldn't argue with a Chief Councillor.

"Directly," Silvanius repeated. "Thank you, that will be all."

"Very good, my lord." Diogenes stalked off.

"Well done, Clarus. He's been throwing his weight about ever since they got here."

Clarus shrugged. "So I gathered from your lad Victor. He also said Lady Sempronia is a little—ah—a little...."

"Difficult?" I finished, suspecting that Titch would have used a more colourful description. "Yes, she is."

"She's used to getting her own way?"

"Exactly. And doesn't see the need to be polite about it."

"Ah well, that's often so with these old aristocratic families." He glanced at the door. "I'd best not keep her waiting. But, Aurelia, I'm sure you realise what a visit from such important people could do for us here at Oak Bridges, if we can make them welcome. To have a personal acquaintance with the Governor's relatives…."

"Oh, I agree. We'll keep them all happy somehow, though it's going to be hard work. The tension over the murders, and refusing consent for Candidus to marry Albia—you can imagine, they're not the happiest party we've ever had at the Oak Tree."

"Perhaps I can help a little to—ah—ease the tension. But I don't want to offend you."

"You could never offend me, Clarus. What have you in mind?"

"Do you think it might be more suitable for Plautius and Sempronia to stay at my villa? We've plenty of room there, and with Saturnalia almost upon us, we can look after them perhaps more easily than you can here."

"I think it's a brilliant idea, if you're sure you can cope with them all. There are nearly twenty altogether, counting slaves. Won't your sister mind having to entertain so many people at short notice?"

"Clarilla will love it. She was saying only yesterday how she wished we had a house-party to help us celebrate Saturnalia. But I do realise that a group of that size represents—ah—a useful amount of income for the mansio at this slack time of year. So you're sure you won't be put out if I offer them hospitality?"

"Put out!" I laughed aloud. "Clarus, if you can take them off our hands and show them the delights of Oak Bridges, I'll write a paean of praise in your honour and sing it on the basilica steps every time there's a council meeting."

He looked shocked, and then relaxed. "Aurelia, my dear, you are *very* naughty sometimes," he chided gently. "And as long as you're agreeable, there's nothing I should like better than to welcome Plautius and Sempronia to my humble abode." Smiling, he got to his feet. "Excellent! I'll go and see them now."

I don't know what he said, or how gracious or otherwise Sempronia was, but within half an hour Silvanius was back in my study to tell me the visitors had agreed to do him the honour of moving to his villa the following day. I insisted on celebrating by pouring us each a large beaker of our best Gaulish red, the wine I keep strictly for special occasions.

"They'll leave after breakfast," he told me. "Unless the weather is too bad, of course."

"Don't worry, I'll make sure they get to you, if I personally have to clear snowdrifts off every yard of road from here to your villa." I raised my mug to him. "Here's to you, Clarus—thank you, with all my heart. You've no idea what a relief this is to us."

"It's I who should be thanking you. It's a wonderful chance for me to get to know one of the most powerful families in Londinium. Not just because of Sempronia's ties with the Governor, important as those are. Plautius owns a great deal of land in the south, and has estates in Gaul not far from my own." He rubbed his hands together, a picture of satisfaction. "And because of Saturnalia, they say they'll stay with me for several days, so that they don't have to travel home over the festival. They'll be here for my Saturnalia banquet. You and Albia are coming, aren't you? And Lucius?"

I remembered to be cautious. "I'm not sure whether Lucius will be coming home after all. He may be delayed for a while. But Albia and I wouldn't miss it for the world." That was putting it mildly. Clarus' banquets were always superb, thanks to his having plenty of money and a brilliant Italian chef. Then I had a sour thought. "Won't it be a little awkward though, with your new visitors staying? They won't want to see Albia or me there, will they? So be honest, Clarus, and I shan't be offended. Would you prefer it if we made a diplomatic excuse not to come?"

"Certainly not! On the contrary, I insist you both attend, and Candidus too. I think he's a delightful young man. I've always liked him, even though I had no idea he came from such a distinguished family. He and Albia seem very well suited."

"You said all that to Lady Sempronia, of course?"

"Perhaps not in so many words. She's a little—ah—"

"Yes, isn't she?"

"But I spoke at some length to Lord Plautius. I saw him in his room, which meant we could talk alone. He informed me he won't return to Londinium until he's been able to speak to his son once more, before deciding what to do about the matter of his will. And you've undertaken to bring his son to him?"

"I'm sure we can track him down. In time for your banquet, if not before."

"Excellent."

"I almost forgot to ask. Did you convince Plautius that Albia and I are innocent of the murders?"

Clarus nodded. "The public version is that the real culprit has confessed and committed suicide. And although that is not true, Plautius realises you two are not the guilty ones. In fact I don't think he ever seriously considered that you were. *I* certainly didn't. Even if you might be *capable* of murder, you would have assassinated the right man, and not allowed yourselves to be caught at the scene of the crime afterwards."

"What a reputation we must have!" I poured us both more wine.

"I've reassured Plautius that I can keep him well guarded at my villa. He's easier to protect there than in a mansio. But it's a little worrying, nevertheless." He gazed at me pensively. "Have you any idea who could be trying to kill him? Or why?"

"Not yet, but Albia and I are working on it."

"You realise there could be danger in this, my dear? For Plautius, though as I say, I can guard him well at my humble abode. And possibly for you, when the killer becomes aware that you have not been convinced by the apparent suicide, and are still investigating it."

"I know. That's one reason why I'm so grateful to you for offering hospitality to Plautius and Sempronia. The killer will be staying with you, not here at the Oak Tree."

"Indeed. It must be someone in their party—the most likely culprit, to my mind, is a disgruntled servant bearing some kind of grudge." He took a sip of wine. "Lord Plautius is a remarkable man, to be sure. He seems quite unshaken by the attempt on his life. And now," he rose to his feet, "I must hasten home. Clarilla will need as much notice as possible to prepare for our guests."

"And we're off to the market at Oak Bridges." I opened the door for him. "We may see your sister there perhaps?"

"Probably, yes." He looked at me a little anxiously. "But you will be able to spare time to locate Candidus, won't you?"

Despite all his enthusiasm for entertaining the Governor's relatives, Clarus knew it wouldn't be easy. "Don't worry, we'll find him. He'll be at your banquet. It's the least we can do, after all the help you've given us."

He held out his hand. "My dear, you are most welcome. We shall meet again in two days."

Chapter XIV

There's nothing to beat a good market, especially just before a holiday, and Albia and I set off as soon as we could after Clarus left.

To our surprise, Priscus announced he would like to come with us, bringing Margarita and, best of all, little Gaius. "He says he'll come if your horse-boy Victor will come too." Priscus gave me his shy smile. "Could that be arranged, do you think? They seem to have struck up quite a friendship."

So Albia and I rode in our medium-sized raeda, with Titch as driver, and Priscus ordered his mother's largest carriage for himself, Margarita, and Gaius. I'm sure I wasn't the only one who was relieved to be told that Lady Sempronia didn't care for markets and was staying in the mansio, "where at least I can keep tolerably warm." Even better, Diogenes was remaining behind with her.

By the time we set off the sun had come out, the sky was clear, and the ride into town was a real pleasure. I say "town" from habit, but Oak Bridges is really just an overgrown village. It's less than a mile from us, with good roads all the way, first through woods and then passing between fields and small farms. There was still snow on the highway, but there'd been enough traffic heading for the market to trample it down and make the going easy for the horses.

As usual, the market was in the forum, which is what everyone grandly calls the big open space in the middle of town. We parked the two carriages on one of the side roads nearby and walked the few yards to the centre. Nestor, Sempronia's driver, stayed to look after both vehicles, so Titch could come with us.

The market was busy and cheerful, with plenty of stalls, and crowds of people doing their eve-of-holiday shopping. The snow and slush had practically gone from the paving-stones, but the shops and the big basilica still had white on their roofs. Most of the stalls were bright with sprigs of greenery, and loaded with produce of all kinds. I felt happy, ready to forget my worries for the next couple of hours. We were getting rid of our troublesome guests, and we were about to enjoy Saturnalia.

We began to spot friends among the shoppers and the stall-holders, and waved back as people greeted us. "Let's separate while we do our shopping," I suggested, "and meet at the Golden Fleece tavern—just behind that vegetable stall, see? It's the best place for food. Albia and I will be there in about an hour. Now Victor, keep Gaius with you, and make sure you stay in sight of Margarita or us."

The lad nodded solemnly. He took Gaius' hand, and said quietly, "Now you stay with me, and I promise nowt bad will happen. No running off, mind. If you're good, we'll get summat tasty to eat." The two of them set off ahead of us, Gaius looking and pointing everywhere and asking innumerable questions, Titch clearly enjoying his role of elder brother. Margarita and Priscus strolled off a few paces behind the boys, holding hands and chatting happily. Albia and I began to make a circuit of the stalls, checking which traders were here, and comparing prices.

Albia consulted a wax note-tablet. "Cheese, cow's and sheep's. Lagus usually has a good stock."

"And plenty of dates and figs," I said. "Raisins too. The guests have gone through most of the treats we bought for dessert over Saturnalia. I was hoping Philippus would be here. He always has good imported fruit, even at this time of year. But I don't see him."

"Oh, he's here, but he's moved up in the world. There he is, look, right in the middle. His stall's twice as big as usual, and if he loads those trestles any heavier, they'll collapse!"

We spent an enjoyable hour and managed to buy all the provisions we needed, except for sheep's cheese, which wasn't to be had anywhere, so we made do with two different types of cow's cheese instead. By the time we lugged our shopping-baskets to the tavern it was full and busy, crowded with laughing, noisy customers. But in a far corner Priscus and Margarita had managed to save us a small table and some stools. We pushed our way through and thankfully sat down, just as Titch and Gaius appeared, grinning broadly and chattering away like monkeys.

Margarita leaned over and said softly in my ear, "It's wonderful to see Gaius so happy. Victor has made a terrific difference to him. I must find a way to thank him."

"I'm glad. He told me Gaius reminds him of his little brother, who died of a fever."

"I've been trying to order some food," Priscus grumbled. "But they seem incredibly busy, and I can't attract anyone's attention. I think we must be invisible!"

I looked round for Afrania, the owner's wife, and signalled to her to bring us wine and cakes. She's a good friend of ours, so the refreshments didn't take long to arrive. The wine was nothing special, though welcome because it was warm, but the cakes were something new: they were shaped like little animals, horses and pigs and cats and ducks, with raisins for eyes and slivers of almond for mouths. Everyone had some, but of course it was the boys who ate most of them. We all thought they were delicious, and I suggested we buy a basket of them to take home. They'd make excellent small Saturnalia treats for the younger slaves.

Albia had a better idea. "Let's just take a few samples back with us and ask Cook to make a big batch. I'm sure he can, and if I handle it right, he'll think it's his own idea."

Yes, I thought, Albia always has the right touch with Cook. How am I going to manage when she's not there to get the best out of him?

As we ate, Margarita looked round the tavern appraisingly. "This is a nice place, but they could do with more barmaids. Their girls are struggling to keep up with all the orders. They'll be losing trade if they're not careful. They're not the only tavern in the forum—I noticed a couple of others quite close by."

I glanced at her in surprise, and she gave me an embarrassed smile. "Sorry, force of habit. I used to work in a tavern in Londinium. Until—until Priscus found me."

Priscus smiled at her and poured her more wine, then belatedly remembered to serve the rest of us as well.

"I'd never have guessed you worked in a bar, Margarita. You don't look like…." Oh, me and my big mouth! Telling someone they don't look like a tavern slave is hardly the most effusive compliment, even if it's true.

She wasn't offended. "Thanks. But then you don't look like an innkeeper."

"Fair comment! Just as well for both of us, isn't it?" Innkeepers are supposed to be raddled old hags, and tavern girls brassy young tarts. "And you're right about this place being under-staffed, but they're only ever this busy when there's a market. The other twenty-odd days in every month, it's a lot quieter in here."

"Oak Bridges seems a pleasant little village," she said, a touch wistfully. "Londinium is so big and noisy. It's exciting of course, always something going on day or night. But when I see a small place like this, I know that deep down I'd prefer to be in the country."

Priscus touched her hand. "One day we'll have a house somewhere like this, if it's what you want."

"Perhaps. One day." She turned to Gaius. "Now, let's hear what you two lads have been up to. Have you seen anything interesting?"

Gaius told us eagerly about the stalls, the juggler, the flute-player, and the live birds and animals for sale, including a big tank full of fish. I suppose if you've always regarded markets as the stuff of nightmare and never even visited one before, the colour and excitement of the pre-Saturnalia shopping must be a marvellous surprise. Margarita and Priscus asked him all sorts of questions, delighted to find he had enjoyed himself so much. Titch sat back and let him rattle on, like a benign brother who's much too old and wise to be impressed by a mere collection of stalls.

It was a happy, relaxed meal, enjoyed by all of us. But eventually Gaius had run out of chatter and breath, and he and Titch had demolished a whole farmyard of animal cakes.

"We'd better get you home before you burst," Margarita said. "And I expect her ladyship will have found a whole pile of jobs for me to do. Aurelia, Albia, have you finished your shopping now? Shall we wait for you, or go on ahead?"

"You go on ahead," Albia answered. "I've just a couple more things to buy. We shan't be far behind you."

"Can Victor come with us?" Gaius asked. "Oh please, Mistress Aurelia, can he drive our carriage back? Nestor can drive yours. Oh, *please!*"

I looked at Titch. "Victor? Is that all right with you?"

"Aye, fine, Mistress. I'd like a crack at driving them good-looking horses."

"All right. On one condition."

"What condition?"

"That you carry our shopping baskets back to our carriage for us on your way."

He grinned at the heavy load. "I think that's the thirteenth labour of Hercules, Mistress. But anything he could do, I'm sure I can manage!"

Priscus insisted on paying for our meal, and then the four of them walked off towards their carriage, Priscus and Margarita holding hands, while Titch and Gaius followed behind them.

Albia sighed. "They're sweet together, aren't they? A real little family. Oh Relia, do you think Candidus and I will ever have a family of our own? Everything seems to be against us!"

"Of course you will. It'll take a little while, but it'll all work out. Now first things first. Have you really got more shopping to do, or are we going straight to Candidus' house?"

She giggled. "You've guessed! I thought we might snatch half an hour and go and see him, if he's there. I must just pick up the oysters, they're keeping them for me on the stall. Then we can go. You don't mind, do you?"

"I don't mind a bit. In fact I promised Plautius this morning that we'd find time to go there, so it's our duty, isn't it?"

Candidus lived a little way outside Oak Bridges. We told Nestor to drive back to the main road, then turn right in the direction of Eburacum, instead of left towards the Oak Tree and the Long Hill. It didn't take long, but when we got to the house, it looked deserted—closed door, shuttered windows, and no smoke rising from the roof. Nestor got down and knocked loudly at the door, but there was no answer. We alighted too, and walked round the garden and outbuildings that Candidus proudly described as his smallholding. Still there was no sign of anyone.

Albia took it stoically. "He must be in Eburacum, or on the way there or back, moving all his things. But he usually leaves a boy here to keep an eye on the place."

"Maybe he has." I put two fingers in my mouth and whistled, the way my father had taught me, and then told me I should never do anything so unladylike. The loud shrill note echoed round the buildings, and the door of one of the small sheds creaked open.

A skinny boy came out, followed by a large grey dog. Both boy and dog looked at us silently.

"Hello, Nasua. We've come to see Master Candidus," Albia said. "Is he here?"

The lad shook his head.

"Has he gone to Eburacum?"

Nasua nodded.

"When will he be back?"

He opened his mouth and seemed to be trying to say something, but no words came out.

"Answer the lady!" Our driver strode forward and caught the boy by the tunic. "Show some manners to your betters, boy."

"H - h - he said…" Nasua stammered, then broke off when Nestor gave him a clip round the ear. The dog growled, but the boy put a restraining hand on its head.

"Ow! P - p - please, sir…."

"Don't do that, Nestor," Albia said sharply. She went quietly up to the boy and smiled. "It's all right, Nasua, we just need to find Master Candidus. When will he be home again?"

"I d - don't know, M - Miss Albia."

The driver raised a threatening hand, but Albia said, "No, leave him. He's new. He probably doesn't know much. Now, Nasua, when he comes back again, will you tell him I called to see him?"

The boy nodded. "He won't be b - back today. He told me to feed the ch - chickens and d - d - ducks tonight."

"All right. Now, if you're feeding the ducks, I've got something here you might like." She went back to the carriage and brought out one of the little cakes we'd bought in town. It was shaped like a duck, and the boy's eyes lit up when he saw it. "Here. This can be your first Saturnalia present."

"Oh, th - th - thank you, Miss Albia." He ran back into his shed, clutching the cake as if it were made of gold.

As we drove away, I said to Albia, "I think I recognise that boy. Where's he from, do you know?"

"He turned up on Candidus' doorstep a couple of days ago. He was with that group of men who helped save our hay-stack, but they used to bully him because they thought he was stupid, so he ran away. Candidus realised he's not stupid at all, he just has trouble speaking, as you heard. So he's taken him on as a servant."

"It's a bit risky, isn't it, leaving a new lad on his own here?"

She smiled fondly. "Candidus says if you trust people, they'll show you they are worth trusting. It seems to be working with that little waif, anyway."

"Quintus would say there's such a thing as being too trusting. Candidus is honest and genuine, but you can't assume that everyone else in the world is."

"That's the second time you've mentioned Quintus lately," Albia teased. "Not missing him by any chance, are you?"

"Me? No, of course not."

We drove home, and Albia talked happily about what it would be like to live in Eburacum, but I listened with only enough attention to say "yes" and "no" in the right places. I was still thinking about Quintus. Seeing other couples, even though their roads of love were twisted and uneven, made me realise how much I missed him. I knew he was working in the south of the province and couldn't spare time to visit us for the holiday, and he'd promised to come in the spring. The weather would be better then, and we could take a little time off together. Spring was a much more sensible season to travel north. But I wanted him now.

The sky had clouded, and as we neared the mansio it started to snow again. Whipped by the north-east wind, it was unpleasantly cold. Despite the weather, a small handful of riding-animals were tied to the railings on the forecourt. Good—the market had brought us a little trade at least. Among the small native ponies there stood one vehicle: a light, fast gig. The horse-boys were just unharnessing two sturdy mules from its shafts.

"Army transport," Albia said. "I wonder whose?"

"At least an officer's, with a smart turnout like that."

She giggled. "Handsome and dashing, with a bit of luck. Yes, I know I'm not interested in officers these days—but *you're* footloose and fancy free. Or are you?"

I said nothing, because I didn't know what to answer.

The bar-room was comfortably warm and noisy, with a dozen or so native customers, mostly peasants drinking beer. At a table near the fire sat Horatius, and with him were two Romans, clearly the people who'd arrived in the military gig. They were a handsome couple, a tall fair-haired man and a dark young woman.

I couldn't believe my eyes. The man was Quintus Antonius. I didn't know his companion, but she was one of the most stunningly beautiful women I'd ever seen.

"Quintus!" I called, overjoyed. I felt like a child who's just received a most magnificent present, or had a prayer answered by the gods. Quintus was *here!* If he'd come to us for Saturnalia, my happiness really would be complete. I started towards him, and only the presence of the other customers kept me from running across the room straight into his arms.

But when he looked up at me, his dark-blue eyes were colder than ice, and he didn't smile or stir from his chair. "Aurelia, how good to see you. And Albia too. Are you both well?"

I stopped in my tracks. I felt as if he'd thrown a bucket of freezing water in my face. His words were the kind of distant greeting you'd use to a mere acquaintance, not to someone you loved, and they cut me worse than a tirade of abuse.

But I've never thrown myself at any man if he wasn't prepared to catch me. "I'm very well, thank you, Quintus Antonius." I matched his distant, cool tone, and even produced a distant, cool smile to go with it. I hadn't the remotest idea what was going on, but if he could play at being strangers, then so could I. "This is an unexpected pleasure. Won't you introduce your companion?"

"May I present Fabia Jucunda, the fiancée of Decimus Plautius Curio." He smiled and put a hand lightly on her arm. "I've had the pleasure of escorting her here to join Lady Sempronia's party. Fabia, these are the excellent innkeepers of the Oak Tree, Aurelia and Albia."

"Excellent innkeepers" indeed! Who does he think he is? Not the old loving Quintus Antonius, that's for sure. But why? What have I done to deserve this coldness? Or is it because he's sitting next to someone whose classic beauty probably has sculptors and painters standing in line begging her to be their model?

I stepped forward. The young woman extended a slender white hand, and I shook it. "I'm pleased to meet you," I said. I've always been a good liar. This woman was the fiancée that Sempronia had chosen for Candidus! What was she doing here? Why was she with Quintus? And why, in Diana's name, did she have to be so unbelievably, astonishingly gorgeous? Seeing her and Albia together was like comparing an attractive bright star with the golden sun.

"Thank you. I'm sure I'll be very comfortable." Fabia had a sweet voice—well she would, wouldn't she?—and the lovely smile she gave me was charming, if rather reserved. After all, to her, I was just another innkeeper. And Albia…did she know who Albia was? Was she even aware she had a rival for Candidus' affection?

Horatius was in his usual mellow state, but even he noticed the chill in the atmosphere, though he completely misunderstood it.

"I'm afraid we're putting you to even more trouble, m'dears," he said to me and Albia. "We're going to be a bit short of space tonight, but we'll squeeze in somehow. Margarita and Diogenes can move into your slave block, to make room for these two."

"Margarita and Gaius can sleep in our wing, as they did last night," I told him.

"Good, yes!" the lawyer exclaimed. "And tomorrow we'll all be out of your way, when we move to the Chief Councillor's villa."

"I might stay on here," Quintus said. "The Chief Councillor is a splendid fellow, but a bit heavy going. I'll probably be more comfortable at the mansio."

"I don't blame you," Horatius smiled, reaching for the wine-jug. "They look after you very well, and there are one or two pretty little maids who can keep a man warm at night."

"Are there? You'll have to introduce me."

So there it was. Quintus was making it absolutely clear that whatever had existed between us was gone. We'd been lovers and friends. I'd never deluded myself that he lived a life of celibacy when he was away from me, and I'd always considered myself free to do as I liked when he wasn't around. But in the four years since we'd met, when we were together, we were a couple. Not any more.

Horatius was telling Quintus the story of how Priscus had found Margarita in a tavern, and they were making silly man-of-the-world jokes. I wanted to break up their silly male chatter, but couldn't think how.

Then Diogenes appeared, and for once he was a welcome distraction. He approached the table and bowed first to Fabia, then to Quintus.

"Lady Sempronia will be pleased to see you now, Miss Fabia, if you'll be good enough to come with me. Master Antonius, her ladyship asks if you'll join her later this afternoon?"

"Thank you, Diogenes." Fabia gave him an impersonal nod. I thought, she called the Weasel by name, which means she must know at least some of Sempronia's household. So she was rich, well-connected, attractive, *and* known to Candidus already! This situation was getting worse and worse.

Horatius got to his feet. "I'd better come with you, Fabia. Fill you in on the latest developments about Decimus." He helped her up, and even in the simple act of rising from her chair, she was as graceful as a dancer. She took his arm and they walked towards the main door, and she made the customers' heads turn as she passed. Diogenes followed at a respectful distance, but not before he'd cast a sharp sneering glance at Albia.

Quintus said softly, "There's a man I shouldn't trust an inch. He got thrown out of the Governor's office for corruption. I don't know what exactly he did, but it must have been something serious. Fabia says Sempronia relies on him, which if true, is a mistake on her part."

I was shocked into forgetting my cool manner. "Horatius? Are you sure? I know he drinks too much, but...."

He started to laugh, then stifled it. "No, Diogenes, of course." His purple-blue eyes lost their cold stare. "Horatius is a good lawyer, when he's sober enough. Which is less and less often nowadays, I'm afraid."

I began to relax a little. This was more like the old familiar Quintus, the man I'd worked with, laughed with, loved. Had his distant behaviour been only for Fabia's benefit?

But when he leant back in his chair and said, "Will you join me for a drink, ladies?" the smile he gave us was as impersonal as Fabia's.

I was tempted to tell him exactly where to put his drink, but resisted the impulse. I felt hurt and confused, but I couldn't just walk off in a sulk without trying to find out what was going on. "Thank you." I fetched myself a beaker and sat down opposite him.

Albia, with her usual quickness, realised why I hadn't brought two mugs, and said, "I'll join you later, if I can. First I'd better go and sort out the new sleeping arrangements for tonight."

Quintus helped himself to more wine from the large jug on his table, and then poured some for me. A small but calculated gesture of rudeness that the Quintus Antonius I'd known before would never have committed.

But I said nothing, and raised my beaker to him. "Welcome back to Brigantia. What brings you to the Oak Tree at the worst time of the year?" Oh yes, if it's polite impersonal chit-chat you want, I can do that till the cows come home.

He lifted his mug in response. "Sempronia asked me to escort Fabia up here to meet her fiancé, Decimus Plautius. I gather he's run away from home and is threatening to marry a Brigantian peasant girl. Sempronia thought he needed a reminder of what his true fiancée is like. Quite a looker, isn't she?"

"Yes, she is. Are you staying in Brigantia long?"

"I have business in Eburacum after the holiday, so I'll be in the district for a few days. And I'm hoping while I'm here to get news of your Lucius. I'm told he's been a naughty boy and isn't working for the Governor any more. What's he been up to? And what's he up to now, come to that?"

"I don't know much really. Some trouble over a woman, I gather." I must tread carefully. Lucius had told us that nobody, not even good friends like Quintus, was aware of his real situation, and keeping that secret was easy enough. But Quintus would guess that Lucius must have got in touch with me to give me some sort of explanation.

"That's what I heard. Pinched the wife of one of the Procurator's men, they say." Quintus smiled properly this time.

"The husband isn't best pleased, and he's got powerful friends in Rome to back him up."

"My brother's been a stupid idiot. He wrote and told me the bare bones of it, but I don't know where he is now, he just said he'd got to lie low for a bit." I sipped some wine, relieved that Quintus seemed to have accepted the story.

"He's certainly an idiot if he's lost the Governor's support. I've no time for investigators who let their personal lives interfere with their work."

"Is that so?" The words were out before I could stop them, but he didn't react, and I hurried on to a safer subject. "Lucius did say that he thinks one of the powerful men in Rome who's stirring up trouble for him is the Shadow of Death."

Quintus nodded. "Yes, I'd heard that. It seems he's found his way into favour at Caesar's court. He was always plausible, wasn't he?"

"Aurelia, forgive me for interrupting." It was Timaeus, approaching our table with his usual irresistible smile.

I returned the smile with enthusiasm. "Ah, Timaeus, let me present Quintus Antonius Delfinus. This is Timaeus, Lord Plautius' physician. I'm sorry we couldn't talk earlier, Timaeus. Is now a good time?" Let's see how Quintus would like *that!*

He grinned. "Any time's a good time, but first his lordship would like a word please, if you'd come along to his room."

"Certainly. Excuse me, won't you, Quintus Antonius?" I followed Timaeus out of the bar.

When we were in the hall, Timaeus turned to me, still grinning. "Is that the officer who brought Fabia up from Londinium?"

"Yes."

He asked casually, "An old friend of yours, is he?"

"More a friend of my brother's," I said, hoping I sounded equally casual.

"I see." He smiled and moved a little closer. Twenty-four hours ago if he'd made a pass at me I might have been only too pleased, but now I wasn't in the mood.

I took a slow step back. "Does Plautius really want to see me?"

"Not just now. But I do need a word, if you've time." He followed me into my study. "It's about the murder of poor Leander."

"Suicide," I corrected. "Very sad, of course, but Albia and I have said all along that we were innocent."

"It wasn't suicide, I'm afraid. Lord Plautius showed me the note that was found beside Leander's body. But Leander didn't write it."

"Why do you think that?"

"Because I know who did."

I felt a surge of excitement. "Who was it?"

"Gaius. I saw him do it."

"*Gaius?* You're mad! Gaius wrote a suicide note for Leander?"

"Of course not. Whoever killed Leander was clever enough to make use of something the boy had written which was a kind of confession."

"A confession? To what, for the gods' sake?"

"The first morning we stayed here, do you remember Gaius let out that dreadful cat of her ladyship's? The fluffy yellow object she calls Medusa."

"I remember. Sempronia threatened that Diogenes would have to climb the oak tree to get her back. I'd have sold tickets for a spectacle like that, but the cat came down of its own accord."

"All the same, Sempronia was pretty annoyed with Gaius, and was making her usual threats about getting rid of him. So Margarita told him to write out twenty times a message saying sorry and asking for forgiveness. It took him ages, poor kid, but he did it, and it mollified Sempronia. All the messages were written on old scraps of papyrus, and Leander's so-called suicide note had been torn from one of them."

"I thought the papyrus was an odd shape. Have you told Plautius?"

"No."

"Are you going to?"

"Yes, but I thought I ought to talk to you first. After all, if Leander killed himself, then you and your sister are no longer suspects. But if he didn't...."

"Thanks, Timaeus. I assume from that, you don't think we are murderers?"

"I think my next line should be, you're far too beautiful to be a murderer."

"Who else besides you and Margarita and Sempronia knew about Gaius' confession?"

"Well...Diogenes did, and Priscus. Some of the slaves too, probably. Is it important?"

"Not when as many people as that were aware of it, no. Look, I expect you know that Plautius wants me and Albia to find out who the murderer is. I could use your help there, if you're willing. You know the family, but you're not too close to them."

He nodded. "I'll help if I can. So you don't think *I'm* a murderer either?"

"Definitely not. You're far too beautiful to be a murderer."

There was a tap at the door, and Diogenes stepped in without waiting to be asked. "So this is where you're hiding. I wondered why you weren't in the bar-room." He gave me his supercilious sneer. "Getting a little medical advice, are we?"

"Timaeus was just reminding me to make sure nobody in the kitchen meddles with the meals that he prepares for Lord Plautius. Nobody at all."

"I'll bet he was! And it's all such nonsense, not allowing anyone else to serve the master."

"Did you want me for something, Diogenes?" Timaeus asked. "Or are you just snooping around as usual, seeing what you can overhear?"

"I'm looking for Margarita. Do either of you know where she is? She's had enough time off for one day, and her ladyship wants her in her sitting-room now. When is she returning from the market?"

"She already has," I said, surprised. "She and Priscus and Gaius left Oak Bridges before my sister and I did, so they should have got back ages ago."

He frowned. "Well none of them are here, and neither is the carriage. It's too bad of her, it really is. My lady gets so agitated when things aren't just so…." He went on grumbling as he left the room.

"I'd better get back to Plautius," Timaeus said. "But any time you want us to put our beautiful heads together, you know where I am."

By dark Margarita and the others still hadn't returned, and Sempronia wasn't the only one to be agitated. We all were.

Chapter XV

My first thought was the obvious one, that their carriage had lost a wheel or broken an axle, or one of the horses had gone lame, so they had had to abandon their transport and walk from Oak Bridges. They'd go at a slow pace, to suit young Gaius. Or perhaps, because of the snow which was still coming down periodically, they'd decided to stay in the shelter of their carriage, but then Titch would have got home somehow to bring us word.

After the first hour of darkness, I had to admit there must be some other explanation. They'd had time to walk all the way from the market to the mansio and back again.

"I don't know what to do next," I said to Albia, as we stood by the fire in the bar-room, which was now empty of customers and even of Horatius. "At least they've got Titch with them. If there's been an accident, perhaps someone's been taken ill, surely he'd come home to get help."

She kicked at a log in the hearth, sending up a shower of sparks. "You know, Relia, I'm beginning to wonder whether they've run away."

"*Run away?* From Sempronia, you mean?"

"Yes. Do you think they enjoyed their day out together as a family so much that they decided to disappear for a while? They couldn't vanish for ever, but if they could get far enough away from Oak Bridges to be by themselves for even a couple of days, they might think it was worth the trouble they'd get into when they came back."

"You read too many Greek love stories, Albia! Priscus, making a bid for a few stolen hours of romance? I can't see it myself. He finds it hard to disobey Sempronia even in small things. He'd never dare take a risk like that. It would end with Margarita and Gaius being sent off to market."

"I suppose you're right. So what shall we do? We can't just wait around doing nothing but worry."

"I'll send some of our men out to search."

Secundus offered to set off straight away, taking our largest carriage and plenty of torches and blankets. Four of our farm boys rode with him on horseback, carrying cudgels and lanterns. Their instructions were to check the road to Oak Bridges, the market area, and the street where we'd parked the carriages. They were also to ask for information, if they could find anyone to ask at this time of night. The Golden Fleece would probably still be open, but not much else, especially since the snow was now continuous. The wind was rising again, and I didn't need to warn Secundus to be as quick as he could, before the weather turned to a real blizzard.

Then I took my courage in both hands and set off to see Plautius. He had to be told that his son and two of his slaves were missing. But as I was crossing the hall, Quintus came out of the guest wing, and smiled when he saw me.

"Aurelia, I've just heard that Priscus and two servants have disappeared. Can I be of any help?"

"I think Albia and I will manage, thank you. You were kind enough to observe that we're excellent innkeepers."

"I know you're far more than that. But this latest development is in my line of business, it seems to me. I presume you've realised what has happened?"

"I'm still investigating the various possibilities."

"Including," he came close and spoke almost in a whisper, "the possibility, or probability, that Priscus and his party have been taken hostage?"

"*Hostage?* Who by, for the gods' sake?"

"Someone who reckons that Plautius and Sempronia will pay a sizeable ransom for their son and two valuable slaves."

I moved a pace back. It unnerved me to be so close to him and yet not touch. "That's ridiculous, Quintus. This is a safe area, and anyway they were travelling in broad daylight. No, my money's on some kind of accident, made worse by the fact that it's snowing, and they either couldn't or wouldn't walk home. They're probably taking shelter in a native roundhouse even now, wishing they could get back here for a hot bath and a good dinner."

"But your boy Titch is with them, isn't he? A first-class lad, as I remember. He'd have made contact with you by now if that was the explanation."

"He's very likely on his way. It's all under control. So thank you for your offer of help, but Albia and I can handle this."

He shrugged. "Whatever you wish. But the offer's still there, if or when you need it. And I've got a good man with me, the best servant I've ever had. His name's Rufus. Feel free to call on him, if he can be of any use."

"Thank you. One thing you should know, if you're advising the family. You've heard that someone tried to kill Plautius, but got the wrong man?"

"Yes, and then killed himself. They told me. They said you and Albia were suspected of the first attack for a while."

I nodded. "We were the ones who found the body in Plautius' bed."

"I suppose they all realised soon enough that if you two had decided on a murder, you'd have made a decent job of it."

"Why does everyone keep saying things like that?" I couldn't help a smile, but then remembered I was supposed to be annoyed with him. "The suicide was no suicide. I know that for a fact. Plautius knows it as well, but we decided to keep it quiet and try to catch the killer off his guard."

"You're sure?"

"I just said so, didn't I?"

"Sorry, yes. You've taken me by surprise, that's all. So the real murderer is still somewhere around. Any idea who it could be?" He was looking at me intently, with that suppressed excitement he often showed during an investigation. I knew it so well.

"In the words of one reliable source, it could be almost anyone in Plautius' party."

"Oh, a nice simple problem then. Why?"

"Plautius is in the throes of making a new will, mainly to disinherit Candidus, but there are various other provisions which are causing bad feeling."

"Bad enough to turn someone into a murderer?"

"Who knows? Oh, and one more thing. We think Titch's dog may have attacked the murderer, possibly bitten him. So if you see anyone nursing a dog bite, will you let me know? Well, don't look like that! You may notice something when you're in the bath-house. One of the things a woman can't do when investigating a crime is share a bath with the male suspects."

"H'm. Well, thanks for that." He smiled again, and the smile reached his purple-blue eyes. "We make a good investigating partnership, you and I."

"We used to."

"Remember I'm there if you need me."

"Right." That was all I could trust myself to say. I turned away and headed for the bar-room. I felt in need of a drink.

The room was empty, so there was nobody to see the time it took me to recover my cheery expression. But I did recover it, and I sat by the warm fire, making a determined effort not to brood on what had once been, but was no more. I'd enough to think about, with two murders and now three missing guests.

As I got up to fetch a drink, there was a crash and a blast of freezing air as the main door burst open. A small snow-covered figure staggered in, barely recognisable because his clothes and hair were white, and his body was stooped forward as if he was about to collapse.

"Titch! Thank the gods!" I rushed across to him. "Are you all right? Are the others with you?"

He didn't answer, but struggled to push the heavy oak door shut behind him against the storm. As I helped him, he stumbled, and would have fallen to the floor if I hadn't caught him. He was shivering, and looked utterly exhausted. "Sorry," he muttered, "I'm so sorry, Mistress." He staggered again. I more or less carried him across the room and sat him on a bench by the fire.

"It's all right, you're home now. Here's a warm fire, and I'll get you some wine. Are the others with you?" I repeated the all-important question as I fetched a lamp and looked at him properly. He was blue with cold, his cloak soaking wet and covered with half-frozen snow. He had bruises on his face, and what looked like a knife-cut across the back of his right hand. He leant towards the fire's heat, while I helped him off with his cloak and brought him some wine.

He gulped half a beaker, which made him cough, but he managed to say, "I'm sorry, Mistress. I couldn't stop it. There were too many of them to fight off."

"Tell me what's happened. Where are the others?"

"They've been kidnapped. While we were driving home. They've been taken hostage." He bowed his head and began to sob.

"*Merda!* Hostage? Why? And who by?" But I thought I knew the answer to the last question. The Wolf-pack was paying us out for not giving them a den.

"I recognised two. Two of the lads who helped with the fire." His tears fell faster, and I realised my anxiety had come out as anger.

"Victor, this isn't your fault," I said gently. "I'm certain you did everything you could. But I need to know the whole thing from the beginning. You were driving home, you say?"

He wiped his eyes with his hand. "Aye, just quietly trotting along, nothing unusual. We'd got into the thickest part of the woods, and there was an old man in the road, trying to drive some sheep along, but he hadn't a dog, and they were all over the place. I slowed down so's not to scatter them even more, and then four men jumped out on us and took us prisoner. Master Priscus and I did our best, and even Margarita got in a kick or two, but they had swords. They got hold of Gaius and said they'd cut his head off if we didn't behave. It was Master Priscus they wanted first off, but then when they got a good look at Margarita and Gaius, they said such a beautiful pair of slaves would be worth a gold piece or two. They weren't so bothered about me. They said I wouldn't fetch much ransom."

"Ransom. So this is for money, then?"

He nodded. "They said Priscus would be worth plenty, because of being from an important family, and the other two might be worth summat to the family as well, or they could be shipped down the river, whatever that meant. I told them I'm a citizen, but they just laughed, and I thought for a bit they were going to kill me, till one of them said I could bring their message back to save them having to risk it. And all the while I kept trying and trying to think how to get us all out of it, only it was getting dark, and snowing so hard, and I couldn't."

"You hadn't a chance against four. Here, finish your wine. That's better." I poured him some more, but he shook his head. "Now, tell me the rest. Do you know where Priscus and Margarita and Gaius are being held?"

"Nah. In a native hut for tonight, they said, and then they'd be moved on tomorrow, but they didn't say where."

"Were they hurt in the ambush?"

"Not much. Priscus got a bruise or two when we tried to fight them off at the start. But the leader told the others to treat them gently, and not to try anything on with Margarita or Gaius, else they wouldn't be worth so much. I don't think they'll come to any real harm."

"And what happens now? You said something about a message?"

"They gave me a note for Lord Plautius. They said it's all in there." He tried to open his belt-pouch, but his fingers were too stiff and cold, and the cut on his hand began to bleed again.

"All in good time. First I'm going to get you some blankets and warm clothes. Will you be all right here by yourself for a little while?"

"Aye, I'll be fine. It's just so good to be here. When they caught us, I thought—well, it didn't happen. But I promised Gaius no harm would come to him. I've let him down. I've let everyone down!" He began to sob again quietly. He was still little more than a boy, despite his seventeen years and his confident manner. I wanted to give him a hug, but he wouldn't have liked it.

"You certainly haven't let anyone down, Victor. You've come through a snowstorm to bring us news, and you've delivered their note. Now stay close to the fire and get yourself warm. I'll be as quick as I can."

In the kitchen they were about to serve dinner to the depleted party of guests: venison stewed in red wine, roasted piglets, and some of our best marinated asparagus. But Albia herself wasn't involved in serving the food, preferring to keep well out of the way as we'd agreed. So she set about organising blankets and dry clothing, and a beaker of some steaming hot herbal concoction. Meanwhile I sent one of the maids into the guest wing to find Quintus. "Ask him," I told her, "to please come to the bar-room as soon as he can, before the beans are burnt."

"The what?" The girl looked blank, but I hadn't time to explain about Quintus' favourite password.

"Just give the message as I've told you. Repeat it now, to be sure."

"Please to come to the bar-room as soon as you can, before the beans are burnt. But they aren't having beans for dinner tonight!"

"*Merda,* girl, just do it and don't argue."

Albia and I went back into the bar-room and got Titch into dry clothes. He wrapped a blanket round his feet, which he said were still numb, but otherwise he was looking better and regaining his usual cocky manner. When Albia gave him the herb drink, he took a sip and made a face.

"Miss Albia, if this is what you're serving the guests for their dinner, they'll all be off to join the hostages!"

"Less of your cheek, or I'll fetch you a second mug of it. Drink it up, it'll stop you getting a chill. Every drop now, or you won't get any dinner."

The bowl of venison stew that she brought him when he'd finished the medicine put a grin back on his face. "Ah, this is better. I must get meself caught in a snowstorm more often."

"Venison stew, eh?" Quintus strode through the door, followed by a tall, tough-looking servant, with red hair and beard, and plenty of muscle.

Quintus smiled at me. "Aurelia, you used my password, so I assume it's something urgent. Why, hello, Titch! Are you the cause of this cryptic message about beans?"

The lad jumped up, forgetting his food. "Master Quintus, it's good to see you."

"And you. I'm surprised to find you still here. Aren't you supposed to be joining the cavalry?"

"Aye, in the spring. I want to get into an auxiliary unit, maybe north of here, or else on the Rhine. There's always trouble in Germania. I want to see some real fighting."

Quintus came over and shook Titch by the hand. "We've got trouble enough on our doorstep, I'd say. Now finish your meal while it's hot, or I will. The smell of it's making me hungry. And let me introduce Rufus." He indicated his servant, who grinned widely and made a mock-bow to all of us. "Aurelia and Albia and Victor here are good friends, Rufio. If they need our help, they get it, without question."

"Pleased to meet you ladies, and you, young trooper. The master's told me a lot about all of you, and none of it too bad. If you ever need me, I'll come galloping up like the Parthian cavalry, only I'm not so smelly."

We all laughed, and I felt as if a great weight was lifted from my shoulders. This was the old Quintus, not the cold, boorish stranger I'd encountered earlier. He might not want to be my lover, but he'd help us, and he'd treat all of us as professionals when it came to an investigation.

Titch gave his account of the ambush, and finished by producing the kidnappers' message. He undid his pouch easily now, and handed the note to Quintus. It was an ordinary wax note-tablet, tied with a cord, and the knot was sealed with a roughly circular piece of wax. Attached to the cord was a crude label, just a small torn piece of papyrus, with the words, "Lord Plautius. Urgent."

Quintus examined the tablet carefully, but didn't open it. "This apology for a seal has some sort of drawing on it. If you apply a bit of artistic licence, it could be a wolf's head. Does that mean anything to you?"

"There's a small criminal gang who call themselves the Wolf-pack." I told him about Hawk's warning, and the fire, and Otus' visit.

Titch added, "I heard the gang mention the Wolf's Head tavern in Eburacum a couple of times, just chatting among themselves. It sounded like somewhere they knew well."

"Then it looks as if this is a straightforward affair," Quintus said. "Distressing, of course, but simple. Crooks trying to raise some easy money by ransoming a wealthy man." He picked up the note. "I'd better take this to Plautius straight away. Aurelia, would you come with me? If we're going to plan tactics, we'll need your help."

We heard voices out in the hall, and Quintus swore softly. "They're going to dinner, and they'll wonder where I am. Rufio, take a look in the hall and tell us when the coast's clear. Then go in there and give my apologies to Lady Sempronia. Tell her I'll be just a little late for the meal, so they're to start without me."

Rufus made a face. "Can't you give me something easy to do, like crossing the Pennine hills with a train of elephants?"

Once Sempronia, Horatius, Fabia, and Diogenes were all safely seated, with their slaves in attendance, Quintus and I hurried across to the guest wing. We found Plautius not only awake, but out of bed. He was in the sitting-room, and Timaeus was waiting on him as he ate a frugal meal of bread and boiled eggs.

Quintus did most of the talking, and Plautius listened carefully, taking everything in his stride and showing no particular agitation. His only question was to me.

"Aurelia Marcella, this young man Victor. Is he to be trusted?"

"I'd trust him with my life, and I'm not exaggerating. He has saved my life. He's a smart lad, honest and loyal. You can believe what he says without hesitation."

"Good." He opened the note-tablet and read the brief contents aloud in a measured, calm tone, which made them all the more chilling.

> If you want your son back alive, send one messenger alone with twenty gold pieces to the Druids' clearing near Oak Bridges at the second hour tomorrow, to wait for further orders. No tricks, or they will all die.

Plautius sighed. "I was afraid of something like this. I can manage twenty gold pieces, but they'll want a large ransom, I assume."

I nodded. "Titch says they discussed ransoms, but didn't name an exact sum."

"I can't take risks with my son's life. I suppose I'll have to pay whatever they demand."

"Not necessarily," Quintus answered. "We could try to negotiate, string matters out for a few days, while we find out who's behind this. It's possible we could catch them, but we need time. For a start, you could tell them you can't get more gold till after the holiday, which is probably true, isn't it?"

"Oh I can get it if I have to. The garrison commander at Eburacum is a friend of mine. The criminals wouldn't know that, of course." He was silent for a while, and then scratched his grey head and smiled. "There is one possibility, of course. Sempronia might not like it. Or perhaps in fact she would welcome it. Yes, it's definitely worth thinking about."

"What have you in mind?" Quintus asked.

"Let me give it a little more thought first. And talk it over with Sempronia too. Technically the decision is mine, but she has a right to be included in the discussion."

I kept my face blank. Best not to speculate what Sempronia would do if she wasn't included in a decision as important as this.

Quintus nodded. "I'll tell her what's happened and ask her to meet you here after dinner, shall I?"

"Yes, please." He lay back on his couch. "Gods, if only I felt stronger. Ah well, we must do the best we can. If you don't mind, I'd like a little time to rest now."

So Quintus went in to dinner, and I returned to the bar-room.

Chapter XVI

Albia told me she'd sent Titch to his bed in the horse-boys' loft above the stables. "There's nothing wrong with him that a good night's sleep won't put right. He's a tough little tyke, as well as a brave one. Oh, he asked if you could feed Poppaea and check on the pups, but I explained you'd probably be too busy, so I told Castor to do it."

"Thanks. I don't fancy going out in the snow again."

We were sitting by the fire eating some of the venison stew, when we heard raised voices in the dining-room—or to be accurate, one raised voice, Sempronia's. Without a word we left our meal and moved to stand close to the connecting door. We'd have looked pretty silly if anyone had come through, but they didn't, and we could hear perfectly.

"It's outrageous!" her ladyship barked. "Preposterous! These bandits, these *criminals,* simply can't be allowed to hold a senator's son, *our son,* to ransom!" There was more of the same, and for once I didn't blame her for being angry.

"It's no good ranting and raving." That was Horatius' voice, soothing and only slightly slurred. "These things happen. We'll just have to pay up, and guard ourselves better in future."

"They're bound to ask for a preposterous amount of money," she snapped, "if twenty gold pieces is their opening price. That's about all the gold we have with us, and we have no chance of raising any more by tomorrow."

"Not by tomorrow," Quintus agreed, "but by the day after, if necessary, so Plautius says. And there may be another way."

"You think so?" Sempronia sounded sceptical.

"I've suggested to Plautius that we might be able to catch the gang," Quintus answered. "If we can buy ourselves a little time."

"Catch them? That sounds promising," Horatius said. "Of course, I keep forgetting you're one of the Emperor's investigators. This is right up your street, isn't it? What's the best way to play it then?"

"*Play!*" Sempronia almost shouted. "Horatius, we are not *playing* at anything. This isn't a game."

"Sorry, sorry. Just a manner of speaking. Well, Antonius?"

"I suggest we try to string out our negotiations with them as long as we can. Give them the twenty gold pieces now, and agree to their demands, which will presumably be for a large ransom. We must let them think we definitely mean to co-operate, but tell them we can't get hold of the gold until after the holiday. That gives us four days, which with luck should be time enough to track the gang down. Oh, and Plautius says he has an idea for delaying tactics too, and he wants to talk to you about it, Sempronia."

"Good." Sempronia sighed. "It's ironic, isn't it? I've been wishing for some time I could find a way of getting rid of that girl Margarita. But I don't want a serious breach with Aulus, and he's besotted with her. He has to make a political marriage eventually, he knows that, and yet he keeps putting it off because of her. Now she's removed by force, but because Aulus has been captured too, we shall have to pay for the privilege of having her restored to us. Unless…." There was a short silence, and then she said thoughtfully, "Slaves are property, after all, and expendable. I wonder if we should perhaps ransom Aulus, but tell the gang they can keep the two slaves."

We were both shocked by this chilling thought. Granted, slaves are property, but they're still people. How could she describe Margarita and Gaius as *expendable,* or contemplate even the possibility of not paying their ransom?

Our silent disgust was given voice by Horatius. "Sempronia, don't even think such things. Margarita and Gaius are part of your household, and your only honourable course is to get them back, whatever it costs."

"Yes, you're right, I suppose. But it's a pity. Gods, I've already got one son trying to escape his duty. I cannot let Aulus do the same."

There was silence for a few heartbeats. Then suddenly Sempronia exclaimed, "Of course!" and there was a crash—she must have thumped her table. "Gods, how blind I've been! It's obvious, isn't it? Antonius, you're an investigator. Don't you see what's behind all this?"

"Apart from a band of kidnappers taking the chance of easy money? No, I don't."

"But hasn't it occurred to you that the obvious person who would want to take Aulus hostage is his brother? This whole affair is Decimus' doing!"

"Decimus?" Horatius clearly didn't find her conclusion at all obvious.

"But why?" Quintus asked.

"He's trying to exert pressure on us over his proposed marriage. You'll see! When we enquire what his demands are, he'll agree to release his hostages in return for our giving consent to his marriage with this innkeeper girl."

By my side, the innkeeper girl hissed, "What rubbish!"

"I don't think that's the answer," Fabia said gently. She'd been so quiet I'd almost forgotten she was there. "Decimus loves his brother. He'd never hurt him. And he knows you wouldn't give in to that sort of blackmail."

"It does you credit that you defend him, my dear," Sempronia said. "And I'm sure you're right, he wouldn't actually hurt Aulus. So all we have to do is stand firm, and he'll release them all. No, take it away! I can't think of eating anything else just now. This is all far too provoking. I must talk to Plautius."

"We'll all go," Quintus answered. "That is, if I may join you in a family meeting, Sempronia? I've some professional experience of this kind of situation."

"Yes, yes, all right," she said shortly.

"We'd probably better ask the innkeeper to join us," Horatius suggested. "We'll need directions to this meeting-place, what was it, the Druids' clearing? I sincerely hope there are no Druids there now!"

"I agree," Quintus said. "I'll see if she's in the bar, shall I?"

We moved quickly back to the fireside, grateful for the warning. He must have known we'd be eavesdropping. He began to open the door slowly, but Sempronia snapped, "No, Antonius, I'm having no outsiders at a family council as important as this. Especially as she's bound to be on Decimus' side, because of her sister. Come along now, let's go and decide what's to be done."

Quintus made a face, then turned back into the dining-room, closing the door carefully behind him. They all began to troop into the hall.

"What an appalling family," Albia breathed. "I can't believe I'm thinking of marrying into it. That Sempronia can blame Candidus for the kidnapping, and if it isn't Candidus, she can seriously suggest not paying a ransom for Margarita and Gaius!"

"Plautius won't let it happen," I answered. "And Quintus will catch the gang. He's still a good investigator, even if…." I paused. "Even if he's stopped caring for me" was the end of that sentence, but I didn't want to say it aloud.

"Oh, Relia, I'm sorry. I've been so wrapped up in my own problems, I haven't been thinking about yours. I couldn't believe the way he behaved to you this afternoon. And yet when he was in here with Titch and just you and me, he seemed like his old self. I don't understand it."

I didn't understand it either, so we talked of other things for a while, until the man himself came in, looking harassed.

"Gods, I swear those two will drive me mad!"

I poured him some wine, and he drained a whole beaker and then sat down on the bench opposite us.

"That was a short meeting." I refilled all the mugs. "I thought you'd be stuck in the guest wing for hours while Plautius and Sempronia argued. What have they decided?"

"I don't know. Plautius insisted on talking to Sempronia in private."

"In *private*? For the gods' sake why?"

"I don't know," he said again, shaking his head. "They agreed to negotiate with the kidnappers for as long as they could, but when they started on the details, Plautius said they preferred not to discuss their family finances in the presence of outsiders, and asked me to leave. I don't like it. I wish I knew what they're up to." He looked at me. "You've had several conversations with the old man, I gather, Aurelia?"

"I have. And whenever I see him, he manoeuvres me into doing something he wants, that I'd much prefer not to do."

Quintus nodded. "He's a force to be reckoned with. He comes across as a gentle, mild old patrician, doesn't he? But there's a will of iron and a heart of stone under that courteous exterior, even now, when he's so ill. How else has he managed to control Sempronia all these years?"

"From what I've seen, I wouldn't say he controls her exactly. It's more that he prevents her from controlling *him*."

"It's a mystery to me why he puts up with her," Albia said. "Such a horrible, bad-tempered harpy, most men would have divorced her long ago."

Quintus shrugged. "Plautius has money, but it's Sempronia who has the political connections. Even before her nephew got the governorship here, she was the one with the really powerful family. He'll put up with a lot of bad temper for that. And she's better than some patrician wives, she doesn't hold orgies, or have affairs."

Albia giggled. "Who'd want her?"

"She was handsome enough as a young woman, they say. Mind you, perhaps they daren't say anything else!"

I smiled, recognising a touch of the old Quintus. "Let's stick to tonight's private meeting. Did you pick up anything about their plans?"

"They're sending a messenger to the Druids' clearing tomorrow morning as instructed, taking twenty gold pieces. He'll try some kind of delaying tactics."

"Who are they sending?" I asked.

"Diogenes."

"*Merda,* Quintus, that's as good as giving in to the gang straight away. He's bound to do some separate deal of his own with them. Margarita told us he's been trying to get his hands on her and Gaius for months."

Quintus nodded. "I wouldn't trust him as far as I could throw him. We'll just have to watch him closely."

"But how? The instructions are, one messenger to go alone."

He smiled. "I did get one sensible decision out of Plautius and Sempronia. I'm going with Diogenes tomorrow to guide him to the meeting-place."

"Guide him?" I repeated. "The Druids' clearing isn't very difficult to find."

"*I* know that, but he doesn't. Perhaps I can do something useful while I'm there—eavesdrop on what he says, and have a look at the other members of the gang. They'll come in force, even if we're supposed to be sending only one man."

"It's not safe for you to go," I objected. "Even though they don't know you, they'll tell by your manner that you're someone with military training, someone in authority, not just a guide. I've a better idea. I'll go. They won't see me as a threat, the way they would you."

He laughed. "If only they knew you, they'd realise that you're at least as much of a threat as I am!"

Yet again, a glimpse of the old Quintus, and the feeling that had once been so good between us. These occasional reminders of how things used to be made the present situation all the worse. Ridiculously, I suddenly felt so miserable I could have cried, and I took refuge in brusqueness.

"No doubt they'll just assume I'm helping a customer, like any excellent innkeeper. So is it agreed? I'll go instead of you?"

"Aurelia…."

"I said, is it agreed?"

"If you're sure, yes. It's a good idea."

"Thanks for the compliment."

"Relia, you're not going with only Diogenes for company," Albia put in. "I don't trust the Weasel, and we certainly can't trust the kidnappers."

Quintus nodded. "Of course you're not. I'll come along too, as far as the turning that leads into the woods, and then I'll follow you in, but keeping out of sight. If you can divert their attention as much as possible, it'll make it easier for me to get up close and look around." He relapsed into thought, staring at the glowing logs. Then he smiled, and asked, "Is Hawk still hunting in these woods?"

"Now that," I said, "is a *really* good idea."

Chapter XVII

We were late setting off for the Druids' clearing. Plautius and Sempronia were moving out to Clarus' villa, and there was an enormous amount to do, much of it involving Diogenes. I suggested Sempronia send another messenger instead of her indispensable secretary, but she wouldn't hear of it, so we had to wait until he was ready. At least that gave me time to do my usual rounds outside, and to make sure someone was feeding Titch's dogs. But I needn't have worried, because Titch was there in person, complete with cheeky grin and assurances that he felt none the worse after his ordeal yesterday.

I insisted that we rode rather than drove, to be more mobile if we needed to make a quick escape. Also, I confess, the idea appealed because I was sure it would disconcert Diogenes, who did all his travelling in carriages. So it did, and he complained loudly, but Sempronia reinforced my instructions. "You'll be going through snowy woods without roads, Mustela. A carriage is hardly appropriate, is it?" I don't know which pleased me more, the wicked gleam in her eyes or the brief spark of anger in his.

It was a grey, cold morning, and though the snow had stopped, it looked liable to begin again at any time. We took tough riding-mules, and wrapped ourselves up warmly. Quintus and I wore cavalry breeches under our heavy tunics and fur cloaks. Quintus announced to everyone that he'd accompany us as far as the point where the track to the clearing left the main road. He didn't tell Diogenes that he'd be following us on foot, and of course neither of us mentioned Hawk, but it was comforting to know he would be watching.

As we made our silent way down the main road, I found my thoughts going back to the last occasion when Quintus and I had visited this hidden clearing together, an August night four years ago. We'd gone in disguise to a Druid ceremony, and hidden among the crowds there. We'd had to witness the hideous sacrifice of a boy, and then…. I wrenched my thoughts back to the present, just as we reached the large holly-bush that marked the turning.

Quintus pulled up his mule. "I'll wait for you here. Good luck!"

I led Diogenes into the woods at walking pace. The track was only a small one used by woodland animals, or sometimes a courting couple seeking a bit of privacy. It wound among the oak trees, which were fairly close together, with scrub and thorn-bushes beneath them. It was simple enough to ride through, as long as you were alert for raised roots masked by the snow, and overhanging branches at head height. The path twisted and turned a bit, but though there was no sun showing to give direction, there was no question of getting lost today. The little track was already marked with two sets of footprints.

The clearing looked familiar, yet also eerily different from the picture in my memory. It was completely empty, and the snow had changed its whole appearance. It was a wide space perhaps a hundred paces across, with trees growing thickly all round its edges, except along the side that adjoined the river. There, the open area sloped right down to the water, which looked almost black against the white snow. Near where the path entered the clearing was an old tumbledown roundhouse. Of course—it was an ideal place to hide hostages. Perhaps we should have brought a larger party, to attempt a rescue. But the kidnappers had been insistent on "no tricks".

We halted in the centre of the clearing and sat our mules, gazing around and listening.

"There's nobody here." Diogenes sounded a trifle petulant, as if even kidnappers should have been waiting respectfully for him to arrive. But to do him credit, he looked relaxed and unafraid, surveying everything with his usual haughty expression.

I matched his air of confidence, but said softly, "I assume we're being watched though."

We waited a while in silence, but still there was nothing to see apart from game-tracks in the snow, and nothing to hear but the wind sighing through the leafless trees.

"Let's have some action. I haven't got all day." I shouted out, "Hello? Is anybody here?"

A noise made us spin round to face the old house, and six men came out of it. They were dressed like native Brigantian peasants, and all heavily armed with swords and daggers. At least three of them looked like soldiers, including Otus, the tall black-bearded army veteran who had visited the mansio. He led the group as they walked towards us.

Then we heard someone call out from the old house. "Help! Help us, please!" There were two different voices, a man's and a woman's—Priscus and Margarita, I was sure of it! But they only managed those few words before one of the natives walked back into the roundhouse, snarling a warning to be silent. Margarita gave a stifled scream, and we heard the wail of a terrified child as the native came out and barred the door. The sounds made me shiver, but at least it meant our friends were all here.

Otus walked up to me, while his henchmen stood in a group a few paces away, waiting for orders. "Aurelia Marcella! We meet again!" His tone was almost conversational, and he spoke Latin as before. "You've taken your time. I was beginning to think you weren't going to show up. And I said only one messenger. Why have you brought *him?*" He gestured towards Diogenes.

"Good morning, Otus." I was pleased to find my voice was strong and confident. Dealing with natives is like dealing with wild horses—if you show any fear, you're done for. "The fact is...."

"The fact is," Diogenes cut in, "that I'm the one handling this business. The innkeeper is here only as a guide. I'm Diogenes, Lord Plautius' confidential secretary, and I've a message for you from his lordship." Just for once I approved of his arrogant tone and the way he looked down his nose.

"Is that so?" Otus glanced at Diogenes, and growled at me, "Then get out of here while I talk to him." He beckoned two of his men. "Take her to the main road and keep her there till we've finished with this one. Stay out of sight. Usual signal if there's anything suspicious."

I couldn't stop them removing me, but I could try to distract their attention and give Quintus more time. "I'm staying here. Do you think I'd leave him with you, and trust you to bring him back safe to the road? You're just as likely to cut his throat, or else turn him loose somewhere in the woods miles from anywhere, hoping he'll freeze to death."

"Don't worry, I'll treat him like the consul's mother," the giant jeered. "I need a messenger, don't I? So I'll keep him safe and use him. But I don't need an innkeeper, so if you've come here with some daft notion about spying while we negotiate, you can forget it." He nodded to his two men. The shorter one, little more than a boy, seized my mule's bridle, and began to walk back along the track, but the taller one drew a long dagger and pointed it towards me. "Wait. Get down off that mule."

"Certainly not!" I blustered. "And don't come too near, this animal kicks."

"I said get down!" The man jabbed his dagger into my leg, tearing the thin fabric of my trousers and drawing a few drops of blood. Reluctantly I slid from the saddle and let them march me away. There was nothing else I could do.

When we reached the main road, the lad said, "Which way's this mansio of hers then?"

"Towards the Long Hill." The taller native jerked his head to the left. "Not a bad place, but I doubt we'll be welcome there now." He laughed, then abruptly stopped laughing. His eyes were fixed on the cleared strip of ground between the trees and the highway. There on the snowy surface, as clear as day, were three sets of mule-tracks crossing from the road into the woods. Two were close together—Diogenes' and mine—and they continued along the game-track. The third set headed into the woods in a different direction. The natives didn't need to be exceptional trackers like Hawk to draw the obvious conclusion.

"Someone came with you," the taller man accused. "Who?"

"One of Sempronia's bodyguards," I improvised. "She wanted to make sure the message got delivered. She thought her slave might be tempted to come part-way and then go home again, saying he couldn't find you."

He raised his dagger. "Where's this man now?"

"At the mansio, I suppose. He had orders to escort us as far as this, and then go straight back."

The native swore. "I'm not stupid! There's no tracks going back up the road, is there?" I silently cursed the snow, which was giving away far too much information for my liking. "Stay here," he barked at the boy, "and don't let her go, else I'll have your guts for catapult-springs." He followed Quintus' tracks into the trees, and before long appeared again leading Quintus' mule.

He threw the reins to the lad and lunged at me, grasping my hair with one hand and pressing the dagger to my throat with the other. I gasped, but managed not to cry out. His expression was angry, and he frightened me. I'd been foolish to involve myself in this business. I'd wanted to impress Quintus, I realised, and that was stupid. How impressed would he be if this cut-throat killed me here and now?

"I'll ask you again," he snarled, "where is this man now?"

I was too terrified to answer straight away, but a shred of common sense in my head told me he wouldn't kill me without a direct order from his leader. So I took a deep breath and said with a show of casualness, "How should I know? Gone behind a tree for a leak, I expect."

"We better tell Otus," he muttered. "Come on."

About halfway along the track to the clearing, the tall native halted us and gave a shrill howl, very like a wolf's. When we finally reached the open space, we found two men on guard by the house, while Otus and two more natives were standing in the middle with Diogenes. They were all holding beakers, and appeared to be drinking a toast. They looked comfortable together, much more like conspirators than enemies. I felt cold inside as I contemplated what sort of treacherous deal Diogenes had concluded, that allowed him to share a drink with men who should have been his enemies.

"You back again?" Otus' hand dropped to his sword. "What's up?"

"They came with a bodyguard," the tall native answered. "We saw his tracks in the snow, and this is his mule. He's somewhere nearby, trying to spy on us I should think."

Otus shrugged. "Just one man?"

"Aye, just the one."

"One man can't do us much harm. And we've finished anyway, haven't we?" He turned to Diogenes.

The Weasel nodded and smiled. "I'm sure my lord will agree we've come to a very satisfactory arrangement."

"Good." The tall native beside me smiled. "So you're releasing the prisoners now?"

"All in good time. There's a little matter of completing the payment first. The young lord can go today, but we're keeping the slaves for a while. Valuable property, those two. And no trouble, neither."

Anger made me incautious. "You scum! Let them go straight away! If you've hurt either of them, I'll...."

"You'll what?" He stepped close to me and slapped me across the face, hard enough to make my head ring and my eyes water. "We've done nothing that won't mend. Like I say, they're valuable, a good-looking pair like that. Worth a lot of money, so I don't intend to spoil their beauty. Or yours!" Suddenly he reached out and gripped my arms. "Tie her up," he ordered my two captors.

I was taken completely off guard. I kicked and struggled to pull free, but they were too strong, and soon had my arms roped behind my back. I was helpless, and my anger melted into bitter misery.

I turned to Diogenes, and saw he was smiling. "Don't just stand there, Diogenes. Tell them to release me at once!"

"As Otus said, all in good time." The secretary looked down his nose at me. "You're to stay here for now. Don't worry, you won't come to any harm as long as you behave."

"But that's outrageous!"

"You surely didn't imagine they would let Master Priscus go without some security in exchange, did you? I'll come back with the rest of the gold as soon as my lord can get it, then you'll be free."

"Plautius has agreed to this?" I couldn't believe the way I was being betrayed.

"Of course. I hope it won't take him too long to raise the rest of the ransom. That house doesn't look anything like as comfortable as the Oak Tree."

"No, Diogenes, this is nonsense. Get me released at once. I'm not part of this deal, I'm just here as a guide!"

"Maybe so," Otus interrupted, "or maybe you thought you'd do a bit of snooping, you and your bodyguard who's mysteriously vanished in the woods. I said no tricks, and I meant it. You didn't listen, so now you'll learn your lesson." He gestured to my two captors, and followed them as they marched me unceremoniously towards the roundhouse. He unbarred the door and leaned into the dark interior, calling, "Lord Priscus, you can come out now."

I heard Priscus say, "Thank the gods! Come along, Margarita, Gaius, it's going to be all right!"

"Not the others," Otus barked. "Just you."

"I'm not leaving them here," Priscus protested, but Otus simply went into the house and dragged him out, as my two captors steered me towards the door. I got a fleeting picture of his white face covered in bruises, and the way he staggered and blinked in the white snow-light. Then the natives pushed me inside the house and banged the heavy door shut behind me. I heard the bar slide across. I stood still, trying to accustom my eyes to the near-darkness, and my mind to being a prisoner.

From the shadows at the far side of the room, Margarita spoke. "Who is it?"

"Aurelia."

"Oh, Aurelia! What's happening? What are they doing to Priscus?"

"Releasing him, I think. Are you and Gaius all right?"

"Yes, give or take a few bruises." She sounded weary and miserable, and looked unsteady on her feet as she came towards me. Her hands were tied, and she was pale and dishevelled. Gaius trotted by her side, his hands tied too. His golden curls were matted and his tear-stained face had a purple bruise on one cheek. In spite of it all, they both smiled at me.

"It's good to see you," Margarita said. "What are you doing here? And Priscus—you say they're releasing him?"

"I think so, yes. I'm his replacement, as surety that the rest of the ransom will be paid."

"You put yourself in danger for us? Oh, Aurelia, that's wonderful of you!"

Not all that wonderful, I thought. I'd much rather have been on my way back to the Oak Tree with Priscus.

"Did you hear that, Gaius?" Her voice was full of relieved happiness. "Master Priscus is being taken home now, and he'll arrange for you and me to go back very soon."

"Hooray!" the child cheered, and I hadn't the heart to cast any gloom on this version of events. But if Diogenes had arranged some deal of his own, would the two of them be going back soon? Or ever? Diogenes knew Sempronia wanted Margarita out of the way. But no, I would look on the bright side. I must.

"Let's try and be comfortable for a bit." I began to move towards where they'd been sitting. "It's bound to take Priscus a while to get things organised."

"There's some fairly clean straw at the back." Margarita led the way. "It helps to keep out the draughts, so it's not too bad." Together we all sank down, leaning our backs against the wall.

"Better than nothing," I agreed, "and it's quite warm, considering there's no fire. But I can hear some rather disturbing rustling noises. Have we got mice?"

"Yes, *and* fleas," Gaius announced proudly. "Hundreds and hundreds of them! I've been bitten all over, and the bites itch like anything, only I can't scratch with my hands tied up."

We laughed, and the boy sat huddled close to his mother while I told her about the message brought by Titch, and how Plautius and Sempronia had sent Diogenes to negotiate, but it would take a day or two to collect the full amount of the ransom. I tried to make it sound hopeful, despite my own serious suspicion of what Diogenes had been up to, drinking a toast with the kidnappers. And I was careful not to mention Quintus or Hawk. I knew they'd bring us help if they could, but if there was a guard outside our prison, we might be overheard.

Margarita was delighted with Priscus' release, and pleased to see me. If she had any darker thoughts, she kept them to herself, and I knew we must both stay cheerful for the boy's sake.

"I'm hungry," Gaius announced. "Will they bring some food soon?"

"I expect so, love."

"The food's *awful*," he told me cheerfully, "but Mamma's promised we can have some animal cakes when we get home, like we had yesterday. Oh—is Victor all right? They made him go back by himself in the snow and dark."

"He's fine, Gaius. You'll see him again soon."

"And Poppaea and the puppies?"

"They're fine too. I saw them this morning. They're growing fast."

"Good." He stood up. "I need a wee. I'll go over in that corner, where I went before." He turned away, and I smiled in spite of everything. Margarita had done well to keep his spirits up like this, so that he regarded the whole dreadful experience as some kind of adventure.

I leaned close and whispered to Margarita, "We must find a way to loosen these ropes. Then if there's any chance to break out, we can get our hands free quickly."

"I've looked round," she whispered back, "to see if there's some sharp spike, or a nail, so I could try to rub the knots against it. But there's nothing."

"Hey!" Gaius gave a squeal of mixed excitement and fear. "Mamma, there's a mouse in the straw! I almost wet him! He won't bite me, will he?"

"No, darling, he's more frightened of you than you are of him. He's sheltering from the snow, just like we are."

Thinking of the mouse started me pondering how we could escape. Maybe we could bite each other's ropes loose? No, that would take too long. Well then, maybe we could make ourselves a way out of the house, our own version of a mouse-hole?

As if in answer to my thought, Gaius called, "I've found the mouse's hole, Mamma. It's in the wall. He ran out into the snow through it. If you lie down and put your eye there, you can see the snow outside, and a few trees. It's here under the straw."

I went to look. It was quite a large hole, big enough to get a hand through, if any of us had had a hand free. The mud that had been used to plaster over the woven wood structure was flaking off, and the wood itself was flimsy and loose. Well, if I didn't have the use of my hands, how about my feet? I sat down and stretched out my right riding-boot. Yes, my big toe fitted into the gap, and by wriggling it around, I could enlarge the hole a little. It would be slow work, but maybe I could make it big enough to crawl through.

Margarita came over and watched me, half questioning and half amused. I nodded and whispered "Shhh!" as I settled down to the laborious process of enlarging the gap, inch by painful inch.

I saw Margarita bend close to Gaius and whisper something, and the boy grinned and nodded. "I'll be as quiet as a mouse," he said, in his normal shrill voice. I managed not to laugh, and she whispered to him again. This time he simply nodded.

I kept at it for what seemed like hours, till I was tired and chilled from the cold wind blowing into the house from the enlarged hole. Margarita took over for a while, and then it was my turn again. I'd just got the gap large enough to slide one leg through up to my knee and begin pushing with my other foot, when close beside me, but outside the roundhouse, a man's voice shouted, "Hey! They're trying to break out!"

There was an answering shout, and the sound of running feet. The door was unbarred and flung wide, and Otus burst in with two natives on his heels. By that time we were all three sitting demurely among the straw, well away from the hole, but they weren't fooled.

"That settles it," Otus growled. "We can't wait till dark to move them to the safe house. We'll have to do it now. Up you get, you three. We're going for a nice walk in the woods. And shut that brat up," he added, as Gaius began to cry.

We were a sombre little procession, three pathetic-looking prisoners shambling along, surrounded by six grim-faced natives, all mounted and armed to the teeth. Two were riding our captured mules, and the others had quite reasonable mounts, presumably also stolen. I sent a quick silent prayer for help to Diana, my special goddess, that Hawk and Quintus were still in the vicinity watching us, and would be able to carry word to the Oak Tree. I remembered that Hawk prayed to Epona the horse-goddess, so I asked for her aid too.

Depression settled over me along with the cold as we took the track towards the main road, the three of us walking slowly, the mounted men surrounding us in a travesty of a bodyguard. The light was beginning to fade, and the trees pressed in close. Their roots across the path were hard to see beneath the snow, so we kept tripping and stumbling. Gaius was sobbing almost continuously, complaining that his feet were hurting. Mine weren't too comfortable either, shod in boots designed for riding, which let in the snow like sandals. Our progress got even slower, till any slug or snail not sleeping away the winter could have followed us with ease.

"Where are we going?" I asked Otus.

"Never you mind."

"Well I hope you're not expecting us to walk far in all this snow."

"No, you'll have your own private transport once we get to the road." They all laughed. "Keep quiet, and save your breath."

So we'd at least be travelling along the road. And he couldn't walk us along the highway as we were—our appearance would arouse suspicion if we met any Roman travellers. He'd probably arranged for a cart to pick us up, where we could lie safely hidden under sacks or hay. Would we be heading up the Long Hill into the wold country, or in the opposite direction, to Oak Bridges or even to Eburacum?

We halted just inside the tree-line, in sight of the road—that's to say we could see any travellers on it, but they couldn't see us. "Rest your horses," Otus ordered. "The others'll be here soon."

As we stood there, I tried to find a scrap of hope in the situation. If Hawk was following us, and perhaps Quintus too, this respite might give them time to fetch reinforcements, even to attempt a rescue. But thinking about Quintus depressed me even more. He'd offered to accompany me to the meeting with the kidnappers, and I'd hoped that one reason was so he would be there to help if things went wrong. But he hadn't been there, and perhaps he didn't consider that things *had* gone seriously wrong. Priscus was on his way home, and I assumed I'd be released eventually, because I'm a free citizen. Though I'm not wealthy enough to produce a big ransom, even kidnappers must know the trouble they'd be in if I disappeared completely. But Margarita and Gaius were different. What was to happen to them?

There was a sudden commotion of shouts and footsteps in the trees to our left. An arrow whizzed out of the gloom, catching Otus a glancing blow on the shoulder. He rocked forward but managed not to fall, as two spears came flying, and two men tumbled from their mules. Dark figures erupted from the trees—two, three, four of them—and surrounded the group of riders.

And Quintus' voice, pitched to a parade-ground yell, called out, "All right, everyone. Stand still. I said STAND STILL!"

The two natives at the rear turned tail and rode back into the woods. Two were on the ground, wounded. But two were left, including Otus, who leaned down and scooped Margarita up onto his horse. She tried to resist, but her hands were tied, and he growled, "Keep still, or the kid'll suffer."

"Come on!" he shouted, and set off at a reckless gallop along the road. The remaining man bent from his saddle to snatch Gaius, but the boy dodged out of reach, and miraculously Titch was there, bringing a cudgel down hard on the man's outstretched left hand. The horseman fled, and Titch took Gaius in his arms in a bear hug. "There now, young Gaius, you're all right!"

But the child was terrified and screaming, and didn't seem to recognise him. "Mamma!" he yelled. "Mamma, wait for me! Wait for me! I'm coming!" He kicked out at Titch, catching him in the balls, so that he doubled up with pain and relaxed his hold. Gaius wriggled free and set off at a clumsy run after the two retreating horses, still crying "Mamma!" at the top of his voice.

Titch, in spite of his pain, tried to follow, until Quintus yelled, "No, Victor! Don't be an idiot!"

"I'll not leave him!" But his legs went from under him, and he collapsed, staring helplessly in the direction Gaius had gone.

"Shall I try, sir?" For the first time I realised Quintus' red-haired servant was one of our rescuers.

"No, Rufio." Quintus strode quickly over to me and cut my hands free. "Check those men we speared, tie them up if they're still alive. Victor, you can't do any more, it's too risky to go after them. We'll have to leave it for now."

I ran to the road, and even as I watched, Otus' companion was galloping back to Gaius and hoisting him onto his horse. "They've caught Gaius," I called, and walked sadly back to the others.

Titch swung round angrily to face Quintus. "We were so close! Why didn't you follow and get him? You could have caught him, he's only little. I promised I'd look after him!"

"Too dangerous." Quintus put a hand on Titch's shoulder, but the lad shrugged him away. "We'll get him free, I promise you, but not like that. Whoever had gone after him would have run straight into a trap, don't you see?"

"No, I don't see. I think we've been cowards!"

Quintus ignored the insult. "Use your brains, lad. Yes, I could probably have caught up with Gaius, but one of their men was already coming back for him. Say I'd ordered him to surrender, threatened him with my sword. All Otus would need to do was start to hurt Margarita, and I'd have had to let Gaius go. And surrender myself, probably, so they'd have got another hostage."

"He's right," I said gently. "Don't feel bad. There are no cowards here. You all did everything you could."

Titch turned away and wiped a hand across his eyes. Then he squared his shoulders and faced Quintus again. "I suppose so. Sorry."

"Nothing to be sorry for. Now I think we need to get Aurelia home. Will you fetch the carriage?"

"A carriage!" I couldn't believe it. "You've really brought a carriage?"

"Aye. It's parked just down the road." Titch hurried away.

Quintus came and took my hands, which were so numb with cold that I could hardly feel his touch. "We had to bring transport. We weren't sure what state you'd all be in. Gods, you're as cold as ice. We'll soon have you warm again. Titch will drive you back, while Rufus and I see to these prisoners." He glanced at his servant. "Are they dead, Rufio?"

"One is. The other's alive, the spear only got him in the thigh. And conscious too, aren't you, pal?" He kicked the native in the ribs, and got a groan as answer. "I'll take that as yes. I've got their weapons, but there's nothing else worth having. No money, nor anything to say who they are."

"We'll find out." Quintus looked grim, and then smiled as Titch drove up in our medium-sized raeda. "Now here's the carriage. May I assist madam to take a seat?"

"You may. In fact I think you'll have to. My feet don't feel as if they belong to me any more." With his help I clambered aboard, and gratefully lay back on the cushions. There was a woollen rug there, and he leaned in and wrapped it gently around me. For a few heartbeats we were alone in the confined space.

"Thanks for coming, Quintus," I said softly. "You took quite a risk."

"Of course I came." He held me close and kissed me full on the mouth. "And I would have taken any number of risks." He squeezed my hands, and then drew back, grinning. "Perhaps you'd better ask that handsome Greek doctor to check you over. I don't want you catching a chill from being in the cold."

I grinned back. "Maybe I will. They say Timaeus has a remarkably fine bedside manner."

"So have I." He jumped down, and the carriage started for home.

Chapter XVIII

It was so good to see the Oak Tree again. Albia and Priscus were waiting for me, but otherwise the mansio was wonderfully empty now our visitors had gone. The comforting warmth of the bar-room was blissful as I began to take off my sodden cloak and boots, and I felt so happy I wanted to sing, even though physically I was numb with cold and bone-tired.

Priscus started to ply me with questions, but Albia stopped him.

"First she needs to get warm. Time enough for questions later. Come on, Relia, here's a beaker of warm wine, and you're to drink it while you have a hot bath."

"No chance!" I knocked back the mug of wine in one go. "That's better. I'll take a second one into the bath-house, or maybe a whole jug. I wouldn't mind some food too. I'm starving!"

"Please." Priscus was close to tears. "Just one question. You haven't brought Margarita and Gaius back with you?"

"No. I'm sorry, Priscus. The kidnappers still have them."

"Ah." He suppressed the tears with an effort. "Diogenes said that might happen. But are they all right?"

"They've not been hurt since you left, but they're being moved to a new hideout. I don't know where."

"Enough!" Albia exclaimed. "Priscus, please let Albia get out of these freezing cold clothes. Then she'll answer your questions, *if* she feels up to it."

"I'm sorry," he said humbly. "Yes, of course. At least you're back safely. Presumably Diogenes gave them money to get you released?"

I decided to dodge that one for the present. "Where's the little turd now?"

"Gone to Silvanius' place to report to her ladyship," Albia answered. "Now come along, Aurelia Marcella, or you'll find yourself kidnapped by me, and force-marched to your bath!"

She came with me to the bath-house, and when she'd helped me undress, she looked me up and down. "Thank the gods you're in one piece, Relia. I've been imagining them doing all sorts of awful things to you."

"They didn't hurt me. They didn't have time." I eased myself into the hot water. "This feels wonderful! They hadn't much in the way of heating in that roundhouse."

She said seriously, "Poor Margarita. And little Gaius too. If you're chilled through after a few hours there, I don't want to think what it must be like for them."

"I know. I'd like to get my hands on those bastards. I hope Quintus and Hawk can find out where they've gone."

"Quintus? Ah, that explains the silly smile you've had on your face ever since you got home. You were rescued by a certain Quintus Antonius Delfinus, I gather?"

"Quintus was there, yes. So were Titch, Rufus, and Hawk."

"Oh I forgot, you always wear a silly smile when you see Titch, Rufus, and Hawk!"

The memory of Quintus' kiss stayed with me through that hot bath, and a second and third beaker of wine which I drank by the bar-room fire. At last I was warm all through, and feeling more like going to sleep than talking, but I was curious about Priscus' presence.

"I'm surprised to find you still here, Priscus. I thought you'd be with the rest of your party at Silvanius' place."

"I wanted to wait for news." He ran a hand through his sandy hair. "I won't be a nuisance and plague you with questions when you're tired. Victor has told me what happened. But there's one thing…."

"Yes?"

"I want to apologise, Aurelia. For my family, and for that little swine Diogenes. He should never have agreed to your taking my place as a hostage. I feel ashamed that you were put into such danger for me."

"I don't think it's you who should be apologising. I assume you had nothing to do with the negotiations."

"Nothing at all. Apart from not wanting to involve you, do you think I'd have agreed to be ransomed if Margarita and Gaius weren't released with me? The thought of them all alone with that band of cut-throats! But by the time Diogenes had negotiated with them, it was too late for me to change anything. The little toe-rag exceeded his authority, which is no great surprise. But I'm truly sorry that you were involved."

"Don't worry. Thanks to Quintus Antonius, I got away without any serious harm. I went along to the clearing to try and eavesdrop on the negotiations, but I couldn't, so you probably know more than I do. What did Diogenes tell you he'd agreed to?"

"He said that he would return with enough money to get you released today, but there probably wouldn't be sufficient to free the others. He doubted if Father could raise the whole ransom till after Saturnalia." Suddenly he stopped, then leapt to his feet. "Listen! Is that horses I can hear outside? Perhaps there's some news!"

Albia and I hurried to the door, expecting to see Quintus and Rufus. Instead we found one of Silvanius' carriages, with two mounted guards riding alongside it, and its driver placing steps ready for someone to descend. "Holy Diana," I prayed, "don't let it be Sempronia!"

Out came, of all people, Horatius. He carried a box of papers, and his grey-haired servant followed him down, bearing a clothes-chest. So he must be planning to stay, just when we'd nicely got rid of them all.

"Horatius!" Priscus had come to stand beside me at the door. "What in the gods' name brings you here? Is there any news?"

"News?" he repeated vaguely. "Oh, you mean about Margarita? No, not a thing. Here, let me get inside. This cold seeps right into your bones."

We all went back into the bar-room and stood awkwardly just inside the door. "I hope it's not putting you out too much, m'dears," Horatius addressed Albia and me, "but I'd like to stay here tonight. Just tonight. I'll go back in the morning. Fact is, I've had a bit of a row with Sempronia, and I need to keep out of her way. You don't mind too much, do you?"

"Er—no, of course not." But I did mind, and he wasn't too drunk to know it.

"I'm sorry." He sounded as if he meant it. "I can see it's inconvenient. But you'll hardly know I'm here. My man will look after me, and I'm quite well-behaved, you know, when my irritating relations aren't around to provoke me."

I couldn't help smiling. "If you promise you've brought no irritating relations, you're very welcome."

"Thank you." He turned back to the door, where the carriage driver stood waiting. "You can go back to the villa now. Pick me up from here at noon tomorrow. And if the fun and games start again, I'll expect a full report, all right?"

The slave grinned. "Very good, sir. But I think the show's over for tonight."

"Fun and games?" Albia asked, as I shut the big door and we trooped over to the fire. "What have you been up to, apart from having a quarrel with Sempronia?"

"Oh, wait till you hear!" He turned to his slave. "Take my things to the room I had before. That'll be all right, won't it, m'dear?"

Albia nodded. "I'll get someone to put a brazier in there. And I'm afraid we've nothing very grand to offer you for dinner. Or have you had a meal at Silvanius' already?"

"Not yet. But you've got some of that excellent Campanian red wine, haven't you?" He sat down, rubbing his hands.

"I daresay we can find a mug or two for a valued customer. Especially one who likes the stuff so much he's driven through the winter snow for it!" Albia fetched a wine-jug and beaker, and poured the lawyer a drink.

Priscus said to Horatius, "So you've heard nothing more about Margarita and Gaius?"

"No, 'fraid not. But I have one piece of news that will please you, I think. A certain confidential secretary got what he deserved today."

"If you mean the Weasel," Priscus remarked, "what he deserves is a sound thrashing."

Horatius chuckled. "And that's what he got. Timaeus gave him a good beating."

"Timaeus! You're right, that does please me. But why?"

"Because Diogenes didn't get Margarita and Gaius released. In fact he accused the Weasel of making a deal with the kidnappers, that the two of them wouldn't ever be ransomed, but would be left with the gang. Diogenes denied it, of course, and kept insisting he'd just done the best he could." Horatius took a long drink of his wine.

"He's an evil little rat," Priscus said, "and I agree he overstepped his authority when he let them take Aurelia. But surely he'd never betray Margarita and Gaius like that? Sempronia and Plautius would have his hide, wouldn't they?"

"Ah, but that's not all. Timaeus really laid into him. I thought he was going to kill him at one stage. He had him on the floor in a stranglehold, and kept demanding that he admit what he'd done. And Diogenes suddenly changed his tune and said, 'All right, I admit it. I've got rid of those two for good. It's what my lord and lady wanted, and I've done it.' Well naturally, that made Timaeus madder than ever, but by then somebody had run and told Sempronia what was going on, and she sent a couple of the bodyguards in to stop the fight. I was rather sorry myself."

We were all digesting this when Quintus strode in through the main door. "Any chance of some service in this bar?" He glanced round the room in surprise. "Well well, quite a reception

party. I expected Priscus, but you, Horatius? Has Silvanius run
out of wine already?"

"Sempronia's turned it all sour," the lawyer grunted.

Quintus gave me a smile and a nod, and discreetly squeezed
my hand as I helped him out of his cloak. He thanked me
politely when I handed him a beaker of spiced wine. Oh well, I
thought, we're back to the starting-gate. Whatever his reasons,
when there are other people about, he's distant and cold with
me. But when we're alone…. I resolved to get us alone again as
soon as possible.

Priscus shook Quintus' hand, reminding me that the two of
them hadn't met yet, at least not on this journey. However, they
obviously knew one another slightly.

"Antonius, it's good to see you. And I thank you for rescuing
Aurelia. I'm ashamed of the way she was treated, just to get me
released."

"It's not your fault," Quintus answered, sitting down by the
fire. "It was Diogenes who left poor Aurelia in the lurch. And
now, I'm very much afraid, Margarita and Gaius are in an even
worse situation."

"What's happened? Do you know where they are?"

"No. Hawk and I followed them as far as we could, till it got
too dark to see. That's why I didn't come back sooner." He took
a long draught of wine. "Gods, I've been dreaming about a good
spiced drink all day! The natives rode towards Eburacum, but
they hadn't got far when a farm cart came up the road to meet
them, with three more riders. There was some arguing, because
apparently the cart should have been waiting by the holly-bush.
We have to be thankful it wasn't," he added, smiling at me. "They
loaded Margarita and Gaius into the cart and covered them with
some sacks, and all moved off together. I'm afraid there was
nothing we could do to stop them. They went straight past the
Oak Bridges turning, so they may be heading for Eburacum, or
probably somewhere closer for tonight. It was full dark by then,
so it was pointless to search any more tonight."

Priscus was dismayed. "But how will we know where to find them? To hand over the rest of the ransom and get them back? I suppose they'll send us a message. *Merda,* more waiting! And my poor Margarita and Gaius, prisoners all night in the cold!"

"Prisoners for good, I'm afraid," Quintus said gently. "There's no easy way to tell you this, Priscus, but I think you'll be lucky to see either of them again."

"But Diogenes said he'd be taking the rest of the ransom to the gang as soon as Father could raise the money. He told me it would only be a matter of days…. Why are you looking at me like that, as if you don't believe a word I've said?"

"I don't believe a word *Diogenes* said, and neither should you. I'm afraid I've got some information that will upset you, Priscus. Diogenes has arranged for you to be released, but for the kidnappers to keep Margarita and Gaius."

"Keep them? But when Father sends the rest of the money…."

"He isn't going to send any more money."

Priscus shrank away, as if he'd received a physical blow. "You mean—he's agreed that the gang will keep Margarita and Gaius *for good?*"

Quintus nodded. "Yes. But more likely they'll be sold rather than kept. They'll fetch plenty at the Eburacum slave market."

"No! No, I can't believe it. How in Jupiter's name do you know all this?" Priscus sounded almost accusing. "Did the kidnappers tell you? Or Diogenes?"

"Of course not. But I caught most of their conversation. After Aurelia was marched out of earshot, Diogenes and Otus and a couple of his men held a meeting in the clearing, to discuss what to do with you and the others. They assumed they were safe from eavesdroppers, standing in the middle of a wide open space."

"You managed to overhear them? I don't see how! We couldn't catch anything they said from inside the roundhouse. We tried."

"I couldn't hear their voices, but I watched their lips move." He smiled at me. "Aurelia, you've heard me speak of my old Aunt Antonia?"

"Yes. She lives in Rome, and spoils her nephew disgracefully."

"More to the point, she's stone deaf. She has been for years. But she's learned the art of interpreting what people say from the way their lips move, without needing to catch the sounds. She taught the trick to me when I was a boy."

"I don't believe you, you cocky bastard." I mouthed the words soundlessly, and he laughed.

"Aurelia says she doesn't believe me because I'm a cocky bastard. Well, I'm a cocky bastard who can read people's lips. I managed to follow most of Diogenes' negotiations with the gang, except for one man, because he stood with his back to me the whole time."

"How thoughtless of him," I mouthed.

Quintus nodded. "Yes, Aurelia, it was extremely thoughtless, but one has to put up with these things." He became serious again. "Priscus, are you satisfied that I can give you a reasonable account of what was said today?"

Priscus hesitated, then mouthed a few silent words.

Quintus nodded. "He says, 'I'll believe you if you can understand me, otherwise it's just a trick.'"

"Very well, I'm convinced," Priscus agreed. "Go on."

"Wait," Albia cut in suddenly. "There's something I need to see to in the kitchen before we start. Relia, could you come and help me please?"

Priscus began to object, but I recognised that Albia had something urgent to say, so I got up to follow her. "I expect it's about the beans," I said, for Quintus' benefit. "We won't be long."

"Gods," Horatius muttered, "Sempronia isn't the only woman who likes ordering everyone around."

"These two usually do it with more tact than Sempronia," Quintus answered.

I mouthed something very rude in his direction, and we went into the kitchen. There, calmly sitting at the big table, was Candidus. They both laughed when they saw my surprise.

"Sorry, Relia," Albia said. "He arrived at midday. He'd heard rumours about the kidnapping, and wanted to be sure I was all right. We were going to tell you."

"And I'm the Queen of Brigantia! You just enjoy sneaking around like a couple of sixteen-year-olds avoiding a disapproving father."

"It has its attractions," Candidus grinned. "But I'm not sure whether I should stay out of the way tonight. I don't want to upset my brother any more than he's upset already."

"Why should your being here upset him?"

"I'm afraid he may resent what I've done, running away and everything. It dumps all the family responsibility onto his shoulders."

"Listen, *children.*" I wagged my finger at them. "You can't play hide-and-seek like this. And I for one am glad to see you, Candidus. It means you'll be coming with us to Silvanius' banquet tomorrow, doesn't it?"

"I doubt it."

"Of course it does. Clarus wants you to be there, and more important, your father wants to see you. He asked me to get a message to you, only with all this hostage business I hadn't done it. He says he won't consider going back to Londinium until he's had a chance to talk to you."

"Which means," Albia put in, "that your parents may be trailing round Brigantia for months, just because you're being stubborn. Your father's ill. Your mother's…."

"Giving everyone a hard time," Candidus finished. "I suppose, if you put it like that, I'd better come. After all, what harm can it do? I've only got to see him, not change my mind about anything."

I expect my sigh of relief was audible in Oak Bridges.

"Meantime," he looked at Albia, "do you think Aurelia's right, and I ought to go in there and have it out with Priscus?"

"I'm always right, it's a well-known fact. Get it over, that's my advice. And I think you'll be pleasantly surprised. I believe

Priscus rather admires the stand you and Albia are taking. So you might find you have an ally against your parents."

When Candidus entered the bar-room, there was a stunned silence for a few heartbeats. Then Priscus jumped up and ran to him, and they embraced like—well, like long-lost brothers. Far from resenting Candidus, Priscus was overjoyed to see him. They hadn't set eyes on each other for three years, and it was good to see the happiness their reunion brought them.

We ate dinner sitting round the bar-room fire, and Albia and I brought the food in ourselves, so we could talk without any of the servants overhearing. The meal was simple compared with the fare we'd given our guests on previous nights: venison stew with vegetables and fresh bread, followed by cheese, nuts, and raisins, and washed down with Falernian.

While we ate, Quintus told us about the exchange he'd heard—or should I say seen?—in the clearing that morning. "Otus and Diogenes did most of the talking. Diogenes began by saying he had his master's authority to negotiate, and he even produced a papyrus to prove it."

"You couldn't see that, surely." Priscus was clearly still sceptical.

"No, but Otus read it out to the other two men. It appeared to be from Plautius, giving Diogenes full power to act for him and Sempronia."

"Do you think Father could have written something like that?" Candidus looked at Priscus.

"I don't know. Perhaps. Or perhaps the Weasel forged it. I'll find out. Sorry, Antonius, go on."

"First of all Diogenes offered the twenty gold pieces he'd brought along as full ransom for all three prisoners, and Otus laughed in his face. So Diogenes suggested that they should release Priscus in exchange for the twenty aurei, and keep the other two, to do as they liked with. He made a point of how valuable they were."

There was a shocked exclamation from Candidus, and Priscus used some barrack-room language to describe Diogenes.

Quintus took a couple of mouthfuls of stew. "Otus liked that idea, and his two men seemed happy with it. One of them asked Otus what he proposed doing with Margarita and Gaius. He said he'd sell them to a slave dealer he knew, who'd either auction them in Eburacum, or maybe send them for sale down south, where they'd fetch a good price. Whatever money is made will be divided up among the gang."

"Down south!" Priscus repeated, appalled.

"One of the men, the one I couldn't see, seemed to be insisting the prisoners should belong to the gang as a whole and be used by all of them, but Otus said he would punish anyone who laid a finger on either prisoner. Not from moral scruples, of course, but they'll be much more valuable if they're sold in good condition."

"That's something, I suppose," Priscus said sadly.

"Did you happen to see any discussion about why they decided to capture me?" Well, naturally I was curious.

Quintus smiled grimly. "Oh yes. Diogenes told Otus to imprison you for a day or two to teach you a lesson, then let you go even if no ransom was paid. It seems he doesn't like you much."

"It's mutual."

Priscus turned and asked me, "When's the next slave auction?"

"Four days from now, I think."

"In the middle of the holiday?" Horatius was scandalised. "They can't do that, surely."

"We only celebrate Saturnalia for three days in this district," I explained, "because of being quite near the frontier. There's always a slave auction a day or two after the holiday, and before the beginning of January."

"Then if they're being sold there, we can buy them back," Priscus said.

"That certainly seems like the simplest solution," Quintus agreed. "Not the cheapest, though. Especially if you find yourself bidding against the pimps the army officers use." He saw Priscus wince, and added, "Sorry, Priscus, but we've got to face it. And there's always the chance that Otus may decide to send them down south instead."

"I'll find them," Priscus said. "Wherever they go, I'll find them, and whatever it costs, I'll get them back." He looked at us all with cold fury. "I call on the gods to witness, I won't rest till they are safe again. And if anything happens to either of them, Diogenes will pay for it. I swear it!"

There are few things more frightening than a mild man provoked beyond endurance. As our grandmother used to say, when a worm turns, it changes into a crocodile.

We finished our meal in silence, and I'm sure I wasn't the only one who thought about the two prisoners out in the cold somewhere, and wondered what, if anything, they were eating tonight.

Horatius, now well lubricated, broke the pensive mood by telling Candidus about the fight between Timaeus and Diogenes.

"Is that why you came back to the mansio?" Candidus asked. "Mother was in one of her rages, and you thought you'd be safer out of the way?"

"She was in a bit of a mood, yes. But usually I don't mind her. I'm used to her, and you generally just have to sit tight and wait till she calms down." He sighed. "But this afternoon I had a serious argument with her, and for once I wasn't prepared to let her bully me. It concerned you two boys, in a way."

Priscus asked, "What was it about? Or would you rather not say?"

"On the contrary, I think I'd like you to know." Horatius glanced uneasily at me and Albia. I realised he'd prefer to talk to the others privately, and I couldn't think of any reason for including us in the discussion, much as I wanted to be there. So I got to my feet. "Would you like us to leave?"

But Candidus put an arm round Albia. "Albia is as good as family now. If she leaves, so do I."

"And Aurelia," Quintus said, "is an excellent investigator, and is involved in your family's affairs, after today. She should stay too. I can vouch for her discretion."

"All right. It was about Plautius and his will. You all know Sempronia wants Plautius to alter it, to disinherit Decimus. Apart from a few minor legacies, the whole estate will be divided between Priscus and Sempronia herself, and Decimus, you won't get a copper coin."

"I know," Candidus answered, "and I couldn't care less. I had all this out with Mother yesterday."

"The argument was about whether he ought to make a completely new will, or alter the existing one. Sempronia wants him to include some other changes too, and thinks it would be simpler and tidier to draw up a fresh document."

"What changes?" Candidus asked.

"She wants him to free Margarita, for one thing. And *not* to free Diogenes, for another. The existing will frees the Weasel, and it bequeaths Margarita and Gaius to me."

"To *you?*" Priscus exclaimed. "I never knew that."

"Sempronia wants her out of your reach for good, so she's pushing Plautius to free her, on condition she leaves your household and has nothing more to do with you. She thinks that then you'll agree to make a political marriage."

"I won't."

"You will, you know. I've said it before, you'll have to give in one fine day, and accept an arranged marriage."

Priscus looked at him sharply. "Mother told me once that she thought Father ought to put a clause in his will cancelling all your debts to our family, and leaving you a decent legacy. That was after the business of the senator's nephew and the gladiators, when we had to—well, never mind. Would there be a clause along those lines in the new version?"

Whether Horatius blushed, I couldn't be sure, because his face was already so red. "Yes, actually there would. But that's irrelevant."

"Is it?"

"Yes, it is. Because I've refused to draw up a fresh will. Plautius doesn't want it, and I don't think it would be fair on him. Any changes that are needed will be made to the existing will, by way of a codicil. I told Sempronia this, and she exploded. But I'm insisting on it."

Priscus looked puzzled. "I don't see what difference it makes, Horatius. Why is it so important? New or old, Father's so ill now, he isn't in a position to sign any will, is he?"

"That's the whole point. He's very weak, and he knows it. He can only concentrate on family matters for a short while, then he has to rest. To get to grips with a completely new will would be too much for him until he's got his strength back. And he's afraid Sempronia might manage to force him to sign and seal it anyway, even if he hadn't been able to give it his full attention."

"Could she do that? What about the witnesses?"

"She could make it look as if she's helping him—guide his hand to sign it, use his ring to seal it. If I wasn't present, the witnesses wouldn't realise."

"It would be tantamount to forgery, though," Quintus said. "You're saying Sempronia is capable of that? It's a serious charge, Horatius."

"Believe me, I'm not making it lightly. And that's why I've promised Plautius that there will be no new will, until his health improves and he can instruct me in person, in writing, and I'm satisfied that he's lucid. But if he wants to add to the old one, even alter it a little, I'll help him do that. It will be easier for him, because he's familiar with what it says, and we can make any alterations slowly, one at a time, when he feels up to it."

Candidus said, "May I ask if he's made any alterations yet?"

"No. He was in no state to do it today. Any sort of travel tires him out, you know. Tomorrow—well, we'll see."

"It sounds to me," I said, "as if he doesn't want to make the new changes that Sempronia is so keen on, and this is his way of avoiding them."

Horatius chuckled. "You've got it, m'dear. He doesn't. He may or may not decide to cut Decimus out of the will, but as for the other bequests, he says he prefers to leave things as they stand for now."

Priscus sighed. "I spoke to Timaeus about Father's health yesterday. He isn't optimistic, I'm afraid. I must say I was hoping that if anyone could cure Father, Timaeus could. He's a good doctor, and is devoted to Father. Until we started all this travelling, he seemed to be getting better, and his mind's never lost its sharpness, even when his body is weak. But now—well, it doesn't look so hopeful."

"No," Horatius agreed. "If he continues as he is today, Plautius will have to use all his strength to exercise his authority as head of the family. But a man should be master in his own house. He's told me what he wants, and I intend to see that his wishes are carried out. I hope you two boys accept that." He glanced enquiringly at Candidus, then at Priscus. They both nodded.

"Is he well guarded at Silvanius' villa?" I asked. "He was worried about his safety. He's a brave man, but the attempt to murder him here upset him more than he wanted to admit."

"That was all cleared up, surely," Priscus said, "when Leander committed suicide and left a note confessing that he'd tried to murder Father."

"It wasn't suicide," I corrected him. "Someone killed Leander and left a forged confession."

Priscus turned on me angrily. "That's outrageous! You knew this, and you didn't tell anyone? So the real murderer is still free, waiting for another chance to kill my father?"

"It's the way your father wanted things. He thought we had a better chance of catching the murderer if we could put him off guard. He asked me not to tell anyone, so I haven't, till now."

"She's right," Quintus confirmed. "Plautius made the decision. Aurelia followed it."

"He is the most extraordinary man," Horatius said. "I remember once, when we were all in Italia…." He embarked on a long family reminiscence, but I felt my attention wandering, as a feeling of utter weariness crept over me. The combination of a hard day, a warm room, and plenty to eat and drink was making me sleepy. The conversation flowed around me in an increasingly meaningless blur, until I felt a hand on my shoulder and found Albia bending over me. "Relia, you're almost asleep. Come on, let's get you into bed."

I was only too grateful when she led me to my room and helped me into bed. She tucked my blankets round me, and I was asleep almost before my head touched the pillow.

Chapter XIX

The next morning the snow had more or less gone, leaving the ground wet and slushy under a blue sky. As I stepped out onto the forecourt, I thanked the gods that our journey to Silvanius' villa was to be along good Roman roads, properly drained and serviceable in all weathers. The muddy native so-called roads are simply beaten tracks, a mess all winter long. But excellent though it was, our main road hadn't a man or a beast on it, and I guessed the mansio would have another quiet day, with only a handful of customers.

I did my morning rounds, and stopped at the stables to make sure Secundus knew we wanted the large raeda ready two hours after noon. He asked if we'd like a couple of mounted men along as guards.

"Yes, that's a good idea, as things are. They can come back here in plenty of time for the party."

Our servants were holding their own Saturnalia feast in the evening. It was an annual event, and as usual Albia and I had been invited. As usual we'd politely refused, no doubt to everyone's relief. I'd given them permission to use the bar-room, and a generous allowance of wine to make the party go well, with the customary warning to the senior servants—Cook, Carina, Secundus, and Ursulus—of the dire consequences they'd face if I found any damage in the morning.

"Who do you want as driver?" Secundus asked.

"I'd like to take Titch. But after the other night I don't know whether to ask him. The attack on the hostages seems to have shaken him up. Do you think he'll be willing to come?"

"Of course he will, if you want him. He's no coward, and I'm not going to turn him into one by mollycoddling him. I'll tell him."

"No, just this once I'll ask him myself. I won't make it an order, he can choose whether he comes or not. So just tell him I want to see him, would you?"

He nodded. "I'd bet any money that he'll do it."

"He did well yesterday, helping Quintus Antonius. But I know he was upset about losing little Gaius when he'd so nearly got him back."

Secundus sighed. "He blames himself, though I've told him it wasn't his fault. If Quintus Antonius couldn't rescue them, then nobody could. Gaius was a nice little feller, a bit like one of my other sons who died young."

"Let's not say 'was'. There's still hope. The gang won't kill them when they can get good money for them."

Secundus would have won his bet hands down. When I eventually found Titch and asked if he'd drive us to the banquet, his face lit up.

"Why, I'd love to! I thought you mightn't want me to, after I let them kidnappers get away with Gaius."

"You've got that all wrong. It's because you tried so hard to rescue him that I very much want you to. But it'll mean you miss the party tonight. We're staying over at Councillor Silvanius' place." The least I could do was give him a good excuse for not driving us, if he needed one.

"But I don't have to stay too, do I? I can drive you to your banquet, and then come back here for the night, and collect you again in the morning. I can be there whenever you want, real early if you like. Though if it's a good party, you might not want reveille to sound too soon, eh?"

"Neither might you. Right then, you can collect us from the villa at noon tomorrow."

Breakfast felt almost like a family affair. Albia and I joined Candidus, Priscus, and Quintus (Horatius was still asleep), and Cook had made some lovely little ginger cakes, shaped like animals—the same idea as the ones we'd eaten at the Golden Fleece, but much better done. I complimented him, and managed not to catch Albia's eye when he told me they were all his own idea.

He said he was making a large batch for the party—farm animals for the outdoor slaves, horses for the stable hands, and even a little dog for Titch. "Only I can't think what to make for the young barmaids," he grunted. "They're not interested in animals, only men. Maybe I'll do some small images of Priapus!"

Gods, I thought, I don't know when I last heard Cook make a joke, so even he's getting into holiday mood. I wished I could have shared it. I tried to look forward to the banquet, thinking of Silvanius' superb chef and the sumptuous hospitality of a luxurious villa. But I knew that though the dinner would probably be a spectacular party, the glamour and glitter of it all would be as fragile as ice on a lake, which entices you to step out onto its shining surface only to let you fall to destruction in the depths.

After breakfast Priscus and Candidus sat in happy conversation by the bar-room fire. Quintus prowled restlessly about, apparently unable to settle to anything, which made me restless too. I went to my study to check the hair I'd put across the hinges of my document chest, though I realised there wasn't much point now, with Diogenes and the others safely in Oak Bridges. But I saw with a shock that the hair was gone.

I don't know whether I actually spoke aloud, but Quintus came into the room and looked at me enquiringly. "Something wrong?"

I pointed at the hinge. "I put a hair across there. It's gone now."

"Has anything been disturbed?"

I opened the chest carefully and looked at the papers stacked inside it. Albia was right, my filing system left something to be desired, but I could tell if anything had been touched. "No, they haven't been moved since I last looked at them."

"Which was when?"

"Yesterday, before going out with you and Diogenes. I thought with all of them moving on, I could stop worrying about snoopers, but it seems I was wrong." I felt a perverse sense of satisfaction that someone had fallen into my simple trap, but it was mixed with worry. Only a few of Sempronia's party had been here at the mansio last night: Priscus, Horatius, and his slave. If the spy was among the visitors, it must be one of them. But then I reflected that the guests hadn't fully moved out before Quintus and I left yesterday. One of them could have sneaked in after I'd gone. The only person who couldn't have done was Diogenes, because I'd been with him the whole time.

"You have nice hair," Quintus said, smiling. "Look, Aurelia, we need to talk."

"Do we?"

"I want to explain why—well, why I'm having to keep my distance from you when the others are about. It's because of Lucius."

So that was it! Everything became suddenly clear to me. Lucius' disgrace was the reason for Quintus' change of attitude. He preferred not to be seen as my friend, now my brother had fallen from favour. He didn't want his own reputation tarnished by association with us. Yet he wasn't averse to stealing an occasional kiss when he got the chance. I supposed from his standpoint it made sense, but it was disappointing, and it angered me.

"No explanation is necessary," I said stiffly. "You're a free agent, just as I am. You must behave just as you like. I quite understand."

"No, that's just it. You don't. You see…."

"I don't want to be rude," I cut in, as rudely as I could, "but will you excuse me now? I've several important things to do before I leave the Oak Tree. We'll meet again tonight."

He left without another word.

Sempronia's carriage arrived at noon and carried Candidus, Priscus, Horatius, and Quintus away to the villa. I waved them off with a show of cheerfulness, but I was glad to see the back of them all.

As the echo of their wheels faded, Titch came up to me. "Mistress, I've got something for you, but it's secret. I've hid it out of the way. It's in the small hay-store, where the pups are now."

I went with him to the store, and waited while he crossed to a far corner and plunged his hands into a pile of loose hay. He felt around blindly, then pulled out a small folded note-tablet, scruffy and worn and without a seal. He handed it to me. "From Master Lucius. He was here this mornin', and he gave it to me when I was down in the trees, far end of the big paddock."

"Here? I wish I'd known. Didn't he ask to see me?"

Titch shook his head. "He said it was too risky, with all the people about. He wanted to, that's why he came, but he hadn't reckoned on Priscus and Horatius being here. He couldn't wait around for long, so he told me to give it to you when it was safe, and keep quiet about it to everyone else. Which I have, and I will."

"Good. Thank you, Victor. I wasn't expecting to hear from him so soon."

"Is he in some kind of trouble, the master?" He looked at me without his cheeky grin. "People are saying that the Governor's kicked him out in disgrace. And this is the second time he's come here secretly."

"I can't tell you much. You know the sort of work he does."

He brightened. "I thought so. He's on an investigation, then?"

"All I'll say is that he knows what he's doing, and we can trust him. And he can trust us to keep his movements secret, I hope."

"Aye, of course. Sorry, I shouldn't of asked, should I?" He went over and crouched down by the puppies, and stroked the bitch's head affectionately. "I must get Poppaea fed. She's hungry about six times a day. Oh, one more thing the master said."

"Yes?"

"He said, 'Send Aurelia and Albia my love and wish them a happy holiday.'"

I went straight inside and through to my study. I glanced round to make sure nothing had been disturbed, but everything was where it ought to be. I sat down and read Lucius' note.

WUXVWTKHLVKHUHWRKHOS

I might have known he'd disguise it. He and I have played around with simple codes ever since we were children. I sometimes joke that he only became an investigator so he could get to use more complicated versions in his job. But this note, I knew, would involve a simple cipher, and the likeliest was the one that was invented by Julius Caesar—well, according to army legend, anyway, though I've always thought the Divine Julius must have been too busy conquering Gaul and altering the calendar and seducing other men's wives to have time for codes. If he had that much energy, he deserved to be made a god.

You treat the alphabet as a list of letters, and you replace each letter in your message by another one located a few places further down the list. Caesar was supposed to have favoured three places further along, so I tried that first. I took out a wax tablet and laboriously began to transpose:

W. I counted three letters backwards and got T. Next U: that became R. X turned into U, and V into S. And another W, which meant another T. So the first word was TRUST.

Soon I'd written out the whole message.

TRUSTQHEISHERETOHELP
TRUST Q HE IS HERE TO HELP

I stared at it in a mixture of surprise and gladness. Q must stand for Quintus. Of course we know other people whose names begin with Q, but nobody who would fit the picture here. Trust Quintus? My brother was saying we could still trust Quintus as we had before. Not only that, he was going to some considerable trouble to say it. And if Lucius trusted Quintus, then so did I. Yet the message didn't explain Quintus' efforts to keep his distance—or did it?

Yes, it did! I'd been right in concluding that his hostile manner, his rudeness, were all on account of Lucius. But not because he refused to let himself be tainted by association with a disgraced investigator. Quite the contrary! He'd said to me when he first saw me, "I'm told your brother's been a naughty boy." In plain Latin, "I know your brother's in trouble, and I can't be seen to help him." Which wasn't at all the same as saying he *wouldn't* help him.

I thought back over the short time since Quintus had arrived. He'd done his best to make it plain to me. Every time he'd treated me with disdain, we'd been in company with others. When we were alone, or had only Albia or Titch with us, he was much more like his old self. And in the carriage yesterday he'd been very much his old self. So he was on an investigation, and because of it he had to appear to be not just neutral towards our family, but positively hostile. But he was ready to help if we needed him.

When I had the chance to show the note to Albia on her own, she smiled delightedly. "I'm so glad, Relia. If Quintus is Lucius' friend, that makes him ours as well, even if he's behaving like a bear with a sore tail."

I explained my theory on that score, and she nodded enthusiastically. "Yes, that makes sense. So he'll presumably keep up his act as a boorish oaf, and *you* must pretend to be annoyed and hurt by the way he's carrying on."

"That'll be easy enough. However he feels about Lucius, he's also here to accompany the fabulous Fabia, and he's enjoying it a bit too much for my liking. But at least if we can co-operate over dealing with the Plautius family, I'll be glad of his help."

Albia said, "I'm going to start getting ready. Do you know, I've spent the last couple of days dreading this banquet, but now I'm looking forward to it, in spite of everything. We'll at least get some important things sorted out. Candidus and I will have faced Sempronia. You can find a private corner to make friends with Quintus again. You won't be able to sit next to him at dinner, though."

"No. But now I know why he's being so rude, I'll rather enjoy giving him a taste of his own medicine."

She produced a small package from her belt-pouch. "Look, let me show you what Candidus has given me." Her eyes shone as she unwrapped a silver ring with blue lapis lazuli set in it. "My betrothal ring. Isn't it beautiful?"

"It's lovely, Albia. But you're never going to wear it tonight, in front of everyone?"

"Of course I am. Candidus insists on it."

"Good for you! And good for him." That young man was proving to have more backbone than I'd given him credit for.

An hour later we were bathed and dressed in our best. Albia was wearing a new sea-green tunic with a paler green over-tunic, embroidered with a design of sea-shells and waves, and the silver ring Candidus had given her stood out proudly on her left hand. My tunic was pale peach, and my matching over-tunic had bronze coloured embroidery in a pattern of swirling curves. I'd planned to wear the gold ear-rings that Quintus had given me last year, but instead found some silver ones decorated with bronze coloured enamel.

We came into the bar-room to tell Carina we were leaving, and yes, to show off our glad-rags to the customers there, including some of the servants who had decided to start their party early. We both looked good, though I say it myself, and we got a gratifying round of applause.

As we were about to go outside, one of the young kitchen maids brought us beakers of steaming wine, "to warm you before you set off, Mistress." She looked very neat and tidy and pleased with herself, and remembering what day it was, we sipped warily. Sure enough, the wine tasted disgusting, having been flavoured with fish sauce instead of honey. Everyone laughed as we pretended to be astonished by this hoary old prank, and the little rascal grinned widely, delighted to have caught us out. I knew what came next. I, as the mistress, was expected to wait on my slave.

I went to the bar for a fresh mug of wine and said, "Well, now it's your turn for a drink. Would my lady like to be seated, and have a beaker of our excellent spiced wine?"

There were cheers and whistles from the slaves at the bar, and the girl sat down. "Yes, thank you, innkeeper. That is, if there's anything drinkable to be found in this dreadful place. Which I seriously doubt!" It was a recognisable imitation of Sempronia, and got a good laugh. "I expect the wine will be very poor stuff. Is it really, *really* hot?"

I handed her the mug. "Oh yes, my lady, it's just come from the kitchen. Our kitchen maids are a lazy lot, I'm afraid, but they do know how to warm up a pan of wine."

Another round of applause followed us as we went out to our carriage. I felt my spirits suddenly lifted. Families could fight and feud, lovers could go and come, but Saturnalia and its simple pleasures were still there to enjoy.

Chapter XX

It was a pleasant ride to Silvanius' villa, through Oak Bridges and out on the northern road. The afternoon sunshine gave us the illusion of warmth. We chatted about light, trivial matters, and in no time at all we were turning into Silvanius' long drive.

Clarus had built his villa five years ago, arousing a mixture of awe and envy. Feeling the dignity of his position, the Chief Councillor had gone to a lot of trouble to create the kind of large, elegant residence that a rich Roman gentleman would live in, whether he hailed from a province of the Empire or Italia itself. Since then yet another extensive wing had been added. It was far and away the largest and grandest villa for miles.

The drive had wide gardens on either side as far as the eye could see. There were no flowers at this season, but the winter dullness was relieved by some fine trees and statues. The white-washed stone of the house walls stood out sharply against the blue sky, and in front of the main door was a large gravelled circle where vehicles could turn. Titch pulled our carriage up smartly and placed a set of steps for me and Albia. As we descended, a servant opened the house door and invited us to step inside while he fetched his master.

The hall had been beautifully decorated. The mosaic floor was covered with thick red-patterned wool rugs, and there were dozens of torches in wall-brackets, giving out a rich golden light. The holly and laurel boughs were even bigger and more spec-tacular than ours, and the ornamental fountain, though it wasn't flowing, had green garlands all around its marble basin. It looked festive and welcoming, and must be Clarilla's work. Clarus had been a widower for many years, and his large, impressive home had lacked a woman's touch until a year ago, when his sister had come to live with him after her husband died. She'd added just the right amount of warmth to the richness and luxury.

Clarus came bustling through to greet us, and his beaming smile was infectious. Either he was a very good actor, or he was managing Sempronia's visit with less trouble than I'd expected. "Aurelia, Albia—welcome, welcome. Come through into the large sitting-room. Clarilla is there, with Lady Sempronia and our other guests. Albia, I'm so very glad you persuaded your fiancé to join us today. This is a time for families to be together, isn't it?"

"It is," I agreed. "And I wish my brother could be here too. He asked me to apologise to you. He isn't able to get home for the holiday, as we'd all hoped."

Clarus nodded gravely. "I heard he was having a somewhat— ah—difficult time just now. But I'm sure it will all come right in the end. Whatever people are saying, I am positive your brother would never do anything dishonourable."

"Thank you, Clarus. It's at times like this that you realise who your true friends are." I resisted the temptation to ask what exactly people were saying. I could imagine well enough, and this wasn't the time or place. Lucius had warned us that rumours of his disgrace would be widespread, and I supposed that was good, if it was what he wanted.

We followed our host down the passage to a spacious sitting-room, which faced south-west so the last of the sunlight streamed in through the windows. Here too the greenery had been very well displayed, and there were wall-lamps and candles enough to make sure the big room would be as bright as noonday when darkness came. I was pleased to see there were at least twenty people here, including several of the leading lights of Oak Bridges as well as Sempronia's party. So the guests had already separated into small groups, and we could circulate among our friends and not have too much to do with Sempronia or Diogenes. After my brief career as a hostage, the less conversation I had with them the better.

Clarilla was sitting on a couch talking to Fabia, but got up at once as we came in. Not for the first time, I was struck by how like her brother she looked, only a few years younger. They were both tall and stately in build, fair-skinned and fair-haired, with the instinctive air of authority that the old native aristocrats still have. She hadn't acquired Clarus' pomposity though.

"How good to see you both!" She spread her arms wide in greeting. "It's ages since you were here, but I know how busy you are. Aurelia, I heard about your adventures yesterday. I hope you're none the worse?"

"I'm fine, thank you. Just in the mood for a party. You've got the house looking marvellous! I thought our decorations were good, till I saw yours."

"I love your new hairstyle," Albia said. "With those ivory combs, and the curls, it really suits you."

Clarilla's smile was mischievous, and she dropped her voice to a stage whisper. "My cousin Melina lent me her hairdresser. She's just back from visiting Italia, you know, so her girl is up to date with all the latest fashions. I promised I wouldn't copy Melina's style too closely, and in return she promised she wouldn't lend the girl to anyone else till after Saturnalia."

I noticed Albia glancing round scanning the faces, and Clarilla saw it too. "You're looking for Candidus, I expect. He's with his father. Plautius seems a good deal better, and he promises to come to the banquet tonight, at least for a while." Again she lowered her voice. "I hope it all works out for you, Albia. You and Candidus are made for each other."

Albia held out her left hand, and Clarilla smiled broadly. "Good for you. We've been doing our best to tell the visitors what a wonderful daughter-in-law you would make."

"Aurelia Marcella!" That was Sempronia's unmistakeable gravelly growl. Reluctantly I walked over to where she sat on a couch next to Horatius.

"Good afternoon, my lady," I said formally.

"I want a word with you," she began, and then paused, looking at me coldly.

I waited. Whichever word she wanted, I didn't expect to like it.

"I heard what happened to you yesterday. *Most* unpleasant."

"Most."

"And I...." Again she hesitated.

"Oh do get on with it, Sempronia," Horatius put in. "The poor girl hasn't even got a drink of wine yet. Don't keep her standing about all afternoon."

"Yes." She cleared her throat. "It seems I owe you an apology. For the way Diogenes allowed you to become involved as a hostage. He went well beyond his instructions. It should never have happened."

"Allowed" was good, I thought, but I let it go. "Thank you, Lady Sempronia. I accept your apology. It was a bad experience, not only the actual imprisonment, but feeling I had been betrayed by someone I was trying to help. But I'm quite over it now." I decided to chance a shot in the dark. "Will Margarita and Gaius be released soon?"

She sighed deeply and shook her head. "We are still negotiating. The criminals seem disposed not to release them, but sell them for money themselves. Very upsetting, not to say inconvenient. Once again, Diogenes acted on his own, without authority. Of course, we shall do our best."

You disgusting hypocrite, I thought, but I merely said, "We shall hope for good news," and turned away to beckon one of the wine slaves.

The wine was excellent—no surprise there, it had been supplied by us, and I always made sure that Silvanius got the very best. The beautiful wine-glasses were new, and I guessed were another of Clarilla's innovations. Drinking-glasses were rare and precious, two qualities which made them very desirable for an ambitious Chief Councillor.

I went and chatted to several of our friends, complimenting Melina on her hairdresser, enquiring how Saturninus was coping with his new baby, listening to Tullius expounding on the trials and tribulations of a farmer's life. I noticed Quintus trying to catch my eye, and ignored him. Clarilla must have spotted this too, because she came up to me and said quietly, under all the noisy chatter, "Aurelia, tell me to mind my own business, but have you and Quintus Antonius fallen out?"

"Yes."

"I'm sorry to hear that. I'd arranged for you to share a couch with him at the banquet."

"Ah. Is it at all possible to alter the seating plan?"

"That's why I'm mentioning it now. Quintus took me on one side this afternoon and asked me, as a great favour, not to seat you two next to each other. So I haven't. You're sharing with Horatius."

"Thanks, Clarilla. Your party's going so well. I don't want our silly row to spoil anything."

As I finished chatting to Clarilla, I saw Albia and Candidus disappearing into the hallway. Evidently Candidus' meeting had finished, for good or ill. Diogenes entered the room and went to Sempronia's couch, bowing apologetically and saying a few quiet words in her ear. She nodded and waved him away. He started to come towards me, limping a little. I hoped that was Timaeus' doing, but I wasn't going to risk having to chat to him, so I strolled over to the window and gazed out at the garden, tinged red now by a beautiful sunset.

All at once Quintus was beside me. He said softly, "Aurelia, can we call a truce for tonight? I need your help."

"What's happened?"

"Plautius has received a death threat."

"When? How?"

"I'll explain somewhere private."

"All right. The truce isn't public, I assume?"

He smiled, looking out at the sunset so that only I could see his face. "Certainly not. Public hostilities will have to continue for a while longer."

I smiled back. "So that you can sit next to Fabia tonight?"

His eyes were full of mischief. "Of course." Then he became serious again. "There's an empty room along the corridor to the right, a small sitting-room. I'll wait there for you."

He walked leisurely out of the room, and I flounced across the floor a few paces, exclaiming, "The cheek of that man!" to nobody in particular. Then I wandered out into the passage and found the small sitting-room. It had decorations, and lamps lighted, and even a jug of wine and a tray of glasses on a small table. And it had Quintus. I closed the door and sat down beside him on a reading-couch.

"You look wonderful," he murmured. "Let's skip the banquet and just stay here all evening."

He was looking pretty good himself. I smiled at him for a couple of heartbeats, then I shook my head. "Fabia would miss you dreadfully."

"Who cares? Aurelia, I'm so sorry...."

"No, don't say any more. I'll help you. I don't know what you're up to, and I don't need to, so let's stick to the point. This threat to Plautius. When and how did he receive it?"

"A note was pushed under his door this afternoon." He produced a small piece of papyrus from his belt-pouch.

I read its brief message.

EAT, DRINK, AND BE MERRY, FOR TONIGHT YOU DIE.

"How has Plautius taken it?"

"He's still insisting on coming to the banquet. But he's worried, naturally enough, with all the gossip and bad feeling about the hostages."

"I can't believe he authorised the Weasel to give away Margarita and Gaius. I think Diogenes forged some sort of message, knowing it was what Sempronia wanted."

"Oh yes, he authorised it. I asked him, because it may be relevant to the death threat. I don't doubt that Sempronia encouraged him, but the paper that Diogenes showed to Otus was genuine."

"How *could* he!"

"As I said the other night, he's a lot tougher than he looks."

"And he thinks this latest threat comes from someone who is angry with him for not getting Margarita and Gaius released?"

"He does, but I'm not sure I agree. He told me he's been worried about his safety ever since he left Londinium, and someone did try to kill him while he was with you at the mansio. Didn't he give you any idea who he's afraid of?"

"None. When I pressed him, he pretended to go all vague on me and said he was just an old man letting his imagination run away with him. I didn't believe it though. He's as sharp as a spear, despite his physical weakness."

Quintus sighed. "Then let's assume the worst possible case: an attempt on his life will be made sometime during the banquet. Which, being a special celebration, is likely to go on for hours."

"Hours and hours, yes."

"Plautius may not stay for the whole evening, but he's determined to attend for as long as his strength holds out. After that, once he's in his room, it will be easier to guard him. Our main problem is during the party itself, when there'll be all sorts of people milling about—dozens of table slaves, and the guests as well. So we must be vigilant the whole time, ready for anything."

"Who else knows?"

"Horatius—he was there when the note came. Timaeus—Plautius wants him to be the only one who serves him with food and wine. And maybe some of the slaves overheard, in which case everyone else too."

"We're assuming the murderer will use poison, are we?"

"It's the most likely weapon, at a banquet."

"But supposing the killer is Timaeus himself? He was angry enough to beat up the Weasel."

"I don't think so. When the food comes to Plautius' table, Timaeus has offered to sample everything first, before Plautius eats it."

"Gods, that's what I call devotion to duty! How about guarding the dishes while they're in the kitchen? That's the most likely place for someone to try to interfere with the food."

"Timaeus will choose what's to be served to Plautius in the kitchen. Until it goes out to the table, the head bodyguard, Hector, will stand over it all the time."

"You seem to have covered everything. And you've warned Clarus, presumably?"

"Yes. Plautius doesn't want anyone else told about it, he says he doesn't want to worry the family. But I think I'm going to tell Sempronia at least, whatever he says. She has a right to know." He stood up and crossed to the door. "I'll go and find her now, before...."

"*There* you are, Relia!" Albia burst into the room, looking flushed and agitated, and almost knocking Quintus over. "I've been hunting everywhere for you. Oh, hello, Quintus," she added distractedly. "You may as well hear this too. We're going home. Candidus has seen his father, and they've had a huge row. I knew they would. Plautius is still refusing his consent for us to marry, and still threatening to disinherit him. It's all Sempronia's doing, I know that, but he could say no if he wanted to. I'm so angry, I could murder the pair of them! How dare they meddle in our lives like this? How *dare* they?"

"Oh, Albia, I'm so sorry," I said. "But it's only what you expected."

"I was still hoping against hope. But it's too late for that now. We don't want to stay under the same roof with them, so we'll go back to Candidus' Oak Bridges place tonight. Tomorrow he's taking me with him to his new house in Eburacum. If you need me, that's where I'll be."

I was alarmed. "Now wait awhile, Albia, and calm down. This isn't the best way to make important decisions...."

"It's the *only* way! Don't try to stop us, Relia, we know what we're doing. If we can't have a proper wedding, then there's nothing to stop us living together straight away. And if Candidus' parents don't like it, they can lump it, or they can drop down dead for all I care!" She left, slamming the door with a bang that rattled the glasses on the table.

Quintus said, "I'd offer to go after them, try and persuade them not to leave. But this Plautius business means I've got to stay here."

"Thank you, but there's no point talking to them till they've cooled down a bit. They've made up their minds, and if they want to gallop off into the night, there isn't anything we can do."

"I suppose not." He sat down again. "Poor Fabia. This will be hard on her."

"Fabia? Oh, I'm sure you'll be able to console her."

"Mi-aouw! What's the unlucky girl ever done to you?"

"Nothing at all. She's just not the type to be my bosom friend. Fortunately she seems to have found a friend in you."

"I like her well enough. But mostly I feel sorry for her."

"Oh yes, and I'm the Queen of Brigantia! Don't forget, I saw you together that first day at the Oak Tree, and I'd say you were being more than merely sympathetic." The jealous words were out before I could prevent them. I realised I'd shattered the friendly working atmosphere between us, but I didn't care.

"Aurelia, don't be such a bitch. It's not like you."

His sharpness stung me. "I'm sorry? I find a man I—I used to regard as a friend, showing off to a stunning-looking girl by treating me like a servant, and you're surprised that it brings out the worst in me?"

"It's that poor girl," he said deliberately, "who's been badly treated. She's been ordered to marry someone who doesn't want her...."

"We all know arranged marriages are normal for senators' children. They're brought up to accept it."

"Oh, she accepts the marriage. In fact she wants it. She loves Candidus, and has done since they were children together."

"What? But I thought she hardly knew him."

"They know each other well. They were childhood sweethearts, apparently, and everyone took it for granted they'd marry, until Candidus grew out of childhood and wanted a different life. I'm not blaming him, these things happen. So now Fabia's been ordered to come to Brigantia to persuade him to go back south with her. Her father and Plautius have even signed a marriage contract, and Plautius and Sempronia say they intend to drag their son home again and proclaim that he and Fabia are married."

"They'll never succeed."

"Let me finish. What does Fabia find when she gets here? The groom completely refuses to have anything to do with her. It's not just that he doesn't care for her. He cares so much for Albia that he's prepared to be cut off from his family rather than lose her. How do you think that makes Fabia feel? How would you feel in her place? Humiliated? Miserable? Friendless?"

"She doesn't look humiliated or miserable, and certainly not friendless."

"Of course she doesn't. I repeat, how would you feel? The man you love rejects you and goes off to live his own life with another woman. Would you crumple up like a broken doll and let everyone see how hurt you are? I don't think so! And neither will Fabia. It doesn't mean she isn't hurting."

"I hadn't looked at it like that."

"No. So if she indulges in a bit of harmless flirting, what do you want me to do? Let her know how little I care about her, and humiliate her still more?"

"I suppose not." I wanted desperately to believe him, to accept that he could be kind to an unhappy girl without being in love with her.

The door opened slowly to admit Clarus' elegant Greek major-domo. "Sir, Madam, dinner is being served in the new dining-room. Would you care to come through and be seated?"

"Of course," we both said, in our best party manner.

The new dining-room was enormous, and set in its own wing of the villa. As we began to walk down what seemed like half a mile of corridor, I realised I was dreading the dinner now. This latest threat to Plautius had changed everything. I even found I was taking deep breaths, like someone preparing to dive into a cold river, and illogically, I wished that after all I'd be sharing a couch with Quintus.

I said softly, "May the gods protect us." Then I strolled into the grand banquet as if I hadn't a worry in the world.

Chapter XXI

The dining-room looked magnificent. There were green branches everywhere, and even pink roses, which I discovered later were made of silk, so realistic you wanted to pick them. The air was heavy with rose scent, and alive with music. The dining-couches, placed all round the edges of the room, were draped with embroidered linen, and the small tables in front of them were set with silver-handled knives and spoons, and beautiful drinking-glasses. A huge table waited in the centre for the first course to arrive. It was all as bright as day, thanks to dozens of bronze lamp-standards festooned with small hanging lights.

A slave showed me to my place. It wasn't at the very top of the room, but quite respectably close. Sempronia was sharing with Clarus and Priscus, while Clarilla sat with Quintus and Fabia. Plautius was there, reclining on a smaller couch on his own, with Timaeus seated nearby on a stool. I was in the middle section of the room with the dozen or so local guests—senior town councillors and their ladies—and at the far end sat several favoured freedmen, mostly Clarus' clients. Where Candidus and Albia would have been placed I couldn't tell. The furniture had been tactfully reorganised.

A couple of dozen pretty boys and girls carried in the appetisers, and delicious food aromas competed with the rose scent. But before they served us at our tables, there was a charming bit of festive play-acting, a typical example of how Clarus managed to honour the old Roman traditions while not letting them get in the way of his modern daily life. At a truly traditional Saturnalia dinner, the slaves should have been seated while their masters and mistresses waited on them. This wouldn't have gone down at all well with important guests, and Clarus had arrived at a compromise which kept everyone happy. From the smooth way it was managed, it probably happened every year. Of course, being Clarus, he had to make a speech.

"Honoured guests! I'd like to welcome you all to my humble abode. At this season of convivial joy, we must not forget the old customs which have made Rome great. I shall have the pleasure of waiting on my servant here, my major-domo. Please come and be seated, Dimitrius." He stood up and beckoned, and the man approached with a gravity and dignity that would have made a high priest envious.

"Thank you, my lord." He sat carefully on Clarus' own couch, but didn't attempt to recline full-length like the rest of us. Sempronia, who was in the place of honour to the right of the host, looked on stonily as Clarus poured wine into a glass and offered it to his slave. Dimitrius drank the whole of it and held it out for a refill, which Clarus poured, smiling. "Thank you," he said. "An excellent wine." He looked round the guests and raised his glass. "May I propose a toast—to a happy and peaceful Saturnalia." We all drank, then he rose and slipped back into his major-domo role, while Clarus resumed his position on the couch. It was very well done.

I was sharing with Horatius and Gemellus, one of our local Roman landowners. They were both good company, and when I told Horatius how Gemellus was winning an impressive reputation as an orator in court cases in Eburacum, the two of them became instant friends. Horatius wasn't aware how easy it is to win an impressive reputation as an orator in a small place like Eburacum.

The food was wonderful. A touch showy, of course, but I can put up with that, as long as it's also mouth-wateringly delicious. First there were oysters and snails, quails' eggs and crabs, dormice, and lettuce—how had his gardeners managed lettuce in mid-winter?—all accompanied by fresh bread and warm wine. Then for the main course, four slaves carried in a whole roast sow. More servants brought smaller trays of roast piglets, which they arranged round the sow, and platters decorated like birds' nests, containing chickens, ducks, geese, and doves. All this was set out on the central table in a wonderful display, before the carvers began to cut up and distribute the meat. I lost count of the different kinds of vegetables, and as for the choice of wines—but this isn't the place for a complete menu. The sweet course is the only one that needs a detailed description.

As I ate and chatted to my two companions, I glanced around often, as if taking in the glittering scene, but in reality watching Plautius. He looked better than at any time since we'd first met, and was eating solid food, though sparingly. If you observed closely, you saw that he only ate from dishes that Timaeus fetched and sampled, but it was discreetly done. Timaeus was wearing a white tunic, like the table slaves. So was Quintus' man Rufus, who was hurrying about among the tables, doing quite a credit-able job as a waiter, and presumably keeping both eyes open for anything suspicious.

There was a longish pause between the appetisers and the main course. Some of the guests, like Gemellus, got up to walk about the room and chat to friends, but Horatius and I stayed put and watched the entertainment. Three bronze-skinned African girls, supple as snakes, bent their bodies into impossible shapes and did complicated acrobatic dances. They were accompanied by a girl drummer wearing nothing but a short leopard-skin kilt, and making enough noise to let me snatch a few private words with Horatius.

"You heard that Lord Plautius received an unusual message earlier today?"

He nodded. "A bit worrying, after we thought all that assas-sination business was finished with. What do you make of it?"

"I don't know. All we can do is be on the alert."

"He's safe enough with all these people around him, isn't he? It's good to see him here." He signalled to the wine slave to refill his glass. "Delicious, this white wine. Must be from Italia somewhere."

"Yes, from near Neapolis." I decided to venture a question that might sound rude if I asked Sempronia or Plautius directly. "Well, now that Decimus is found, I presume you'll all be leaving to go home soon?"

"Don't ask me, m'dear. I'll be the last person to be told!" He looked across at Sempronia, who was eating with apparent enjoyment, and smiling as she talked with Clarus. "At least she's in a better mood tonight. She's done nothing but moan all day about how her slaves are all useless compared with Margarita. She misses her more than she expected."

Serves her right, I wanted to remark, but said instead, "I saw Albia just briefly before she left. She said Decimus and his father had an argument."

He gave a snorting laugh and took a long sip of wine. "*Argument!* That's a good one! Full-scale battle, I'd call it. Old Gnaeus doesn't often lose his temper, but by the gods, he did this time. I think he genuinely hoped he could persuade Decimus to give up this marriage. I could have told him the boy has made his mind up and won't budge. He finished by storming out and yelling, 'Goodbye, Father. I hope I never see you again. Remember, men are only mortal, but love goes on for ever!'"

Gemellus came back to his place just then. "It's a good thing Silvanius serves a hearty first course," he remarked. "This is likely to be a long interval. Apparently it's chaos in the kitchen."

Horatius shrugged. "It's bound to happen at Saturnalia. The slaves are having high jinks, are they?"

"Yes. Only the usual sort of foolery, as far as I can make out. One of the junior cooks has been elected King of the Kitchen for the night, got himself drunk on the cooking wine, and started ordering everyone about. Most of them have had a few drinks more than they ought, seemingly. The chef's having a tantrum and threatening to walk out."

"I wish I'd a gold piece for every tantrum our cook has thrown!" I said, wondering what my own slaves were up to at the Oak Tree. "But how did you discover all this, Gemellus? Everything here looks so calm and efficient."

"I heard Dimitrius apologising to Clarilla and Clarus. And I heard Clarus say that if anything goes wrong, Dimitrius will be in for a flogging."

The second course, when it finally came, was worth the wait. If Gemellus hadn't told us that the kitchen was in uproar, we wouldn't have guessed. Perhaps some of the table slaves looked a little red in the face, and there was one small accident when a girl knocked over somebody's glass, but nothing that doesn't happen sometime at any party in the Empire. It was a triumph. Everyone sent compliments to the chef, and Clarus and Clarilla smiled and smiled, supremely happy.

Before the sweet course, there was a musical recital. A handsome eunuch with a clear, sweet voice sang love poetry which he accompanied on a lyre, and then two girls played flutes while two boys performed sinuous dances. Once again we had time to stretch our legs, and nearly everyone got up to stroll around, except Plautius and Sempronia, and the host and hostess. Several people disappeared briefly, presumably to relieve themselves, and the rest of us ambled about the room chatting to our friends. I even greeted Fabia as I passed her couch, and she replied with a sweet smile. Quintus smiled too. I approached Lord Plautius— slowly, in case he wasn't wanting company—but he beckoned me closer. He looked well, if a little tired.

"Aurelia Marcella, thank you for arranging for my son to come here this afternoon. I'm sorry to say we couldn't agree, but I was glad of the chance to talk to him. I wanted to give him a fair hearing."

"I'm pleased if I was able to help. But you know, I'm sure, that he came back to the Oak Tree of his own free will, when he heard that Priscus and the others had been kidnapped. I don't want to take the credit which should belong to him and his family loyalty."

"Yes, so I understand." He sighed. "I still haven't completely decided what to do. Disinheriting my son is a very big step. Yet it's what his mother wants. Well, we shall see." He cleared his throat, indicating that the topic was closed. "A dreadful business, this kidnapping of innocent people. And I'm sorry that you were compelled to be involved in it."

Gods, two apologies in one evening! Was he merely being polite, or was he feeling guilty about the instructions he'd given his messenger?

"I was lucky to escape with very little harm done. It's a pity your trip to Brigantia has been spoilt by so much violence. You'll be glad to get home, I daresay."

He smiled. "I can't deny it. We'll be leaving tomorrow, if the weather permits. Silvanius' sister is lending us her house in Eburacum for the first stage of our journey."

There was no time for more. The flute-players brought their final piece to a triumphant conclusion, and the applause warned me I should return to my couch.

The slaves began to bring in the final course, a large and mouth-watering selection, mostly sweet. There were rich custards in individual bowls, and fruits to go with them, peaches and cherries in wine. Hazelnuts and walnuts, ready shelled, were brought round on silver trays, and I counted nine kinds of cheese, offered with fresh warm bread. I don't know who had enough appetite left to do justice to those, but I regretfully realised that I hadn't. However I couldn't resist a few of the special almond-paste treats that the chef was famous for. They were shaped and coloured like miniature fruits—apples, pears, and peaches, and even, as a comic alternative, carrots and cabbages.

Last and sweetest of all, there were dates stuffed with almond paste, each one topped with a sliver of almond. Horatius' eyes lit up when he saw these, and he told the boy to put half a dozen onto his plate. "I adore them," he explained with his mouth full. "So do Sempronia and Plautius. I think a sweet tooth runs in our family. Look," he dropped his voice, "she's getting her own special supply of them. So's Gnaeus. You'll see, I won't be the only one making a pig of myself."

He was right. Diogenes had just brought in two oval silver dishes of the dates, and as soon as he placed one on Sempronia's table, she began happily cramming them into her mouth. Greedy old sow, I hoped they'd give her a belly-ache later. Diogenes took the second dish to Plautius, who looked at it doubtfully. Sempronia leaned across from her couch and smiled, urging her husband to try them. I noticed Plautius' dates were slightly different in their decoration from Sempronia's, as if they'd been prepared specially for the old man.

Diogenes offered Plautius the dish, and the old man glanced at Timaeus. Gods, I thought, he's certainly taking no chances about his food. Timaeus took a date, ate it, and smiled. This satisfied Plautius, and he ate three of the sweets in succession before waving the dish away. There was still a half-eaten custard on his table, but he lay back, wanting a rest now, and settled himself comfortably for an after-dinner snooze.

I wished I had the nerve to do the same. I knew that the next event of the evening would be a speech by our host. Clarus, despite his Roman education, had never managed to be more than a moderate public speaker. He had a good voice which he projected well, and his words were fluent, but his turn of phrase was unimaginative, ranging from slightly pompous to very *very* pompous. Well, it was a small price to pay for a superb meal. I picked up my glass and gazed round at the other guests.

People's attentiveness for the next quarter-hour was in inverse ratio to their status. The table slaves were fully alert, making sure everyone had enough wine and food, and in between whiles listening carefully to their master's speech. The freedmen at the far end of the room were wide awake, laughing at the jokes (I mean joke—there was only one, and it wasn't very funny) and applauding whenever it seemed appropriate. The guests of medium importance, like Horatius and Gemellus, listened politely without nodding off or yawning. The same went for Priscus and Fabia. But Plautius lay dozing, and very soon

Sempronia was sound asleep and snoring. The exceptions were Clarilla, who smiled encouragingly, and Quintus, who looked ready for anything, despite a casual pose. And I tried to be ready for anything too.

At long last Clarus drew to a close, and was rewarded with loud clapping. Well, it was his party. Now it was time for the final toast. Priscus glanced at his father, realised he was asleep, and rose to propose it himself. "My friends, I know you'll all agree this has been a wonderful occasion, a most generous and delightful Saturnalia party. I thank our host and hostess on behalf of everyone. Please join me in drinking their good health. Hail, Silvanius and Clarilla!"

We drank the toast, and everyone tactfully refrained from noticing that Plautius and Sempronia weren't joining in. Clarus and his sister rose, and she announced that there would be more wine, food, and entertainment in the sitting-room, and led the way out. The party began to break up as diners left their tables and moved slowly towards the wide double doors. Now, I thought, might be a dangerous time for Plautius, with everyone milling about in disorganised groups. I got up and began to make my way steadily through the press of people towards his couch, where Timaeus was bending over him, talking gently. He'd rolled over onto his stomach, and the physician reached out to turn him onto his side. At the neighbouring couch Priscus crouched down beside Sempronia, gently shaking her and murmuring "Wake up, Mother."

Then Timaeus snatched away his hand and jerked upright, giving a small shrill cry. He stood up, and said distinctly, "Help, somebody, please. My lord is ill!" He seized Plautius' left wrist in his fingers, for all the world as if he was feeling for a pulse.

I moved fast, and so did Quintus, and we reached Plautius at the same time. Quintus felt for a pulse at his neck, and I turned his head to see his face. It was a ghastly greyish-blue colour, and there were flecks of foam around his mouth.

Quintus muttered, "I can't find a pulse. Can you, Timaeus?"

"No, I can't. But he's only asleep, surely. Just taking a nap after a good meal...." He began shaking Plautius, gently at first and then more roughly, murmuring, "My lord, wake up. Please, my lord!" But there was no reaction from the still figure.

The room was still half full, but had gone unnaturally quiet. Everyone heard Quintus' next words. "I'm sorry. I'm afraid he's dead."

Chapter XXII

I don't know how everyone stayed so calm. Well, yes, I do: the famous Roman virtue of self-discipline came into its own. At times of crisis you realise how Romans have come to be masters of the world.

Silvanius and his major-domo managed to clear the remaining diners from the room with speed and courtesy but no panic, which was a minor triumph in itself. Sempronia awoke, and Quintus went to her and told her quietly what had happened. She sat on her couch bolt upright, as white as marble, but didn't speak or cry. Priscus seated himself beside her, holding one of her hands, and began to weep silently.

Fabia stared blankly and then began to tremble, and sat down on the nearest couch. Horatius went to stand next to her, still clutching his glass of wine. Timaeus was crying, and Diogenes began to wail loudly, and tore his tunic in the ritual gesture of grief. But his devotion to Plautius had been mainly for show, so perhaps this display was too. Clarus stood like a statue, his face a picture of astonishment, soon changing to alarm. Clarilla had tears in her eyes, but she controlled them with an effort and said she would go to the sitting-room to see to the other guests.

I stayed slightly apart from the rest, keeping silent because I didn't know what to say, and feeling like an intruder in the family's private grief. I looked round for Quintus and saw him talking urgently to Rufus, who nodded twice and then hurried from the room. To my relief Quintus came to stand beside me, but his first words were gloomy. "I've failed him, Aurelia. I promised I would protect him, and I haven't."

I briefly touched his hand. "You did all you could. And it may be his illness that killed him. We don't know for certain yet."

"I do," he muttered. "But you're right, we must go through the formalities." He turned to Clarus. "Clarus, you're the senior magistrate in this area, and as you know, I carry the Governor's authority to investigate anything unusual, such as a sudden death. I'll help you in any way I can. Have I your permission to examine Plautius and establish how he died?"

Clarus nodded. "By all means, Antonius. But surely it was his illness? He's been unwell ever since before he left Londinium to come north. That's what has caused this tragedy, surely…." He trailed off, glancing quickly at Sempronia.

"It's our duty to be certain," Quintus answered. "Plautius was an important man, of senatorial rank, and the Governor will want to be assured that we checked everything properly. Now, I'd like to spare the ladies as much distress as I can. Clarus, perhaps you'd escort her ladyship and Fabia to one of your sitting-rooms, and find a maid to sit with them?"

"Willingly, yes. My lady—Miss Fabia—I think we should leave Antonius and Timaeus to do what must be done. Will you come with me please?"

They went quite meekly, glad to have someone to tell them what to do. Diogenes sniffed noisily. "I'll go with my lady, in case I can be of service. There's nothing I can do for my master now." He followed them out.

"Spare the ladies?" I mouthed at Quintus, and then asked aloud, "Shall I go too?"

"No, stay, please, Aurelia. I had to get rid of her somehow, didn't I?" he added in an undertone.

I nodded. The last thing we wanted was Sempronia watching our every move.

We sat down, and there was a depressed silence until Clarus returned. "Clarilla will look after them. All our other guests have left, or are leaving now. The snow has started again, so they were anxious not to delay."

"I think that's for the best. None of them were involved in this sad business," Quintus said.

Horatius stirred himself and asked, "What's in your mind, Antonius? You're wondering about the note Plautius received today?"

"I think it must have a bearing," he answered.

"What note?" Priscus asked sharply. "I've heard nothing about any note."

Without a word, Quintus produced the papyrus he'd shown me earlier. Priscus read it and burst out, "Why wasn't I told about this? Why was he allowed to attend the banquet, with so many people about, when he was in such danger?"

"He wanted to attend," Quintus said gently. "And he didn't want his family worried, as he thought, unnecessarily, so he only told Timaeus, Horatius, and me. Now, first things first. Was this a natural death, caused by his illness? Timaeus, come over here please."

We all moved to the couch and looked down on the dead man.

Quintus asked the physician, "What was the nature of his illness?"

"He had a diseased heart, and congestion of the lungs."

I pointed to the foam around his mouth. "Was that one of his usual symptoms, when he was ill?"

"No, it wasn't."

"And this bluish colour in his face?" Quintus asked.

Timaeus replied slowly, "Yes, I have seen something like that before, but not so extreme. He gets—he used to get bad chest pains and have trouble breathing. Sometimes he almost seemed to be choking, gasping for air, and then his face went greyish, perhaps with a tinge of blue. But not like this."

"In your opinion," Quintus asked, "has he died as a result of his illness?"

After a long pause, Timaeus answered, "No."

"Let's be absolutely clear," Quintus persisted. "It's your opinion that he did not die a natural death?"

"No, he did not."

A shiver went through us all. Before our eyes, on what should have been a happy, peaceful occasion, Plautius had been murdered.

"What exactly did he have to eat tonight?" I asked Timaeus.

"One step at a time," Quintus said. "I see where you're driving, Aurelia, but let's go carefully here. Timaeus, can you make a suggestion as to what caused his death?"

"Aurelia's right. It looks like poison. But the gods alone know how it was given. I was extremely careful. He ate a little of the meat that everyone else had—the pork, which we saw carved in front of us. The rest of his meal, a selection of appetisers and vegetables and sweets, I prepared with my own hands, and I tasted a sample of each one before I'd let him eat it."

"You got the food ready in the kitchen beforehand?" Priscus asked.

"Yes."

"Could someone have tampered with any of it while it was waiting in the kitchen?" Quintus suggested.

He shook his head firmly. "I left Hector guarding it."

"Ah, now we're getting to it," Horatius exclaimed. "The kitchen was quite disorganised tonight, with some sort of Saturnalia horse-play. Isn't that right, Chief Councillor?"

"Yes, just seasonal fun and games, you know," Clarus agreed. "I had to speak sternly to my major-domo to make sure things did not get out of hand."

"Well, Timaeus?" Quintus asked sternly, "Can you swear that nobody could have interfered with your master's food? Can you be sure that Hector wasn't careless, letting his attention wander when the others were running amok? You can't, can you?"

The physician had gone deathly pale and seemed unable to speak.

Priscus said, "Gods, I wish I'd known about the threatening note that Father received. I'd have taken better care of him!

Whoever actually committed this foul crime, I'm holding you responsible, Timaeus. You should have guarded him better."

Timaeus bowed his head. "Yes, my lord. I know I've failed him."

I thought this was unfair of Priscus. "I think Timaeus did everything he possibly could. Your father was well aware of the risks he faced. Whoever killed him was clever, and well-organised, and determined. This was his second attempt, remember, and he also killed Leander. I'm saying 'he', but there could perhaps be more than one person involved."

"You should rather say 'he or she'." We all turned to the door and saw Sempronia standing there. Her first reaction, weakness or shock or whatever it had been, was clearly over. She strode into the room, erect and angry, with Diogenes following at her heels.

"Mother," Priscus objected, "you shouldn't be here. Please wait with Fabia until we've finished."

"Nonsense, Aulus! Where else should I be? This is in effect a family council, and I have a right to be here." She walked over to her dining-couch and sat down. We all moved to stand in a group round her, like courtiers around a monarch.

"Now, you're discussing how my poor Gnaeus died, and from what I heard as I came in, you've concluded that his death wasn't a natural one. Is that correct?"

"I'm afraid so, Sempronia," Quintus said. "It seems he was poisoned sometime during the banquet."

"May the gods of the Underworld receive him kindly." Her composure almost slipped, but then she was in control again. "There's no doubt who's responsible. I assume you all agree. So what are you doing to arrest her?"

"Her?" Priscus echoed blankly.

Horatius said, "Who d'you mean, Sempronia? You know who's done this dreadful thing?"

"Isn't it obvious? It's that girl Albia." She turned on me. "Your sister!"

"*What?* Don't be ridiculous!" I took a step towards her, but Quintus put a hand on my arm, and I stopped and said more calmly, "Albia is no murderer. She couldn't, and she wouldn't, do something like this."

"Of course she wouldn't," Quintus put in. "I know you don't like her, Sempronia, but that doesn't make her a killer."

"You think not? Then allow me to show you how wrong you are. Albia has made up her mind to marry Decimus, regardless of where his duty lies, and against his family's wishes. She came to realise she couldn't do so while Plautius was head of the family and refused to give consent. So she decided that killing him was her only way of achieving what she wants. Well, she may think she's achieved it, but let me tell you here and now, I shall never accept a murderer as my son's wife."

This brought me up short. I'd been so preoccupied with how Plautius had died that I hadn't thought about the implications. Candidus was now the head of the Plautius family, with freedom to do as he liked, whatever his mother said, and she would certainly continue to say plenty. His father's death had released him to marry Albia. I knew my sister would never resort to killing. But Candidus—was it remotely possible that he'd been so enraged by his father's intransigence that he'd made up his mind to poison him?

No, it wasn't even remotely possible. But it wasn't surprising that the burden of suspicion was being thrown onto him and the woman he'd chosen. Everyone knew there had been violent disagreements, culminating in tonight's argument. What was it Horatius had told me? "He finished by storming out and yelling, 'Goodbye, Father. I hope I never see you again. Remember, men are only mortal, but love goes on for ever!'" How many other people had heard the words?

As if she read my thoughts, Sempronia said, "The girl might even have lured Decimus into helping her. He was always an impressionable boy. But she's the one who is truly guilty. She's the murderer. And I don't understand why you're all sitting around like a gaggle of old wives discussing the price of fish. Get after her! Find her! Bring her back here, and Decimus too, if you have to!"

Thank the gods, I thought, the old horror has just shown me the obvious way to prove Albia's innocence. "They left here just before the banquet began, didn't they? About—what, three hours ago?"

"Yes," she agreed. "So they can't be far away. If we get a party on the road now to pursue them…."

"Just hear me out, please. Supposing for the sake of argument that Albia was the kind of person to commit murder, she couldn't have poisoned Plautius at the banquet. *She wasn't here.*"

"Oh, that is irrelevant. She wouldn't necessarily do the killing with her own hands. In fact she almost certainly would use a servant. What slaves did you bring with you?"

"None."

"*None?* How extraordinary! But you must have had a carriage driver."

"Yes, and I sent him home again. He'll collect me at noon tomorrow."

"Then she used one of the Chief Councillor's slaves, or perhaps one of ours. She tried to murder Gnaeus at the mansio, and then she killed another of our men in a pathetic attempt to cover her tracks. You see? It all fits together."

"If you please, my lady," Diogenes spoke up, "I don't know what happened tonight, but I'm fairly sure that Margarita must have been involved with the earlier attempts to kill the master."

"*Margarita?*" we all exclaimed. I glanced quickly around. Everyone else looked as astonished as I was, even Sempronia.

The Weasel said, "I may be wrong of course. Perhaps I shouldn't say any more, now that Margarita is gone anyway."

"Stop rambling, Mustela," Sempronia barked, "and tell us what you're talking about."

"Yes, my lady. Young Gaius told me he'd seen a bloodstained cloak hidden away in the woods. A blue cloak, belonging to one of our slaves. He was reluctant to tell me, because he thought the owner would get into trouble for dirtying his uniform, and I didn't want to press him too hard. He's so easily frightened." I didn't like the gloating expression in those weasel eyes. "So I asked Margarita about it. She denied all knowledge of it, which made me suspicious. After all, if Gaius was speaking the truth, I can't believe he wouldn't tell his mother of something like that. More likely he was only giving me part of the story, and it was Margarita who hid the cloak in the first place."

I was both angry and alarmed. How had he managed to get that choice bit of information out of Gaius? Surely the boy wouldn't willingly have given away the secret, so what had Diogenes done, or threatened, to make him tell? Or maybe the Weasel knew about the cloak anyway, because he was the one wearing it when the bloodstains were made?

But Sempronia was convinced. "You think, Diogenes, that this blue cloak the child saw was worn by whoever tried to kill your master?"

He nodded. "It grieves me to say so, my lady, but yes, I do. And it was also worn by whoever killed the guard Leander. There was a good deal of blood, according to the child."

"What do you mean, whoever killed Leander?" she snapped. "Leander killed himself, and left a note confessing to attempted murder."

Diogenes shook his head. "With the greatest respect, my lady, I don't think he did. The note was a forgery."

"Forgery?" Sempronia pounced on the word like a cat on a rat.

"I only found out today," he said meekly, "and I haven't had time to tell your ladyship. Leander didn't know how to write."

"Indeed?" She sat thinking for a few heartbeats, and then turned to me. "If we needed additional proof of your sister's guilt, we have it. With or without help from Margarita, she committed two murders while at the mansio. She failed to kill Gnaeus then, so she made another attempt tonight. And perhaps she had assistance from you also. Well? What have you to say to that?"

"What I have to say to that isn't fit for polite company." I looked at the Weasel, determined to wipe that gloating smile from his face. "Diogenes, you seem to know a great deal. How did *you* come by the information about the bloodstained cloak?"

But Sempronia ignored my question. "Don't attempt to change the subject. There's no doubt in my mind that both you and your precious sister are murderers. Antonius, kindly arrest Aurelia now, and send men to find Albia and bring her here. What are you waiting for?"

"Arresting Aurelia would be a waste of time," Quintus countered. "Time which we should be spending apprehending the real murderer."

"So you consider," Sempronia demanded, "that Albia acted alone? Or even with help from Decimus?"

Quintus faced her calmly. "It has to be a possibility, I admit, but not a strong one, to my mind. Plautius told me he'd been worried about his personal safety for some time. *For some time,*" he repeated with emphasis. "I took that to mean, before you ever came to the Oak Tree."

"He told me the same," I put in. "On the first night that you stayed with us. And Albia proved to his satisfaction that she couldn't have killed either Idmon or Leander. If she'd killed Idmon, she'd have had traces of his blood on her person, and she had none. And on the evening Leander was killed, she and I were both under surveillance."

"By Margarita!" Diogenes crowed triumphantly, "who was in possession of a bloodstained blue cloak. I said she was involved, my lady! Perhaps she didn't wear the cloak herself, but she was helping Albia and Aurelia by hiding it."

I couldn't fault his reasoning, though it must have a flaw somewhere. Whatever the provocation, Albia wouldn't have killed anyone. I knew she wouldn't—but I also knew that was hardly a convincing argument.

Sempronia was smiling at the Weasel. "Good, Diogenes! That's well argued. Antonius, do you agree now that Albia has a case to answer?"

"Ye-es, I think she has," he said slowly. "And Decimus too. I'll bring them here for questioning tomorrow. It's snowing now, so we can't do anything tonight."

"But they could be miles away by tomorrow," she objected.

"I doubt that. The snow will stop them travelling far. I imagine they'll stay the night at Decimus' house, don't you think, Aurelia?"

"Albia told me that's what they were intending to do."

"Very well then. Now, Sempronia, you must put aside your personal prejudices, at least where Aurelia is concerned. I know her, and I personally vouch for her innocence. And her accuracy—she's given you a correct account of events. Plautius told me that he'd asked both her and Albia to investigate the murders. They have some useful experience in this sort of thing, so it wasn't an unreasonable idea."

He glanced at me, but I said nothing. *"Some useful experience"* indeed!

"When I arrived here," he went on, "Plautius asked me to help in the investigation myself, and I agreed. I said it was better nobody was told, so I could ask questions without arousing the killer's suspicion. I made a start, but what with the kidnapping, rescuing Aurelia and trying to find Margarita and Gaius, I regret I haven't had much time."

Sempronia considered, and at last said grudgingly, "Very well, Antonius. If you vouch for Aurelia, *your* word is good enough, of course." She looked at Priscus. "Isn't it, Aulus?"

"I suppose so. I mean, yes, I take your word about Aurelia. But Albia? My brother and Albia resented Father's attitude to them very much, you know. They could have been driven to violence."

"They could. But resenting isn't the same as killing." Quintus gave a profound sigh. "I'm a professional investigator, as you know. I'd like nothing better than to capture the murderer, present him or her to the Governor, and hear you all say, well done, Antonius, you haven't lost your touch when it comes to solving crimes. I'll try my best to do it. But it's not as simple as it looks, I'm convinced of that. There's a lot of work to be done before I can be sure. To begin with, I must question everybody."

"Everybody? You mean *all* of us?" Sempronia didn't like that.

"Everybody," he repeated firmly. "Starting with the obvious people, that is the servants who handled the food tonight. The kitchen staff, and the slaves who waited at table. Have I your permission, Clarus?"

"Certainly, Antonius. But you're not planning to torture them tonight, are you?" From his troubled expression, I guessed poor Clarus was wondering how he could protect his valuable chef.

"Torture's the only way to get admissible evidence out of slaves, legally speaking," Horatius put in.

"I know that, but I'll stick to straightforward questioning to begin with."

"If you seriously think any of the slaves are implicated," Sempronia said icily, "you have probably left it too late. Anyone with a guilty conscience has had ample time to make his escape from the house, snow or no snow."

"I've posted my man Rufus outside, with some of your body-guards," Quintus said. "No one will leave the house."

"That was well done," Clarus said, and even Sempronia looked impressed.

"One more thing," Quintus said. "I'd like Aurelia to help me in my investigations. She's worked as my assistant in the past, and an extra pair of hands will be useful now, in fact essential, if we're to make any real progress. I trust nobody objects to that?"

Nobody did, though one or two of them appeared less than ecstatic. I probably didn't look overjoyed myself. *She's worked as my assistant...an extra pair of hands...*oh, really? We'd been a partnership of equals, and I opened my mouth to tell him what I thought of his patronising, arrogant manner. Then it struck me that his public coldness towards me was to my advantage. They'd all seen how he treated me over the last few days, and nobody could possibly argue that he was defending me out of friendship, let alone affection.

Yet he *was* defending me, that was the crucial point, and I must give him all the help and information I could. To do that, I needed to get him alone. And that was exactly what he was suggesting. Gods, sometimes I'm so slow, I'd have trouble catching a tortoise.

"If you'll excuse us, we'd better begin straight away," Quintus said. "We've half a legion of slaves to interview. The quicker we start, the quicker we'll finish."

"I'll find you a room to use as an office," Clarus offered. We followed him out.

Chapter XXIII

"Before we talk to anyone, I'd like you to tell me as much as you can about the Plautius household." Quintus and I were sitting together in the small room that Clarus had lent us, and now that we were by ourselves, Quintus was as relaxed and friendly as in the old days.

"Of course. But I must ask you first, you don't believe Albia is involved in this, do you?"

"No, I don't, nor Candidus either. But you must see I can't refuse to investigate the possibility. And now there's this evidence from Diogenes about the blue cloak."

"I knew about the cloak. Titch's dog dug it up, and Gaius saw her with it. I was there."

"You *knew* about it?" He didn't hide his exasperation.

"Yes. Gaius agreed to keep it a secret, because he said whoever had got his cloak dirty would get into trouble. I don't like to think how the Weasel got the information out of him—scared the poor little brat somehow, I suppose."

"Why didn't you tell someone you'd found it? Me, for instance?"

"I didn't see any need to. I told Plautius at the time."

"Look, Aurelia." He reached out to take my hand. "Promise me there'll be no more secrets from now on. You and I have to combine our resources if we're going to get through this."

"I promise. No more secrets."

"Good." He let go my hand and sat back on his chair. "That's the first thing we need to be clear about. The second is: are we sure this murder tonight and the killings at the Oak Tree were all the work of the same person?"

"I'm certain of it. It's too far-fetched otherwise—I can't believe in two people in the household trying to murder the old man. Now if we were talking about Sempronia...but we're not."

Quintus rubbed his cheek thoughtfully. "I agree. And are we certain that the murderer *is* somebody in Plautius' household—either servant or relative?"

"Whoever planned the murders must be. But he or she could well have used a second person to carry them out. Tonight, for instance, if I'd wanted to poison someone's dinner, I'd have got one of the food servers or kitchen slaves to do it—as Sempronia suggested."

"Again I agree. Now, of the people in Plautius' entourage who might have murdered him, Timaeus had by far the greatest opportunity. He was with him most of the time, and tonight he was the one who chose and served his food."

"Perhaps. But I'm sure it wasn't Timaeus."

Quintus smiled wryly. "Why? Because of his bedside manner?"

"Why else?" I smiled back. "But I have got two other good reasons. First, if he'd wanted to kill Plautius, there were a hundred ways he could have done it discreetly and made it look like a natural death. Everyone knew how ill Plautius was, and nobody would have been very surprised if he'd died quietly in his sleep one night. Why take the risk of poisoning him in front of a roomful of people? And when they stayed at the Oak Tree, why cut his throat instead of slipping something into his food? Wait, that makes it three good reasons. Timaeus was one of the few people who knew Plautius wasn't sleeping in his own bed that night."

"Yes," Quintus said. "I'm with you so far. Your other reason?"

"The most likely cause of this murder, in my view, is the proposed alterations to Plautius' will. And Timaeus wasn't expecting any legacy at all."

"The will," Quintus repeated. "I wondered when we'd get to that."

"Several people had good reasons for wanting, or not wanting, the will to be changed. Timaeus told me he wasn't concerned, because he wouldn't get a bequest whatever happened. He joked about how people shouldn't make wills in favour of their doctors."

"Perhaps he was lying. If his lordship had promised him a bequest in a new will, Timaeus might have thought it wisest not to mention the fact. Do you think Timaeus is carrying a torch for Margarita? Could he have been so angry with Plautius for handing her over to the kidnappers that he decided the old man deserved to die?"

"It's not impossible, but I doubt if Margarita has given him any encouragement. She's keen on Priscus, she said so."

"We should regard him as a possibility."

"Fair enough. But if we're considering men who are keen on Margarita, we mustn't forget Horatius. He becomes her master under the existing will. I suppose that's one of the reasons he was glad that Plautius didn't want to make any major changes." I thought back to the previous evening's conversation round the bar-room fire. "Wait now, Priscus made some remark about Horatius possibly having his debts paid off. Does he owe much, I wonder?"

"Yes. The sort of sum the governor of a province might use to start a medium-sized war. From gambling at the races, mostly."

"Oh? I didn't know you moved in those circles."

"No, but Fabia does. She gave me some entertaining snippets of gossip while we were travelling north. Horatius owes so much money these days that he has trouble even getting credit with the tradesmen. He might have decided to cultivate a wealthy relative who's not long for this world."

"But surely then he'd have tried to include a bequest to himself in the will. And I was with Horatius for the whole banquet, don't forget. He was relaxed, happily half-drunk, and I'd swear he was as surprised by Plautius' death as I was. I don't believe he's a good enough actor to have behaved so calmly for a whole evening, if he'd organised a murder."

"Perhaps not." He gave me a half-smile. "Fabia is about the only member of the party who I'd say can't have anything whatever to do with Plautius' death. She wasn't even in Brigantia when the first two murders happened, and as for tonight, she wanted Plautius alive and well, to compel Candidus to marry her."

"Or perhaps she didn't."

"I'm sorry?"

"Maybe she doesn't want Candidus any more than he wants her. She's been pretending to love him, or she's stopped loving him because of the way he's behaved. Perhaps she killed Plautius because he was determined to force Candidus to marry her. She saw his death as her only way of escape."

"Rubbish! It wasn't any such thing. Candidus has made it clear he won't marry her under any circumstances. If she doesn't want the marriage either, all she has to do is sit tight. If she does want it, why murder the one man who might help her to achieve it?"

That was logical, and I managed to admit as much with reasonably good grace. "Then let's get back to the matter of Plautius' will. Who else had an interest in keeping it as it is, not making any changes?"

"Diogenes did. He gets his freedom now, doesn't he?"

"I'm afraid so." It was a depressing thought. "He's been odious enough as a slave. When he's free he'll be unbearable."

"He will. But wanting his freedom could give him a very strong reason for wishing Plautius dead. Nobody else had the power to free him while Plautius lived, and if Sempronia managed to get the will changed, he wouldn't be freed after Plautius died. It had to come through the existing will."

"He was an inveterate eavesdropper," I pointed out. "Suppose he overheard some snatch of conversation which made him think Plautius was going to add a codicil to disinherit Candidus, *and also* put in some of the changes Sempronia wanted? If he was afraid he could lose his chance of freedom forever, he might panic and decide to murder Plautius before the changes could be made. And he had plenty of opportunity to poison Plautius tonight. He was serving Sempronia at the next couch, and going in and out of the kitchen as he liked. He's a nasty piece of work. Unfortunately, the mere fact that I dislike him doesn't mean he's a murderer."

"It doesn't mean he isn't," Quintus answered grimly. "Now, can we work out how the poison was given to Plautius? To start with the obvious first, I think we can assume it was in food rather than wine or water."

I pictured the big dining-room in my mind. "The drinks were served from large jugs, taken round by the slaves from table to table and poured out as the diners wanted more. I don't see how just one person could have been given poisoned wine or water. We all drank the same."

"I suppose it could have been done using sleight-of-hand," he suggested. "You could slip a little powder or liquid into a glass, if you were clever enough."

"Not easily, with Timaeus keeping such a close watch. No, we can forget the drinks."

"By the same reasoning we can rule out all the various meats that were carved from large joints, and the big bowls of vegetables, and the cheeses. Too difficult to tamper with only one portion."

"Surely the poisoned food was part of the dessert course?" I said. "After all, the desserts were the last thing Plautius ate."

Quintus nodded. "And there were so many individual dishes, custards and pastries and sweets—those imitation-fruit things, and the dates. Somebody could have poisoned any of those small items, either in the kitchen or when they were on the central table, while the servers were hurrying round among the couches."

"Plautius ate half a custard. The remains of it were on his table. And Sempronia persuaded him to have some of those stuffed dates."

"So she did." Quintus' blue-purple eyes flashed. "Yes, so she did."

"Quintus, you're not seriously suggesting that *Sempronia* poisoned him?"

"We can't rule her out. She wouldn't be the first wife who murdered her husband to get her own way. She's strong-willed enough, and intelligent, and there wasn't much love between them. And if she wanted a willing helper, she could have called on the devoted Diogenes."

"But she had ample opportunity to do away with him quietly and make it look like an accident. Her precious nephew the Governor would have helped keep it quiet, to protect the grieving widow, that sort of thing. She'd have much more of a problem hushing up a poisoning at a grand banquet given by an important Roman citizen."

He smiled. "If people committing murders always chose the most rational course of action, an investigator's life would be very much easier."

"I think Priscus is at least as likely as Sempronia. He's another man who was angry over Margarita's betrayal. He loves her enough to want to live with her, and he told me he wants to adopt Gaius as his son."

"His *son!* Is he in fact the boy's father, then?"

"I don't know. But you can see how he loves Margarita, and she says she loves him too. When we were all at the Oak Bridges market, they were like a charming little family together."

"In the proposed new will, Margarita was to get her freedom," he mused.

"Yes. Provided she left Sempronia's service."

"So wouldn't Priscus want to keep Plautius alive till the new will was made, or the old one changed? As things are now, Margarita and Gaius are bequeathed to Horatius."

"If they're ever found."

That sad thought made us both pause for a while. Eventually Quintus said, "I think we've cleared the ground as far as we can for now. It's time to start interviewing the slaves."

We talked to more than forty slaves, but we got very little out of them. The kitchen contingent were all frightened, and either drunk, or sobering up at the prospect of being blamed for Plautius' death. The dining-room slaves were simply frightened.

The chef was a tall Athenian, with greying hair and a long nose, down which he looked in a manner at least as haughty as Sempronia's. He couldn't escape answering our questions, but he made it clear that he and his cooks were above suspicion, and he certainly wouldn't demean himself to volunteer any extra titbits of information. I suppose he was allowed to get away with this sort of insolence because he was supremely good at his job.

Yes, he said, he had prepared or supervised all the food. No, he hadn't poisoned any of it. No, he didn't know who had. Yes, his staff, though a pack of incompetent cretins, had performed well enough, and he trusted them all completely.

He added just one small point of interest, and then only because he could make it into a complaint. "The visitors' slaves were a nuisance, coming in and out of my kitchen all night. And one of them hung about the whole time, looking after the special diet for the sick old lord. They kept getting under our feet. I don't like strangers in the way when I'm working."

"Which slaves kept coming in and out?" Quintus asked.

"I don't know their names," the chef retorted. "There was the physician, and he was at least polite enough to ask my permission. But the others wandered around without a by-your-leave."

"Would you recognise them again?" I prompted.

"I doubt it. They all look alike in that ridiculous blue livery."

The assistant chef, Florus, was a welcome contrast, a round, jolly man, and disposed to be helpful. When we asked him to describe what went on during the banquet, he grinned. "Chef was going mad and throwing things, but he often does, when there's an important dinner. Dimitrius kept threatening all sorts if we made a cock-up, but he often does that too, and in the end Chef bawled him out and he left us alone. Big banquets are always chaos. We just get used to coping."

"What about the lad who was elected King of the Kitchen?" I asked. "Someone told us he was ordering everyone about. That must have made things even more chaotic."

He laughed. "Gito? No, it was all just harmless fun. The only orders he gave were that we should all eat and drink as much as we could. He had a bet with another boy that he could eat something from every single dish and drink at least a beaker of each wine, without being sick." He laughed again. "I don't know if he managed it. He passed out just after we'd finished clearing the desserts. He's under a table now, sleeping it off."

"We'll talk to him later," Quintus said. "Thanks for your help."

The interviews went on, and it felt as if we were trying to piece together a mosaic floor, where we had a lot of small tiles and only a hazy idea of the final picture they would make. The kitchen slaves could tell us fairly clearly who had prepared and cooked which foods, or assembled the dishes that didn't need cooking. They all confirmed that Timaeus had been adamant about preparing his master's food, and that Hector had remained on guard and hadn't allowed himself to be distracted. Well they would, wouldn't they? I'm sure they were all praying to their gods that we'd find the guilty person among the visitors' household, and quickly too, before anyone took the more drastic measure of torturing them for their evidence.

The boys and girls who'd waited on us in the dining-room seemed genuinely to have trouble recalling details of who had served the many different items. Each one knew which dishes he or she had taken to the big central table, but when we asked who had served a particular delicacy to a specific guest, we got mostly blank looks. None of the servers were assigned to wait on particular couches or tables, except that Timaeus served Plautius, and Diogenes looked after Sempronia. Otherwise the boys and girls simply took plates and dishes wherever they were needed or requested. They'd all had plenty of experience of large banquets, and they just got on with it.

Finally we decided we should go and inspect the kitchen complex and interview its temporary King. We found the place busy, as the lower-ranking slaves were still cleaning dishes and polishing silver. The chef was nowhere in sight, but his cheerful assistant greeted us with a smile.

"Have you come for a word with His Majesty? He's under there, taking his ease like the King of the Persians." He nodded towards a large table, which was piled high with mountains of left-over food. Gito, having sampled its contents, had crawled into the corner under it, and all we could see of him was his sandaled feet. "Here, I'll pull him out for you. Come on, Gito boy, you've got visitors. Somebody get a bowl over here, he'll probably want to throw up." He bent and hauled the slave out feet first.

Gito was perhaps eighteen, a handsome boy with glossy black hair and a full mouth. He was wearing a gaudy red cloak that looked like a piece of curtain, and on his head was an elaborate crown made out of an old bit of papyrus decorated with red and blue daubs of ink.

He didn't throw up. He didn't move at all. As we looked down on his bluish-grey face and staring eyes, we both went rigid with horror. He wasn't sleeping off his excesses now.

"Poor boy," I said, but my voice was drowned in a scream, as one of the girls dropped the bowl she was fetching him and ran to crouch by his head. She was a pretty blonde, one of the table slaves we'd already seen, but now her face was twisted with fear.

"Gito! Oh, no, no, my Gito!" She began to cry. "I said you shouldn't have had the extra dates. I told you you'd gone far enough! Who cares about the stupid bet, I said, you'll make yourself ill with all this nonsense."

"Extra dates?" Quintus asked sharply. "What extra dates?"

The girl was sobbing hysterically, so I turned to the assistant chef. "What's this about extra dates, Florus? Were those the dates with almond paste stuffing?"

"That's right. We got a good batch of them ready this afternoon, stuffed with paste and decorated with slivers of almond. Then wouldn't you know it, just before the main course, when everyone was flat out, an order came through from the old lady, saying they were one of her favourites, and one of her husband's favourites too, but he didn't like almond pieces, and would we do some more with cherry decorations for him. I suggested we just whip the almond slivers out of some of the ones we'd prepared and bung the cherries on instead, but Chef's such a perfectionist. He said no, if the lady had asked specially, we'd best make some more. She's got quite a temper on her, that old—Lady Sempronia. So I gave it to Gito to do. He'd had several beakers by then, it was about the only thing I thought he couldn't mess up. We had plenty of dates and paste, and I fetched him a jar of preserved cherries. No great problem, just a nuisance. The dinner went on so long, we could probably have gone all the way to Africa for more dates, if we'd had to."

"And Gito ate some of this second batch, just before he died?"

"Don't ask me. His girlfriend seems to think so." Florus bent and touched the weeping girl's shoulder. "You've got to help us now, lass. Dry your tears and answer the lady and gentleman's questions."

She raised her head and wiped her eyes on her sleeve. "I'll try."

I knelt down beside her and examined Gito's face carefully. Yes, there were traces of foam around his mouth. "I'm so sorry," I said as gently as I could. "This is a dreadful thing. You see we don't think that your Gito died from eating too much. I'm afraid that he was poisoned by something in the food. Like the old lord at the banquet. So it's important we know what exactly he ate. Now, this second batch of stuffed dates. Did he eat any while he was getting them ready?"

"Oh, no, ma'am! Chef never lets us eat any of the food before it goes through. Leftovers only, we're allowed." She sniffed.

"Gito'd been stuffing himself like a pig all night. He had this silly bet." She started to sob.

"So when the dishes were brought back in here, he had some of the original batch with the almonds on them, and then some of the extra special ones with the cherries?"

She nodded. "Just showing off—stupid, stupid! He said, well, after all the trouble I had to make them, the old man hasn't even finished them all up! And he grabbed a few—maybe three or four, I don't know. And then he said he felt sick, and his belly hurt him. I'm afraid we all just laughed and told him it served him right, and to lay down somewhere and keep out of everyone's way. Oh, poor Gito!"

I looked at the table with the left-over food, counting the stuffed dates: five with cherry pieces, and eight with almond slivers, lying on a big silver tray.

Quintus said, "Some of these were put onto smaller dishes, weren't they? I saw one on her ladyship's table, and one on Lord Plautius'."

"That's right. Two oval silver dishes. One with almond slivers for the lady, and one with the new batch for the lord. Course, it was all carried through and set out on the central display along with everything else, while the music was going on. I showed the two dishes to Dimitrius and a couple of her slaves, the doctor and that slimy secretary. I said the ones with cherries were special for their master, and it was their job to make sure he got them. All the other guests got the ones with almonds, served off the big dish."

"I did, certainly," I agreed. "They were delicious. Weren't they, Quintus?"

He nodded. "Florus, who gave you the order for the cherry decorations? Surely not Lady Sempronia herself?"

"No sir. Mistress Clarilla told Dimitrius. I don't know who told her."

"Right. Please put those last few dates with cherries in them into a small covered dish, and secure the lid on it somehow. We'll take them away and keep them safe for now. There might still be one or two poisoned ones left, and we can't take any risks."

We waited while he carefully transferred the five sweets to a square wooden platter, using a small pair of serving-tongs which he ordered one of the boys to wash immediately. He put an earthenware cover over the board and tied a cord round to hold it in place. We thanked them all for their help, and were glad to leave the sad spectacle of the dead King of the Kitchen.

Chapter XXIV

When we got back to our makeshift office, someone had brought in a small brazier, and there was a tray of refreshments on the desk. Neither of us felt hungry or thirsty, but Clarus' hospitality was as impressive as ever.

Quintus carefully placed the covered platter of poisoned dates on the desk. "I'd better find somewhere safe to store these. I wonder how many make up a fatal dose?"

I flopped wearily onto a couch. "More than one, I presume. After all, Timaeus tasted one before Plautius did, and he's showing no ill effects."

Clarus' major-domo knocked and came in, bowing to us in his usual unhurried way. I wondered what, if anything, could ever disturb his composure, if he could remain so calm even after a poisoning at his master's festive table. "The Chief Councillor sends his compliments, and requests that when you have a little time, you'll please come to his study. He's anxious to know how your enquiries are proceeding."

My heart sank at the thought of having to face Clarus just now, and Quintus must have felt the same. "Please tell him we'll come very soon," he answered. "We need a short time to check over our notes." That sounded professional, and Dimitrius couldn't know that neither of us had put stylus to tablet all evening. "And perhaps you could do me a service, please, Dimitrius?"

"Of course, sir."

"I'm sorry to say we've just found out that one of your kitchen slaves is dead. Poisoned, we think, in the same way as Lord Plautius."

He frowned, but it didn't seriously change his bland expression. "How terrible. You'd like me to inform the master?"

"If you would, please. And tell him we'll be with him as quickly as we can."

"Before you go, Dimitrius," I said, "could you answer a question for us?"

"Certainly, madam, if it's within my power."

"Florus mentioned that an extra batch of stuffed dates was prepared, with cherry decorations instead of almonds, and that it was you who took the order to the kitchen." I smiled a knowing smile. "I bet you were popular, arriving with that sort of request when they were flat out serving the meat course."

"There was some grumbling, yes," he admitted, "but I gave them all a piece of my mind, and they settled down and got on with it."

"Do you know who it was who asked for the special dates? Was it Sempronia?"

"Yes, she sent a message by one of her maids. I don't know her name. They all look alike in those blue tunics."

"And she definitely said Lord Plautius preferred cherries to almonds?"

"Yes, she did. Apparently his teeth are—ah—not what they once were."

"Thank you, Dimitrius, that's very helpful."

"Thank you, madam—sir." He bowed himself out.

I yawned and stretched and told myself I didn't feel tired. "Considering we've talked to so many people, we don't seem to have got very far."

Quintus pushed both hands through his fair hair, and rubbed his eyes. "We've made a start. We know the poison was in the dates with the cherry decorations, because both Plautius and the kitchen boy died quite soon after eating those."

"Yes, and several people were aware that Plautius would be getting his own special sweets, different from the others, several people who maybe hated the old man enough to want him dead…. So what do we say to Clarus? That the murderer could be any one of half-a-dozen people, including the Governor's aunt?"

Quintus laughed wearily and stood up. "We do what investigators always do when they're not sure. We tell everyone we're close to a solution, they'll see justice done very soon, but we can't go into details at this time. Come on, let's get it over."

We found our host and hostess sitting glumly together. Glasses of wine and plates of fruit lay untouched on a citrus-wood table, and Clarilla courteously offered us refreshments as we sat down, but neither of us had any appetite.

"Lady Sempronia has gone to her bed," Clarilla told us. "She was more shaken by what happened tonight than she wanted us to see. Though I don't know why she should try to hide away her grief, it's only natural."

"Horatius is in bed too," Clarus added. "He'd become rather—ah—emotional, which of course is understandable."

"Drunk, in plain Latin," I said.

Clarus nodded. "But Priscus is still about, with Fabia. I believe they're in the library. Shall I fetch them?"

"Not yet, I think," Quintus answered. "I'd rather we told you privately what we've found out. Then you can help us decide what we should do next."

Clarus, for all his pomposity, was no fool. "Do I gather that you fear one of the family might be implicated?"

"It's a possibility," Quintus said cautiously. "But we're still not absolutely certain, and we don't want to name any names until we are."

"Of course, I understand. I suppose you're aware that Lord Plautius added a codicil to his will this afternoon? I was one of the witnesses."

"Did he?" I glanced at Quintus, but he made no move to join in. "Plautius' health must have improved under your roof,

Clarus. Horatius was insistent that he wouldn't allow any alterations to the will unless he was sure Plautius was thoroughly alert
and able to understand what he was doing."

"Indeed yes. But I can assure you he was thoroughly alert, and
surprisingly cheerful, considering that changing one's testamen-
tary arrangements is—ah—a somewhat solemn business."

And considering that he was cutting off his elder son without
a copper coin, I added to myself. Or was he? I thought he'd said
to me earlier that he hadn't finally made his mind up about the
will, but either I'd misunderstood him, or he'd lied for some
reason. Yes, that must be it: he was letting it be thought he
hadn't come to a decision, because he feared someone might
kill him once he had. Well, we'd all know tomorrow, when the
will was read.

Quintus and I reported what we'd concluded so far: that the
poison was in an extra batch of stuffed dates, prepared part-way
through the banquet in response to an order which the kitchen
staff thought came from Clarilla.

She said she remembered giving the instruction. "Dimitrius
came and told me that Sempronia had requested a different gar-
nish for the dates," she said. "He was a little reluctant to ask the
kitchen staff at a time when he knew they'd be at their busiest,
especially with their silly Saturnalia foolishness going on. But I
told him it was his job to crack the whip and get the staff under
control, and provide whatever the guests wanted."

There was a loud knock at the door, which opened abruptly
before anyone had time to answer. Rufus stood there, with a
white coating of snow on his head and shoulders, and an expression of suppressed anger on his face.

He bowed quickly to Silvanius, then saluted Quintus. "Excuse
me, sir, but it's urgent. Two people have escaped from the house.
At least two, maybe more."

Quintus swore. "And what were you doing, Rufio? Having
an after-dinner nap?"

"No, but somebody was, for sure. There were six of us covering the outside of the house and slave quarters. I was by the

kitchen. Hector, that big fellow in charge of Plautius' guard, was by the main front door, and I thought I heard a noise coming from there, and went to see. I found him just now, flat on the ground with his head bashed in."

"Dead?" Quintus asked.

"No, just knocked senseless, or even more senseless than he was already, stupid bastard."

"Did any of you spot anyone suspicious?"

He shook his head. "Nobody as far as we could see, which wasn't far, because it's snowing quite hard. I made out some footprints on the ground, coming out of the main door and then leading off down the drive—looked like more than one set of boots. There didn't seem much point trying to follow, because the way it's coming down, the tracks will soon be gone. So I came to you. I'm sorry, sir. I don't understand it. Hector seemed one of the better trained ones. How could he let himself get caught like that?"

"Perhaps the attacker was someone known to him," Silvanius suggested. "Someone he would not suspect until too late."

"That must be it," Quintus agreed grudgingly. "Well, it can't be helped, Rufio. You may as well bring the men in now. Get the doctor to have a look at Hector if his wound's bad. We'd better start checking to see who's missing. Clarus, would you please come with me while I search the house? We have to assume that anyone who's run away has had something to do with the tragedy tonight, and we must find out who's gone even if we can't get after them till daylight. Aurelia, could you and Clarilla make sure all the women are here?"

Clarilla looked scandalised. "Is that absolutely necessary, Antonius?"

"Yes, I'm afraid so. Poison is said to be a woman's weapon, after all."

"But I'm sure none of the women here are involved!"

"We can't be sure, Clarilla," I cut her short. "That's the point."

Ours was the quicker search, because there were fewer women at the villa than men. They were all present and correct: Clarilla's personal maids and kitchen girls, Sempronia's two remaining female slaves, and Fabia and her maid. Sempronia too, of course, though I confess that neither of us ventured into her bedroom to check that she was there in person. Her maid Ebrel, Margarita's replacement, assured us that she was in her bed, and we could hear loud snores from outside her door.

Before I left Sempronia's suite of rooms, I took the chance to ask Ebrel whether she'd been the girl who carried the message from her mistress to Dimitrius, asking for extra stuffed dates.

"Why, yes, I did," she said at once. "Stuffed dates with cherries in then. My lord's favourite."

"When did Lady Sempronia ask you to order them?"

"At the beginning of the banquet, only I was too busy serving till we'd got the first course dished out. But it wasn't my lady as asked me, not personally. It was Master Priscus."

"Priscus? The major-domo said it was Sempronia."

She nodded. "I told that haughty Dimitrius it was her ladyship, cos she scares him out of his—that's to say, she's so well respected."

"Indeed she is." I suppressed a smile. "By the way, I hear one of my lads' dogs has bitten one of Sempronia's servants. Do you happen to know who it was? The boy wants to give them a little Saturnalia gift to say sorry."

She shook her head. "Not one of us girls, for sure. We all bathe together, I'd have noticed any bites. Dog bites or otherwise," she smirked. "And if the dog belongs to that red-headed horse-boy, tell him from me—no, the gods forgive me, I shouldn't joke. Not with poor Leander having killed hisself. He was sweet on me, did you know that? He got me a lovely present, and wrote ever such a pretty little letter with it. I felt awful when he died. I'd no idea he'd even looked at me twice."

"Get on with you," I smiled. "I bet you have a line of lads a mile long queuing up to keep you warm these winter nights."

She laughed. "A girl's got to keep the cold out somehow. And I'm only following in Margarita's footsteps, when all's said and done."

"I thought she was keen on young Master Priscus."

"She is, and he's crazy about her. But she's got a past, has our Margarita, so they say. And she's not short of offers, even now. The Weasel would like to get her into his den—well, he'd like to get all of us, so that's not saying much. But I wouldn't be too surprised to see her fall for a smooth bedside manner, if you catch my meaning."

I steered her back to our present investigation. "Is there anything else you can think of that might help us find out who killed Lord Plautius?"

"No, nothing. But if I were the gambling sort, I'd put my money on Diogenes."

"Why?"

"It's obvious! He's such a scum-bag! If you've got a bad man and a bad deed, they usually go together, don't they?"

I only wish life were that simple, I thought, as we went back to wait for Quintus and Clarus.

"I haven't your experience of investigating," Clarilla said diffidently, "but if that maid is telling the truth, it seems to me that Priscus could have had a hand in poisoning Lord Plautius, or Sempronia could."

"Perhaps. Unless Priscus was simply passing on a message from someone else—someone other than his mother, I mean, who intended to poison Plautius, but was clever enough not to make it obvious."

"That sounds very complicated!" She twisted a fold of her tunic between her fingers. "But for a son to kill his father, it's so dreadful, so unnatural. And so unlike him, from what I've seen of him. He seems gentle, rather shy. Not the kind to resort to violence."

"Gentle and shy," I agreed. "Or to put it another way, weak."

"That's a shade harsh, isn't it?"

"In family matters, I think it's fair. He finds it almost impossible to stand up to his parents, especially Sempronia…. Well, let's not speculate till we see who's run away."

"All right." She smiled suddenly. "You and Quintus seem to be on good terms again. Have you made it up?"

"I think so. I'm afraid I was being unreasonable, and perhaps a bit—well—"

"Jealous of Fabia?"

"You don't miss much, do you?"

"She's a pleasant girl," Clarilla said thoughtfully. "And a real beauty. A good family, too. My brother is quite taken with her."

"Clarus is?" There was something in her tone of voice that caught my ear. "Now what are you up to, Clarilla? Not thinking of match-making, by any chance?"

"Me? No, certainly not. It's just that Publius has been on his own too long. And he's ambitious."

But we couldn't pursue this intriguing topic, because Clarus and Quintus reappeared.

"We've searched everywhere," Quintus said. "And we can't find any sign of either Priscus or Diogenes."

Chapter XXV

"Two runaways!" Quintus groaned, as we walked back to our little office. "And I thought I'd been so careful, posting guards round the house! If it wasn't that Rufio is a first-class man, I'd give him a good hiding for this."

"It's hardly his fault if Hector got caught out. And you can't blame Hector altogether, either. What's the poor man supposed to do? His master comes out of the door and walks up to him, and knocks him unconscious before he realises the danger. Or maybe Priscus just distracted him while Diogenes knocked him out."

"I suppose so." We sat down on a couch. "If they were working together, that is. Or did they join forces just to make their escape? They always gave the impression of hating one another's guts."

"There is one serious question we need to answer straight away."

"Just one? I'd say there were several."

"Which of us is going to wake Sempronia and tell her that either her son or her secretary is suspected of murder?"

"Gods, I need a drink!" He got up and poured us each a glass of white wine from the jug on the table. "This is no way to spend Saturnalia, is it?"

"We're better off than poor Margarita and Gaius." I accepted the glass gratefully and took a large sip of the watered wine. "Ugh, this stuff's not very good. They've given us the rough stuff the slaves normally get! Oh well, I need something to keep me awake." I raised the glass again.

"Aurelia, no! Stop! There's something wrong with it!" Quintus reached out and knocked the drink out of my hand.

"Hey, don't do that!" I grumbled, and got up to fetch some more. Abruptly the room began to spin round me, and I sat heavily down again. My limbs felt like lead, and it was hard to breathe. I tried to ask Quintus to help me, but my mouth wouldn't move. As my mind slowed down, I had only one clear thought: the wine is poisoned.

◇◇◇

I felt like death. Somebody had kicked me in the stomach, and was wielding a hammer inside my head. But I was awake, and that was something.

I was lying on a bed in a small green-painted room, with thin daylight shining in through a high glazed window. It showed me a figure sitting on a stool close to my head. He smiled as he saw my eyes open.

"Hello, Aurelia," he said. "Thank the gods you're awake. You gave us a fright."

I said "Hello, Quintus," but only a croaking sound came out. Whoever had kicked my belly had filled my mouth and nose with sand.

"Don't worry. I'm here, and you're going to be all right." He took my hand and held it. "How do you feel?"

"Not strong enough to answer silly questions," I croaked, and he laughed.

"I'll interpret that as 'I'm getting better, so kind of you to ask.'"

"Where are we? This isn't the Oak Tree."

"We're still at Clarus' villa. You've been unconscious for more than twelve hours. It's good to have you back again."

"Can I have a drink of water please?"

"Here." He held a beaker to my lips. "You must drink as much as you can. I'm afraid it may make you sick."

It did, but after that unpleasantness, I felt better and sat up. Quintus held out a cool damp cloth dipped in rosewater, and I wiped my face with it. He put his arm round my shoulders for a few heartbeats, and I felt better still, comforted and safe. I even began to think I might survive.

The scene in the office came gradually back into my mind. "I drank some wine, and then everything went strange. Was it poisoned?"

"Yes. I noticed the odd smell of it when I was about to drink some. I wish I could have stopped you sooner."

"But how could it be poisoned? There were only the two of us in the room."

"The wine was left in our office while we were in the kitchen. Nobody admits putting it there, and almost anybody could have added the poison to it. I suppose the most likely are Priscus, Diogenes, or Timaeus. Can you remember last night, before you drank the wine? The banquet, and Plautius' death?"

The memories flowed back like a river in full spate. I shivered. "So much death. So much killing."

"I thought I was going to lose you." He leaned close and kissed me. "I never want to lose you."

"Then you won't." We kissed again, until I pulled away and smiled at him, suddenly feeling absurdly happy. "*Now* you can ask me how I feel, and I'll say, 'It's not so bad, thanks, no worse than a nasty hangover.'"

"Good. Because as soon as you feel up to it, we've got work to do."

I sat fully upright, swung my legs out of bed, and stood up. I felt weak and washed-out, and the hammering in my skull beat faster, but then slowed down to an ordinary parade-ground drumbeat. I sat down again on the bed. "I don't seem able to think and stand up at the same time."

He smiled. "Then stick to thinking for now. Do you remember, just before you passed out, we discovered Priscus and Diogenes had run off?"

"Yes. Does anyone know where they went?" I reached for the cool cloth and wiped my face again.

"It snowed hard all last night, so there was no point trying to follow them. But I think Priscus has gone to Eburacum."

"Surely he could just as easily have headed for the coast, if he's running away."

"We don't know that he is. He apparently said last night to Clarus that he wants to talk to Candidus about his father's death. That's one reason. And I assume he'll be at the slave auction in two days' time, looking for Margarita and Gaius."

"Of course—the poor things. There's no news, I suppose?"

"None, I'm afraid. At least Priscus should be fairly easy to pick out in a town like Eburacum. A well-dressed young nobleman, not a soldier, on his own in a place he doesn't know, especially at holiday time. He's bound to attract attention. I've sent Rufio over there today to start looking for him."

"Diogenes will be more difficult to find," I said. "Has he gone to Eburacum too, do you think?"

"That's my guess. He can be anonymous there. He thinks he's a free man now, and he may have saved some money. But having been a slave, he'll know how to travel and live without drawing attention to himself."

"He *thinks* he's a free man? You mean he isn't?"

Quintus shook his head. "Plautius has proved himself a match for Sempronia, right to the end."

"How do you mean?" I reached for the jug of water and poured myself some. It tasted good, and didn't make me queasy.

"You remember Clarus told us he witnessed a codicil that Plautius had written? Well, so he did. It contained instructions to disinherit Candidus. But there was only one alteration in the rest of the document. Plautius crossed out the part about freeing Diogenes. No other changes at all, so Sempronia's beside herself, but there's nothing she can do."

"Good. And typical of the old boy. Gods, who's going to keep Sempronia under control, now that cunning old fox is dead?"

"Not Priscus," Quintus said. "Candidus, perhaps?"

"Perhaps, with a little help from Albia. We ought to go and talk to her ladyship, I suppose. Or have you interviewed her already?"

It was like a scene from a comic play. The bedroom door opened, and Sempronia herself stood there, as if she'd been waiting for my cue. Clarilla, in the corridor behind her, was saying anxiously, "I don't think we should disturb Aurelia, really I don't. She's not even regained consciousness yet." But she might as well have tried to talk an angry elephant out of charging across Africa.

Sempronia came into the room, glaring at Quintus, then at me. She remarked sourly, "It's all right, she's awake. Good. Now perhaps you can proceed with your investigations."

"Yes, I'm awake. But forgive me if I don't get up. I'm not feeling at my best, having narrowly escaped being murdered by one of your household."

Her face reddened. "I *beg* your pardon? How dare you say such a thing! Well, I suppose I must put your rudeness down to your feeling unwell."

"Fine. And I'll put yours down to having about as much sensitivity as a granite obelisk." Of course I didn't say those words, but merely thinking them made me feel good. The anger I'd been carefully keeping in check these last few days welled up, still under control, but giving me strength and purpose. I wanted to shake her arrogant superiority and see what she knew about the tensions and violence that seethed around her.

"I assume," I said, "that you're not accusing my sister or your son Decimus of trying to poison Quintus and me? The poison must have been added to our wine well after they'd left here."

"It seems so," she conceded grudgingly.

"And you'll agree that an attempt to poison us, the investigators, only makes sense if it was made by whoever murdered your husband?"

She thought about it, and gave a reluctant nod. "But nobody apart from your sister and Decimus had reason to kill my poor Gnaeus."

"On the contrary, several people did. Your younger son, or your secretary, or perhaps your husband's physician." Or you yourself, I could have added, but that was going too far even for me.

I braced myself for an explosion, but it didn't happen. Instead she heaved a deep sigh and sat down on a stool by the foot of my bed. "I don't know. I thought that I did, but I don't." She glanced at me without her usual arrogance. "Now, I'd like you both to see this." She held something out towards Quintus.

It was a small piece of papyrus with writing on it. Quintus scanned it and passed it to me, and I felt a shock of recognition. It was a scruffy piece, roughly torn from a larger sheet. I read the words aloud:

I'M SORRY FOR DOING SUCH A WICKED THING. PLEASE FORGIVE ME.

"Where was this found?" I asked.

"Among Priscus' belongings. After he left, I had my slaves search his room thoroughly, to look for some indication of where he's gone. I didn't expect them to find anything. I know why my son has left."

"Why?" Quintus asked.

"Because of Margarita and her son. We should never have agreed to let the kidnappers have them. It seemed a good idea, and of course I never intended Priscus to find out that my husband and I had a hand in their disappearance. But he somehow discovered it, and after he was rescued, he was so angry with both of us, so bitter and hurt. He said we had sold the two people he loved most in the world. He even hinted—you may find this hard to credit—he even hinted that Gaius is his son."

We both sat quiet.

"Of course it isn't true," she hurried on. "It's just a tale that Margarita has told him, to make herself even more desirable to him. But if *he* believes it, it would explain why he turned to…how he could bring himself to…." She couldn't get the word out.

"Murder," Quintus said.

"Yes." It was barely more than a whisper.

"You think this is Priscus' confession, then?" I asked.

"What else can it be?" Suddenly she seemed to crumple, to collapse into herself, and she looked old and frail, nearer seventy than fifty.

I said, "It isn't a confession. At least not to murder."

A spark of her old spirit flared up. "And what makes you so certain of that, pray?"

"Priscus didn't write this. The person who did was confessing to nothing more sinister than letting your cat escape." I told her about the note found with Leander, which was the twin to this one, and about how Gaius came to write his pleas for forgiveness. "I'm a little surprised that you don't remember the incident," I challenged Sempronia. "It was only a few days ago."

"I do recall something, now you mention it. But I did not pay much attention when Gaius brought me his lines to look at. And I never saw the note that was found with Leander." She raised her head and looked at me. "Then I must thank you, Aurelia Marcella."

"For what?"

"You have been instrumental in proving that neither of my sons killed his father. That is a profound relief."

I wonder if I really have, I thought, and was glad when Quintus courteously ushered her out of the room, using my weariness as an excuse.

It was a relief to lie back on the bed. Quintus came and sat beside me, taking my hand. "We seem to be making some progress at last, Aurelia."

"I'm not so sure. There are still four people who could have poisoned Plautius and then left that note to be found in Priscus' room. The two with the most obvious motives have run off. The one with the best opportunity had no motive. The fourth, who had an opportunity and a motive, is related to the provincial Governor."

"Four that we know of." He smiled. "I've faced worse odds than that. Now I don't want to tire you out. Shall I leave you to sleep for a while?"

"No, don't go. I must be on the mend. I feel quite hungry. It's dawning on me that the good side to this situation is being here at Clarus' villa for an extra day, with another chance to sample his chef's brilliant cooking."

"I expect we'll all be eating banquet leftovers today. Just steer clear of any stuffed dates, that's my advice."

"I shall. Probably for the rest of my life."

There was a gentle tap at the door. Quintus got up, saying, "Don't worry, I'll get rid of them."

"No, let's see who it is. If I don't want to talk, I'll lie still as if I'm asleep, and you can send them away."

But when he opened the door I sat up straight, because the visitor was Timaeus.

He came over and looked at me carefully, not like a man gazing at a woman in bed, but like a doctor examining a patient. "How are you feeling, Aurelia?"

"I'll live."

"I heard what happened and I offered to help, but Antonius preferred to look after you himself."

I didn't know whether to laugh or cry. Either the man was innocent, or he had a colossal amount of nerve.

"Aurelia's recovering, as you see," Quintus said, "but she's still very tired. So if that's all you wanted...."

"No, it's not. I want to tell you that I'm leaving for Eburacum today. I have Sempronia's permission to go, and though I don't strictly speaking need yours, I'd rather you know about it. I don't want you to think I'm running away."

"We'll have a better idea what to think when you've told us why you're going," Quintus answered.

"To search for Margarita and Gaius, of course. And to get away from Sempronia. She blames me for not preventing Lord Plautius' death."

"Do you mean she believes that you caused it?" I asked.

"She knows I didn't. She's found a note from Priscus, confessing to the murder."

"No. She's found another part of young Gaius' note, confessing to letting out the cat."

"Of course! I should have realised it might be that! So someone's used the same trick again, trying to put the blame on Priscus this time." He shook his head, and even now I couldn't help admiring the way his wavy chestnut hair shone, and feeling the warmth of his winning smile.

But I hardened my heart. "Where will you stay in Eburacum?"

"At Clarilla's house, for tonight. After that, it depends."

"If you find them," Quintus said slowly, "you'll bring them back, won't you?"

Timaeus paused and gazed at us, completely still for a few heartbeats. "Have my feelings been so obvious?"

"No," I answered. "Not until you decided to pick a fight with Diogenes."

He swore under his breath. "I wish I'd killed the little rat! But I shouldn't have let people see how I...how fond I am of Margarita and Gaius. I was so angry when they were handed over to the criminals, without even a token resistance."

"So angry that you took your revenge on Plautius?" Quintus asked.

"No! I didn't kill Plautius."

"You're the obvious person," Quintus persisted. "Doctors have a good knowledge of poisons, and how to use them. You handled your patient's food last night. You saw an opportunity to kill him, and...."

"No! Don't you understand, I wanted him to get well again. I did everything I could to help him to recover. Because I hoped, one day, I'd be able to persuade him to change his will."

"Did you indeed?" Quintus' purple eyes flashed. "Let me guess. You wanted him to give Margarita and Gaius their freedom, instead of bequeathing them to Horatius?"

Timaeus sighed and lowered his eyes. "Is that such a terrible thing? I know she loves Priscus, and he loves her. But I thought if she's free, there's just a chance she might come to realise how I feel. Now she'll never be free. She belongs to Horatius."

"And you'll bring them to Horatius, won't you," Quintus said gently, "if you find them in Eburacum before anyone else does? Otherwise we'll have to conclude that you murdered Plautius with the intention of running off with two of his slaves."

Timaeus looked straight at us then. "I will."

"You swear it?"

"I swear it, Antonius. I'll bring them back."

"Then good hunting. I'll be in Eburacum myself tomorrow. You can reach me at Brocchus' mansio near the fortress, if you need to."

After he'd gone, I lay back in bed. "There goes an unhappy man. But not a murderer, I'd say."

"I don't know. He's the cleverest of all the people we're viewing as suspects."

Margarita, I thought, arouses love wherever she goes, in all sorts of men. It's a quality to be envied, even if it brings her trouble…. But I saw Quintus watching me, and realised there was no woman I envied just then.

I ate a piece of bread and honey about noon, and then got up, bathed, and went to laze in the sitting-room that looked out over the garden. The snow had all but gone, and the flower-beds and gravel walks were bright in the winter sun. I shooed Quintus off to bed to catch up the sleep he'd missed while nursing me through last night. By now I felt more or less back to normal, except that my stomach was sore still, and I was very tired. I wondered how many other people were in a similar state after their Saturnalia celebrations, and lay down full-length on one of the cushioned couches, ready to doze the afternoon away.

"Ah, you're up and about, m'dear. That's good." Horatius was standing over me, smiling down in the amiable mellow mood he usually reached by this time of day. "How are you feeling?"

Holy Diana, if anyone else asks me that, there may be another murder. No, gently, Aurelia, he means it kindly. I said, "Not too bad, considering everything."

He sat down on a neighbouring couch. "Dreadful, all this. Quite appalling. I feel responsible, in a way."

All at once I was wide awake. "I'm sorry? Responsible for Plautius' death, you mean?"

"No, not quite that! You'd make a good lawyer, m'dear, I'll have to watch my words. What I meant was, I wish I'd taken Gnaeus more seriously when he talked about his secret enemies and how he didn't feel safe."

"But we all took him seriously after someone tried to kill him at the Oak Tree."

He scratched his head. "You know, I've been thinking about that. I don't believe that was an attack on Plautius. The dagger was meant for Idmon himself."

"The bodyguard? But I was told nobody knew he was sleeping in his master's bed, except Plautius himself, and Timaeus."

"Stuff and rubbish! Everyone knew, they were just very careful not to show it. Gnaeus had used a slave as a decoy before, several times. He may have thought it was a closely guarded secret, but you know how slaves gossip."

"Who'd want to kill the guard, though?"

"Ah, now, that I haven't worked out yet."

"So you're suggesting there are two murderers—one who killed Idmon and then Leander, and another who killed Plautius? With respect, that takes some believing."

"With respect!" he mimicked. "I was right, you're almost a lawyer already."

"I think women might make good lawyers, if men would allow them to. We'd cut to the chase when we were making our speeches, instead of spending hours waffling."

"But if we didn't spend hours waffling, how would we justify our fees?"

"You've got a point there." I laughed, and then yawned. "Forgive me, I don't mean to be rude, but I'm a bit sleepy."

"Well, before you have your nap, let me tell you something I think you should know. Only will you swear you won't pass it on to Sempronia?"

"Yes. But I may need to tell Quintus Antonius."

"Oh, I'm assuming you will. Now you know I promised poor Plautius that I wouldn't let Sempronia force him to make a new will."

"I remember. Because he felt vulnerable and could only concentrate for short spells of time. He seemed a good deal better yesterday, I thought."

"He was. But Sempronia never stopped nagging him, cajoling, bullying, on and on. If he wouldn't have a new will drawn up, then would he make the changes she wanted to the existing document? We'd worked out what we would do if she became too insistent, and in the end he agreed to make one change to the will itself, and add a codicil."

"I heard about the change. He crossed out the paragraph that would have freed Diogenes."

"You're well-informed, m'dear. It was the only one of Sempronia's alterations that he felt like making, and of course she was delighted. And then when he added a codicil disinheriting Decimus, she really thought she'd won. But she hadn't."

"But she had, if Candidus has lost his inheritance."

"Ah, but he hasn't. You can't use a codicil to disinherit an important member of the family, like the eldest son. That needs a much more formal procedure."

The phrase "with respect" took on a new meaning. "So the codicil isn't legally binding?"

He chuckled. "No. Never stand up in court, if anyone challenged it, which they won't. Decimus keeps his inheritance, and I've kept my promise."

"Have you told Sempronia?"

"Yes. Not immediately we opened the will, naturally. I let a bit of time go by, during which I 'discovered my error'." He laughed heartily. "She wasn't very happy."

"And she doesn't know that you realised the codicil wasn't valid?"

"No, she thinks I made a foolish mistake, and she's called me all sorts of names because of what she regards as my carelessness.

But if I let rows with Sempronia disturb me, I'd have gone out of my mind long ago."

"This is none of my business, Horatius, but I can't help saying congratulations. I'm sure Plautius' shade appreciates what you did."

He nodded. "When you go to Eburacum and see Decimus, can you let him know what I've just told you?"

"Yes, if you like. But why don't you tell him yourself?"

He looked out of the window, then round the room, anywhere but into my eyes.

"It's awkward, d'you see. If I'd let Sempronia have the changes she wanted, it would have been rather more to my advantage than keeping the old will."

"But I thought the existing will bequeaths Margarita to you?"

He shrugged. "It does, but I'm not such a fool as you all think me. I can't take Margarita, not if Priscus wants her. If we ever find her, I'll give her her freedom, and she can choose for herself. She'll choose Priscus, for certain."

"That's generous, Horatius. You're fond of her, aren't you?"

"I am." He sighed. "But the thing is, I'm financially in rather a pickle just at present. Got a bit carried away betting at the races last summer. It's only temporary, of course. But Sempronia had promised me that if I got the will changed, or a new one made, my debts would be paid off. However, it's not to be. And Sempronia's so annoyed with me now that she won't even pay me the fee we agreed. But Decimus is head of the family, and perhaps if he could see his way…." He tailed off, but I'd got the message.

"I'll make sure he knows that you did the honourable thing, even though it went against your own interests. He's an honourable man himself, and he's also rich now, thanks to you. Leave it with me."

"Thank you, m'dear. You're leaving for Eburacum tomorrow?"

"Quintus and I are, yes."

"So am I. So are we all. Clarilla is letting us use her house there."

"I know. We'll be staying at the mansio near the fortress. You'll be glad to get home to Londinium, I expect."

"I can't say this has been a pleasant trip. Feels like the end of an era, now poor Plautius is gone." He wiped his eyes and sniffed. His mood was slipping gently from mellow to maudlin. "You'll be looking for Diogenes and Priscus?"

"We will, though Quintus doesn't think we've much chance of finding Diogenes. And we'll be searching for Margarita and Gaius too, of course. There's a slave auction the day after tomorrow. If the kidnappers have sold the pair of them on to one of the major dealers, we should be able to buy them back."

"I do hope so. I think Plautius and Sempronia were quite wrong, you know, to get rid of them like that." He clasped my hand for a heartbeat. "I know you'll do your best, m'dear. And now I'll leave you to your nap. You'll need all your strength for tomorrow."

Chapter XXVI

We left Clarus' villa before dawn next morning, to make the most of the winter day. I don't know why the gods, who give Britannia so much beauty, have to be so tight-fisted when they dole out our ration of daylight for the winter months. If you ask priests about it, they solemnly tell you the gods move in mysterious ways, which means they don't know either.

We went back to the Oak Tree first. I'd sent a message there the previous afternoon about our travel arrangements, so all I needed to do when I arrived was have a few words with the senior staff and collect some clothes. The Saturnalia party had apparently been a huge success, and everyone said I should have been there. I answered truthfully, I only wished I had been.

From the mansio to Eburacum is about sixteen miles on good Roman roads. The journey was uneventful, especially for me, because I slept through most of it. Quintus and I travelled in the large raeda, with Titch driving, and Taurus riding alongside as guard. When we set off, I was full of good intentions about making use of the quiet, uninterrupted journey to discuss our investigations. But my tired body wanted to relax. I leant against Quintus' shoulder and fell asleep soon after we passed the Oak Bridges turning.

I woke up as we reached the town, about two hours before dark. The streets were lively, the food-shops and taverns doing good holiday business. Everywhere there were people strolling about in the winter sunshine, and we passed a couple of acrobats

and a troupe of street musicians entertaining the crowds. Brocchus'
mansio was near the fortress, in the civilian quarter—the camp,
as the locals still called it, because that's how it had started. When
we first came to Brigantia half a generation ago, there was just a
higgledy-piggledy maze of unpaved streets crammed with houses
and shops, for the soldiers' families mostly. Then some enterpris-
ing civilians realised what a good living they could make from the
army, and the place was now a thriving little town, with its main
streets paved or gravelled, and an open space for markets.

Titch knew Eburacum well, having been brought up there,
and he drove us straight to the mansio. It was a substantial two-
storey building, with a courtyard behind it and stables alongside.
I knew the innkeeper Brocchus, a wiry curly-haired veteran,
who greeted us cheerfully and showed us into a pleasant set of
rooms overlooking the fortress. The solid military bulk of the
Ninth Legion's headquarters was very Roman and reassuring,
but being used to the country, I found it strange to be in the
middle of so many buildings. I felt that if we'd been much closer
to the fortress, the sentries on the ramparts would have been
able to watch us in bed.

We went down into the bar, where Rufus was waiting for us,
and Titch and Taurus had already made themselves at home.

"The food's good here," Rufus greeted us, "and the wine's
not too bad."

Brocchus came over to join us. "You'd like a bite to eat, I
expect, and something to drink. What can I get you?"

The others looked hungrily around the crowded room,
and I was hungry and thirsty too, but I didn't want to have
to spend the meal fending off Brocchus' questions. So I said,
"We'll have a stroll first, and come back later. Brocchus, which
is the quickest way to the warehouses for the cargo-boats that
trade down-river?"

"They're a bit of a way down-stream, on the main river.
There's a path of sorts runs along by the water. Who is it you're
looking for?"

"A friend of ours called Candidus. He's set up as a trader, and gone into partnership with a river pilot they call the Skipper. We thought we'd pay him a visit while we're in town."

"I heard something about them joining forces," Brocchus said seriously. "If you don't mind a bit of advice, tell your friend to be careful. The Skipper isn't a man *I'd* want to be in partnership with."

"Why not?"

"He's fine most of the time. He's a bit of a rascal, no worse than any other boatman, but he's over-fond of his wine. Drinks too much, too often, sometimes for days at a stretch. When he's drunk, he's too fuddled to work, but he still has enough energy to get into fights."

"Sounds like an innkeeper's delight," Quintus joked, "as long as he's got the cash to pay his bar bill."

Brocchus shook his head. "I don't let him in here no more. Causes too much trouble. I don't know where he drinks these days, but they're welcome to him."

After he'd gone, Rufus said quietly, "He goes to the Wolf's Head. I saw him there yesterday. Scruffy place, and dreadful beer, but cheap."

"Good. We'll pay it a visit," Quintus said. "Have you found any trace of our two runaways?"

"Not a sign so far, no. I've put the word about, and left a message for—the other man you wanted me to contact."

"Thanks. So where is this Wolf's Head? Is it far from here?"

"Nothing's very far from anything in this town." Rufus looked at me doubtfully. "It's no place for a lady though."

"Then I'd better not look like one, had I?" I'd remembered to bring an old scruffy cloak in case I needed a disguise, and I went and put it on.

Rufus grinned and said, "Quite a transformation! You'll do. But you still sound like a lady when you open your mouth."

"You reckon so, do you, you red-haired toe-rag?" I said in British, with a good Brigantian accent.

Rufus laughed. "You'll do!" He turned to Quintus. "Am I coming along with you? Only I've arranged to try out the night-life with your two lads, if you don't need me."

"Then enjoy it," Quintus smiled. "Just make sure you're all here at dawn tomorrow, ready for a hard day's work."

The Wolf's Head was a small unkempt place which had once been painted a garish red, in a narrow unpaved back street. It was crowded and smoky from poor-quality lamp oil, but we found a small table, and Quintus ordered drinks and a hot meal. An over-painted barmaid brought us pork and vegetable hot-pot, which was greasy and hadn't enough spices, and the red wine was rough. But we hadn't come here for the food.

The customers were mostly soldiers and their women, and the occasional trader. But standing at the bar counter were several men who, to judge from their loud chatter, were river pilots and boatmen. Quintus leaned across the table and said quietly, "Watch that tall fellow in the middle. I'm pretty sure I heard him say Albia's name."

He was a huge man, broad and muscular, with brown hair and beard, and a scar on his forehead shaped like a fish. Not a local from Eburacum, to judge by his accent—I guessed he came from a district further north. He was getting cheerfully drunk when we started our meal, and by the time we finished it we didn't have to make any effort to hear what he was saying, or rather shouting. He was telling nautical stories and jokes, and when he began to sing, one of the men at a nearby table called out, "Shut up, Skipper, you'll crack the mugs with that row."

Could this be *the* Skipper, Candidus' new partner? Or was Skipper simply a title given to boat captains in general? He stopped singing and said loudly, "You're no fun these days, Gavo. Here I am, money in my hand and wanting to celebrate, and all you can do is tell me to shut up!"

"I never mind helping a friend enjoy himself," Gavo said cheerfully, "so you can buy me a drink to make up for that awful noise. What are we celebrating?"

"I've found a partner to invest in my boat at last," the big man said. "Just in time, too. The man who sold it me was getting very impatient for his money. Now I'm going to be rich, lads, rich and respectable. I'm sacrificing a bull-calf to Fortuna tomorrow, to say thank you."

"A bull-calf? Gods, this must be something good!" Gavo laughed. "Does the poor chump know that one bad storm would send your old tub to the bottom to feed the fishes?"

"Rubbish! Solid and respectable, it is, like me. Guaranteed not too leaky, and can't abide being dry." He bellowed for another jug of wine, and several more bystanders gathered round, intent on helping him drink it. To stop him singing again, they asked him about his new partner.

"Just the sort of investor a man wants," he replied, his speech slurring a little. "Up from the south country, plenty of money, nice manners, and innocent as a new-born babe! He believes every daft thing I tell him! Talk about pleased with himself—you'd think I'd given him half the boat, not made him pay through the nose for it. Keeps on and on about the importance of trade, and making the world more civilised." He spat scornfully. "Well I'll trade with any man, as long as he puts gold in my hand. 'Sell the best,' that's always been my philosophy."

"Aye, we all know your philosophy, Skipper," Gavo grinned.

"The only thing I've had to do—no, you'll never believe this!"

He paused till someone obligingly asked, "Go on then, what?"

"Change the name of my frigging boat so it's called after his girlfriend. Of all the crazy ideas! But I don't care, as long as his money's good. So if any of you gentlemen want to find my beautiful boat from now on, look for the *Albia. Albia!* Makes you laugh, doesn't it?"

But Quintus and I weren't laughing. We finished our meal and got out of there as fast as we could without making it obvious.

It was growing dark now, but there were a few torches in brackets on the walls of bars like the Wolf's Head, to attract evening customers. All the same we didn't want to be on the streets after nightfall, so we began to walk back to the mansio. We'd only gone fifty paces or so, when a figure came racing towards us, and Quintus' hand went to his dagger. But he relaxed when we recognised Titch.

"What's the hurry, Victor?" Quintus smiled. "Have you stolen somebody's girlfriend already?"

"I've seen that man Otus," he panted. "Drinking in a bar, and I heard him say he's on his way to the Wolf's Head. Only then he spotted me, so I legged it to warn you. He'll not be far behind."

"Thanks. Let's move. Can we get out down there?" Quintus pointed back the way we'd come.

"Nah, blind alley. Back up here, then first right. I'll show you." He turned and started to run like a hare. As we followed, I looked up the street, trying to see into the shadows, but there could have been half a cohort hidden in the semi-darkness. We reached the small turning and dived thankfully round the corner, and then a voice roared out behind us, "There he goes! He's stolen my money! Stop thief! Stop thief!"

We could hear heavy footsteps pounding along after us, and we headed into an even smaller alleyway. Otus had seen or guessed our line of escape, and he continued to shout as he chased us, but not for long. Nobody in this section of town was going to help apprehend a thief. They'd be more inclined to help one than hinder.

We ran through the shadows along a little lane which twisted between blank-walled buildings. Titch led us confidently on, weaving and winding through a maze of alleys, mostly so narrow you could stand in the middle and touch both walls. But we didn't stand, we raced on, only twice pausing to listen. The heavy pursuing footfalls were still there, but fainter. I thanked the gods that Titch knew this area of Eburacum so well. I'd lost all sense of direction and distance, and the empty little streets all looked the same. It felt like one of those nightmares where you are pursued by a terrifying monster, and you must run for your life. Only this time we couldn't escape the terror by waking up.

Eventually we erupted into a small dim square between high walls. It contained a large rubbish-heap, and several rats fled as we approached. Nobody had put torches up here, and the smell was appalling. But I could feel a misty damp in the air, which must mean we were near the river. Titch stopped so abruptly we almost ran into him. "Quiet now!" he whispered. I held my breath and listened.

Silence. No footsteps pelting behind us, no enraged shouting, no pursuit of any kind. There was just the faint lapping of water nearby, and the sound of our panting, when we all started to breathe again.

Titch whispered, "I think we've lost him."

"That was nicely done, Victor," Quintus whispered back. "Thank you."

We waited a while longer to be certain, but there was definitely nobody chasing us now, so Titch navigated us safely to the mansio. On the way, he told us how he'd spotted Otus by sheer chance, drinking with a group of soldiers in a seedy tavern near the fortress. "And I think he must know the Skipper, from what he was saying. Oh, and I found out the Skipper's name, too."

"I know what name I'd call him," I remarked.

Titch grinned. "Well, if you ever feel like being polite to him, his real name's Ephialtes."

I stopped dead. "It's *what?*"

"Ephialtes. Why, d'you know him?"

"I know it means trouble."

"Why?"

"I despair of the youth of today!" I teased him. "The things you haven't been taught that you ought to know at your age would fill several very large libraries."

"Aye, well, if they're in a library, I can go and read 'em some day. Who's this Ephialtes, then?"

"He was a giant in an old story. He and his twin brother tried to storm Mount Olympus. Remember him now?"

He shook his head. "I'm not very well up in that old stuff."

"Sometimes it's useful. Ephialtes' twin brother was called Otus."

He whistled. "Twin brothers! So that's the way of it." His cheeky grin appeared. "They do say twins are double trouble, don't they?"

I laughed. "Not very often, in my hearing. Now off you go, and thank you."

"Aye, I'll be off. With all this messing about, I've not had time to steal anybody's girlfriend yet." He gave us a wink and a wave, and disappeared.

"He reminds me of myself at his age," Quintus said, smiling. "You'll miss him when he joins the army."

We went to bed early, and I was so exhausted that I fell asleep straight away. Lying in Quintus' arms I felt happy and safe, and slept through a long and restful night. In the morning before it was light, we made better use of our time together, and I finally let myself begin to believe that whatever had been wrong between us was now right again. I didn't understand it and I didn't have time to try. I was simply content to find happiness where and when I could.

Chapter XVII

The sun was burning through the morning mist as we set off for Candidus' warehouse. The day was cold, but pleasant enough for walking, and I tried to push my foreboding of trouble to the back of my mind. At least we had Rufus and Taurus with us—two big men who gave us a reassuring feeling of safety. And we had Titch to guide us, and after last night we had reason to trust his knowledge of the town.

Candidus had been right about Eburacum resembling a building-site. Everywhere we looked there were houses and shops being put up, pulled down, or re-developed. There was precious little actual work going on though. They must indulge themselves in an extended Saturnalia festival here, because the streets were alive with folk on holiday, but not blocked by delivery carts or towers of scaffolding. It didn't take us long to reach the water, and that, too, was almost deserted, with only a few small native row-boats ferrying a trickle of customers across to the opposite bank.

"We don't need to go over the river," Titch said. "The cargo-boat moorings and warehouses are all on this side."

I remarked how fast the brown, muddy water was flowing, giving the oarsmen a tough task to row straight across it. "That's a strong current, isn't it? Fine for boats sailing down-stream, but how do they manage to get back up against a flow like that?"

Quintus said, "This is a tidal river. Most of the time it flows towards the sea as you'd expect, but when the tides flood in at the seaside, they raise the water level all the way up here too. There's a strong current flowing up-river then, and the boatmen are experts at using it to help them."

"But we're miles and miles from the sea," Taurus objected.

"A lot of rivers behave like that in Britannia," Quintus said. "The sea is very strong here. You get used to it."

"It's not natural," Taurus muttered. "Imagine if our sea at home in Italia went up and down like that! You'd never feel safe walking along a beach, knowing it could be under water before night-time."

I agreed with him. I find it disturbing enough to think of the sea advancing on the land twice a day and then retreating again, but the idea of tides that could come up rivers as far inland as this—it was frightening. I sent a quick prayer to Neptune, asking for his protection, and another more general request to whatever gods guarded the river here.

"And when the level gets really high, there's flooding all along the bank," Titch put in. "Most of the buildings get a couple of feet of water in them once or twice in a winter, when the snow melts and the river's full. Like now, I reckon. So best not to get ourselves shut into any warehouses. A friend of me dad's got trapped in one once, stacking boxes and they fell on him and broke both his legs. Next morning there he was, drownded. And another time...."

I cut him off. "Thank you, Titch, that's quite enough! Concentrate on showing us the way."

"We're almost there. The warehouses are just ahead, look." Titch pointed to a row of low buildings seventy paces or so further down-stream. "There's more now than when I was last here."

Each of the warehouses had a wooden landing-stage in front, where boats could load and unload, or tie up while they waited. Several were moored there now. I've not had much experience of boats, except for the big powerful military galley that had brought our family from Gaul to Britannia. Compared with a sleek seagoing trireme, these river craft were unimpressive, dumpy and rounded, built for roominess rather than speed. But

I was being unfair, I realised. I might as well say an ox-cart isn't as elegant as a chariot.

I'd expected to see the place as busy as a hive of bees, but the whole bank appeared deserted. Well, if they could swing an extra day's holiday, good luck to them, I thought, with a twinge of envy. The buildings were closed up, the boats' decks were empty and their sails were furled. There were a couple of piles of boxes in front of one warehouse, and a stack of timber near another, but otherwise the wooden wharves were empty too.

Only one vessel at the end of the row showed any sign of life. A short scruffy native was sweeping out its cargo hold in a lackadaisical fashion. Quintus called out to him, "Which boat belongs to Perennius Candidus?"

The man returned a blank stare. "Never heard of him," he grunted, and went on sweeping.

"Perennius Candidus," I repeated, in case the fellow hadn't understood. Quintus speaks British with an atrocious accent. "He's got a warehouse, and a boat named *Albia* that he shares with a pilot called the Skipper."

"Oh, the Skipper! Why didn't you say?" The man pointed with his broom. "He has his boat further down. About two hundred paces. Likes to keep himself private, does the Skipper."

Quintus tossed him a coin and we tramped on. We were beyond even the outskirts of town now, with fields to our left, bordered by scrubby trees and a narrow cart track that ran parallel to the river. Along the bank itself the path was now just a muddy morass, which, as Titch helpfully pointed out, would be under water at high tide. The river was shallow near the bank, with reeds and rushes growing in it, though their leaves were brown and dead now. Occasionally a bird flew up as we passed, but otherwise it was a lonely spot.

"I don't like the idea of Albia living this far out," I said to Quintus. "Candidus gave the impression his house was in the town."

"Candidus is too much of an optimist," Quintus grunted. "He tends to see the world as he'd like it to be, not as it is."

Taurus pointed ahead. "There's a boat there, Mistress Aurelia. And a building, but it looks a bit tumbledown."

As we drew near, we could see he was right. The warehouses we'd just passed had been workmanlike and solid, whereas everything here looked flimsy and barely finished. The boat wasn't moored by the bank, but floated at the end of a long wooden gangway, like a narrow bridge. Even a nautical ignoramus like me could see why: there was no water near the bank, just smelly brown mud. Until the tide came in, the boat had to stay further out. But, thank the gods, it was the vessel we were looking for. It had *Albia* painted along its side.

There wasn't a person in sight. We walked to the warehouse building, which was little more than an overgrown shed. It was locked, and the lock, at least, looked new and secure. I knocked and got no answer, then Taurus hammered with his huge fist, making a noise like a thunder-clap. I called out. "Hello! Albia, Candidus, are you here?"

"Relia! Oh, Relia!" Albia came running towards us round the end of the building, and flung her arms round me. "Oh, this is wonderful!"

"Albia, we've found you at last!" I hugged her. "You're certainly out in the wilds here. Are you all right?"

"I'm fine. It's so good to see you—all of you. This has made my day. It's lonely here when Candidus is in town on business. He's been away since first light, and I've been longing for some company."

"He hasn't left you here all alone?" Quintus asked.

"I've got Nasua and his dog, and the Skipper will be here later, to take the *Albia* down-river." She smiled at the boat. "Isn't it wonderful, having a boat named after me? But come inside, let's get you something to eat and drink."

The house backed onto the warehouse, so its front door faced away from the river, looking out over marshy fields and the same narrow cart-road we'd seen already. We stepped into a small, dark hallway, with a kitchen and a sitting-room leading off to the left, and another room, presumably the bedroom, to the right. Straight ahead was a stout wooden door which must lead directly into the warehouse.

It wasn't very prepossessing, any of it. I felt sorry for my sister, if this was to be her home with Candidus. But she smiled as she welcomed us in, and I determined I'd make the best of things for her sake.

"Go through into the sitting-room," she said, "while I get some wine. You two," she beckoned Titch and Taurus, "come with me and I'll find you something in the kitchen. Where's your man Rufus gone, Quintus?"

"He'll keep watch outside. I'd like you there too, please, Victor. One of you guarding the back, the other covering the river."

"Right, sir. But if Miss Albia was thinking of giving us a drink of wine to keep the cold out…."

"You're posting sentries?" Albia asked, surprised. "Are you expecting trouble?"

"Just being careful, that's all. We saw Otus last night, and he saw us, so we don't want to be taken unawares. But Victor's got his priorities right. He and Rufio can have a drink while they're on watch."

The sitting-room was shabby and smelled of damp, but there was a table set with bright new wine-beakers, and Albia soon had them filled with a good drop of Campanian white. We drank to wish her joy in her new home, but after only a short time of cheerful chatter, the mood became serious.

"You don't look well, Relia," Albia commented. "You're very pale, and I think your face is thinner. Are you ill?"

So I had to tell her about the poisoned wine, making light of it so as not to worry her. "I'm fine now, just a bit tired. In fact I'm in much the same state that any girl might find herself in after a good Saturnalia party."

"Hardly a good party though, was it?" she corrected. "We heard about the banquet, and poor Lord Plautius being murdered. He wasn't my favourite person, but all the same it was a dreadful business. I'd no idea you were in trouble. I'd have come to you if I'd known."

"Thanks, but as you see, I've been well looked after." I smiled at Quintus. "He makes quite a reasonable doctor."

"Wait till I present my bill," Quintus grinned. "But Albia, who told you Plautius had been murdered?"

"Priscus. He arrived on our doorstep early yesterday morning, having ridden from Oak Bridges through the snow. His poor horse was practically dead from exhaustion."

"Is he here now?" Quintus asked.

"No, he wouldn't stay long, he said this would be the first place anyone would look for him. He said he'd get a room at one of the dockside taverns for now. He thinks Sempronia will send someone to town to find him."

"She has," Quintus nodded. "Me. I'm supposed to be tracking him down and taking him back to Oak Bridges."

"Why? Does the old cow think he's killed his father?"

"He's one of a number of people who could have done it. So, I'm afraid, are you and Candidus."

Albia frowned. "She's bound to try and blame us, even though it couldn't have been Candidus or me. It had to be somebody there on the spot, and we'd very publicly left the villa before the banquet."

"You could have sneaked back, though. Or you could have got someone else to help you." Quintus looked at Albia gravely. "Albia, we don't believe Candidus or you killed his father. But Sempronia thinks it's possible, and I had to promise her that I'd question both of you about your movements the night of the banquet." He continued to gaze at her steadily, and she returned his stare. "So tell me, did you or Candidus cause Plautius' death, or have anything to do with causing it?"

"No, we did not. I swear it. I'll swear it by any god you care to name. So will Candidus, if you ask him to."

Quintus said, "That's good enough." I found I'd been holding my breath, and let it out with a rush. Though I'd always known in my heart that Albia was innocent, it was reassuring to hear her declare it.

"Priscus was too upset to talk much about the banquet," Albia said. "Can you tell me what happened?"

She listened in silence while we described the evening. Quintus ended by saying, "Priscus is making things worse for himself by running away from everyone. Have you really no idea where he is?"

"I truly don't know. I'd tell you if I did. He told us he'd come to Eburacum to tell Candidus that Plautius was dead, and to go to the slave auction tomorrow to find Margarita and Gaius. So I suppose we'll meet him there."

"Did he have any ideas about who killed Plautius?" I asked.

She nodded emphatically. "He was certain it was Diogenes' doing."

"That's what I think too," I agreed. "The Weasel thought Plautius was about to change his will, and he might not get his freedom after all. So Plautius had to be killed with the old will still in force."

"Or perhaps he was carrying out Sempronia's instructions," Albia suggested. "Maybe she ordered him to kill Plautius, and it was what he wanted to do anyway." She frowned, then looked at me keenly. "Relia, you just said that Plautius was about to change his will. Didn't he change it then, before he died?"

"Yes and no." Quintus produced a small scroll from his belt-pouch. "I've brought you a copy, so you and Candidus can see for yourselves. Sempronia tried to force Plautius to make some alterations, but he and Horatius were too clever for her."

He held out the will, but Albia said, "These legal documents get me confused! I'll read it later. Just tell me in plain Latin. Has Candidus lost his inheritance?"

"No." Quintus smiled. "You'll see there's a codicil which appears to cut him out. It was put in under pressure from her ladyship. But Horatius only allowed it to be added because it isn't valid."

Albia was silent for a few heartbeats. "So Relia was right about Plautius being more sympathetic than Sempronia. Apart from that, did she manage to add any other changes?"

"Just one," Quintus answered. "Diogenes doesn't get his freedom now. He stays with Sempronia. It's a kind of justice, isn't it?"

Albia sipped her wine. "I don't imagine Diogenes sees it like that."

"He doesn't know. He's run off too," Quintus said. "At the same time as Priscus."

"Run off? Priscus didn't mention anything about it. How odd! But I suppose just because they left the same night, it doesn't mean they actually left *together*."

"No," Quintus agreed. "We're assuming he's come to Eburacum and will escape either down south, or over to Gaul. I'm supposed to be pursuing him as well, but he'll be much harder to trace than Priscus."

"So in theory, the murderer could be either Priscus or Diogenes," Albia mused. "Or Timaeus, perhaps, as he was the one serving Plautius with food and wine?"

"I think that's unlikely," I said. "Timaeus told us yesterday he'd been hoping that Plautius would get well, and would agree to alter his will so that Margarita would be given her freedom one day, not left to Horatius. He's carrying a torch for her, it seems. So the last thing he'd do would be to murder Plautius, knowing that his will would put Margarita out of his reach for good."

"But *I* think," Quintus put in, "it could well be Timaeus. He's clever, and if he loves Margarita as much as he says, he might well have wanted revenge on Plautius for betraying her to the kidnappers. He might be gambling that he could persuade Horatius to free her eventually, or sell her to him."

We discussed the various possibilities for a while longer. I felt as if we were walking over well-trodden paths, which were no less confusing for being familiar. Eventually I decided to change the subject. "It's not all bad news, though, Albia, is it? Plautius' death cuts both ways, from your point of view. Once Candidus has proved he's innocent, you're free to marry whenever you like. Sempronia will still disapprove, but legally she has no say in the matter. So don't feel too badly about this horrible business. Try to think of the happy future, not the sad past."

"I'll try." She put her head in her hands, and when she looked up again, I was surprised to see how tired and strained she was.

"Albia, I thought you'd be overjoyed that the wedding will go ahead as you planned it. What's the matter?"

"Nothing."

"Yes, something's wrong. Tell us."

"I expect I'm being silly, worrying unnecessarily…but I just wish I knew a bit more about Candidus' business here in Eburacum. The man he's in partnership with, the Skipper—I don't like him or trust him. I believe he's trying to get Candidus involved in something…."

"Something illegal?" Quintus suggested gently. "What makes you think so?"

"He's so secretive—the Skipper I mean, not Candidus, although *he's* starting to be the same now. For one thing, he's so proud of having a half share in a boat, yet he won't let me go on board."

"Some sailors consider women unlucky on boats," Quintus pointed out.

"Perhaps. But he won't let me see inside the warehouse either. What sort of cargo can they be storing there, if it's so secret he doesn't want even his future wife to know about it?"

I remembered him talking about the advantages of water transport as against ox-carts. "He's going to be carrying building materials, isn't he? Limestone from the quarries, and timber, and tiles. And I assume there'll be some less bulky odds and ends that escape the eye of the tax-men. But a bit of small-time smuggling isn't going to bring the province to its knees. Is it, Quintus?"

He grinned. "Gods, I've no love for the Procurator and his tax collectors. As long as Candidus isn't breaking any imperial monopolies, smuggling gold or silver or suchlike, then it's up to the good citizens of Eburacum to control their own river trade."

"It's nothing like silver or gold," Albia answered. "It's the slaves. They sell slaves to the limestone quarries at Calcaria, and bring back stone on the return trip. The Skipper does the actual sailing, of course. Candidus just negotiates the deals, except for some of the slaves, because the Skipper says his contacts are better. But sometimes they sell small numbers of slaves locally. Very locally."

"What makes you suspicious about them?" Quintus asked gently.

"I think—no, I'm sure—that some of the slaves aren't what they seem. I was there yesterday when a batch were loaded on board and taken off down-river. They were kept out of sight in the warehouse mostly, but I saw them walking across the gangway to the boat. They weren't slaves, I'd bet any money. They were soldiers."

"Soldiers?" Quintus said sharply. "How do you know? They weren't in military clothing, surely?"

"Oh no. Just ordinary cheap cloaks, native boots, and no weapons. They had their hands loosely tied behind their backs, and no chains on their feet. They looked like a group of actors *playing* at being slaves, only they weren't actors, they were soldiers. You can tell a soldier a mile off—well I can, after working in a mansio for years. It doesn't matter what they're wearing or doing, there's just something about them. Isn't there, Relia?"

"There is. They're fit and well-fed and carry themselves well. But it's more their attitude that makes them stand out. They look at the world as if they won't take any nonsense from anybody."

"That's it exactly," Albia agreed. "You don't see slaves like that."

"*Merda*," Quintus muttered. "You're right to be worried. It sounds as if this Skipper is helping army deserters escape."

She nodded. "That was the first thing I thought of. We've heard there have been more deserters than usual from Eburacum lately."

"Yes," he said. "A steady trickle over the last three months, legionaries and auxiliaries. It seems they're fed up with the current policy of pulling troops back from the northern frontier."

She nodded again. "That's what Lucius...." She stopped short.

"Lucius?" he repeated.

We both hesitated for a few heartbeats. I wanted to say more, and I thought about my brother's brief message: "Trust Q, he is here to help."

Quintus looked at me squarely. "Do you know where your brother is now?"

"Not precisely. Do you?"

He smiled. "Pretending to be a disgruntled officer in Eburacum, while hunting down army conspirators."

I felt relieved. "Yes. We saw him quite recently. He wanted us to know he wasn't really in disgrace. Thank the gods he's confided in you. He may need your help."

"He's already made contact. Just a short note in code. If I remember right, the exact words were, 'All going well, result soon.'"

"Good," I said. "There's one more thing I should tell you, Quintus—well, both of you. I've had to keep it to myself till now. Albia, I'm sorry, but Lucius warned me that there was a rumour Candidus was involved in something shady. He didn't know what, but he was concerned."

"*Relia!* Why didn't you tell me? What exactly did he say?"

"He said it was tavern talk here that Candidus was mixed up in some sort of shady enterprise—smuggling, evading taxes, not major crime. I didn't want to worry you, and frankly I thought the rumour was probably wrong. Now I'm not so sure."

"The rumour *is* wrong!" she exclaimed defiantly. "One thing I'm certain of, if there's something illegal going on, Candidus doesn't realise it. He wouldn't do anything criminal. If you're right, and the boat's being used to smuggle deserters out, it's the Skipper who's responsible for it. Not my Candidus."

"Then why the secrecy?" Quintus demanded.

She wasn't daunted. "I don't know, but when Candidus comes home, we'll ask him."

"Ask me what?" Candidus was standing in the doorway, smiling his boyish smile. He came into the room and embraced Albia, completely oblivious of the wary looks he got from Quintus and me.

"Albia, my love, I'm sorry I've been so long." He embraced her again, and then turned to Quintus and me. "Thank you for keeping my girl company. And welcome to our new home. Now, what is it you want to ask me?"

"They think…" Albia began, but Quintus cut in roughly.

"We want to know why there were soldiers in your boat yesterday, pretending to be slaves. We also want to know where they were taken."

"That's easy." His composure didn't waver. "They were a bunch of the Skipper's friends, lads from the garrison here. They fancied a hunting trip in the woods further down the river. He'll be bringing them back in a day or two."

Quintus looked unconvinced. "Why were they trying to look like slaves?"

Candidus gave a conspiratorial wink. "I don't think they had full permission for leave of absence. So they thought they'd better come in disguise."

I almost laughed. "You've never been in the army, have you, Candidus?"

"I did a year as a military tribune in Judea. I can't say I enjoyed it."

"Then you should've realised they were telling you a tale. Those men weren't going hunting. They were deserting."

"*Deserting?* They can't have been! The Skipper wouldn't be a party to something like that."

Quintus snapped, "Are you sure? How long have you known him?"

The two men stared at each other. Finally Candidus dropped his gaze. "Not all that long, I suppose. A month perhaps."

"Long enough to learn his name?"

"Yes, of course. His Christian name is Clemens. Not that anyone ever uses it."

"His *Christian* name?" Quintus almost shouted. "This gets worse and worse. You're telling me he's a Christian believer?"

"Yes," Candidus answered proudly. "He is, and so am I, which is why I'm sure I can trust him. I'm not fully initiated yet—baptised, as they call it. But I believe in their philosophy. I learned about it when I was serving in Judea. It's the main reason I decided against a political career. You see I can't regard the Emperor—any Emperor—as a god. Christians believe there is only one."

"Holy Diana protect us!" I was horrified. "I don't know much about Christians, but what I do know is appalling. They drink blood at their ceremonies, and they don't believe in any of our Roman gods. Albia, did you know about this?"

"Of course. I'm not one of them myself, but there's no harm in their philosophy that I can see. Their main beliefs seem to involve treating everyone with respect, and obeying the law."

"How can you say that? Everybody knows they burnt down most of Rome in Nero's time."

"It's not true, Aurelia," Candidus answered gently. "They were made scapegoats. The Roman people were angry after the fire, and some of them said the Emperor himself had started it. Nero diverted their hostility away from himself by blaming the Christians."

"Let's not get into a historical debate," Quintus growled. "So you're a Christian sympathiser, Candidus. And the Skipper claims to be one too?"

"Yes, and so are the men who were in his boat last night. If you want the truth, he said they were going down-river to visit other Christians there. They were afraid to meet in Eburacum itself, because so many people react to them as Aurelia does. I took him at his word. After all, he's proved himself with the work he's doing to help slaves find new homes."

"What slaves?" Quintus interrupted.

"Children mostly, and sometimes young women. We send them away to a better life."

I couldn't believe Candidus was so naïve. "*Merda,* he's helping runaway slaves too?"

"No, not runaways. We buy them, and then sell them to good homes down in the south—Christian homes, where they'll be kindly treated and given their freedom as soon as they're old enough."

"We?" I pounced on the word. "You're paying money into this hare-brained scheme?"

"Yes, we share the purchases equally."

"And the profits too, I suppose?" Quintus asked scornfully.

He looked shocked. "We don't make a profit on the children. As long as we get our money back, it's enough to know we've given them a chance of freedom when they're older."

"What proof have you of where the slaves end up?" I knew what the answer was.

"Well—nothing in writing...."

"Or where they come from in the first place?" Albia interrupted. "What if they've been kidnapped, like Margarita and Gaius?"

"But the Skipper's as committed to helping them as I am. You must meet him, then you'll see."

"We have met him, or anyway seen him," Quintus answered. "A big man with brown hair and a scar like a fish on his forehead?"

"Yes, it sounds like him."

"Last night he was drinking in the Wolf's Head, boasting that he's going to sacrifice a bull-calf to Fortuna to give thanks, because he's about to make a lot of money."

"That can't be true!"

"We heard him bragging to everyone," Quintus went on relentlessly, "how he's recently acquired a new partner, who, he says, has the great merit of being 'innocent as a new-born babe, and believes every daft thing I tell him.' The only thing he'd had to do to satisfy his new associate was to re-name his boat the *Albia*."

Candidus sat speechless, but Albia exclaimed angrily, "There, I was right not to trust him. But I never dreamt it was anything as serious as this. Tricking you into helping deserters! It's death for both of you, if you're caught."

Candidus still didn't reply, but his white, scared face gave us all the answer we needed.

Albia went to him and put her arms round him. "It's all right, love. We'll help you straighten things out." Then she turned to us. "What's best to do now? Candidus is giving you all the information he has, and you can see he's as horrified by what you've just told him as you are. How can we get him out of this mess?"

"Mess is right." Quintus frowned and picked up his beaker, twisting it between his hands with such force I thought he'd break it. "Candidus, will you help us catch the Skipper in the act of carrying a cargo of deserters, or dealing in stolen slaves? If you do, I can keep you out of trouble by saying you were acting as an undercover agent for me."

Candidus shook his head. "Antonius, I know you're trying to help. But you're putting me in a very difficult position. I still can't believe everything you've told me. It's all suspicion and hearsay, isn't it? You're asking me to betray my partner, to consider him as a criminal. I will if he's breaking the law, but I'm not satisfied about that yet. First I'd like some proof, some solid proof."

There was a pause while the two men confronted one another. Then the howl of a wolf split the silence. I jumped and stared round the room, half expecting Otus and his men to come pouring in.

"Is that some sort of signal?" Quintus asked.

Candidus nodded. "It means the Skipper or his men are here now. They always give us warning." The sound came again, a little closer.

Quintus said, "That same signal is used by the band of criminals called the Wolf-pack. Perhaps you've heard of them?"

"The Wolf-pack? Not…not the gang that took Priscus and the others?"

"The same," he growled. "Now, I'll ask you once more. Will you help us catch the Skipper?"

Candidus nodded miserably. "God help me, what have I got myself into?"

Chapter XXVIII

"First," Quintus said, "tell us exactly what's going to happen. This is one of your human cargoes, I take it?"

Candidus nodded unhappily. "Some soldiers are being marched down here disguised as slaves. The Skipper or one of his boys will be with them, acting the part of overseer. He'll lock them in the warehouse, and they'll stay there out of sight for now. The Skipper will take them down-river later, as close to dark as he can, but it depends on the tide. He doesn't go far—he says they're meeting with their Christian friends a few miles from here. If you're right, they presumably disembark somewhere quiet, then wait to be picked up by another boat which will carry them down to the sea, or wherever they're escaping to. He'll sail the *Albia* back here as soon as the ebb tide slackens tomorrow."

"So all we have to do is wait till they're safely in the warehouse, and then catch them," Quintus said. "Rufio and Titch are outside, but they've got the sense to stay hidden."

It was frustrating not being able to see what was going on. We could hear muted shuffling sounds and hushed voices which gave nothing much away. Then a heavy door banged, and after a silence there was a final wolf-signal, coming from some distance off. Then silence.

The quiet was broken by a sharp rap at the door, and Rufus came in.

"Things have started, sir. You'll have gathered we've got company?"

"We heard the signals. How many?"

"Eight."

"Eight! All soldiers, I presume?"

"Mostly, I'd say. Disguised as slaves, but not very convincing."

"There'll be no garrison left if they keep disappearing at this rate. They're in the warehouse now?" Quintus stood up.

"Yes. An old grey-haired man came with them and locked them in. He's gone again now. He told them to relax till tonight, but keep out of sight. He said the Skipper will be down later."

"Then let's go and see. Where's Titch?"

"Outside still, keeping watch in case they try to leave. A good lad, that."

Candidus got up and went to the door. "If we're doing this, let's make a decent job of it." He reached down a heavy brass key from a nail in the wall, and handed it to Quintus. "I suggest we go in from this end, through the house. The door's narrower—easier to block, if anyone makes a run for it."

"Good," Quintus approved. "Rufio, you and Titch go round to the river entrance, in case anyone tries to get out that way. There's a small window, isn't there, Candidus?"

"Yes. It's high up, though."

"Catch anyone you can, but don't risk your lives. And make sure you guard the boat. If there are eight half-decent soldiers in there, some of them are bound to get away, but we can stop them going by water. If necessary, cut the mooring-rope and let the boat drift."

"I'll go outside too," Candidus said. "If the boat's in danger, then I want to look after it."

Quintus nodded. "Have you any weapons here?"

"No swords, I'm afraid. But there's an axe, and a couple of good cudgels."

"I've got a small dagger." I touched the spot where it was hidden under my cloak. "How about you, Albia?"

"I'll fetch mine."

"Oh no!" Candidus was horrified. "You two girls must stay out of harm's way. Barricade yourselves into the kitchen and wait there till this is over."

"I'll do no such thing," Albia retorted. "I'm not missing all the action! I don't know who or what you'll find, but you're not going in there without me."

"Or me," I agreed. "Candidus, if you're marrying my sister, you've got to realise that we Aurelius girls don't appreciate being left behind 'out of harm's way'."

"Don't argue with them about it, that's my advice." Quintus smiled ruefully. "I've tried, and I never win."

While Rufus and Candidus went outside, the rest of us collected in the small hallway, facing the warehouse door. Quintus and Taurus stood shoulder to shoulder in front, Quintus with a dagger and Taurus holding an axe. Albia and I, with our daggers drawn, were the rearguard. Quintus fitted the key gently into the lock, and looked round.

"Ready?" he whispered.

We all nodded. He turned the key and flung the door wide.

It was a big box of a place, the walls made of crude planking, the floor just coarse gravel. In the light from the high window we made out six men sitting round a makeshift plank table playing dice, while two more sprawled on a pile of blankets by the left wall. They were strangers, except one: Diogenes.

As the door banged open, they glanced up casually, and then leapt to their feet. "Everybody stand still! Hands on your heads!" Quintus bellowed, but they ignored him. Suddenly they all had daggers in their hands and were rushing for the big door at the far end.

Two of them wrenched at the handles of the solid door, but the strong lock held. They all faced back into the room. We four were still bunched together in the doorway, blocking their escape route into the house.

"The window!" One of the men leaped for the small unglazed square next to the door. It was above shoulder height from the ground, and only just wide enough for a man to squeeze through, but these were fit young soldiers, and the first of them was out in the blink of an eye, with one of his comrades giving him a helpful shove from below.

"Stop them!" Quintus yelled, and he and Taurus charged across the floor. Two men turned and grappled them, while their comrades climbed out through the window. That left Diogenes, who took one scared look round and ran straight for the door where Albia and I were standing. He was holding his dagger as if he knew how to use it.

He charged at us, and we both instinctively moved apart, just enough for him to push through between. But I stuck out my foot to trip him as he passed. He stumbled, then almost regained his balance, till Albia kicked out at him and he fell face down on the gravel floor.

"Keep still, Mustela!" I yelled, and threw myself down to kneel on his back, pressing my dagger point into his neck. Albia sat down hard on his legs, which caused him to cry out in pain.

"No, please! Don't hurt me!" He began to moan like a hurt animal.

"Stay quiet!" I yanked his head back by the hair and pricked the dagger into the soft skin near his throat till it drew blood. "What's up with him, Albia? Is he injured, or just shamming?"

"His right leg's badly swollen," she answered, "and he's got a bandage on it. He has an infected wound there, I'd say, quite a bad one. How did you come by that, Weasel?"

He said nothing.

"Well?" I jerked his head back hard.

"One of your mules kicked me. Get off my leg, you're hurting me."

Albia didn't move. "When was this?"

"I was in the stables at the mansio."

"Spying, you mean? Looking for evidence against Albia and me?" I was suddenly shaking with anger, almost out of control. I wanted to hurt him badly, to make him suffer for everything he'd done to us and our friends. "Albia, I'd hate to see Diogenes come to any harm because of one of our mules. Why not try lancing that leg of his with your dagger? I'm sure it's the right medical procedure."

"No! Please, no!"

Quintus' voice came from behind us. "We've got two of them, and you have the pick of the bunch there, by the looks of things. He's making a lot of noise. What have you done to him?"

"Nothing yet," I said, "but we're just about to start. Apart from betraying Margarita and Gaius, he's been spying on us at the Oak Tree, trying to incriminate us."

"I haven't!" Diogenes whimpered. "Please, tell them to stop hurting my leg. I can't stand the pain."

"Give us some truthful answers," Quintus said, "and I'll consider it."

"Who sent you to spy on us?" I asked.

"I haven't been spying, I swear it!"

"Albia, I do think that leg would benefit from a little surgery, don't you?"

Albia told me later she didn't even touch his wound, but his scream brought Candidus into the warehouse at a run. "What's going on, is someone hurt? Diogenes! What are you doing here, trying to escape among a bunch of army deserters?"

"Save me, Master Decimus, please!" the Weasel whined. "They're torturing me. I've told them the truth, but they won't leave me alone!" He stretched out his hands towards Candidus' boots.

"Save you?" Candidus stepped back. "After you let Margarita and Gaius go to the Wolf-pack? I won't allow anyone to torture you, but I'm sure they weren't doing that in any case. Otherwise you'll get no help from me."

"We'll take him into the house," Quintus decided, "and the other prisoners can stay in here for now. How many did you catch, Candidus?"

"Two. The others got away, heading towards town."

"We've got four altogether, then. That should be enough for Lucius."

"Lucius? You mean Albia's brother? What's he got to do with this?"

"I'll explain later. For now, can I borrow some strong rope, please?"

Quintus and Rufus tied the four prisoners up. They began to protest loudly and forcefully that they were soldiers, but Quintus merely shrugged. "You're not in uniform, you're dressed as slaves. Why should I believe you've suddenly turned into free men? I'll take you back to the fortress, and we'll see what your officers have to say." That quietened them down, and we left them in the warehouse, guarded by Rufus.

The rest of us walked through into the sitting-room, Taurus keeping a tight hold on Diogenes. "I'll tell Nasua to go outside and keep watch," Albia said. "He'll warn us if he sees anyone coming."

Quintus turned to Titch. "Victor, I need you to take a couple of messages into town for me urgently. One for the duty guard commander at the fortress, and the other for Lucius."

"Right, sir. Except I don't know where Master Lucius is."

"Neither do I, but the innkeeper at the Wolf's Head will be able to contact him. The password is Midas."

"Midas. Is Master Lucius out of trouble now?" Titch asked.

Quintus grinned. "After today he will be."

"That's good."

"It is," I agreed. "Very good."

Diogenes was sitting against the wall, with Taurus towering over him. He was shivering, though it wasn't cold. I wondered if his infected leg was making him feverish.

Albia saw me looking at him. "I wish you'd let me clean that wound for you, Diogenes."

"No, don't touch me!" he cried out, and tried to shrink away from her.

So much the better, I thought. I don't care if his leg rots, especially if it's followed by the rest of him.

Quintus looked down at the prisoner. "Diogenes, if you've murdered your master, I can't save your life. But if you tell us everything you can, I'll make sure you get a quick clean death."

"I didn't murder him. And I'm a free citizen now. You've no right to hold me against my will." It seemed the Weasel had begun to use his wits. "I shall appeal to the local magistrate. To the Emperor, if need be."

Quintus was equally calm. "What makes you say you're a free man?"

"My lord Plautius gave me my freedom in his will." He spoke slowly, as if explaining something to a particularly slow child. "I mourn for him, of course, but now that he's gone to the Underworld, his last wish should be carried out."

"Oh, it will be," Quintus answered. "He insisted that the will he already had, the one everyone calls the 'old' will, should stand."

"I know. With a codicil to disinherit Master Decimus."

"That's correct. And there was one more change to it."

Diogenes stiffened. "What change?"

"Plautius crossed out the clause granting your freedom."

"He wouldn't do that. He promised!"

"All the same, he did."

Diogenes stared at him, then relaxed and smiled. "You're lying, trying to catch me out."

Without a word, Quintus got up and fetched the copy of the will that we'd brought for Candidus and Albia. He opened the scroll out and held it, and Diogenes read it.

"I haven't been given my freedom?"

"No."

"You swear this is true? It's not some kind of trick?"

"I swear it's true."

"Master Decimus!" Diogenes turned to Candidus, his calm giving way to panic. "You're an honest man, I know you are. Do you swear this is what the will says?"

"I swear it, Diogenes."

"Gods," the Weasel muttered, "how they've used me!" He looked as if he might burst into tears—tears of rage, not grief. "All these years I've served them, tried my best to please them. 'Yes, my lord! At once, my lady!' I've done everything they asked of me, and more, and in return I was promised my freedom when the master died. I was *promised!* And now he's broken that promise. He's betrayed me." Two tears ran down his face, but he shook his head angrily. He spoke so quietly he was almost whispering. "You may as well kill me now. I don't want to live any more of my life as Sempronia's slave."

I had some sympathy with that, and even felt sorry for him briefly. But he was still a weasel by nature as well as by name, and I saw how we could turn his disappointment to our advantage. "Candidus," I said, "could I have a word with you outside please?"

We went into the hall, and I briefly outlined what I wanted to do. He agreed readily, as I'd expected. We rejoined the others in the sitting-room.

"Diogenes," Candidus said. "I intend to find out who killed my father. Was it you?"

"No, Master Decimus. *I* didn't kill him."

We both picked up the slightly odd emphasis on the word "I". Candidus asked, "Do you know who did?"

"I can make a good guess."

"Will you tell us who it was?"

"Why should I?"

"I thought," Candidus said, "that you wanted your freedom. I'm prepared to give you the chance to earn it."

He took the bait. Even the craftiest weasel will take bait, if it's sufficiently tempting, and this one had nothing to lose. His dejected look vanished and he stared into Candidus' pale blue eyes. "What are you suggesting?"

"It's simple enough. If you help us catch the man who killed my father, assuming it wasn't you yourself, then I'll grant your freedom. I promise I will."

"You'd do that?" He was pathetically eager, like a child who's been offered a treat when he expected a beating. Then he controlled his emotions and became the Weasel once again. "But how do I know I can trust you?"

"Have you ever known me to break a promise?" Candidus countered.

He thought about it. "No. You've always been honest. And there are witnesses here." He glanced round at the rest of us.

"We're all witnesses," Quintus agreed. "Give us information that leads to the murderer, and when he's caught, you'll go free."

"All right. I think the person who stabbed Idmon and Leander also killed my lord Plautius," Diogenes said slowly. "And I know for certain who murdered the two slaves. That was Timaeus. But killing Idmon was a mistake. He was trying to kill *me*. He thought I was sleeping in my lord's bed that night."

I said, "Horatius told me that Plautius arranged for different servants to sleep in his place when he felt afraid for his safety. That night it was your turn, was it, Diogenes?"

He nodded. "Timaeus didn't know I'd swapped with Idmon, nobody did. We only changed late at night, because I had stomach pains and felt unwell."

"Why did Timaeus want to kill you?" Candidus asked.

"Because of Margarita. We both wanted her, and he was afraid she would prefer me."

Frankly I thought the Nile would freeze over first, but that might not stop Timaeus fearing a rival. "He was jealous enough to try to kill you? Is that what you're saying?"

The Weasel nodded again. "Of course he denied it. When I confronted him with it, he admitted he meant to kill Idmon, because they were rivals for that little maid Ebrel. I suppose it's possible, but I didn't believe him. Anyway, the point is he didn't intend to kill the master."

"And then," Quintus said, "when he realised he'd stabbed the wrong man, he killed Leander and tried to make the death seem like suicide?"

"That's right." The Weasel licked his lips. "Could I have a drink of water, please?"

While Taurus fetched it, my brain was racing, filling in the gaps in his account. Odious as Diogenes was, I realised he could be telling the truth. It all fitted together. He and Timaeus clearly hated one another, they'd made no secret of it. Rivalry over Margarita might be enough to turn Timaeus into a murderer.... Except somehow it didn't feel right. But then Quintus would say I was letting my personal liking for the handsome doctor get in the way of the truth, and perhaps I was.

"Let's accept that Timaeus killed the two slaves," I said. "Why did he go on to murder Plautius?"

"Because he was so furious that my lord allowed the kidnappers to take Margarita and Gaius."

"I understood that was Sempronia's idea," I said.

"Originally it may have been. But it was my lord who had the power and gave me instructions to make a deal with the Wolf-pack if I could. That was the way they often worked, my lord and lady. She made the arrows, and he shot them."

"And you were quite happy to let Margarita and Gaius go to the gang, weren't you? Because Margarita had made it absolutely clear that she preferred Priscus' advances to yours."

"I had ways of making her go with me when I wanted," he said bitterly. "But Priscus could do what he liked with her any time, and she said she loved him. So yes, I admit it—when my lord sent me to negotiate with the kidnappers, I was happy enough to carry out his instructions."

Quintus moved on to more practical matters. "Where are Otus' gang holding the two of them now? What do they intend doing with them?"

"I don't know where they are now, but Otus is going to ship them out of Eburacum and sell them in Londinium or perhaps Glevum, where they'll fetch a better price. The Skipper will take them on the first part of the journey."

I heard Candidus gasp, but Quintus went on relentlessly. "When?"

"I don't know. I had wondered if they might be sailing out with us." He smiled unpleasantly. "I'd have enjoyed that."

"You're sure they aren't going to be sold at the auction here?" Candidus asked.

He shook his head. "Otus thinks he'll get a better price for them in the south. Some of the high-class brothels down there will pay a consul's ransom for a mother and son as attractive as those two. And the Skipper has plenty of contacts, apparently. He takes regular cargoes of slaves down the river." He glanced at Candidus. "Isn't that so, Master Decimus?"

"He rescues slave children, and I help him, now we're partners. But we don't sell them for profit. He arranges for them to go to good homes, where they'll be well treated and eventually freed."

"Oh he does, does he?" The Weasel sneered, and then seemed to recollect that he was talking to the man who could give him freedom, and said more calmly, "Master Candidus, that's not what he tells his friends at the Wolf's Head. 'Sell the best and burn the rest,' that's his philosophy when it comes to the slaves."

"Burn the rest?" Albia repeated, appalled. "What does that mean?"

"After the pretty ones have been sent south to make a fat profit, the less attractive specimens are sold off to the Druids. I don't think they fetch much money...."

"The Druids are outlawed!" Candidus exclaimed.

"But they still have power with the natives," Diogenes insisted. "And they still sacrifice children to the old gods at some of their ceremonies. They put them in wicker cages and set fire to them. The children are caught by Otus, and sold by the Skipper, and they both share the proceeds."

"No!" Candidus protested. "You're lying, Diogenes." But he wasn't, and we all knew it.

"*Merda,*" I said. "So these are your good Christian homes, Candidus? Life in a brothel, or death in a Druid cage?"

"May god forgive me," Candidus muttered. "I had no idea." He looked at the Weasel. "Diogenes isn't the only one to have been betrayed."

Chapter XXIX

Titch came back soon after, with a note from the fortress duty commander. Quintus scanned it quickly, and growled, "They can't spare any men to fetch the deserters in. There's been some sort of minor riot in town, and they're having to patrol the streets. Flavius asks if we'll bring the men to the fortress ourselves." He stood up. "Well, we can manage that easily enough, I suppose. Rufio and I, and you, Taurus, please. We'll take Diogenes with us too, and deliver him back to Sempronia. She's still at Clarilla's house, I assume?"

"But Master Decimus said he'd free me!" the Weasel objected.

"When my father's murderer is caught," Candidus agreed. "Not before. But I'll come with you, Antonius, and while you see the soldiers safely into custody, I'll take Diogenes back to Mother and explain what we've discovered. I'll talk to Timaeus too, if he's there. But if Diogenes has told us the truth, I suspect he'll have made a run for it." He sighed. "I ought to see Mother anyway, now that my father's dead. Whatever differences we had, he was still my father, and I'm still his eldest son. I've a duty to arrange the formalities of mourning."

"All right. What about you two girls?" Quintus looked enquiringly at Albia and me.

"I'm staying here," Albia said firmly. "They may bring Margarita and Gaius down today."

"It's too dangerous, love," Candidus objected. "You must come with me."

"There's no danger if I'm careful. And I want to be here just in case. It's all right, I'm not planning to rescue them single-handed. But at least I can watch what happens, and make sure they aren't brought here and then taken away again without our knowing."

"You're not doing anything single-handed," I said, "because I'll stay here with you till Candidus gets back. As you say, we need to keep an eye on things, and four eyes are better than two."

"I don't like it," Quintus said doubtfully. "You shouldn't be alone here without a man to protect you. If the Skipper comes, anything could happen. Leave with us now, and we'll all come back together later."

"Nonsense, Quintus. Albia and I will be fine. You've got the difficult job, getting the prisoners safely into the fortress in the middle of a riot. All we have to do is sit quietly and wait."

He shook his head. "What if some of the gang come here? No, it's too risky."

"I'll stay, shall I?" Titch offered. "I'll keep them safe. And if Gaius shows up, I want to be here to look after him too."

This solution satisfied us all, and I was glad of Titch's company, especially after the men had all gone. It seemed unnaturally quiet, and Albia and I were unsettled and jumpy, listening for unfamiliar noises. But Titch was cheerful and reassuring, and when Nasua offered to run into town to fetch some fresh bread and pastries, we all realised we were hungry.

I suppose people of a romantic turn of mind would say the warehouse's surroundings were pretty, with the river sparkling in the bright midday sun, reflecting the blue of the sky. Birds flew in and out of the reeds, and the tide was coming in fast now, so the water level was high enough to conceal the ugly mud close to the bank. Behind the house the fields were dotted with trees, including a couple of holly-bushes to remind us of our Saturnalia decorations at home. But to me, the remoteness seemed threatening rather than relaxing, and the cold was still biting. We didn't linger long to admire the scenery, but went indoors, leaving Titch outside as our sentry.

We'd hardly had time to sit down comfortably when he came running in. "Miss Albia, I've heard funny noises coming from the boat. I think there's someone inside it."

"On the boat?" She shook her head. "No, there's nobody there. We'd have seen them."

"Mebbe we wouldn't if they're in the cargo space, under that big leather cover. There's room for a few folk to sit or lie hidden there. Not very comfortable, mind."

I asked, "What sort of noises did you hear?"

"Like a girl's voice, but sort of muffled, and I couldn't make out the words. Could be she's gagged, trying to shout out."

"Most likely a bird," I suggested. "A gull or something?"

"I don't reckon so. But come and listen for yourselves."

"Candidus told me there was nobody there last night," Albia said thoughtfully. "But someone could have loaded a small number of people aboard this morning early, after he left. I wouldn't have seen them from here in the house." She jumped to her feet. "Could it be—you don't think—oh, let's go and look! If there's anyone there, we must get the poor things out straight away."

"Wait, Albia. It could be a trap. We need something to defend ourselves."

"I've got the axe," Titch said, "and I found a couple of spears outside. Old army issue. I don't know why they're here, but they'll do for you two ladies."

Albia and I collected one each as we went out. They were long and unwieldy, but heavy and comforting, and they'd do at a pinch.

We stood on the bank and looked at the boat. The tide was still coming in fast, and the *Albia* now floated level with the wooden gangway, rocking very slightly at its moorings. There wasn't a sign of life on it. I called out, "Hello, is anyone on the boat? Margarita? Gaius? It's Aurelia and Albia and Victor, come to get you out."

I thought I saw a tiny stir of movement under the heavy cover, but there was no sound.

"It's me, Aurelia. I promise you're safe."

"And me, Albia. We're going to come onto the boat and get you. Margarita? Are you there?"

"Mmm," came a female voice, muffled and wordless.

"Margarita? Answer if it's you."

"Mmm."

"Brilliant!" Titch exclaimed. "Have you got Gaius there too?"

"Mmm."

"You sound as if they've gagged you," Albia said.

"Mmm."

I called, "Don't worry any more. Albia and I are coming to get you free. Titch will go and fetch help."

"I can't do that!" he protested. "I can't leave you here alone."

"You must. The Skipper will be coming soon, ready to take them away. But he won't sail on this rising tide, so we've got—I don't know, two hours, maybe three, before he can leave. I want plenty of help here by then. Find Quintus or Rufus at the fortress if you can, or Candidus—he'll be at Clarilla's house. Priscus too, if he's turned up there. Preferably all of them. Hurry!"

"But I've got to stay. Master Quintus would never forgive me if I didn't...."

"Victor, *I'm* giving the orders now, and this is an order. As my father used to say, stop talking and start doing. Straight away, please."

He gave me a salute and a grin. "Yes, *sir!* And I'll be as quick as I can." He set off at a run.

We hefted our spears and walked out along the plank jetty, which was now almost under water. This was going to be an exceptionally high tide, with the river already fuller than usual because of melting snow. Typical of the Skipper's badly built gangway, I thought, that anyone boarding his boat at a very high tide would get their feet wet. As we went we talked to the prisoners, telling them we were coming, reassuring them that they'd soon be free. We stepped onto the raised stern deck, and together bent and unfastened the heavy leather sheet that stretched over the whole central area, where the cargo would usually be stowed.

Margarita and Gaius lay huddled in the bottom of the boat on a pile of straw. They were tied hand and foot, and gagged with strips of cloth. We hugged them both tight, and then used our daggers to cut away the gags.

"Aurelia, Albia, thank you! Oh thank you...." Margarita was incoherent with relief. Gaius lay silently, staring at us with huge, scared eyes.

"You're safe now. We'll soon have you ashore." Albia and I began to cut the ropes that tied them, while Margarita thanked us over and over, and we all tried to reassure Gaius, who remained as still as a statue. Freeing them was slow work, because the tight bonds had cut into their flesh, and the last thing we wanted was to hurt them. And our excited chatter stopped dead when we all clearly heard the howl of a wolf on the bank.

"Oh no," Margarita whispered. "Otus and his men!"

"Or the Skipper." My mind raced. "Who brought you here to the boat, Margarita? Was it Otus?"

"Yes. At dawn. Now he's come back for us." She began to shiver, and there were tears in her eyes.

"No, I think it's his brother who's coming. And he may not know for sure that Otus has brought you yet. You must stay out of sight in the boat, and we'll tell them you aren't here. We just have to keep them talking until help comes."

"No! Please, don't leave us!"

"You'll be absolutely safe. We can hold them off for long enough. It's easy to stop anyone coming across that flimsy plank gangway. We can do it, can't we, Albia?"

"Yes, we'll do it. Now let's get this cover back in place...."

"No! We're not staying here on our own again. We'll jump in the river, try to swim for it. Anything's better than sitting waiting for them." She stood up unsteadily, and reached down a hand to pull Gaius to his feet.

My heart sank. If we couldn't hide them, we were all done for.

Albia said briskly, "Swim for it? What nonsense! That's really doing it the hard way. Here's what we'll do. I'll stay in the boat with you, while Relia goes and talks to them. I've got a spear, look, and my dagger. You'll be all right if I'm here, won't you?"

"Well, I suppose so. Will you, Albia? Otherwise I can't face it!"

"We'll face it together." Albia looked at me. "All right, Relia?"

Hardly how I'd have described it, but I took a deep breath. "All right. I'll tell them the whole place is deserted, except for me. I can keep them talking till Titch brings us reinforcements. I'm a good talker. Ask Albia."

"But you'll never stop those men all by yourself!" Margarita wailed.

"Yes I will. I'll stay on the gangway, so they can't touch me or come past me to the boat. I've got a spear, and my father taught me how to use it. Now hurry, let's get you hidden."

"She'll be like Horatius Cocles," Albia added, "guarding the bridge across the Tiber to save Rome. Remember the old story? He held back a whole army."

Horatius had been a hero of ours when we were children, and in a quick flash of memory I saw the three of us re-enacting his heroic victory in our games. Well, now I'd be doing it in earnest. It was a desperate plan, but it was the only plan available.

"Crouch down with me in the straw," Albia was saying cheerfully. "You too, Gaius. Relia will hide us. We're the secret reserves, here to help if we're needed. But we won't be."

I was proud of my sister, so brave, so outwardly confident. The least I could do was match her courage and her air of assurance. "Just stay quiet. Albia, if I have to fall back, I'll signal to give you as much warning as I can." I deliberately used military jargon, because that's what we'd done in our childhood games. Anyway it sounded better than, "I'll yell if I can't hold them off, and you're on your own." I stooped and pulled the cover into place, but didn't fasten it. "Don't worry now. Help will be here any time."

There was nobody in sight as I walked gingerly towards the bank, using my upended spear as a staff, because the planking was completely under water now. It felt slippery and treacherous, the cold river lapping round my feet, and I was glad to reach solid ground.

As I got to the bank, two tall figures came out from behind the warehouse: Otus and the Skipper, the two men I least wanted to meet in all the world.

I raised my spear and faced them, taking a step backwards onto the jetty. They strode towards me, and I moved back slowly, feeling the way with my feet, not daring to look round. I stopped midway between the bank and the boat. That meant I was a good ten paces from where they stood at the river's edge. I felt the comforting solid spear in my hands, and waited.

"Aurelia Marcella! You here again?" Otus growled. "Every-where I turn, you keep getting in my way. Time we taught you a lesson."

"More than time." The Skipper smiled nastily and put a foot on the plank. "And it won't take long dealing with one stupid woman all alone. Your friends have deserted you, from the looks of things. So we can do what we like with you."

"They've gone for reinforcements. They'll be back here any time." I was pleased to find I could keep my voice almost con-versational.

"If you mean your boy, he's gone nowhere," Otus retorted. "We caught him easy. Now he's what you might call tied up." They both laughed at this witticism.

I tried not to show the fear that shot through me. They'd caught Titch! I'd been banking on him getting through, and now they'd captured him! How long would it take for rescue to come, with nobody to raise the alarm for us?

I gripped my spear and looked across at them. "Help's on its way already. And they're coming for you two. Get out while you can, that's my advice, if you want to save your skins. And the gods help you if you've done anything to hurt that boy!"

"He hasn't complained yet," Otus jeered. "Well, how could he? You could tear him in pieces, and with that stammer, he'd never be able to object till it was too late. He always was a stupid little runt."

I felt a huge surge of relief. The boy they'd captured must be little Nasua, on his way back from the baker's. I didn't wish him any harm, but the important point was that Titch was still free.

And for all their bluster, the brothers were continuing to stand at their end of the gangway. They were reluctant to challenge me, and I must convince them they were right to be cautious. Though they were ruthless, I was counting on them not being reckless. As long as I had my spear and kept my nerve, I could hold them where they were. I took a deep breath. "If you're expecting to see Candidus, he isn't here."

"We don't need him. We've come to check on our property," the Skipper answered. "So out of our way, while we get on board my boat. You can come ashore or you can jump in the river, I don't care. Just go."

"You haven't seen Candidus today, then?"

He scowled. "What's it to you?"

"He told me not to let anyone onto the boat till he gets here. So I'm afraid you'll have to wait on the bank there till he comes."

"*What?*" he roared. "What nonsense is this?"

"Not nonsense. I'm not letting you aboard." I levelled my spear.

"She's bluffing." Otus spat towards me. "She can't stop us. She doesn't know how to use that thing." He pulled out a large dagger.

The Skipper drew a blade that looked like a butcher's cleaver, and held it towards me. "I said get out of our road. *Now.*"

"No."

He took three steps towards me and seemed to be measuring the distance between us, perhaps wondering if he could run at me and throw me off. Otus was close behind—at least there wasn't room for them to advance side by side. But as the planking moved under their weight, I suddenly felt very scared and very alone. The gangway was three fingers deep in water, and my feet were numb with cold. It would be easy to slip. And, being realistic, I knew these strong, determined men would sooner or later find a way to pull me to the bank, or push me into the river. The water didn't frighten me, I'm a strong swimmer. But if they got their hands on the others…. I gathered my courage for a last stand.

I raised my spear a fraction and said, "That's far enough. Don't come any closer." They didn't try to, which gave me confidence. "And don't even think about trying to rush me. My father was an army man, and he taught me how to use a spear for close combat. I can trip you up, or stick you in the eye, or spike you in the balls, before you've got time to yell for help." It sounded good, and the Skipper shuffled back a little, making Otus step back too. One up to me.

Otus lost his temper. "You interfering bitch, I'm sick of you sticking your nose in my business! That's my brother's boat, and it contains property of mine. Let us on board now, or we'll put you in there with the others. The dealers down south pay plenty for females in good condition. Or maybe we'll have a bit of fun with you first, and if we spoil your looks, we can always sell you to the Druids. Come on, brother, let's get this finished."

But the Skipper didn't move, and Otus' words, far from frightening me, made me angry. Threatening me like that, and describing those two terrified people as "property"! And my sister was there with them now. They were all depending on me, and I wouldn't let them down. I *couldn't!* I felt a sudden fierce rush of energy, like fire racing through my veins and leaving no room for fear. This was a battle, and I was elated, and knew I was invincible.

"Don't be stupid! You know you can't cross to this boat if I say not." I was shouting now, loud and exultant. I pointed my spear at Otus. "As for the people on the boat, you won't lay a finger on them. I'm guarding them till Candidus gets here. He'll have something to say about crooks who steal slaves." I shifted my weight and took a pace forward, daring them to come within my reach. "And as for you, Skipper Ephialtes, we know all about your foul trade with the Druids, and how you've been helping army deserters. You're the worst kind of scum, the pair of you, and you'll get what's coming to you. You'll die in the arena, and the slower the better."

The Skipper swore. "Right, that's enough. I'll count to ten. If you haven't shifted by then, I'm coming for you, and you're dead." He began to count aloud. "One...two...three...." I crouched, preparing to give him a low blow. Perhaps I could trip him, use his own momentum to pitch him into the water.

"Four...five...six...." Holy Diana, help me now! As if in answer, into my mind came the image of my hero Horatius, guarding his bridge against an invading army. I'm a Roman, I thought, and Romans don't give in.

"Seven...eight...nine...."

Then I pictured the heroic warrior Horatius standing next to Sempronia's drunken lawyer who shared his name, and I laughed aloud. It must have looked like mad bravado, or simply madness, and it goaded them into action.

"TEN!" The Skipper started along the gangway, with Otus at his heels. He took three paces, and he was almost within my reach.

And then, incredibly, he stumbled and swayed, and came no further. He put a hand up to his neck, and I saw there was an arrow sticking out of him. He grunted and tugged at the shaft, and it came free in his hand, releasing a stream of blood. Then he fell backwards, straight onto Otus.

Otus shouted and staggered sideways, thrown off balance by his brother's heavy weight. As I stared in astonishment, both of them tumbled into the river with an enormous splash.

I looked beyond them to see where the arrow had come from. Timaeus stood on the bank, carrying a hunting-bow. He had Titch and Taurus with him. I let out a yell of delight.

They stopped a safe distance from where the two men stood chest-deep in the river, clinging onto the submerged planking. Timaeus yelled, "Stay down, you two. If you try to get out, I'll shoot."

"Mistress Aurelia!" Titch called. "Are you all right?"

"Fine, Victor, thanks to you three."

"Where's Gaius and Margarita? And Miss Albia?"

"In the boat. We'll go and get them. Taurus, can you go into the house please, and find Nasua. These two tied him up. Then come back out here and stand sentry on the bank. If anyone comes in sight, anyone at all, we want fair warning."

Taurus nodded. "Very good, Mistress. But take care, these two aren't done yet."

"I'll watch them." Timaeus gestured with his bow. "Aurelia, can you and Victor get the others out?"

"No, wait," Titch cut in. "Let's not take any chances. Let's catch these bastards first."

I looked down at the two brothers. Otus was struggling and splashing, and I realised he was pulling off his heavy cloak. As he got himself free of it, he shouted, "Come on, Ephialtes, swim for it!" and letting go of the jetty, struck out strongly for the other side of the river. The tide was at its highest, and there was no real current flowing either up-stream or down, so he made good steady progress.

But the Skipper stayed where he was, holding onto the planking. The water around him was red with his blood. "Let me out of the river!" he called up to Timaeus. "I'm hurt. I'm done for."

"Stay where you are," Timaeus ordered. "Victor, watch him, will you, while I try and deal with Otus." He raised his bow and shot at the swimmer. He missed, but not by much. Quick as lightning he fitted another arrow and shot again, and this time hit Otus squarely on the back of the head.

"Good shooting!" I exclaimed. But Otus was strong, and he swam doggedly on, not pausing to remove the shaft, which stuck out of his thick black hair. He was more than halfway across the river now, and looked as if he would make his escape. Then another arrow caught him, this time in the back of the neck. He stopped swimming, twisting a hand behind him to try and shift it, but he couldn't. We saw him desperately splashing as the water around him turned red, and then he sank.

Chapter XXX

"Help!" The Skipper was clawing feebly at the planking close to the bank. "Help me! I can't get out of the water. I'm done for. I won't give you any trouble! Help me, please!"

"Stay where you are," I ordered. "See if you can find a rope, will you, Titch? There may be one in the house."

"There'll be some on the boat, for sure." The lad ran onto the gangway, leaping lightly over the place where the Skipper's hands were still desperately holding on.

I hurried to the boat, shouting, "Albia, Margarita, Gaius, you're safe now! We're coming!" Titch was behind me, and together we jumped on board and pulled back the heavy leather covering.

"Aurelia! Oh, thank the gods!" Margarita was laughing and crying at once as she stood up and looked around.

Gaius stayed where he was for a couple of heartbeats. Then he saw Titch and gave a joyous shout. "Victor! Victor, you've come!" Titch crouched down, holding the boy tight and saying gently, "There, young Gaius. You're safe. I've come for you, just like I promised. You'll be all right now."

Albia looked over their heads at me and said quietly, "Good work, Relia."

"You too. They wouldn't have stayed here without you. Are you all right?"

"Yes. Thanks to you."

"Thanks to Timaeus. He's the one who saved us."

"Timaeus?" Margarita moved to stand on the raised stern deck. "Is he here?"

I pointed. "On the bank there."

"Oh, this is wonderful! I can hardly believe it—we're safe! It's been a nightmare. I can't describe it." She gazed at the river and the shore. "Where are we?"

"Just outside Eburacum. That's Candidus' warehouse, and his house is just behind."

"Eburacum?" she repeated, surprised. "They wouldn't tell us where we were, or where they were taking us. Gods, what's that?"

We heard shouting on the bank, and looked across in alarm, which swiftly turned to relief. Taurus had hauled out the Skipper, who lay unmoving on the ground, either unconscious or dead. Now Taurus was shouting excitedly and pointing up-stream. A tiny rowing-boat had rounded the bend and was pulling rapidly towards us, with Candidus and Priscus at the oars.

Titch gave a whoop of triumph, and carried Gaius to the bank. The brothers disembarked, and Albia rushed across the gangway into Candidus' arms. I reached out a hand to help Margarita, thinking she was still too weak and stiff to manage the treacherous planks alone, but she waved me aside and ran nimbly across. I thought, Venus is giving her feet wings, as I saw Priscus waiting at the end of the gangway, his arms open wide to receive her.

But she flew past Priscus without even seeing him. She ran to Timaeus, who took her in a fierce embrace. They clung together as if they'd never let go.

I walked from the boat to the bank, too astonished to say anything. Priscus was standing as if he'd taken root, watching Timaeus and Margarita, who were too absorbed in one another to be aware of him or of anyone else.

"I don't understand," Priscus breathed. But his white face and staring eyes told me he understood only too well. He was seeing the girl he loved, happy in the arms of the man she loved.

"Margarita's mine!" he exclaimed. "I love her. She said she loved me. Why is she with him?"

I couldn't think what to answer. What can you say to a man whose heart is breaking?

"It's all been for nothing then," he muttered. "All for nothing." He raised his voice. "Margarita! *Margarita!*"

She broke away from Timaeus and came to him, her face full of sadness. "I'm so sorry, Priscus. I should have told you, but I didn't know how."

"Told me what?" He sounded dazed.

"Since Timaeus came into the household, I've realised I love him. I can't help it. We belong together. We knew each other years ago, you see, before your mother bought me."

He stared at her. "You knew each other before? You mean you were lovers?"

"Yes. But it stopped when I came to you. I swear it."

"You said you loved *me!*"

"I cared for you very much. You made me happy, and I wanted to make you happy too."

"All these years we've been together, and I've loved you so much. I refused to marry, I wouldn't go into politics, all because I loved you. And now I find that you—you've been lying to me!" He was shouting, and everyone had turned to listen to him. With the tail of my eye I saw Titch pick up Gaius and carry him round to the house. This was no scene for a young child to witness.

"It wasn't like that," Margarita said gently. "After your mother bought me, Timaeus left Londinium and went home to his family in Crete. I wasn't free to follow him, and I was sure I'd never see him again. I thought I could make myself forget him. And you were so good to me, so gentle, I believed that with you I'd found a different kind of love. But now I've met him again, and…. The gods know I never meant to deceive you."

"So every night, when we made love, were you dreaming of Timaeus?"

"Never, I swear it."

"Yet you didn't forget him."

"I thought of him sometimes." She couldn't meet his eyes. "Oh my dear, I can't lie about this. Gaius is his child."

"No! You swore that you stopped seeing him when you came to me."

"But I was already with child when your mother bought me."

Priscus gave a low moan, like an animal in pain. It made me turn cold inside.

"I'm truly sorry," Margarita said. "Please believe me, I never wanted to hurt you. You've every right to hate me."

"I don't hate you!" he burst out. "I wish I could, it would be so much easier! No, I love you more than anything else in the world. Gods, I've killed my own father for your sake, doesn't that tell you how much I love you?"

"You killed your father?" She stepped back in horror. "But why?"

"Because Father told Diogenes to hand you and Gaius over to the kidnappers. He hoped when you were taken away from me I'd forget you. So I poisoned him."

"Did you kill the two slaves as well? Did you murder three people, thinking that would show you loved me?"

"No, of course I didn't. They had no power to hurt me. Only Father had that. And now you. If I've lost you and Gaius, I've lost everything!"

Before we realised what he was doing, he ran along the gangway and sprang onto the deck of the boat. "I've killed my father. I can't undo it, and I can't regret it. Now I have only one honourable choice." He pulled a dagger from his belt.

"No!" Margarita screamed. "Priscus, that's not the way!"

He turned his back on us, so we didn't witness how he used the blade. But we saw it fly through the air, dripping with blood, as he flung it away from him, and then he plunged into the river. It was deep there, and he sank like a stone, straight down without moving.

"Help him!" Margarita shrieked. "Somebody help him!" She ran forward, but I stopped her. She was too weak after her long ordeal. She stood statue-still, like the rest of us. We seemed to be held motionless by some force outside ourselves. We saw Priscus' head show once above the water, but still he made no effort to save himself. He sank a second time, and didn't surface again.

Candidus said, "It's best, perhaps. He's done a dreadful wrong, but may god give him peace now." He made a sign like a cross in the air, and there were tears in his eyes.

Albia came and stood next to me. "I believe Priscus," she said softly. "Why would he lie? He killed his father, but not the others."

"I believe him too," I agreed. "But I'm still not convinced by Diogenes' account, are you?"

"No."

"Let's hear Timaeus' version." I looked over to where he and Margarita stood together, hand in hand. "Timaeus, will you answer us a couple of questions?"

The sternness in my tone made him release Margarita and come to stand in front of me. "Yes, of course, Aurelia. What is it?"

"I want to know about the first attack on Lord Plautius. At the Oak Tree, when Idmon was acting as decoy in his bed. Whose turn should it have been to sleep there?"

"Mine. But I swapped with Idmon because my lord was so ill. I wanted to be ready if he needed me in the night."

"I thought it was Diogenes' turn."

"Gods, not him! He only ever did one night as decoy, and then he refused absolutely to do another. Plautius ordered him to, but he always found an excuse to get out of it—he wasn't well, or he needed to be on hand in case Sempronia called him. But he was just plain afraid. He's a born coward," he added, with scathing contempt. "Look at the fuss he made over that little dog bite, refusing to go anywhere near the stable block after it happened...."

"Dog bite?" I said, hardly daring to breathe. "What dog bite?"

"On his leg. He got bitten by Victor's dog. He said she attacked him, but I don't know why. He must have been upsetting her, or the pups."

"Did he ask you to treat the bite?"

He nodded. "I put some ointment on it, and a bandage."

"When did he come to you about it?"

"The morning after Leander was killed. Look, do you need me any more? I must get back to Margarita."

"Just one more question, Timaeus. Were you and Idmon rivals for a maid called Ebrel?"

"Ebrel? Gods, no. A nice enough lass, but—all right, I can guess where you're driving. You've seen me flirting, playing the part of the carefree lad who likes a good time. But it was just an act. I tried hard, but I couldn't feel anything for any other woman, once I'd seen Margarita again."

◇◇◇

By the time we got to Clarilla's house, Quintus and Rufus had arrived there, and Diogenes had confessed to murdering Idmon and Leander, and helping to poison Plautius.

The two events weren't connected. I expect Quintus could have found a way to make the Weasel talk, but he'd never have come up with anything more frightening to Diogenes than Sempronia in a rage. She'd bullied the truth out of him, or as much of the truth as he was ever going to reveal. He'd killed Idmon, mistaking him for Timaeus and jealous of the growing attraction between the doctor and Margarita, and stabbed Leander to try and cover his tracks. Later he'd helped to poison Plautius, fearing his master would alter his will and deprive him of the chance of freedom.

Sempronia was still in a fury over her slave's treachery when we got there, but her rage turned to bitter weeping when she heard how Priscus died.

"I can't believe it!" she kept repeating. "That dear Aulus should kill his own father! His *father,* who was willing to give him everything he wanted…" and more of the same, till Quintus and I had had enough.

"This is a Plautius family council," Quintus said gravely. "We've no place here, Sempronia. We'll be on our way. If you need us later, you can contact us at Brocchus' mansio."

That made her angry again. "But your investigation is not complete."

"I think it is. We've established that Diogenes killed your two slaves, and that Priscus poisoned your husband. Now Diogenes has admitted to helping him. Candidus offered to free him if he told us the truth, but only if he was innocent."

"To *free* him? How dare you, Decimus? You've no authority!"

"I have, Mother. I'm head of the family now, and I have the power to free our slaves if I choose." He paused to let her take this in. At last she nodded, and he went on. "But there's no question of releasing him now. He must be put to death, after what he's done."

"But exactly what *has* he done?" I asked. "Did he poison Lord Plautius' dates?"

"He did," she answered grimly, "all but one. And he saw to it that Timaeus chose to eat the only one that was safe. How he did that, I do not know. Unless Timaeus was in the plot too?"

"He wasn't." I made myself recall the scene in the brightly lit dining-room. Timaeus took a date from the oval silver dish and ate it, and nodded, and then Plautius reached for the sweets....

"I think I see how it could be done." I glanced round the room. On a side table stood an oval plate of small pastries. I chose one at random, and scratched a small mark on the underside of it with my thumbnail. I showed it to Albia. "That's the poisoned cake. Now I'll arrange the dish so you pick it out." I carefully kept my back to them all, blocking their view while I placed the little cakes in an oval shape round the edges of the dish. At either end of the oval, the pattern came to a point, and I put the marked pastry at one end as part of the design. When I held the dish out with the narrow end towards Albia, one pastry stood out invitingly, and she chose it.

"Yes," she agreed, checking that she'd selected the marked one. "With an oval shape, Diogenes could make it almost certain that Timaeus would pick the one that was safe. Perhaps he put in two safe sweets, one at each end."

Candidus turned to Sempronia. "So you see, Mother, they've completed the investigation, and we've no right to detain them. Antonius…Aurelia…thank you for everything. I've learnt some useful lessons in the last few days. You can safely leave this family's affairs in my hands." He smiled at Albia. "And you can trust me to take very good care of my girl."

The sun was going down in a misty red blaze as we strolled along towards the mansio. Halfway there we met Horatius, weaving an unsteady course up the street and singing to himself. He greeted us with a big smile. "Antonius! Aurelia! How splendid! Come and have a drink. I'm celebrating, but Sempronia says it's in bad taste to be enjoying myself in a house of mourning, so I had to come out to find some cheerful company."

"Thanks, but we're on our way back to the mansio," Quintus smiled. "There's somebody there we have to meet, just before dark."

"What are you celebrating?" I smiled at him, remembering how he and that other Horatius had helped to give me courage on the jetty.

"Some good news. D'you know what Plautius did before he died? No, course you don't. Before he left Londinium, he wrote to his bankers, cancelling all my debts to him, and giving me a big enough sum of money to pay off my other creditors. I only found it out when I was going through his papers today. He left me a note, to be opened if he died, explaining what he'd done. He must have had a premonition about ending his life here." He laughed. "I shouldn't laugh, but I can't help it. He said in the note that he hadn't told me before we left home, because he was afraid I'd refuse to travel with them if I didn't need to earn a fee. He was probably right. But wasn't that a fine thing to do?"

"It was," Quintus agreed. "And you deserve it. You were a good friend to him, and behaved honourably. Will you go back to Londinium with Sempronia now?"

"Yes, I expect so." He hiccupped noisily. "But not tonight. Tonight is for having a good time. Come and join me later, if you like. I'll be the one buying all the drinks!" He waved a farewell, and meandered on his way.

"I wouldn't want him as my lawyer," I said as we entered the mansio, "but he's not a bad old stick. Now who's this we're supposed to be meeting—or was that just an excuse?"

"No, it's someone I know you'll be pleased to see."

He was right. Waiting in the bar-room was my brother.

"Lucius! This is wonderful!" We hugged one another, while Quintus ordered a jug of wine.

"I just looked in to make sure you're all in one piece, Sis," my brother said. "Quintus says you've been getting into scrapes, but you look as if you've survived. And thanks to your help, I've finished the business that brought me up here. Thank you both." He picked up a beaker. "Let's drink a toast—to a happy future for us all."

It was the first of many toasts, and the evening developed into a party. Well, why not? Like old Horatius, we had something worth celebrating. And like him, we were the ones buying all the drinks.

Chapter XXXI

Albia and Candidus were married in Eburacum, on a glorious blue April day of birdsong and spring flowers. It was a perfect wedding. Albia, Lucius, and I stayed the night before at Clarilla's house, so we could walk in procession from there to the groom's home as custom demanded.

And the groom's home was no longer the damp, cramped quarters behind the warehouse down-river. Candidus had bought a bright new house in the centre of town, and Albia had helped him choose the decorations and furniture for it. "Nothing but the best for my girl," he'd assured us, and it was clear he meant it.

My sister looked radiant, supremely pretty and happy, her brown eyes sparkling and her dark brown curls showing up beautifully against the flame colour of the wedding veil. I felt extremely proud of her, as well as overjoyed that all the trials and tensions of the last few months were behind us. I also had a tiny twinge of sadness because I was losing her, but I put aside thoughts of how much I should miss her. Nothing was allowed to dim the joyful atmosphere today.

The guests assembled at Clarilla's house just before noon. Lucius and Quintus were resplendent in gleaming togas, and I'd made sure my new peacock-blue tunic and matching over-tunic were fashionably eye-catching. My sandals were in the latest style, and gave me fashionably painful blisters.

We weren't a large party of guests, but you'd go a long way to find a happier one. Clarus and Clarilla were among the friends who'd made the journey from Oak Bridges, along with a large contingent from the Oak Tree. Timaeus was there, with his new wife and his son, and a handsome group they were, as well as a joyful one. Margarita was free now, and she and Gaius shared in our excitement as if they were part of our family. In a way they almost were, because the three of them had taken up residence in Oak Bridges so that Margarita could be my housekeeper at the Oak Tree. She could never be Albia, but she would be a pretty good substitute.

Even old Horatius had come north for the occasion, and cheerfully endured our teasing about the distance that some folk will travel just to get free drinks. We also had a military presence, in the shape of a dashing red-headed young cavalry trooper—still a very new recruit, but as cocky and proud as any victorious general leading his triumph through the streets of Rome.

The only notable person missing was Sempronia, though of course she'd been invited. She declined in a reasonably polite note, explaining that she was too old and tired for the long road north. She had the grace to wish the young couple well, and I didn't hear anyone lamenting her absence.

The sun shone warm as we paraded through the streets, with all the traditional trappings. There were torch-bearers, musicians, and dancers, and we were accompanied all the way by the usual crowd of small boys, who always know by instinct where to find a wedding procession. They cavorted about shouting ribald jokes and making so much din that everyone for several streets around knew this was a special day.

Candidus waited for us in his new house, which was bright with flowers and green spring leaves. He made a handsome bridegroom, and when he embraced Albia and then carried her over the threshold, the cheering made the whole street echo. I felt my eyes fill with tears.

There followed a wonderful party, with food prepared specially by Cook, who had forsaken his kitchen at the Oak Tree for the day to provide Albia's wedding feast. He was ably assisted by

Nasua, who under Candidus' gentle care was blossoming into an excellent servant.

The celebration broke up towards evening, when it was time to leave the happy pair to themselves. Quintus and Lucius and I were to stay at Clarilla's for the night, but none of us wanted to go there yet, so we wandered down to the river to watch the boats on the water. I was supremely content to be in the company of the two men I loved best in the world.

"I hope they'll be happy," Lucius said, as we paused to watch a duck leading her ducklings down to the water's edge. "Albia deserves a good man. Candidus came out of the whole business better than I expected, in spite of all his weird philosophical ideas."

"They'll be happy." I felt sure of it now. "Albia's always wanted a home of her own and children, and she'll never find a kinder man than Candidus to share her life. That's enough for most women."

"But not all?" Quintus smiled into my eyes. We'd had this conversation before.

"Some of us want more," I answered.

"So if I were to ask you to marry me, what would you answer?"

"That it's the wine talking. You're not the marrying kind, any more than I am."

"Gods," Lucius laughed, "if the conversation's going to take a romantic turn, I'll be off. Three's a crowd."

"No, don't go yet. I've something I've been meaning to ask you, brother. You're back as one of the Governor's bright boys again, aren't you? Completely reinstated, all the rumours of treachery dead and buried?"

"Yes, I am. With a little help from you and Quintus."

"I'm not fishing for compliments. When you came to see us in December, you said something about a spy being sent to the Oak Tree, to investigate us and try to catch us out. Did someone come? Was it one of Sempronia's people? I assumed it was Diogenes, but I never knew for certain, and there were several others it might have been. Were any dire reports ever sent back to the Governor?"

The two men glanced at each other. "Didn't you tell her?" Quintus asked.

"No, I thought you had."

"You'd think she'd have worked it out for herself." Quintus smiled at me. "After all, she claims to have some experience as an investigator."

My brother nodded solemnly. "Yes, she should have done. Downright disappointing, I call it."

"All right, boys, what's going on? What am I supposed to have worked out?"

Lucius laughed. "Who the spy was, of course, and why you've no need to be worried about his report."

"It wasn't one of Sempronia's people?"

But they just exchanged knowing smiles, and then Lucius slapped Quintus on the shoulder. "You're too modest, that's your trouble. You must learn to blow your own trumpet now and then."

"Oh, Jupiter's balls!" I suddenly saw where they were driving. "Quintus, the spy was *you?*"

"At your service." He bowed.

"Well if that doesn't beat everything! I don't know whether to hug you or push you into the river."

"Do both," Lucius suggested.

"Maybe, but first I'd like to know how you fixed it, Quintus. You truly came up to investigate the Oak Tree?"

He nodded. "The Governor wanted someone to be in Brigantia in case this brother of yours needed help. So we arranged it that I'd escort Fabia Jucunda to the Oak Tree, and then stay in the area and at the same time cast an eye over your activities at the mansio."

"But surely the Governor knew you and I were old friends, so you wouldn't exactly be an impartial observer."

"He's a new Governor, remember, since all that business with the Shadow of Death. I told him we were former lovers who'd fallen out, and let him think I'd be delighted to catch you out, if there was anything to catch."

"But there wasn't?"

"Of course not. I gave you and the Oak Tree a glowing endorsement." His blue-purple eyes were laughing.

I turned to my brother. "And you knew about this, Lucius?"

"Not at the time. He told me afterwards."

"Well, it was a brilliant solution. But what about the Shadow of Death, stirring up trouble for us in Rome? Have you convinced the Governor he's not to be taken seriously?"

"I think so," Quintus said.

"You *think* so? You're not certain?"

"Nobody has the luxury of certainty, with Domitian Caesar on the throne," he answered gravely.

"That's quite enough serious talk for now," Lucius said. "This is a day for being happy."

Quintus agreed. "I suggest we all go and drink a beaker or two to Albia and Candidus. Then I'll think of something to amuse Aurelia for the evening."

And he did.

About the History

People who call history a dead subject couldn't be more wrong. The past can't change, but our knowledge of it alters all the time. For anyone writing historical fiction, this is fascinating and simultaneously frustrating. However hard you try to get the history right, you run the risk of being overtaken by new discoveries.

That's especially so with Eburacum—modern York. At present we haven't anything like a detailed map of the town in the 90s AD, though we know a fair bit about the fortress, which was its reason for existence. (Eburacum, by the way, is the correct spelling of its name in its early days; the more familiar Eboracum came later.) Historians and archaeologists are working hard to uncover more and more of its first-century life, but all we can say with certainty at present is that Aurelia would have found a rough-and-ready garrison town, not the prosperous provincial capital that developed later.

Then again, we don't know for sure who was Governor of the province of Britannia in 95 AD. I find this surprising, as the bureaucracy that ran the Empire then was quite efficient, and loved paperwork as much as any modern civil servant. The best guess is Metilius Nepos. He may well have had an aunt or several, but Sempronia is fictitious.

Oak Bridges and the Oak Tree Mansio are fictitious, but I've placed the Oak Tree in a real location, alongside a Roman road which ran from the coast to York, and which is still a main highway two thousand years later. The other places mentioned in the book were and are real.

We know quite a lot about how Roman law dealt with family matters like marriages and wills, but then as now, people often did not stick to the exact letter of the legislation. The power of the *paterfamilias,* for instance, was awesome. In law he had tyrannical authority over his whole family, even his grown-up children with families of their own. His rights included the power of life and death. But by the end of the first century, heads of families very rarely executed their children, and a mother would expect to be involved in major family decisions along with her husband. The position of most women seems in real life to have been less restricted and oppressed than the laws decreed. As in all eras and cultures, an intelligent and strong-minded woman could wield considerable power, inside and outside her family.

Code enthusiasts will recognise the alphabet cipher used by Lucius. It was indeed favoured by Julius Caesar, according to Roman sources, but I've applied it to the modern English alphabet. I couldn't find a simple way for Aurelia to explain that her alphabet had only 23 letters (no J, U or W). I mvst ivst hope that the Latin pvrists among vs vill forgive me.

Finally, for the people who want to follow reading Roman fiction by reading Roman fact, I've listed a few of the books that I've found useful. They form just the tip of a large iceberg, because for me, reading about Roman history is as much fun as writing about it.

Roman Authors
Agricola, by Tacitus. Tacitus' account of a general and Governor who spent much of his time in Britannia

The Twelve Caesars, by Suetonius. A wonderfully gossipy account of Roman court and political life

Letters of the Younger Pliny. Not about Britannia, but very much about the Roman mind-set

The Satires, by Juvenal. These show clearly how like us, and yet how different, the Romans were.

Modern Authors
A History of Roman Britain, by Peter Salway

Life and Letters on the Roman Frontier (Vindolanda and Its People), by Alan K. Bowman

Women in Roman Britain, by Lindsay Allason-Jones

The Roman Family, by Suzanne Dixon

The Finds of Roman Britain, by Guy de la Bédoyère

The Landscape of Roman Britain, by Ken Dark and Petra Dark

The Classical Cookbook, by Andrew Dalby and Sally Grainger

What the Romans Did for Us, by Philip Wilkinson

Roman York, by Patrick Ottaway

To receive a free catalog of Poisoned Pen Press titles, please contact us in one of the following ways:

Phone: 1-800-421-3976
Facsimile: 1-480-949-1707
E-mail: info@poisonedpenpress.com
Website: www.poisonedpenpress.com

Poisoned Pen Press
6962 E. First Ave. Ste. 103
Scottsdale, AZ 85251